MADELINE BAKER

**Winner of the *Romantic Times*
Reviewers' Choice Award
For Best Indian Series!**

"Lovers of Indian Romance have a special place
on their bookshelves for Madeline Baker!"
                                    —*Romantic Times*

VISION OF LOVE

As Shadow Hawk lay there, his eyes closed against the pain, the Spirit Woman's image appeared before him. He had not been able to see her face clearly, only the glow of the sun-gold skin and a riot of curly hair as black as the wings of his spirit bird. And even as he watched, the shadow of the black hawk he'd seen in his vision seemed to merge with the woman, and he heard a voice echo in the back of his mind, the voice of the shadow hawk.

She is waiting for you. The words were no more than the merest whisper, yet they rang loud and clear in his mind. *You cannot fulfill your destiny without her.*

Who was she? Why did her image intrude on his prayers and dreams? What power did she have over him, that he could not forget her; what magic did she possess that made him think of her day and night? What did she want of him?

MADELINE BAKER

THE SPIRIT PATH

LEISURE BOOKS NEW YORK CITY

LOVE AND HUGS
TO
MY DARLING DAVID
We missed you while you were gone and
we're ever so glad to have you back!

A LEISURE BOOK®

March 1993

Published by

Dorchester Publishing Co., Inc.
276 Fifth Avenue
New York, NY 10001

Copyright © 1993 by Madeline Baker

Cover Art by Pino

Printed in the United States of America.

He walks in my heart
  This man of Yesterday;
He stands tall and proud
  This bronze god of mine.

Is he only in my mind,
  And in my heart?
Or is he out there, somewhere,
  Waiting?

Did he leave this world
To walk among the stars?

I see him standing tall
  Against a pink and purple sky,
His bronze skin aglow
  In the evening light;

His strong and rugged face
  Shows no emotion;
His eyes are black as midnight.
  If you look deep, you can see into his soul.

There is pride and love there,
  For this land and his people;
For who he is, and where
  He was born.

Is that a tear I see
Gleaming in his eye?

Is it for people who
  No longer roam this land,
For battles lost, for a way of life
  That can never be again?

My heart cries for you...
My Lakota warrior.

—Mary Lou VonMeter

Chapter One

Dakota Territory, 1872

"She is not here."

Shadow Hawk frowned at the aged medicine man sitting across from him. "Not here? I do not understand."

"She is not here. She is not of the People."

Shadow Hawk was silent a moment. Not of the People. What did it mean?

But before he could put the question to Heart-of-the-Wolf, the wizened old medicine man leaned forward and gazed intently at Shadow Hawk, his dark eyes probing deep into the younger man's soul. "How brave are you, *Cetán?*"

Shadow Hawk cocked his head to one side, puzzled by the question. Then, with a hint of a smile, he lifted a hand to the necklace of bear claws at his throat, then dragged a well-callused thumb across the ragged Sun Dance scars that adorned his chest.

Heart-of-the-Wolf nodded. "You are a man of strength. You have killed *matohota* and sacrificed your blood and your pain to *Wakán Tanka*. But I ask you again, Shadow Hawk, how brave are you?"

In a movement uncharacteristically graceful for such a tall man, Shadow Hawk rose to his feet, his hands curling into angry fists as he glared down at the medicine man. "I do not understand your answers or your questions." He thumped his chest with his fist. "I am Shadow Hawk. I have proven my courage at the Sun Dance Pole. I have counted coup in battle. I have taken the scalps of our enemies, the Crow and the Pawnee. Why do you question my courage now?"

Heart-of-the-Wolf nodded, unruffled by the younger man's outburst, and after a moment, Shadow Hawk sat down again.

Heart-of-the-Wolf took a deep breath and exhaled slowly. When he spoke, he chose his words carefully. "I have been the eyes and ears to the future of our people for more than forty years, *Cetán*, but each day it grows more difficult for me to guide the Lakota. The strength is going from my legs, my eyes grow dim; only my heart remains strong.

"These are trying times for our People. I fear the *wasichu* will soon cover the land of the spotted eagle like the prairie grasses in the summer. Our People look to you to be their next holy man. And so I ask you once again, Shadow Hawk, how brave are you? Do you possess the courage to travel the Spirit Path and see what the future holds? Are you strong enough to make the journey? Are you brave enough to enter the Sacred Cave and seek the vision that lies within?"

Shadow Hawk gazed at Heart-of-the-Wolf, wondering at the sudden chill in the lodge. Had the small fire crackling in the center of the lodge lost its warmth, or was it the medicine man's words that had turned his blood to ice?

The Cave of the Spirit Path. Its legend was woven deep into the fabric of his people's history, but he knew of no one who had entered the Sacred Cave and returned to tell the tale. . . .

He looked at Heart-of-the-Wolf sharply. "You have been to the Sacred Cave! That is how you knew we were in danger two summers ago. That is how you knew the *wasichu* were coming last fall."

Heart-of-the-Wolf nodded. "I fear worse things lie ahead. I need you to be my legs, my eyes."

Shadow Hawk lifted a hand to the necklace of bear claws at his throat. There were many kinds of courage. Did he possess the kind of courage required to follow the Spirit Path, to face the unknown? The proud words he had spoken earlier tasted like ashes in his mouth.

"You need not answer now," Heart-of-the-Wolf remarked softly. "What I ask is not easy, but remember, I do not ask it for myself, but for the People."

Chapter Two

Leaving the medicine man's lodge, Shadow Hawk caught his big calico stallion and rode into the hills. He needed time alone, time to think.

Shadow Hawk gave the horse its head, and *Wohitika*, the Brave One, ran effortlessly, its long legs eating up the miles as it climbed higher and higher, gliding over the low, grassy hills like an eagle skimming the sky.

Shadow Hawk put the medicine man's question from his mind. He knew the answer to that. What Heart-of-the-Wolf asked of him might not be easy, but it was a great honor, and a sign of the old shaman's faith in him, that he would trust such a momentous responsibility to another. Shadow Hawk would go to the Cave of the Spirit Path when the time was right and look

14

into the future, but it was not the future that haunted him, it was the woman in his vision.

Shadow Hawk drew Wohitika to a halt at the crest of a tree-studded rise. It was here he had first seen the Spirit Woman. He had been fourteen at the time and earnestly seeking a medicine dream to guide him on the road to becoming a warrior. Even now, eleven summers later, he could remember that day.

It had been *Wazustecasa wi,* The Moon When Strawberries Are Ripe. The sky had been blue and clear, the air warm. Clad in nothing but a clout and moccasins, he had stood on the blanket his mother had made for him, his arms raised, his head thrown back as he gazed up at the sun. Three nights and four days he had waited for a vision. He had offered tobacco to the four directions, to Mother Earth, to the Great Spirit Above, but he had seen nothing, heard nothing.

Weak with hunger, his mouth and throat dry from lack of water, he had uttered a final prayer to *Wakán Tanka,* begging for a sign, a vision, to guide him through life. He had been about to give up when the shadow of a huge black hawk had fallen over him. Mesmerized, he had stared at the shadow on the ground and, gradually, his image had merged with that of the shadow of the hawk, until they were one. He had legs and wings, hair and feathers. And he could see for miles, as though he were looking through the far-seeing eyes of the hawk. Time lost all meaning and he felt as though he were soaring, gliding, chasing the wind.

For a long while he was alone in the skies and then, to his surprise, he was leading other birds—sparrows and jays and one lone eagle, leading them away from the blood-stained claws of a vulture. Using the keen eyes of the hawk, he had searched for a haven of safety, away from the sacred land of the Lakota into a land northward. But before he could find refuge, the eagle overtook him, and then, before he had time to wonder what it meant, the shadow of the hawk was gone and he stood on the mountain, alone.

He had stared after the hawk until it was out of sight and then, too weak to remain upright any longer, he had dropped to his knees and closed his eyes. It was then he had seen the Spirit Woman's shadowy image for the first time.

He had not mentioned the mysterious woman to Heart-of-the-Wolf when he told the medicine man of his vision. Perhaps he had only imagined her, after all.

Old Heart-of-the-Wolf had interpreted his medicine dream. The first part of the vision meant that he would be as strong and wise as the great black hawk so long as he followed the life path of the Lakota.

"And what of the second part?" Hawk had asked.

Heart-of-the-Wolf had not answered right away. When he did speak, his voice was troubled. "You will lead our people away from our enemies."

"I hear doubt in your voice."

Heart-of-the-Wolf nodded. "It may be that you will not lead the people yourself, but that you will

16

lead the eagle who follows in your shadow. But know this, you have been chosen by the Great Spirit to be a leader of our people. You shall have a new name. From this day forward you shall be known as Shadow Hawk."

He had been twenty when he saw the woman's ghostlike image a second time. It had been summer again, during the time of *Wiwanyank Wacipi*, the Sun Dance. Tethered to the sacred pole by two lengths of heavy rawhide fastened to skewers embedded in the muscles of his chest, he had danced forward and back, offering his blood and his pain to *Wakán Tanka*, beseeching the gods of the Lakota to bless the People through the coming year.

Staring at the sun, he had pulled against the rawhide, his teeth tightly clenched to hold back the groan that rose in his throat. One last jerk against his tether and his skin had given way, freeing him from the Sun Dance Pole. He had stumbled backward, then dropped to the ground, his chest warm with his blood.

As he lay there, his eyes closed against the pain, the Spirit Woman's image had appeared before him. He had not been able to see her face clearly, only the glow of sun-gold skin and a riot of curly hair as black as the wings of his spirit bird. And even as he watched, the shadow of the black hawk he'd seen in his vision seemed to merge with the woman, and he heard a voice echo in the back of his mind, the voice of the shadow hawk.

She is waiting for you. The words were no more than the merest whisper, yet they rang loud and

17

clear in his mind. *You cannot fulfill your destiny without her.*

He had seen her for the third time just before going to Heart-of-the-Wolf's lodge that morning and he could not attribute the vision to fatigue or loss of blood this time. He had gone into the woods to pray and as he gazed heavenward, he had seen her face, her mouth full and red, her eyes as blue as a midsummer sky. Who was she? Why did her image intrude on his prayers and dreams? What power did she have over him, that he could not forget her; what magic did she possess that made him think of her day and night? What did she want of him?

One mystery at a time, he thought with a wry grin. He would venture into the Cave of the Spirit Path and seek the answers to Heart-of-the-Wolf's questions, and then he would seek to unravel the mystery of the Spirit Woman.

His mother, Winona, was waiting for him when he returned to his lodge. She never seemed to age, only to grow more beautiful with the passing years. He smiled at her as he took a seat and reached for the bowl she offered him.

"You have seen the woman again," she said, and it was not a question.

"Yes."

"Could not Heart-of-the-Wolf tell you what it means?"

Shadow Hawk put the bowl aside. "We did not speak of her. He wishes me to go to the Cave of the Spirit Path."

Winona stared at her son, one hand over her mouth to cover her astonishment.

Shadow Hawk smiled at her. "He wishes me to be his legs and eyes."

Winona shook her head. *"Heyah!"*

"I must do it."

"Heyah," his mother repeated. "No."

"What would you have me do?"

"No one but a holy man must enter the cave. For another to do so means death," Winona said fervently. "If Heart-of-the-Wolf has lost his power, then it is time our people found a new medicine man."

"He has not lost his power. His heart and his mind are still strong. Only his legs and his eyes grow weak." Shadow Hawk gazed at his mother for a long moment. "I will be the next medicine man."

"He has made his decision, then?"

"Yes."

Winona stared at her son for a long moment, and then she smiled, her eyes filled with quiet pride. "It will be good, to have a holy man in my lodge."

Shadow Hawk nodded soberly. To be a *Wicasa Wakán*, or holy man, required much learning and carried a great deal of responsibility. Holy men had to be able to interpret dreams and visions, to settle disputes, to be well versed in knowledge of the Lakota gods. *Wakán Tanka* was the supreme God who ruled over all; four gods ruled beneath him: *Wi*, the sun, ruled the world; *Skan*, the sky, was a source of power; *Maka*, the Earth, was the mother of all living things; *Inyan*, the Rock, was the protector of households. It was *Skan* who judged a man's spirit at the time of death.

Shadow Hawk took a deep breath. He had learned much from old Heart-of-the-Wolf and he felt a deep sense of pride that the old medicine man considered him worthy to succeed him, but it was the Spirit Woman who occupied his thoughts most often these days.

"When I return from the cave, I will ask Heart-of-the-Wolf to tell me of the Spirit Woman," he remarked, putting his thoughts into words. "She troubles me, *Iná*, I would know what she wants of me."

Winona shook her head as she squeezed her son's arm affectionately. "Sacred caves and spirit women! Wagh! Forget this *wasicun winyan* who haunts your dreams. It is time you took a wife."

Shadow Hawk took a deep breath and loosed it in a long sigh. His mother was right. It was far past when he should have taken a wife. But none of the Lakota maidens drew his eye. Many were beautiful. Many had looked at him with warm eyes. All would make fine wives and mothers. But his blood did not heat at their nearness, his heart did not beat fast for any of them. And so he remained alone, a man apart. He had war honors. He had been gifted with a vision and endured the pain and the reward of the Sun Dance. But he had not found a woman to share his lodge.

Perhaps the fault lay in him. Perhaps he was meant to live alone, or to be one of those men who was neither man nor woman.

Shadow Hawk shook his head in disgust. He was a warrior. He had proven himself in battle many times. He had counted coup more than any other man in the village. He would not sit with the women. He would not live his life alone.

A wry grin turned up the corner of his mouth. Perhaps his mother was right. Perhaps it was time to take a wife.

But first he must travel the Spirit Path.

Chapter Three

Old Father *Wi* had crossed the sky five times and now Shadow Hawk sat in the lodge of Heart-of-the-Wolf again, learning the things he must know before he could venture into the Cave of the Spirit Path.

"You must not eat or drink for one full day before you enter the sacred cave," Heart-of-the-Wolf said quietly. "You must not wear coup feathers in your hair, nor adorn yourself with enemy scalps. You must not carry any weapons, nor should you wear the claws of *matohota*. One must be humble to enter the realm of spirits. Wear only a clout of deerskin and your oldest moccasins. You must not braid your hair, or wear paint of any kind."

Shadow Hawk nodded solemnly.

"When you enter the cave, you must offer

sacred pollen to the four directions, then to the Great Spirit, and then to our mother, the earth. When that is done, you must sit down facing east. It will be dark in the cave, but you must not light a fire, and you must not speak. You must think of the future, nothing more. In your mind and heart, you must ask *Wakán Tanka* to show you what the next year holds for our people."

"Perhaps the Great Spirit will not reveal the future to me," Shadow Hawk remarked. "Perhaps I do not possess the power to communicate with Man Above."

Heart-of-the-Wolf placed a gnarled hand on Shadow Hawk's shoulder. "You will not be in the cave alone. My prayers will join with yours. My spirit will be there, beside you."

"When?" Shadow Hawk asked. "When do I go to the cave?"

"The night of the next full moon."

Three days, Shadow Hawk mused, and felt his insides grow taut.

The next two days passed slowly. Shadow Hawk spent many hours contemplating what he was about to do, wondering if he had the courage to enter the cave, if his medicine was strong enough to summon the power of the spirits. Heart-of-the-Wolf had taught Hawk all he knew about healing, instructing him carefully in the many chants and rituals a medicine man must know, imparting to Shadow Hawk the knowledge he would have passed on to his own son if he'd had one. Shadow Hawk had listened attentively to everything Heart-of-the-Wolf said.

He had learned that a wise man sought out *Hunonpa*, the bear, who was a source of knowledge and wisdom; that *Tatetob* was four gods in one, representing the four winds, and that *Tatetob* ruled the weather and the directions; that *Yumni* was the god of the whirlwind.

He knew that red was the color of the sun, blue represented the sky, green signified the Earth, and yellow was the color of rock. A red forked zigzag was the sign of *Wakinyan*, the thunderbird. Sage smoke could drive away certain evil forces; a buffalo skull contained the power of *Tatanka*.

Shadow Hawk had learned well; he had passed all the tests required of him, and now he faced the biggest test of all. His courage and his confidence had always been strong. He prayed fervently that they would not fail him now.

The evening before the chosen time, he went down to the river to be alone.

A chill wind blew down out of the mountains, whispering to the cottonwood trees, sighing as it danced over the tall grass.

Shadow Hawk took a deep breath. He refused to admit he might be afraid to enter the sacred cavern, that the calling of a holy man might not be his.

He squared his shoulders and shook off his doubts. If Heart-of-the-Wolf could travel the Spirit Path and return unharmed, so could he.

Shadow Hawk smiled faintly as he recalled years past, remembering how awed he had been at the old medicine man's unerring predictions of the future. Heart-of-the-Wolf had always known when it was time to move the village, where to find the buffalo, how to avoid the white men who ventured into their country.

Shadow Hawk had marveled at the old man's powers, but now he knew where those powers had come from. Now he knew that the Cave of the Spirit Path was more than just a legend.

And tomorrow night he would enter the cave and learn its secrets.

Shadow Hawk shivered as a gust of wind embraced him, whispering in his ear that once he crossed the threshold of the sacred cave, he would never be the same again.

Standing there, gazing at the starlit sky, he saw a great black hawk soaring overheard. Closing his eyes, he willed his spirit to join with that of the hawk and he felt himself soaring upward, felt the power and wisdom and patience of the hawk flow through his soul, and he knew that no matter what happened at the cave, his medicine spirit was still with him, still strong.

Gradually, the spirit of the hawk faded, leaving him feeling refreshed and at peace. Tomorrow night he would enter the Cave of the Spirit Path. . . .

Chapter Four

Shadow Hawk left his mother's lodge early the following morning, walking purposefully toward a quiet bend in the river to offer his Dawn Song to *Wakán Tanka*. It was a song of joy that lifted to the sky like the sacred healing smoke from a holy fire; a song that told of the earth and the sky and the great circle of life with the Great Spirit in the center, and man yearning to be a part of it.

"*Hee-ay-hee-ee!*" he cried, lifting his arms overhead. "Help me, *Wakán Tanka*, guide my steps."

He lowered his arms, listening to the sound of the river as it eddied and swirled at his feet, to the carefree song of a bird as it flitted from tree to tree. In the distance, the vast Lakota horse herd grazed on the short yellow grass.

Looking up, he gazed at the clear blue sky, felt the warmth of the new sun caress his bare shoulders and chest, and once again he lifted his arms overhead.

"Hear me, *Wakán Tanka*," he murmured earnestly. "Grant me the courage to do what must be done to help my people."

He stood there for an hour, his heart and mind sending silent prayers to the Great Spirit as he prepared himself to do what must be done.

At the appointed time, he went to the *sintkala waksu* with Heart-of-the-Wolf. The medicine man had dug a small *iniowaspe*, or pit, in the middle of the sweat lodge to hold the sacred stones, which were called *inyan*. The pit made a circle within a circle, representing life which had no end. The door of the lodge faced the setting sun, the floor was covered with a blanket of sage. The dirt which had been removed from the *iniowaspe* was used to make a small mound about two paces from the entrance. The mound was called *hanbelachia*, the vision hill.

Between the pit and the hill, the dirt had been cleared to form a path called the smoothed trail, which symbolized the path Shadow Hawk would travel to find his vision. Tiny bundles of tobacco were attached to sticks and placed on the west side of the vision hill; the sacred pipe was also placed on the hill, its stem facing east.

Naked, Shadow Hawk entered the sweat lodge. Heart-of-the-Wolf's nephew, Black Otter, remained outside to tend the fire and pass the heated stones into the lodge.

Shadow Hawk took a deep breath and released it slowly as Black Otter passed in the first four stones, lifting them with a forked stick.

With great ceremony, Heart-of-the-Wolf took the pipe and touched the stem to one of the stones. "All four-footed creatures," the medicine man murmured reverently, for his power came from the wolf.

He passed the pipe to Shadow Hawk, who puffed it four times and passed it back to the medicine man.

This was done four times, until the tobacco was gone, and then Heart-of-the-Wolf reverently returned the pipe to the *hanbelachia*. Pipes were smoked to prevent storms, to ensure a successful hunt, to invoke the blessings of the gods, or to denote peace and friendship. They were considered sacred, their smoke carrying the prayers of the people to *Wakán Tanka*, and thus they were handled with great care and respect.

"All four-footed creatures," Heart-of-the-Wolf intoned solemnly, and taking up a spoon made of buffalo horn, he tossed cold water on the stones.

He did this four times, as four was a sacred number. There were four directions to the earth, four elements above the earth: sky, sun, moon, and stars. There were four seasons to the year. There were four classes of animals: flying, crawling, two-legged, and four-legged. There were four parts to plants: roots, stem, leaves, and fruit. And, finally, a man's life was divided into four parts: infancy, childhood, adulthood, and old age.

As great clouds of steam filled the lodge, Heart-of-the-Wolf began to chant, begging the spirits to purify them.

Shadow Hawk gasped for air as the heat engulfed him. The cold water and the hot stones united him with the earth and the sky, the water of life and the sacred breath of the Spirit. As he inhaled the steam, he inhaled the water of life, praying for strength, for courage, for wisdom.

And suddenly she was there, the woman of his vision, her curly black hair falling about her shoulders like a dark cloud. Her lips were the color of ripe berries; her eyes, as blue as the wildflowers that covered the hills in the summer, were filled with tears.

She was sitting in an odd-looking box with big wheels like those on the wagons of the bluecoats. Behind her, Shadow Hawk could see a drawing of a tall Indian man sitting astride a big calico horse. The Indian wore a necklace of bear claws; the horse looked exactly like Wohitika. Despite the stifling heat within the lodge, Shadow Hawk felt a sudden chill spiral down his spine.

"Do you see her, old one?" he whispered, hardly daring to speak aloud for fear of chasing the image away.

Heart-of-the-Wolf grunted softly, astonished by the clarity of the vision, troubled by the Spirit Woman's ability to manifest herself to Shadow Hawk within the sacred circle of the sweat lodge, and even more alarmed that he was able to see another's vision. What manner of white woman was this, to have such power?

29

Heart-of-the-Wolf leaned forward, his gaze focused on the drawing behind the woman. No, he thought, it could not be Shadow Hawk. . . .

"You must put her from your mind," the medicine man said sternly. "You must think only of the cave, and the vision that waits for you there."

Shadow Hawk nodded. "I hear you, *Tunkasila*," he murmured.

As soon as he spoke, the image of the Spirit Woman began to dissolve, until all that remained was the memory of the unhappiness he had seen in her eyes.

Chapter Five

Shadow Hawk reached the entrance to the Cave of the Spirit Path as the sun began its descent behind the distant mountains. His heart was pounding like a Lakota war drum as he took a deep breath and exhaled it slowly.

The cave was located on a narrow plateau near the crest of the hill, surrounded by trees whose branches were woven so tightly together they blocked his view of the sky, leaving the face of the cave shrouded in darkness and mystery.

He took another deep breath, for courage. He had done all that Heart-of-the-Wolf had commanded. He had not eaten for one full day. He carried no weapons, he wore no coup feathers in his hair, nor did he wear his bear claw necklace.

Clad only in a deerskin clout and moccasins, his hair falling over his shoulders, he took his first step into the cave, which was cut into the side of the hill.

For a moment, Hawk stood just inside the entrance, letting his eyes adjust to the darkness, which seemed blacker than the night. He had expected the cave to be musty and damp; instead it was cool and sweet-smelling.

He took four steps, his moccasined feet whispering over the ground, the sound of his heartbeat echoing in his ears. He had known fear before, but nothing like the nameless anxiety that brought a fine sheen of sweat to his brow.

Reminding himself that Heart-of-the-Wolf had entered the cave and survived to tell the tale, he took four more steps, and then four more before he stopped, deep in the heart of the cavern.

Removing a small deerskin bag from his belt, he reached inside and withdrew a handful of corn pollen, scattering a small amount to the east, the west, the north, and the south, to the Great Spirit, to Mother Earth. When that was done, he poured the remainder back into the bag, then sat down, facing east.

The cave's darkness closed around him, so thick he could almost touch it. Head high, his body tense, he faced the east wall of the cave, silently beseeching the Great Spirit to grant him a vision that he might obtain the knowledge that Heart-of-the-Wolf required to lead the people through the coming year.

Over and over again, he uttered the same prayer. He lost track of time. Indeed, time might have ceased to exist. The darkness seemed to have a life of its own, moving over his bare skin like a caress, its touch probing, testing, challenging.

Hands clenched, Shadow Hawk stared toward the east wall, all his thoughts and energy focused on the future.

Slowly, so slowly he thought he must be imagining it, a faint light began to glow on the face of the cave and at the same time, images began to appear within his mind, images that grew stronger as the darkness within the cave seemed to grow thicker, heavier, until he thought he could feel it sitting beside him, an entity with a life force of its own.

In the back of his mind, he heard Heart-of-the-Wolf's voice warning him to concentrate on the future, only the future.

Shadow Hawk shook off the fear crowding his heart as the glowing light and the images in his mind grew more distinct, and now he saw the Lakota village clearly in his mind's eye. He saw his own lodge, and that of Heart-of-the-Wolf. Snow covered the ground, the sky was gray and lowering. It was the winter camp in the Black Hills, he thought, surprised. The images seemed to fill the cave now and he seemed to be a part of it. He felt the cold wind, inhaled the scent of smoke and roasting meat. He shivered as it began to rain, but the rain was blue and dry and wherever the rain touched the snow, the flakes were stained with crimson.

Startled, Shadow Hawk recoiled, then gasped as he felt something warm and wet slide down his right side.

"A-ah!" he exclaimed, and the images in his mind melted like frost beneath the sun. The light disappeared, the air lost its heaviness, and he felt suddenly empty and alone.

Rising, Shadow Hawk hurried from the cave, surprised to find the sun climbing over the mountains. The early morning sunlight seemed unusually bright after the darkness of the cave; he felt weak and lightheaded, as if someone had drained all the strength from his body. There was a sudden pain low in his right side and when he looked at it, he saw a bright splash of blood just above the belt of his clout. Blood where there was no wound.

Bewildered, he turned to stare at the cave entrance, wondering what it meant, and she was there, silhouetted in the mouth of the cave, her black hair becoming one with the darkness behind her.

The Spirit Woman.

"Not real," he murmured, yet he saw her clearly, sitting as though trapped in the thing-on-wheels, her arms outstretched, her deep blue eyes silently entreating him to come to her. A soft breath of cold air blew out of the cave, chilling him to the bone.

"Not real," he said again, and resisting the urge to run, he turned and started down the mountain, certain he would never be warm again.

Heart-of-the-Wolf listened intently as Shadow Hawk related his experience in the sacred cave. His eyes grew thoughtful, his expression pensive, as the young warrior told of rain that turned the snow to blood.

"Did you see any *wasichu* in your vision, Shadow Hawk?"

"No."

"But the rain was blue and the snow turned red?"

Shadow Hawk nodded.

"It is not good," Heart-of-the-Wolf mused slowly. "I think we will not go to the *Paha Sapa* this winter. The blue rain represents the soldier coats. The red snow is the blood of our people. *Wakán Tanka* is warning us that soldiers will attack our village." He nodded, as if satisfied with his interpretation. "We will find another place to pass the winter."

"Have the visions in the cave always been true ones?"

"*Ai*, if they are interpreted correctly."

"Have you ever been wrong?"

The old man nodded. "Once, long ago. Some visions are not easy to understand."

"How can you be sure you are right this time?"

"The blue rain always means the *wasichu*."

"Perhaps the red snow means the whites will lose."

"Perhaps," Heart-of-the-Wolf allowed. "But we will not take that chance. Did you see anything else?"

Shadow Hawk shook his head. "No."

"Perhaps there was nothing more to see."

"I broke the silence of the cave when I felt the blood trickling down my side," Shadow Hawk confessed guiltily, "and the images in my mind dissolved."

"Ah. Then you must go back. The visions do not always come in the order they will happen. Your vision took place in winter, and it is only spring. There may be another vision waiting for you there."

"Go back?" Shadow Hawk said reluctantly. "When?"

"Tomorrow night, while the moon is still full."

Shadow Hawk nodded. He would go back because Heart-of-the-Wolf required it, but he would not like it. "The blood on my side? What does it mean?"

Heart-of-the-Wolf stared at the dark stain on Shadow Hawk's right side. He had examined the skin beneath the dried blood carefully; there was no wound, not even a scratch.

"I am not sure," the medicine man replied, his expression somber.

Shadow Hawk took a deep breath and released it slowly. "The Spirit Woman was there, at the cave," he said, leaning toward the medicine man. "What does she want of me? Why does she summon me with her eyes?"

Heart-of-the-Wolf shook his head. "I cannot answer these questions now. I must meditate on the vision granted you in the Sacred Cave. We will speak of it when you return."

Shadow Hawk nodded, then rose to his feet and left the old man's lodge. Later, always later, he thought as he walked down to the river and washed the blood from his side. How long must he wait to find the secret to the Spirit Woman?

His mother was waiting for him when he entered the lodge. She had prepared food for him and the air was redolent with the aroma of succulent buffalo ribs, thick berry soup, and strong tea. She did not question him while he ate, but he could feel her concern, her need to know what had happened in the cave.

He smiled at her as he licked the grease from his fingers. "I am well, *Iná*," he assured her. "Let us talk of it tomorrow. I would sleep now."

Winona nodded, her curiosity replaced by motherly concern as she watched her son stretch out on the buffalo robes in the back of the lodge. What had it been like within the sacred cave? Had he seen a vision? What did the future hold for the People?

Chapter Six

A shrill cry of terror shattered Shadow Hawk's sleep. Rolling nimbly to his feet, he reached for his bow, grabbed a quiver of arrows, and hurried out of the lodge.

For a moment he could only stare at the chaos before him. The setting sun cast a crimson shadow over the village, so that everything looked dreamlike and unreal. Men, women, and children ran wildly through the village while the hated blue-clad soldiers rode amongst them, shooting everything that moved. People, horses, and dogs fell prey to the rifles of the Long Knives. The air was thick with the smell of gunpowder. And blood.

Rage filled Shadow Hawk's breast as he reached for Wohitika's reins. Even now, Red Cloud and a handful of the tribal elders were in Washington talking peace. How like the white man, he mused, to hold out the promise of peace with one hand and strike down women and children with the other!

Swinging onto the stallion's back, Shadow Hawk swept his gaze over the area as he searched for some sign of his mother, but he could not find her in the surging crowd.

Wohitika reared up on his hind legs as a blue-clad trooper came hurtling toward him. With a wild cry, Shadow Hawk nocked an arrow to his bow and let it fly, feeling a deep sense of satisfaction as the arrow pierced the man's chest.

Shadow Hawk rode into the midst of the battle, rage building within him as he saw a small child trampled beneath the iron-shod hooves of a cavalryman's horse. He saw his best friend, Red Arrow, plunge a knife deep into the throat of one of the *wasichu*, saw a hairy-faced trooper skewer a child with a bayonet.

A scream of outrage rumbled in Shadow Hawk's throat as he rode the white man down. From the corner of his eye, he saw one of the soldiers struggling with Red Arrow's wife.

Slamming his heels into Wohitika's sides, Shadow Hawk rode the white man down. He caught a brief look of gratitude from Red Arrow's wife, and then she was lost from sight as she grabbed her young son by the arm and ran for cover.

Shadow Hawk scanned the crowd, still hoping to find his mother. His nostrils filled with the smell of dust and sweat, of fear and blood. Off to the right, a lodge went up in flames. The smoke and the smell of burning hides made his eyes water. His ears rang with the noise of battle: horses whinnying in panic, children crying in terror, women shrieking with fear, the moans of the dying. And over all, the shrill, ululating war cry of the Lakota.

He killed two more white men as he rode back through the village and then, to his left, he saw Heart-of-the-Wolf making his way toward the timber at the east end of the village and he rode after the frail medicine man.

Riding up beside Heart-of-the-Wolf, he leaned over the side of his horse, grabbed the medicine man by the waist, and lifted him onto Wohitika's back, then headed for the cover of the trees, intending to leave the old man there while he returned to the village to search for Winona.

"Stay here," Shadow Hawk said, reining the stallion to a sharp halt, but before he could lower the medicine man to the ground, a trio of soldiers rode up behind him, firing wildly.

"Hang on!" Shadow Hawk shouted. His heart pounding with fear for the old man's life, he slammed his heels into Wohitika's sides.

"The cave!" Heart-of-the-Wolf shouted. "Go to the cave. We'll be safe there."

It was in Shadow Hawk's mind to refuse. His people were fighting for their lives and he wanted to be there, fighting with them. But he could not abandon Heart-of-the-Wolf now. When the battle was over, the people would need their holy man.

Shadow Hawk urged the big calico stallion to go faster. He could hear the soldiers hollering as they continued to give chase. The roar of gunfire seemed to grow closer, louder. He felt Heart-of-the-Wolf jerk against him, heard the sharp report of a rifle, and he drummed his heels into the stallion's flanks, knowing their only hope was to outrun the soldiers.

They had reached the hills now. Higher and higher they climbed, driven on by the shouts and gunshots of the pursuing troopers, and then the Sacred Cave was in sight, its yawning maw as black as a winter night.

Reining Wohitika to a halt, Shadow Hawk dismounted. Ignoring Heart-of-the-Wolf's protests, he lifted the old man into his arms as if he were no more than a child and hurried toward the entrance.

"Your weapons," Heart-of-the-Wolf said as they reached the passageway. "You must not take them inside."

Shadow Hawk hesitated only a moment, then he dropped his bow and quiver to the ground and stepped into the shadowed cavern.

Inside, he lowered Heart-of-the-Wolf to the ground. The old man was breathing heavily now and Shadow Hawk put his arm around the medicine man's frail shoulders to steady him.

He tensed as he heard voices, and then he saw one of the soldiers approaching the mouth of the cave.

"Be still," Heart-of-the-Wolf admonished quietly.

"I should have brought my weapons," Shadow Hawk retorted. "We are trapped in here."

"No," Heart-of-the-Wolf said reassuringly. "Only wait and see."

The bluecoat paused a moment at the entrance, silhouetted against the fading twilight; then, with his bayoneted rifle at the ready, he crossed the threshold and stepped into the murky darkness.

Shadow Hawk held his breath, certain he was about to die, and then he felt it, the cave's blackness hovering all around him, a living entity armed for battle.

But there was no battle. Three more steps carried the soldier well into the cave.

Shadow Hawk stared at the white man, barely visible within the darkness of the cave. For long seconds, there was only silence and then, with a strangled sound of pain, the white man collapsed.

Voices at the entrance to the cavern drew Shadow Hawk's gaze, and he saw the other two *wasichu* peering inside, apparently calling for their companion.

Shadow Hawk frowned, wishing he could understand the white man's tongue. But he didn't need words to know the two white men were arguing about whether to enter the cave. It was obvious they were bothered by the disappearance of the first soldier, and Shadow Hawk could see by their expressions that the two remaining white men were hesitant to enter the cave, not knowing what waited for them inside.

After a few minutes, the soldiers shrugged and walked away.

"What now?" Shadow Hawk asked. He turned to face Heart-of-the-Wolf, though he could not see the old man's face in the thick darkness that surrounded them.

"We wait until they go away."

"I must go back," Shadow Hawk said. Agitated, he began to pace back and forth. "The people may need me."

"No. The bluecoats will kill you before you can reach your weapons. You will be of more value to our people alive than dead."

"I should not have broken the silence of the cave during the vision," Shadow Hawk said, his voice thick with self-accusation. "If I had not failed, we would have known of this battle."

"Do not blame yourself. It takes a brave heart to enter this cave. You did well."

Shadow Hawk shook his head. His people were dying because he had failed. Perhaps his mother was dead, killed by the bluecoats, while he hid in a cave like a frightened rabbit.

"I must go back," he said, starting toward the entrance. "I will return for you when the battle is over."

"Wait."

The pain in the old man's voice stopped Shadow Hawk and he returned to the medicine man's side. "What is it?"

"You must not blame yourself for what has happened," Heart-of-the-Wolf said, his voice suddenly weak. "Before this day is over, our people will have need of a new holy man. Remember all that I have taught you."

"*Tunkasila* . . ." Shadow Hawk slipped his arm around Heart-of-the-Wolf's waist, uttered a soft cry of denial as he felt the warm blood oozing

through the back of the old man's buckskin
shirt.

"There is nothing you can do for me, *Cetán*.
May *Wakán Tanka* guide your steps until we
meet again."

"And yours."

Shadow Hawk felt his throat grow thick with
unshed tears as he lowered Heart-of-the-Wolf
to the ground. The floor of the cavern was
smooth and flat, covered with a thick layer of
fine sand.

Heart-of-the-Wolf placed a hand on Shadow
Hawk's forearm. "Your mother is well," he said.
His voice was weaker now, barely audible in the
hushed silence of the Sacred Cave. "*Cetán*, the
Spirit Woman appeared to me in a dream just
before the soldiers came. Listen to her. When the
time comes, she will tell you what to do. . . ."

Shadow Hawk murmured the medicine man's
name as he felt the strength go out of Heart-of-
the-Wolf's grip, and he knew the life had gone
out of the old man's eyes, as well.

He felt a sudden warmth, like a summer wind,
whisper past his cheek and he shivered, wonder-
ing if it was his imagination, or if he'd just felt
Heart-of-the-Wolf's spirit take its first step on
Wanagi Tacaka, the Spirit Path, which led to
Wanagi Yatu, the Place of Souls.

For a long while, Shadow Hawk sat beside
the old man's body. Heart-of-the-Wolf had been
a part of his life for as far back as he could
remember, teaching him, helping him to be a
warrior, answering his questions. And now he
was gone. It seemed fitting, somehow, that the

aged shaman had died deep within the heart of the Sacred Cave.

Shadow Hawk fought back tears of grief and anger as he smoothed the old man's hair from his face, folded the gnarled hands over the narrow chest, gently closed his eyes.

Softly, his heart aching with his loss, he began to chant Heart-of-the-Wolf's death song, beseeching the Great Spirit to guide the old man's steps into the Great Mystery that was death.

He sat there for a long time, his hatred for the whites churning within him, making his blood burn with a need for vengeance.

Rising to his feet, Shadow Hawk walked toward the entrance to the cave, thinking to go back to the village, but the sound of voices changed his mind. The soldiers were still out there, waiting, and he had no weapons with which to fight them. He could see his bow lying where he'd dropped it, and there was Wohitika nibbling at a patch of yellow grass, but he could not see the bluecoats.

Returning to the rear of the cavern, Shadow Hawk sat down with his back to the wall.

For a time, his thoughts wandered and then he stared at the east wall of the Sacred Cave, wondering if he had the power to summon the spirit of the cave without Heart-of-the-Wolf's prayers to guide him.

Closing his eyes, he tried to focus on the outcome of the battle. Instead he found himself thinking of the Spirit Woman, and he seemed to hear Heart-of-the-Wolf's dying words whisper in the back of his mind. *Listen to her. When the time comes, she will tell you what to do.* . . .

But Heart-of-the-Wolf was dead, and he would never learn her secret now. . . .

Shadow Hawk sat up, torn from the brink of sleep as the spirit of the cave settled over him. As though drawn by an invisible hand, he turned his head, saw the east wall of the cave begin to glow as the square house of a white man materialized before his eyes.

"No!" Shadow Hawk shook his head as the spirit of the cave swirled around him, enveloping him, carrying him away into darkness. . . .

He woke slowly, his mind and body feeling groggy, and then, remembering the battle, he made his way toward the entrance of the cavern.

Shadow Hawk paused there for a few moments, listening, and when he heard nothing, he stepped outside.

The sun was rising over the Black Hills, lighting the edge of the eastern sky, streaking the horizon with brilliant splashes of red and gold.

He stood still a moment, every muscle tense, but no bullet came to find him as he left the shelter of the Sacred Cave. There was only the soft sighing of the wind as it danced across the hilltop, and the answering whisper of the leaves from a nearby pine tree.

It was then he noticed that his weapons were gone, and so was the big calico stallion.

Shadow Hawk took a deep breath, his hatred for the white men growing stronger, deeper, with each passing minute. Until today, he had thought of them only as a peculiar race, a people who didn't know where to find the center of the earth, but now he hated them with a rage that was all-encompassing. They had summoned Red Cloud to Washington to talk of peace when they wanted war; they had killed Heart-of-the-Wolf; they had stolen his prized war horse and his weapons.

He drew in a deep steadying breath, released it in a long shuddering sigh. And then he started down the hillside, wondering if anyone had survived the battle, wondering if he would find his people dead and the village burned to the ground.

But Heart-of-the-Wolf had said his mother still lived, and with that thought in mind, he began to run, his heart pounding with hope, and dread.

He was running down a narrow twisting deer trail, dodging left and right to avoid the prickly brush that covered the hill, when something slammed into his right side, knocking him off his feet. He heard the report of the gunshot as he hit the ground. Seconds later, a large buck bounded past him and disappeared into the underbrush.

For a moment, Shadow Hawk stared blankly at the bright red blood welling from the ugly bullet hole in his side. His right side, just above his clout. He felt suddenly cold as he pressed his hand over the wound. But there was nothing cold about the blood welling between his fingers. It was warm and wet.

Hand pressed to his side, he peered down the hill, frowning in confusion when he saw a tall Indian dressed in a skin-tight white shirt and tight black trousers running up the slope toward him. And beyond the Indian, the square house of a white man.

His first thought was to find a place to hide, but his legs refused to support him and he fell back, groaning softly, as a swirling red mist hovered around him, pulling him down, down, into nothingness. . . .

Chapter Seven

Maggie St. Claire sat beside the bed in the guest room, unable to take her eyes from the man lying beneath the covers. It was incredible, impossible, but true nonetheless. He looked exactly like the warrior in the painting over her fireplace.

But it couldn't be him. The man didn't exist except in a dream she'd had years ago. How many years, she thought, frowning. Five? Six? Even now, she could remember that dream, remember the overwhelming fear that had engulfed her as he thundered toward her, leaning over the neck of a big calico stallion to lift her effortlessly onto the back of his horse. They had ridden away into the night, his arm tight around her waist, his breath warm upon her neck, as he carried her to his lodge.

Upon waking, she'd gone into her studio and sketched the man in her dream while his image was still fresh in her mind. She'd modeled several of the heroes in her books after her dream warrior and then, impulsively, she'd photographed the finished painting and sent it to her editor, Sheila Goodman, who confessed that the Indian was the handsomest thing she'd ever seen. They had both agreed he was exactly what the hero of her book, *Forbidden Flame*, should look like. They'd used his likeness on the cover, and on several others after that.

Maggie glanced at the book rack across the room, feeling a rush of pride in what she'd accomplished. Twelve historical romance novels in six years. And the four best sellers were the ones that featured her dream warrior on the cover.

She looked back at the Indian. How was it possible for this man to look exactly like the warrior in her dream? What had he been doing on her property, clad in nothing but a skimpy deerskin clout and soft-soled moccasins? Thank God Bobby Running Horse hadn't killed him!

Maggie's gaze wandered over the Indian again, noting the long black hair, straight black brows, hawklike nose, and strong, square jaw. His skin was like dark copper, smooth and unmarred except for two faint scars on his chest and the ugly wound low in his right side.

Such a wonderful physique, Maggie mused. He had a build to rival that of Fabio, the gorgeous Italian hunk who appeared on so many of Johanna Lindsey's book covers. The same broad shoulders and powerful arms; a face that was beautiful, yet utterly masculine.

Maggie shook such thoughts from her mind. This wasn't one of her romance novels, this was real life. Beautiful or not, handsome or not, she wanted nothing to do with him or any other man. She'd been hurt once in the game of love; she didn't intend to risk her heart a second time.

With the ease of long practice, she turned the wheelchair around and rolled silently out of the spare bedroom.

Going to her desk in the spacious oak-paneled den, she sat in front of the computer, trying to concentrate on the love scene she'd been writing before Bobby hurried into the house, his words running together as he told her he'd shot someone. Maggie had immediately called the doctor in Sturgis, only to learn that he was out on an emergency and wasn't expected back until late that night. Maggie had told his answering service that she was having a little emergency of her own and then hung up. Thank goodness her housekeeper, Veronica Little Moon, had been at the ranch when Bobby brought the stranger home. Veronica had tended the man's wound, assuring Maggie that he'd be all right even though he'd lost a good deal of blood, warning her that he might have a bit of a fever before the night was over. Veronica had offered to stay and sit with him, but Maggie had sent Veronica home. Veronica had a hard-working husband and two teenage sons to care for. And if Maggie needed anything during the night, she had only to pick up the phone and call Bobby, who lived in the guest house out back.

Maggie grimaced. Bobby, who wanted to be a warrior and couldn't tell a man from a deer!

Maggie stared at the blue screen of her computer, but it was no use; she couldn't stop thinking of the man in the other room, couldn't stop wondering who he was, where he'd come from.

Veronica had called the Sturgis police and told them what had happened. An hour later, Lindsey Hollister, the Chief of Police, had come out to look around. He'd questioned Bobby and concluded it was a hunting accident, and then he and Veronica had agreed it would be best not to move the injured man unless there were complications.

Hollister's only concern had been the fact that the Indian didn't have any identification, but in the end he'd decided that the redskin was probably wandering around drunk and that, sooner or later, someone would show up from the reservation to file a missing person's report and they'd find out who he was and where be belonged.

Hollister had hung around the rest of the afternoon, shooting the breeze with Bobby. He had accepted Maggie's invitation to dinner, then lingered for two cups of coffee before heading back to town, apparently convinced that the Indian was out for the night.

With a shake of her head, Maggie turned off the computer and made her way into her bedroom. Undressing, she slipped into her nightgown, then unbraided her hair. In bed, she stared up at the ceiling, plagued by a sudden loneliness as she recalled what day it was.

Blinking back tears, she closed her eyes. It had been two years and six months since the accident that left her crippled and unable to walk. The doctors had told her it was all psychological, that there was nothing wrong with her legs, that she could walk if she tried. It was guilt, they said, guilt that kept her tied to a wheelchair, guilt because she had lived and Susie had died.

Maggie swiped at the tears cascading down her cheeks. Stupid doctors! Did they think she liked being in a wheelchair? Didn't they think she'd walk if she could? Of course she felt guilty because Susie had died. Who wouldn't feel guilty if they'd caused an accident that took their younger sister's life?

A sob tore at Maggie's throat. She'd been driving too fast, laughing at some silly thing Susie had said, when they rounded the curve. Laughing so hard she hadn't even seen the oncoming truck until it was too late. She'd jerked the steering wheel to the right, barely missing the truck. She'd known a brief moment of relief, and then the car spun out of control, sliding down the embankment, crashing into a tree. Susie, who never wore her seat belt, had been thrown out of the car. Knowing her sister needed help, Maggie had crawled up the hill to the road where she'd flagged down an oncoming car, and then she'd fainted.

When she woke up, she was lying in bed in a hospital room painted a sickly green. It was there, surrounded by doctors, that she'd learned

Susie was dead. Susie, who had loved ice skating and dancing and playing tennis, who had found joy in everything, dead at nineteen because her older sister was a careless fool.

Six months after the accident, Frank broke their engagement. He hadn't made any flowery excuses, he hadn't lied to her. He'd simply told her the truth, as kindly as he could. He was sorry, so sorry, but he had to be honest and he just didn't think he could handle living with a woman who was going to spend the rest of her life in a wheelchair.

Maggie had cried for days and then she'd thrown herself into her writing, running away from the present by writing about the past, hiding from her own misery by penning fanciful romances where true love could overcome any obstacle and everyone lived happily ever after.

She'd moved to South Dakota four months later, buying a small ranch located in a grassy meadow between Sturgis and the Black Hills. It was beautiful country. The Hills were breathtaking and she could understand why the Sioux wanted them back.

The Hills seemed to have a life of their own, a presence that she'd felt the first time she saw them. There were eighteen peaks that exceeded seven thousand feet, an island of mountains in a sea of prairie grass and rangeland that covered roughly six thousand miles. She loved the pines and the aspen and the clear blue sky, the rolling miles of prairie grass, the sense of history that she felt each time she looked out her window and saw the majesty of the Black Hills rising in the distance.

The Lakota called them *Paha Sapa*, meaning hills that appear black in color. They also called them *O'onakezin*, which meant a place of shelter, or *Wamakaognaka E'cante*, which meant "the heart of everything that is."

Soon after she moved to the ranch, Maggie put an ad in the local paper, advertising for help. Nineteen-year-old Bobby had arrived at her door the next day and she'd hired him on the spot. He needed the money, he'd said, to help support his brother, and he hoped to go to college and study medicine. She'd hired Veronica the same day, liking her no-nonsense attitude.

With Bobby to look after the ranch and Veronica to take care of the cooking and cleaning, Maggie turned her attention to writing romantic stories of beautiful white women and handsome Indian men. She never saw anyone else, never went into Sturgis, the small town about ten miles south of Bear Butte. Veronica did all the shopping and picked up the mail.

Maggie's love for the land grew steadily. In days past, the Sioux and Cheyenne had come here, to the *Paha Sapa*, to celebrate the sacred ritual of the Sun Dance. She liked to think that Sitting Bull and Crazy Horse, Red Cloud, Hump and Gall had once walked the land where her house now stood. The Hills were a piece of American history made famous by people like Calamity Jane, Wild Bill Hickock, Jim Bridger, and the ill-fated General George Armstrong Custer.

She'd always been fascinated by the Old West,

especially the Indians. She was enchanted by their beliefs, saddened at their ultimate fate. When she'd started writing, it had seemed the most natural thing in the world to write about the Sioux and Cheyenne.

Perhaps feeling that she was a kindred soul, Veronica had offered to teach Maggie to speak Lakota, and Maggie considered it a rare gift, to be able to speak the ancient Sioux language. Veronica had charmed her with old tales and legends, stories of *Iktomi*, the trickster; of the *Unktehi*, who captured men and turned them into beasts; of *Iya*, a monster who ate animals and men. She wished *Iya* would go to L.A. and devour Frank Williams!

Maggie wiped her face with a corner of the sheet, determined never to think of the past again. It was too painful to think of Frank and what might have been.

With a sigh, she closed her eyes and willed herself to relax, to think of quiet blue oceans and the whisper of the wind sighing across the prairie, singing to the tall grass.

Instead, she fell asleep thinking of the Indian sleeping in her guest room.

In her dreams, he came riding toward her as he had once before, a darkly handsome stranger with eyes as black as a midnight sky and skin like burnished copper, but this time she wasn't afraid, and she didn't run away.

Chapter Eight

Sunlight warmed his face. He heard someone singing softly, smelled meat cooking, and he knew it was time to get up, to go to the river to bathe before he offered his Dawn Song to *Wakán Tanka*.

Sighing, Shadow Hawk started to get up, only to be seized by a sharp pain in his right side.

Hand pressed over the bandage swathed around his middle, he sat up, unmindful of the thin blue blanket that slid down his chest and pooled in his lap as he stared at his surroundings. He'd had little experience with the *wasichu*, but he knew immediately that he was inside one of their square houses. Was he a prisoner?

Frowning, he recalled seeing one of the white man's lodges when he'd emerged from the Sacred Cave, but before he could wonder at its presence, he'd been shot. By an Indian wearing the clothes of a *wasichu*.

He stared at the white material wrapped around his torso. It was unlike anything he had ever seen, lightweight, with tiny holes, like a net.

He touched his hand to the mat beneath him. It was firm yet soft, covered with pale blue cloth. A bed, he thought it was called. His cousin Bright Flower slept in such a bed. She had married a white trapper when Shadow Hawk was sixteen and he had gone to visit her several times, just to make sure the *wasichu* was treating her honorably.

He had thought the white man's lodge very strange, its furnishings stranger still. Bright Flower and her husband had taken their meals at something called a table, eating off colorful dishes made of hard-baked clay. She had cooked on a huge black metal object, a stove, she had called it, instead of over an open fire. He had refused to sleep in the narrow bed they offered him; he had sat on the floor instead of the wooden seat called a chair. . . .

Chair, he thought. That was what the Spirit Woman had been sitting in, a chair with wheels. He shook his head, bewildered by the strangeness of the whites.

With his hand pressed against his side, he slipped out from under the blanket and made his way to the door, ignoring the sharp pain that pierced his side with each step. It was time to leave this place, time to go back to the village, to find out if his mother still lived.

The sound of distant voices made him pause and he turned back into the room, moving toward the window, a sudden need to be outside the confines of the white man's lodge making him forget the ache in his side.

He put his hand to the window, marveling at the smooth coolness beneath his fingers. His cousin's windows had been covered with oiled paper. You could not see through them; they did not feel hard and cool, like clear ice. He pushed against the window, but it refused to open.

He tapped it once, twice, and then, hearing voices behind him, he whirled around, his gaze darting around the room in search of a weapon. He was reaching for the three-legged stool at the foot of the bed, deciding it was better than nothing, when he heard a gasp. Looking up, his eyes widened in disbelief as the Spirit Woman entered the room. She was seated in the chair with wheels and it glided silently across the wooden floor.

Shadow Hawk stared at her, and at the strange-looking chair, not believing his eyes, wondering if he was still inside the Sacred Cave. Perhaps there hadn't been a battle. Perhaps Heart-of-the-Wolf still lived. Perhaps this was just another vision.

"Winyan Wanagi," he murmured reverently. "Spirit Woman." She was even more beautiful than she had been in his visions. Her skin was smooth and clear, her lashes long and thick. Her hair, as black as his own, was worn in braids, the ends tied with bright blue ribbons that matched the color of her eyes.

Maggie stared at the Indian. Awake, his resemblance to the warrior in her painting was even more startling. The man in her dream had been a shadow figure, without substance; the man in her painting was merely a flat image depicting what she recalled from memory. But this man was very much alive and he radiated masculinity and strength and a latent sense of danger.

Behind her, she heard Veronica gasp and Maggie knew that the breakfast tray in Veronica's hands had come perilously close to crashing to the floor.

"Good morning," Maggie said, hoping her voice didn't betray her alarm at finding her patient standing in the middle of the room, naked as the day he'd been born. "How are you feeling?"

Shadow Hawk stared at her, wishing he had learned more of the white man's language from his cousin so he could understand the Spirit Woman's words.

Maggie frowned, wondering if he was deaf. "How are you?" she said again, speaking slowly and distinctly so he could read her lips.

"Maybe he doesn't understand," Veronica suggested.

Maggie shook her head. "Why wouldn't he understand? You told me all the Indians from the reservation speak English."

"Maybe he's not from the reservation."

"Where else would he be from?"

Veronica shrugged. "I don't know, but he looks . . . different."

"Different?" Maggie looked at the Indian more closely. His hair wasn't any longer than that of some of the Indian men she'd seen, his skin wasn't much darker than most, and yet he *did* look different somehow. He held himself with a kind of pride she'd never seen in any of the reservation Indians. There was a wildness about him, a feral look in the depths of his dark eyes that reminded her of a cornered lion, or a bird of prey. She frowned at the scars on his broad chest. But surely they couldn't be Sun Dance scars, not in this day and age.

"*Nituwe he?*" Maggie asked, speaking in Lakota. "Who are you?"

"*Mieyebo Cetán Nagín,*" he replied, startled that she should know his language. "I am Shadow Hawk."

"*Tokiyatanhan yahi he?*" Maggie asked, pleased that he could understand her. "Where have you come from?"

"*Wicoti mitawa.*"

Maggie glanced at Veronica. "His village," she remarked. "What village do you think he means?"

Veronica shrugged. "I don't know. There are no villages near here."

With a shake of her head, the housekeeper walked past Maggie and placed the breakfast tray on the bed. "*Wóyute,*" she said, looking at the Indian. "Food."

Shadow Hawk stared at the Indian woman for a moment. She was tall, with deep-set black eyes and black hair that showed a few streaks of gray. She wore a loose white top, a colorful skirt similar to the ones Apache women wore, and beaded moccasins. She returned his gaze as though she were also studying him, and then she gestured at the tray.

61

"*Yúta*," she said in a motherly tone. "Eat."

Shadow Hawk glanced from the Indian woman to the tray on the bed, his dark eyes wary.

"Well, maybe you can find out where he came from," Veronica said. "I have a pie in the oven that's going to be ashes if it doesn't come out soon."

"Veronica . . ."

Veronica glanced at the Indian, who was staring at Maggie, and then glanced at Maggie, who appeared to be staring back at the Indian with equal admiration.

Matchmaking had never been her strong suit, but Veronica thought she'd have to be deaf and blind not to feel the attraction humming between Maggie and the handsome young man.

"I'll be in the kitchen if you need me," she said, thinking perhaps the mysterious Indian was just what the doctor ordered.

Maggie stared at the Indian for a moment, then gestured at the bandage swathed around his middle. "How are you feeling?" she asked, still speaking in Lakota.

"I am all right," he answered.

His voice was like black velvet, deep and soft. Her gaze was drawn toward the broad expanse of his chest and shoulders, then moved to linger on his arms, which were long and ridged with muscle. She felt her cheeks grow hot and quickly returned her gaze to his face, marveling anew at the masculine beauty of his countenance.

Annoyed by her reaction to his looks, Maggie glanced down at her hands and then, feeling more composed, she looked up at him again.

What was the matter with her? She wasn't
a dewy-eyed teenager, for heaven's sake, she
was thirty-two years old, and this stranger, no
matter how handsome he might be, looked to
be in his early twenties, making him much
too young for her, even if she was interested
in knowing him better, which she definitely
wasn't.

But she did wish he wasn't quite so breath-
takingly male, or quite so bare.

"Bobby didn't mean to shoot you," she said,
staring at a point past the Indian's left shoulder.
"He was after a deer."

"Where am I? How did I get here?"

"This is my house. Bobby brought you here."

Her house. Was he in the land of spirits,
then? Shadow Hawk looked at the woman more
closely. He did not feel dead—surely the dead
did not feel pain or hunger. So, he was still
alive and the Spirit Woman had called him to
her side. He had heard ancient tales of men
mating with spirits. The thought of holding
her, touching her, sent a rush of heat surging
through him.

"How long have I been here?"

"Two days. Please, sit down and eat," Maggie
said, feeling her cheeks grow pink under his
prolonged stare. "You must be hungry."

"No. I must go back to my people."

She saw the wariness in his eyes, the tension
that held his muscles taut, as if he were on the
brink of flight.

"*Kola*," she said, tapping herself on the chest.
"Friend. Please, sit down and eat."

Shadow Hawk hesitated a moment and then, with a curt nod, he took the tray and sat cross-legged on the floor, the tray across his lap. For a moment, he stared at the odd-looking food: something white with a yellow middle, several narrow strips of fragrant meat that made his stomach growl loudly.

"Enjoy your breakfast," Maggie said. "I'll see if Bobby has some clothes that will fit you."

Shadow Hawk nodded. He waited until she had left the room, then began to eat ravenously, his mind spinning in circles. He should go back to the Sacred Cave. If any of his people had survived the battle, they would need him. His mother needed him. He could not stay here.

Putting the tray aside, he started for the door, then paused, his need to know why the Spirit Woman had summoned him stronger than his need to get away.

He was still wondering whether to stay or return to the cave when the Spirit Woman returned, gliding into the room in her chair on wheels.

"Here," she said, handing him a bundle of clothing. "See if any of those will fit."

He took the garments she offered him, studied them intently after she left the room. The pants were of heavy dark blue cloth, the shirt of some softer material. There was a white shirt similar to the one he'd seen on the boy, and an odd-looking item of soft white cloth that looked like pants without legs.

Shadow Hawk grunted as he tossed the clothes on the bed. Just looking at them, he could see they were too small, even if he'd been of a mind to wear them, which he wasn't.

It was a mystery to the Indians why the whites covered themselves with so many layers of clothing. In the Lakota village, a man wore only a clout and moccasins during the summer, perhaps a beaded vest. Only in the winter did they wear leggings and heavy shirts against the cold. But the whites covered themselves from head to foot all year long.

It was most peculiar, but then, the *wasichu* were a peculiar people, with their hairy faces and pale skin. They lived in square houses, when every human being knew there was harmony only within a circle. Life was a circle. *Skan* had caused the world to be made in rounds. The sun, the moon, the earth, and the sky were round. The stems of plants and the bodies of animals were round. Everything in nature, save the rock, was round. Thus the Lakota lived within the sacred circle, in harmony with the forces of nature.

Yes, he thought as he fastened his clout, the whites were a peculiar race. Sitting on the small chair beside the window, he pulled on his moccasins, grimacing as he pressed his hand over his wounded side. It hurt to move, and he glanced at the bed. It was softer than the ground yet firm and strangely comfortable, and he thought briefly of resting for an hour, but he was anxious to return home, anxious to return to the village and find out if his mother still lived.

"Didn't the clothes fit?"

"Your Lakota is very good," Shadow Hawk remarked, turning to face her.

"Veronica taught me. She taught Bobby, too."

"He is Lakota. Why did he not speak our language?"

"I guess he never learned."

"Bob-by and Ver-on-ica." He stumbled over the peculiar names.

Maggie grinned. "Bobby's Lakota name is Running Horse, and Veronica's is Little Moon."

Shadow Hawk grunted softly. "I must go now."

"Are you sure? Perhaps you should rest another day."

"I must go back to my village. My people need me."

"Where is your village?"

"On the other side of the Hills."

"There's no village in the Hills," Maggie said, frowning. "Sometimes the Lakota have ceremonies on top of Bear Butte, but no one lives there." She paused a moment. You're not from Pine Ridge, are you?"

"Pine Ridge?"

"You know, the reservation. It's about an hour away from here."

"My people do not live on the reservation."

"Oh. Is there someone I can call to come after you?"

"Call?"

"On the phone." She pointed at the blue princess telephone on the bedside table. "Phone." She said it in English because she didn't know the word in Lakota, didn't even know if there was such a word.

He looked at her with such confusion that she felt a sudden surge of sympathy. Oh, Lord, he was retarded. No doubt he'd wandered away from the reservation and got lost.

"Who are your people?" she asked. "Who's the man in charge of your village?"

"*Mahpiya Luta.*"

"*Mahpiya Luta,*" Maggie repeated. "Red Cloud!"

Shadow Hawk nodded. He was not surprised that the Spirit Woman knew of *Mahpiya Luta.* Red Cloud was a man of wisdom, well known among the whites, though he was not as revered by the Lakota as Sitting Bull, or considered to be as good a fighter as Crazy Horse.

"Red Cloud," Maggie muttered. But it couldn't be *that* Red Cloud. He'd been dead since 1909.

"Do you know what year this is?"

"Year?"

Maybe he had amnesia, Maggie thought. Or maybe he was simple-minded and liked to pretend he was living back in the 1800s.

"Do you know who the president is?" she asked, then frowned. In the old days, the Indians hadn't called him the president. "The Grandfather in Washington," she said, willing to humor him, at least for the moment. "Do you know who he is?"

Shadow Hawk frowned thoughtfully, trying to remember the name of the Grandfather Red Cloud had gone to see. "Grant?"

"Oh, Lord," Maggie murmured. Ulysses S. Grant had been president back in 1872 or thereabouts.

"Have you ever heard of Bill Clinton?" she asked, knowing as she did so what his answer would be.

He shook his head.

"Do you know what television is?"

"No."

"Do you know about cars? Fords, Chevys?"

"No."

Maggie shook her head, refusing to even consider what she was thinking. She'd read books about time travel, people flitting back and forth from one century to another, she'd even written one herself, but it was just fiction. It wasn't possible in real life. Was it?

Yet even as she told herself it couldn't be true, she knew in her heart that it was. He didn't have the look of a deranged person, or one who was mentally deficient. He had the look of a man who was lost.

"Then I guess you probably haven't heard of Madonna, either," she mused, "or Vietnam or the war in the Persian Gulf, or . . ."

Shadow Hawk shook his head, confused by the strange words, by the look of dismay and disbelief on the Spirit Woman's face.

"Why have you called me here?" he asked, determined to find the answer to the riddle before he went back to the cave.

"*I* called you?"

"I have seen you in vision four times." Shadow Hawk stared out the window. Four, he thought. Four was a sacred number. Was that how he came to be here, because he had seen her four times?

"I never called you," Maggie said. "I don't know what you mean."

He turned to face her again. "I saw you on the mountain when I sought my medicine dream, and then I saw you again during the Sun Dance. I saw you in the sweat lodge, and in the Sacred Cave. And each time, I felt you were calling me."

Maggie went cold, and then hot, as she remembered dreaming of this man, painting him, writing of him in her books. Had she somehow summoned him from the past?

"How did you come to be here?" he asked. "Why do you live in the sacred hills of my people? There was no white man's lodge in the meadow when I entered the Sacred Cave two days ago, yet you are here."

Am I? Maggie wondered. Maybe she was dreaming again. She heard him sigh and she realized he looked suddenly faint.

"Why don't you sit down?" Maggie suggested, her mind whirling with questions. "You've lost a lot of blood. You need time to regain your strength."

It was in his mind to argue. He was a warrior, he did not listen to the counsel of women, but he was too weary, too confused, to protest. Moving to the bed, he sat down on the edge of the mattress, his hands resting on his knees.

"You mentioned a cave," Maggie said. "You said my house wasn't here when you went in, but it was here when you came out. I don't understand."

"There was a battle," Shadow Hawk said. "We took shelter in the cave . . ." He wanted to tell her what had happened, to discover why she had called him to this place, but the wound in his side was throbbing monotonously, making it difficult to think of anything else.

Maggie saw the utter weariness in his eyes, the fine lines of pain around his mouth, and knew she should let him rest. But she had so many questions. How had he gotten here? How long was he going to stay? Did he really know Red Cloud? She felt the excitement building within her as she considered the possibilities of conversing with a man from the past. Why, with his knowledge of history, she could write the most authentic historical romances the world had ever seen!

"I must go," he said, but he continued to sit on the bed, as if he didn't have the energy to get up.

"You really should rest," Maggie said. "You're not strong enough to make it to the Hills today. Maybe tomorrow."

As much as he hated to admit it, he knew she was right. He didn't have the strength or the energy to go anywhere.

Stretching out on the bed, he closed his eyes, surrendering to the weariness that engulfed him.

Tomorrow he would ask her again. Tomorrow he would find out why she had summoned him.

Tomorrow . . .

Chapter Nine

Veronica looked at Maggie as if she were crazy. "A man from the past! Are you out of your mind?"

"Maybe."

"Maybe! Maggie, you've been reading too many romance novels. People don't travel through time. It's impossible. He's probably just another drunken Indian who doesn't know what day it is."

"I don't think he knows what century it is."

Veronica shook her head. "It isn't possible."

"He said he'd seen me in a vision. On a mountain. In a sacred cave."

Veronica went suddenly still, the batter she'd been stirring forgotten. "A sacred cave? He mentioned a sacred cave?"

"Yes, why?"

71

Madeline Baker

Veronica shook her head. "Nothing."

"Tell me."

"Among our people, there's an old legend about a Sacred Cave. It was believed that a medicine man with very strong power could enter the cave and see into the future."

"Our future?"

"I don't know. I never believed it, but my father did. There were tales of a medicine man known as Heart-of-the-Wolf who saw visions in the cave."

Maggie felt the same chill she'd felt when Shadow Hawk said he'd seen her in vision, a sense of being caught up in something beyond her understanding, beyond comprehension or rational explanation.

"Did the Indians travel through time?"

"Not that I know of."

"But if a medicine man could see into the future, why couldn't he go there?"

"I don't know," Veronica said. She stared into the bowl of cake batter, then shook her head. "It was just a legend."

"But some legends are based on fact."

"I don't want to talk about it," Veronica said. "It gives me the creeps." She began to stir the cake batter again, determined not to think of it anymore. But she couldn't help remembering when she was a little girl, sitting in the shadows while the ancient ones spoke of the past, of medicine men who knew the future before it happened, of Heart-of-the-Wolf, who had died inside the Sacred Cave. According to legend, his body had been found there, along with the body of a white man. A young medicine man had accompanied

Heart-of-the-Wolf to the cave, but his name had been lost or forgotten.

"Why don't you go see if he's awake?" Veronica asked. "Dinner will be ready soon."

Deep in thought, Maggie left the kitchen and went into the guest bedroom. Shadow Hawk was still asleep and she stared at him, wondering if she was letting her too fertile imagination run away with her. Did she really believe he had come here from the past?

It really wasn't that hard to imagine such a thing, perhaps because she spent so much time living in a fantasy world. Her last book had been a time travel novel about a modern-day Indian who went back in time. She'd received hundreds of letters from fans who said they wished they could go back in time, even a few letters from people who believed it was possible.

She stared at the man in the bed, noting again how handsome he was. Even in sleep, he radiated a kind of restless power, a deep inner strength.

She glanced out the window toward the Black Hills. The Sioux believed they were sacred, that all life had been created there, in the heart of the earth. Was there a cave up there somewhere, a sacred cave, shrouded in the mists of time? If he had traveled from the past to the future, perhaps she could enter the cave and relive the past, change it so that the accident never happened.

She glanced back at the bed to find Shadow Hawk staring at her.

"*Htayetu wasté*," she said. "Good evening."

73

Shadow Hawk nodded. She looked beautiful sitting there, with the changing shades of twilight visible through the window behind her. She wore a pink dress with a long full skirt that fell to her ankles. Her hair was loose about her face and shoulders, like a dark cloud, and he felt a sudden longing to touch it, to touch her.

"Are you hungry?" she asked. "Dinner is ready."

He nodded again.

"Do you want to eat in here, or in the . . ." She had no Sioux word for kitchen, so she gestured toward the door. "Do you want to eat in the other part of the house, with me?"

"Yes," he said solemnly. "With you." His gaze slid toward the round white pot he had been using to relieve himself and then moved back to her face.

"The . . ." She frowned, wondering how to say bathroom in Lakota, and then shrugged. He'd been using a bed pan for the last two days, another night wouldn't hurt. Cheeks red, she left the room.

A few minutes later Shadow Hawk entered the kitchen. He was wearing his clout and moccasins, nothing more. His hair, long and thick and straight, almost reached his waist. Somehow, his mere presence made her kitchen seem suddenly small.

Maggie pointed to the chair at the opposite end of the table. "Sit down."

He did so gingerly, as if fearing the cane-back chair wouldn't hold his weight, then stared at the plate Veronica placed before him. Glancing

74

across the table, he watched as Maggie lifted her knife and fork.

"Meat loaf," Maggie said, spearing a piece with her fork.

"Meat loaf," he repeated. "Of what is this made?"

"Beef," Maggie replied.

Hawk nodded. He knew of beef, the white man's buffalo. Somewhat reluctantly, he took a bite. "*Wasté*," he said, liking the taste of it.

"Yes," Maggie said. "It is good." She pointed to the rest of the food on her plate, naming each item as she did so. "Potatoes. Carrots."

He nodded, wolfing down the meal, drinking the hot black coffee with obvious enjoyment.

Veronica filled Hawk's plate again, and then again, shaking her head as he put away three helpings of meat loaf and two servings of mashed potatoes and carrots, along with three cups of coffee before he sat back, a contented look on his face.

"I always said you were a good cook," Maggie said, grinning. "I'd better send Bobby to the store. I have a feeling our food bill is about to go up." She looked across the table at Shadow Hawk. "Would you like to see the rest of the house?"

"Yes."

He followed her quietly from room to room, saying little as she told him what things were called: coffee table, sofa, footstool, rug, curtains, fireplace, piano, cupboard, desk, computer, stove, dishwasher, pantry, book, mirror. He repeated each name carefully, the English words sounding flat when compared to the words of the Lakota.

He was fascinated by lamps that gave light with the flick of a switch, mesmerized by the refrigerator and the microwave and the television, astonished by the sound of the stereo even though he couldn't understand the words to the songs. Maggie blushed furiously as she tried to explain what the toilet was, and then decided to leave that to Bobby.

By the time they'd seen the living room, den, kitchen, the other guest bedroom, and bathroom, he was looking a little dazed and more than a little tired, so she suggested he might want to turn in for the night.

Sitting on the edge of the bed, Shadow Hawk stared out the window. Where was he? It was obvious he was no longer where he belonged, even though he could see the Black Hills silhouetted in the moonlight. The place was the same, he thought, and yet it was different. He had gone into the Sacred Cave with Heart-of-the-Wolf and when he left it, he had entered another world, the world of the Spirit Woman. Had she called him here to show him what marvels the white man was capable of so that he might go back to his own people and explain it was futile to fight them?

He thought of Veronica Little Moon and Bobby Running Horse. They were Lakota, but they were more white than Indian. They spoke the white man's language and wore his clothes, they ate his food and sang his songs. Was this to be the fate of his people, to become the slaves of the white man, to forget their heritage and turn their backs on their beliefs?

"I guess you're feeling a little confused," Maggie said sympathetically.

Shadow Hawk nodded.

"Veronica told me about your sacred cave, that medicine men went there to have visions. She told me of a legend about a medicine man known as Heart-of-the-Wolf . . ."

Shadow Hawk leaned forward, his eyes intent upon her face. "She knows of Heart-of-the-Wolf?"

"Well, she said it was just a legend."

"No! He was my friend. He died in the cave."

"Veronica said only medicine men were allowed to enter."

Shadow Hawk nodded. "I was to take his place."

"You seem very young to be a medicine man."

"I have seen twenty-five winters."

"You *are* young," Maggie murmured.

"Are you so old?"

"Thirty-two."

"Not so old as the mountains," he said solemnly, though a faint smile tugged at the corners of his mouth.

She'd thought him handsome before, but when he smiled, it was like night turning to day, like rain after a long drought. She stared at him, feeling her cheeks turn pink. She'd never been one to blush, never been one to be caught up in a man's looks. But Shadow Hawk was a singularly handsome man, with a physique like a Greek god and a smile that could light up a city.

77

"Have others of your people ventured into the future?"

"The future? Is that where I am?"

"It would seem so. According to the white man's time, you're traveled over a hundred years into the future."

Shadow Hawk gazed around the room. He knew the names of the unfamiliar objects now: pillow, mattress, sheets, chest of drawers, closet, nightstand, lamp, walls, ceiling, floor. But none of it seemed real, save the Spirit Woman, and he longed to touch her, to see if she was flesh and blood, or spirit only.

He looked at the blue of her eyes, the clear beauty of her skin, and felt a sudden heat pulse through him, a longing for something he had never known.

"Why do you sit always in that chair?" he asked, needing to turn his attention to something else.

"I can't walk."

Shadow Hawk frowned. "You have been injured?"

"Yes, a couple of years ago." She shrugged. "I can't walk any more."

She said it matter-of-factly, but he saw the pain in her eyes before she glanced away.

"You should get some rest," Maggie said. "You lost a lot of blood."

Shadow Hawk nodded, his gaze following her as she left the room.

Lying back on the bed, he stared out the window toward the Black Hills. His mother and his people crowded his thoughts. The battle would be over by now. Heart-of-the-Wolf had assured

The Spirit Path

him his mother still lived, but Hawk knew he would not believe it until he had seen her for himself. And what of his people? Had they all been killed or, worse yet, rounded up and taken to the reservation? The need to know the fate of his mother and his people burned within him.

The cave, he thought, the cave was the answer. On the night of the next full moon, he would go to the cave and see if he could follow the Spirit Path back home.

Chapter Ten

79

Chapter Ten

Shadow Hawk slept most of the next day and then, feeling he would go crazy if he didn't get out of the house, he went outside and walked toward the Black Hills. They rose before him, rugged, beautiful, covered with tall pines, their branches lifting in silent supplication toward the clear blue sky. The Sacred Cave was nestled up there, waiting for his return. If he climbed the hill and entered the cave, would he find Heart-of-the-Wolf's body lying where he had left it?

He pressed his hand to his side as his steps slowed. The Spirit Woman had been right. He was too weak to climb the hills. His wound, though not serious, had drained his strength.

With a sigh, Hawk turned and walked slowly toward the house. The young would-be warrior, Bob-by, was standing near a four-rail corral brushing a big black stallion.

"It's good to see you on your feet," Bobby said, speaking Lakota. "I am truly sorry for what happened. I was after a deer."

Shadow Hawk nodded. "It is all right."

Bobby couldn't help staring at the man. Was he really a warrior from the past? It seemed too far-fetched to be true, but there were many strange legends among his people, mysteries that could not be explained logically. "Will you be staying here very long?"

A wistful smile tugged at Shadow Hawk's lips. "I do not know."

Bobby grunted softly. "Maybe we could go into town when you're feeling better."

Shadow Hawk nodded, his gaze on the horse. It was a fine animal, big-boned and long-legged, with wide, intelligent eyes and a deep chest.

Bobby grinned. Whether from the past or the present, the stranger had a good eye for horse-flesh. "He is a beautiful animal. I have been trying to break him to ride, but I have not yet been successful. He is very strong and very stubborn, and I have the bruises to prove it."

Shadow Hawk smiled, thinking he'd like a chance to ride the black when he was feeling better. He nodded to Bobby, then went into the house.

He paused inside the front door, staring at the painting that hung over the huge stone fireplace. He recognized the location in the background of the painting. It was in the foothills past Bear Butte. And the horse was Wohitika. There could be no mistaking the markings on the big calico

stallion. And he was the man. The knowledge
sent a shiver down his spine.

He sensed her presence even before she came
up beside him.

"Do you like it?" Maggie asked.

"It makes me uneasy. How did you come by
a painting of me?"

"I drew it," Maggie said. "I . . ." She paused.
It sounded so bizarre, so intimate, to say she
had dreamed of him, but he deserved to know
the truth. "I saw you in a dream one night and
I painted you as I remembered." She took a deep
breath. "Do you have a horse like that?"

"Wohitika."

"The brave one."

Shadow Hawk nodded. "You have not told me
why you called me here."

"I didn't. It isn't possible to call someone
through time."

"Perhaps not," he said, flashing that heart-
stopping grin again. "But I am here."

"Yes," Maggie murmured, in English. "You
are." She stared up at his profile, admiring the
strong square jaw, the line of his mouth, the curve
of his cheek. "Maybe you can go back the way
you came," she suggested, and wondered why the
thought of his leaving made her so unhappy.

"I will try," he said, the need to know what had
happened to his mother and his people strong
within him, "but I must wait until the moon is
full again."

"Of course," Maggie said, laughing softly.
"Magic is always done best in the light of a
full moon."

He turned and looked down at her, and she felt the warmth of his smile wash over her like sunshine on a summer day.

"I should get back to work," she said, feeling suddenly flustered. "Veronica has lunch waiting for you in the kitchen."

"Spirit Woman."

Maggie paused at the doorway. "What?"

"Have you a name?"

"Maggie," she answered quietly. "Maggie St. Claire."

"Mag-gie," he murmured, and the sound of his voice, deep and resonant, sent a thrill of excitement down her spine.

"Bob-by has asked me to go into town with him."

"Do you want to go?"

"I do not know."

"Well, if you decide to go with him, you should get dressed."

"I am dressed."

"I mean you should wear the kind of clothes Bobby wears."

Hawk glanced down at his clout and moccasins. "What is wrong with what I have on?"

"Nothing, but most people aren't accustomed to seeing Indians dressed that way. I mean, well, it doesn't cover very much, and . . . never mind, Hawk, I have to go to work. I'll see you at dinner."

He stared after her. She had explained to him about the books she wrote, but he saw no value in them. What was the point of writing something that was not true? He had stared at the covers that

83

showed muscular Indian men holding scantily attired white women in their arms, and been confused. White women were afraid of Indians. The few he'd seen had looked at him in terror. He could not imagine any of them tearing off their clothes and willingly falling into his arms.

That evening, he sat across the table from the Spirit Woman, hardly tasting the food on his plate as his gaze was drawn toward her time and again, mesmerized by the way the candle-light caressed her skin and danced in the thick blackness of her hair. He listened to the sound of her voice, liking the way she spoke his language, though it was often laced with words of the white man which he didn't fully understand. She told him of Veronica's family, and of how much Bobby wanted to be a warrior, a real warrior, like in the old days.

"But, of course, that's impossible," Maggie said, her voice tinged with regret.

"Why?"

"Because the old days are gone. He wants to seek a vision and count coup on an enemy. He wants to ride to battle, like Crazy Horse."

"You know of Crazy Horse?"

"Of course. Everyone does."

"How?"

"It's in the history books. Children learn of him in school."

"White children?" he asked in disbelief.

"Yes."

"What do they learn?"

"That he was a great warrior. They learn about Sitting Bull, too, and Red Cloud." Maggie paused

84

as an idea came to her. "Maybe I could teach you to speak English while you're here."

Shadow Hawk considered her suggestion. He could not go back to the cave until the next full moon. Perhaps it would be advisable for him to learn as much of the white man's tongue as he could in the time he had left. A wise man studied the ways of his enemies.

"Teach me," Shadow Hawk said.

Maggie put her writing on hold and spent the next week teaching Shadow Hawk to speak English. She had thought to spend an hour or so each morning at the task, but one hour stretched into two, and then three, and by the end of the week, they had worked themselves up to almost eight hours each day.

She was glad that Veronica was there to help her, because the sentence structure of English was vastly different from that of the Lakota. There seemed to be no linking verbs in Lakota. Where a white man would say "The grass is tall," the Lakota said *peji hanska*, meaning grass tall. The sun is hot translated as *Wi kata*, sun hot. The dog ate the chicken became *sunka he kokoyahanla tebye*, or dog that chicken ate.

By the end of the week, Maggie was amazed at how much Shadow Hawk had learned. She had only to tell him something once or twice, and he knew it.

Now, sitting across the kitchen table from Shadow Hawk, she found herself staring at him surreptitiously as she did so often. He still refused to wear anything but his clout and moccasins and her gaze was constantly drawn to his broad shoulders, to the vast expanse of his copper-hued chest.

Even more compelling was the haunting magnetism of his deep black eyes and the sensual line of his mouth. She found herself longing to run her fingertips over his lower lip, to trace the faint white scars on his chest. Such a magnificent chest, she mused.

With a shake of her head, she put such thoughts from her mind. It wasn't like her, to fantasize about such things. Even as a teenager, she hadn't been overly interested in boys or making out. A nice girl saved herself for marriage, her mother had always said, and Maggie had been a nice girl. No doubt she was the only thirty-two-year-old virgin in the United States.

She looked up at the sound of Shadow Hawk's voice. "I'm sorry, I wasn't listening."

"Are you tired?" Shadow Hawk repeated, wondering at her long silence.

"No, I'm fine," Maggie said, and then smiled as she realized he'd spoken to her in English.

Shadow Hawk gazed at her thoughtfully for several moments. He'd been keenly aware of her covert stares during the past week. Did she find him desirable, or was she merely curious about a man who had traveled so far through the mists of time?

Desire surged through him as his eyes met hers, and he wished he dared touch her. When he had thought her a spirit only, he had not given any thought to the beauty of her face, the color of her skin, the shape of her mouth. But now he knew she was flesh and it was all he could do to keep from reaching out to stroke her cheek, to bury his face in the wealth of her hair and breathe in the sweet scent of woman.

Abruptly, he stood up. "We will start again tomorrow."

"All right."

Still, he did not move. His gaze lingered on her face and he wondered again why she had summoned him to this place.

Maggie felt her cheeks grow warm under his prolonged gaze. What was he thinking? Why was he looking at her like that?

"Good night, Mag-gie," he said quietly, and his voice washed over her like dark honey, warm and soft and sweet.

"Good night," she murmured, and wished she could think of some plausible reason to make him stay.

Shadow Hawk left the kitchen, reluctant to leave her, yet knowing he needed to get away from her before it was too late, before he did something that would shame her and prove he was not the warrior he claimed to be.

He walked down the narrow hall that led to the living room, pausing for a moment to look at the painting over the fireplace, and then he went outside.

Standing on the porch, he closed his eyes and drew in a deep breath, inhaling the fresh clean scent of earth and grass, the fragrance of the tall pines, the faint odor of a skunk.

He heard the quiet swoosh of an owl's wings, the soft snort of one of the horses, the distant melancholy cry of a wolf. The sounds of home.

Madeline Baker

Opening his eyes, he gazed at the Hills, feeling their nearness, their power.

He thought of Heart-of-the-Wolf. He thought of his mother, and prayed that she still lived, but always his thoughts returned to Maggie. It pained him that she could not walk, that he could not take her hand and run with her through the prairie grass. She was a woman of beauty and sensitivity. She should not be bound to a cold chair with wheels. She should not be living in a square house with only an old woman and a young boy for company. He had seen the sadness in her eyes and knew she longed for the things every woman longed for: a man to love her, a mate to give her children, a companion to walk beside her until life was done.

Standing there, staring into the darkness, he wished that he could be that man.

Returning to the house, he walked quietly down the hallway toward his room. He paused outside Maggie's room, imagining her asleep inside, her hair spread like a dark cloud on the pillow.

He was about to go on down the hall when he heard her crying softly. Impulsively, he opened the door and stepped into the room.

"Mag-gie? Are you all right?"

"Yes. Go away."

"Why do you weep?"

Why, indeed, she thought bitterly. "Please, Hawk, just go away."

He listened to her words telling him to leave, but in his heart he knew she did not want to be alone. Crossing the room, he sat on the edge of the bed and drew her into his arms.

"Let me go!" she shrieked, a sudden irrational fear rising up within her as his arms closed around her.

"Mag-gie, do not be afraid. I will not harm you."

His voice, that beautiful deep voice, reached through the darkness, soothing her. She felt his hand stroke her hair and she laid her head against his chest and closed her eyes. It had been so long since anyone had held her. She could hear the steady beat of his heart beneath her cheek, feel the heat of his body against hers.

"Mag-gie, why do you weep?"

"I can't tell you."

"Why?"

"I just can't. I hardly know you."

His hand continued to stroke her hair, comforting her. "You can tell me," he urged softly.

She shook her head, not wanting to put her fears into words. It wasn't just that she couldn't walk, it was all that it entailed. She missed horseback riding. She missed playing tennis, walking in the sunshine, swimming, shopping. And though she had vowed never to love again, she missed having a man to care for, a man who cared for her. But she couldn't tell him that. To do so would be to bare her heart and soul.

Shadow Hawk continued to hold her, waiting for her to speak, and then, without words, he knew why she wept, why she had called to him. She was lonely and afraid; afraid of growing old alone, afraid of having no one to love, no one to love her. In dreams and visions, he had seen the

89

tears in her eyes, heard the silent yearning of her heart.

Gently, he cupped her face in his hands and gazed down into her eyes. "Do not weep, Mag-gie. You are not alone any more."

She stared up at him, her blue eyes luminous through her tears.

"I don't know what you mean," she whispered.

"There must be no lies between us," he said, using his fingertips to wipe away her tears. "I cannot stay here forever, but while I am here, you will not be alone."

Chapter Eleven

In the morning, she was embarrassed by the way she'd melted into his arms. She hardly knew the man, yet she had snuggled into his embrace, literally crying on his shoulder. She couldn't believe she'd done such a thing, yet there was no point in dwelling on it. Resolutely, she managed to put the incident from her mind, determined to get back to her writing as soon as breakfast was over.

Shadow Hawk was already at the kitchen table when she entered the room. One look at his face brought the events of the night before surging to the front of her mind, the memory of his arms around her almost tangible. Gazing into his expressive black eyes, she knew that he was remembering, too, that he was keenly aware of her inner turmoil, of the aching loneliness that haunted her late at night. Her only escape was her writing, where she could forget the hurt of Frank's rejection, the feeling that life was passing her by.

Being in a wheelchair set her apart from other people. The friends she'd had in Los Angeles hadn't known what to expect or how to react when they came to visit after the accident. Some had stared, not knowing what to say. Some had found it difficult to meet her eyes and looked at everything in the room except her. She could hardly blame them. Most of her acquaintances were people she did things with: ice skating, boating, skiing, tennis. When she could no longer participate in the sports that had bonded them together, she had realized they had nothing else in common and very little to say to each other. After Frank broke their engagement, she left L.A., leaving no forwarding address, so that only her editor knew where to find her.

After saying good morning to Veronica, Maggie concentrated on her breakfast, refusing to meet Shadow Hawk's gaze. She didn't want to see pity in his eyes, didn't want him feeling sorry for her. She didn't want to feel anything ever again.

When breakfast was over, she went into the den and sat at her computer. She knew Shadow Hawk was waiting for her in the kitchen, that he expected her to continue helping him with his English, but she couldn't face him, not after last night.

She didn't hear him enter the room, but she felt his presence, knew he was standing in the

doorway staring at her back, but she pretended
she didn't know he was there and after a few
moments, he walked away, his footsteps as silent
as a cat's.

She wrote a few pages, decided they were
junk, and erased them, only to sit staring at the
blank blue screen. A noise from outside drew her
attention and she went to the window. Peering
through the curtains, she saw Shadow Hawk
swing onto the black stallion that Bobby had
been trying to break for the last three months.
It was a beautiful animal, all black save for a
narrow white blaze and one white stocking.

No sooner had Shadow Hawk settled himself
on the horse's bare back than the animal lowered
its head and began to buck wildly.

Maggie gasped, wondering how Hawk managed to stay on the animal's back. She had
watched Bobby get thrown time and again, and
Bobby rode with a saddle to hang on to. But
Hawk stuck to the stallion's back as if he were
a part of the huge beast, and she thought she'd
never seen anything more beautiful than Shadow
Hawk as he rode the wildly pitching stallion, his
waist-length black hair whipping about his face,
his broad chest sheened with perspiration and
dust, his powerful thighs gripping the animal's
sides.

Abruptly, the stallion raised its head and
reared up on its hind legs, its front feet flailing
the air, its ears laid flat.

With a wild cry, Shadow Hawk brought his
fist down on the horse's head, just behind its
ears, and the horse's front feet hit the ground

and it began bucking again.

I've got to paint this, Maggie thought, awed by the scene before her. Foamy white lather covered the stallion's chest and flanks, its sides heaved with the strain of trying to dislodge the unwelcome burden from its back. And the man . . . she could not tear her gaze from the man. He rode with seeming ease, a smile on his face as he pitted his strength against that of the horse. It was magnificent. He was magnificent.

She felt a sense of disappointment when the battle was over. The stallion gave one final buck and came to an abrupt halt, its body quivering with exhaustion, its nostrils flared, its ears twitching back and forth.

Maggie watched as Shadow Hawk slid to the ground, then went to stand at the stallion's head. Placing his hands on either side of the horse's head, Hawk blew gently into the stallion's nostrils, letting their breath mingle, and then he scratched the horse behind its ears, speaking to the animal all the while.

She sat there as though mesmerized while Hawk walked the horse around the corral to cool it out, then spent twenty minutes brushing the horse until its coat gleamed like black silk.

Not wanting to be caught staring, she turned away from the window when Shadow Hawk vaulted over the corral fence and started walking toward the house.

She was sitting at her computer when she heard the water running in the shower. It was one of the white man's inventions that he had readily taken to and she felt her cheeks flush as she imagined him standing there with the warm water rinsing away the dust and perspiration.

She knew the minute he entered the room.

"Will you teach me now?" he asked. "I still have much to learn."

What was there about the sound of his voice that made her feel warm and safe, that made her long for things which could never be?

Slowly, she shook her head. She was becoming too fond of this man from the past, this man who was too young for her, who might disappear at any moment.

"Mag-gie?"

The sound of her name on his lips melted her resolve to avoid him. Moments later they were seated across from each other at the kitchen table with Maggie saying phrases in Lakota and Shadow Hawk repeating them in English.

"*Hau*," she said.

"Hello," he replied.

"*Toniktuka he?*" she asked.

"How are you?" he said, repeating the question in English.

"*Matanyan yelo.*"

"I am fine."

She was caught up in the sound of his voice, in the clear black depths of his eyes, in the decidedly male scent that filled her nostrils. Her gaze kept straying to his bare chest and she made a mental note to tell Veronica to find him something to wear. A shirt, an overcoat, anything, because it was impossible to concentrate on mundane things like nouns and verbs with that vast expanse of well-muscled copper-hued flesh staring her in the face morning, noon, and night. It was a good thing he'd never gone into Sturgis with Bobby, she thought, because he would have caused accidents all over town as women drivers turned to watch him instead of the road.

She was unaware that Veronica had entered the room until the older woman tapped her on the shoulder. "Hey, you in there?" Veronica queried, one eyebrow arched in concern. "I asked you three times what you want for lunch."

"Oh, I don't care," Maggie said. "Whatever you feel like fixing."

"Sandwiches okay?"

"Fine."

She went on with the lesson while Veronica prepared lunch. She tried not to stare at Hawk as he picked up the thick roast beef and Swiss cheese sandwich Veronica had made. He studied it for a moment, sniffed it before he took a bite. A slow smile curved the corners of his mouth. "*Wasté*," he said, nodding his approval.

Maggie nodded, charmed by the look of pleasure on his face. He quickly ate his sandwich and she gave him half of hers, pleased that he found contemporary food to his liking.

They went back to the lesson after lunch. She was trying to explain the difference between a noun and a pronoun when Shadow Hawk laid his hand over hers, his thumb lightly stroking the back of her hand.

Maggie's breath caught in her throat and she felt the sting of tears in her eyes. His touch was so unexpected, so filled with warmth and tenderness, that it caught her completely by surprise.

Without thinking, she jerked her hand away, confused by her overwhelming response to such an ordinary gesture, and then she stared at him, mute, knowing she'd hurt him. He didn't say anything, only sat there watching her.

"I'm sorry," she murmured. "I . . ." Oh, Lord, she thought, what was he doing to her? Why did he look at her like that, as if he were lost and she were the only one who could save him?

She felt a sudden urge to take him into her arms, to cradle his head against her breast and tell him everything would be all right. Instead, she placed her hand over his. "I'm sorry," she said again.

He smiled at her and then, in a fluid movement, he stood up and walked toward her. Pulling her wheelchair away from the table, he lifted her in his arms.

"What are you doing?" Maggie exclaimed.

"I wish to go for a walk."

"I can't walk."

"I can," he said simply, and headed for the back door.

She started to protest that she didn't want to go outside, that she was too heavy for him to carry; instead, she twined her arms around his neck and rested her head on his shoulder.

It was a beautiful day, clear and warm with a gentle breeze. He carried her as if she weighed no more than a child, telling her of his youth and of the days he had spent in the Black Hills.

"I was born here, in the *Paha Sapa* in the year when we stole the arrows from the Pawnee," Hawk began. "My father was a mighty warrior. He counted many coup against the Crow and the Pawnee. He was killed in my twelfth summer while defending my mother and two small children from a grizzly bear."

Maggie nodded, understanding the things he did not say. That he had been his mother's protector and provider since his father died.

"It was here, in the shadow of the *Paha Sapa* that I learned to be a warrior. Heart-of-the-Wolf taught me to hunt, to track the deer and the elk, to find food and water. He also taught me what he knew of plants and herbs.

"It was here that I fought in my first battle, and here that I killed my first Pawnee."

Maggie listened, mesmerized by the sound of his voice. In her mind, it was so easy to picture him as the boy he had been, tall and lean and strong, eager to learn, excelling at all he did. She did not like to picture him killing anyone, yet it made her heart skip a beat as she imagined him riding to battle, his blood running hot, his face painted for war.

"Heart-of-the-Wolf prepared me to seek my vision, and to participate in the Sun Dance. We came here each summer to celebrate the Sun Dance with our brothers, the Cheyenne. Those were good times, filled with days of feasting and games, and nights of dancing and story-telling. And always, lurking in the back of your mind if you were going to take part in the dance, was the shadow of the Sun Dance Pole."

"Were you afraid?" Maggie asked, staring at the scars on his chest. She had read numerous accounts of the Sun Dance ceremony and thought she understood, at least a little, the significance of it, yet she could not help feeling repulsed by the ordeal.

"Afraid?" Hawk frowned thoughtfully. "I was not afraid of the pain. I knew it would hurt and I think I was prepared for that. I was afraid of failing, of not having the courage to see it through to the end. Mostly, I was afraid of bringing shame to my mother and to Heart-of-the-Wolf."

"Was it as bad as you expected?"

Hawk chuckled softly. "Worse. And better."

Maggie lifted her hand, wanting to touch the faint white scars on his chest, but lacking the nerve to do so.

And then he took her hand in his and laid it over each scar.

"It was you, Mag-gie," he said, his voice suddenly husky. "It was your image I saw when I offered my blood and my pain at the Sun Dance Pole."

Maggie gazed deep into his eyes and she saw it all clearly: the Lakota encampment in the heart of the Black Hills, the sacred Sun Dance Pole made from the trunk of a cottonwood tree, the warriors dancing while the rest of the people looked on. She could feel the warmth of the summer sun on her face, hear the heartbeat of the drum, the shrill notes of an eagle bone whistle. She felt Shadow Hawk's pain as the skewers that had been embedded in the muscle of his chest tore free, and she felt a new love and respect for the people who had lived here so long ago, for the man who held her in his arms.

A short time later, they came to a small stream. Still cradling Maggie in his arms, Hawk sat down on the grass, holding her in his lap.

"You can put me down now," Maggie said, feeling suddenly self-conscious. "I must be getting heavy."

"You are not heavy," he replied candidly, "and I like holding you."

Maggie blushed and looked away. And then she felt his hand move in her hair as he began to speak to her in Lakota.

"Do you see that high mountain?" he asked. "My people believe the great thunderbird, *Wakinyan Tanka*, lives in his tipi on top of that mountain. There are four of them. The *Wakinyan* of the west is the most powerful. He is clothed in clouds. His body has no form, but he has giant wings. He has no feet, but enormous claws. He has no head, but a huge sharp beak with pointed teeth. His color is black.

"The *Wakinyan* of the north is red. The *Wakinyan* of the east is yellow and the fourth is white. He has no eyes and no ears, yet he can see and hear. No one ever sees a whole thunderbird, though very holy men sometimes see a part of it in dreams and visions."

"Have you ever seen him?" Maggie asked.

"No, but Heart-of-the-Wolf once saw his wings."

"Tell me another of your beliefs."

100

"You are not like other whites," Shadow Hawk mused. "You speak our language, you do not frown on our ways. I think perhaps your heart is more red than white." He smiled down at her, pleased that her eyes were no longer filled with unhappiness. "Have you heard the story of how the Lakota came to be?"

"No. Tell me."

"Long ago, when the earth was still young, *Unktehi*, the water monster, fought the people and caused a great flood. No one knows why. Perhaps *Wakán Tanka* was angry with the people. Maybe he let *Unktehi* win because he wanted to make a better kind of human being.

"The water got higher and higher until everything was under water except for one hill where the sacred red pipestone quarry now stands. The people climbed the hill to save themselves, but it was no use. The water swept them all away and everyone was killed. Their blood formed a pool and the pool turned to pipestone and created the quarry. That is why the pipe, made of that red rock, is sacred to our people. It is made from the flesh and blood of our ancestors, the stem is the backbone of those people long dead, the smoke is their breath.

"After the flood, *Unktehi* was turned to stone. Her bones can be seen in the Badlands even today.

"Only one girl survived the flood, saved by a big spotted eagle. *Wanblee Galeshka* carried the girl to the top of a tall tree which stood on the highest pinnacle of the *Paha Sapa*. It was the only place not covered by water. *Wanblee* kept the beautiful girl and made her his wife. Soon she got pregnant and bore him twins, a boy and a girl.

"When the water finally disappeared, *Wanblee* helped the children and their mother down from the rock and put them on earth and they grew up. After the mother died, he was the only man and she was the only woman and they married and had children and became *Lakota Oyate*, a Great Nation."

"It's like Adam and Eve and Noah and the Flood all rolled into one," Maggie mused.

Shadow Hawk looked puzzled. "Adam and Eve?"

"It is our belief that Adam and Eve were the first man and the first woman. God, the Father, put them in a beautiful garden and told them to multiply and replenish the earth. He told them they might partake of the fruit of every tree in the garden, save the Tree of the Knowledge of Good and Evil. But Eve disobeyed God and ate the forbidden fruit, and they were sent out of the garden."

Hawk grunted softly. "And No-ah?"

"He lived in a time of great wickedness and God decided to send a flood to cover the earth and destroy all the children he had created. But Noah found grace in the eyes of Lord and he built a great ship called an ark and saved his family."

Shadow Hawk nodded, his gaze meeting Maggie's, making her pulse begin to race.

"It's amazing, isn't it?" she said. "I mean, imagine two cultures as different as ours producing such similar tales."

She looked at the Black Hills, feeling their magic even as she felt the magic in the hand that rested lightly on her shoulder. She could feel Shadow Hawk's dark-eyed gaze resting on her face, could feel the mysterious bond that had drawn them together growing stronger. Had her loneliness truly called to him across the years? Was that why he was here? And what would she do when he was gone?

She could not, would not, let herself begin to care.

Chapter Twelve

Shadow Hawk was riding the black stallion in the corral the next day when Bobby climbed up on the top rail to watch.

"You did it!" the boy exclaimed, his voice tinged with pride and a bit of envy.

"But only after you took the edge off."

Bobby ducked his head, pleased at Hawk's praise.

"Come," Shadow Hawk said, riding closer to the rail. "Try him."

"Maybe later." Bobby took a deep breath and then blurted, "It's hard to believe you're from the past, I mean, it seems so impossible."

"It is hard for me to believe, as well," Shadow Hawk replied quietly. His gaze strayed toward the Black Hills. Soon, he would go to the Sacred Cave and see if he could find the Spirit Path that would lead him back home, back to his own time, his own people.

"Tell me, Bob-by Running Horse, what is it like to be an Indian today?"

"Not so good, at least not for the people on the reservation. Many are sick in their souls and they look for answers in whiskey, or worse."

"Reservations," Shadow Hawk muttered, his voice thick with disgust.

"They're worse than you can imagine. Our people are poor. Many are discouraged. I was lucky. Miss St. Claire gave me a job here and I have a good life. I send money home to my brother."

"Money?"

"It's what the white man uses to get what he wants."

"And he always gets what he wants. That, at least, has not changed. How is it that you did not grow up speaking Lakota?"

"No one bothered to teach me until I came here. My mother died when I was very young. My father spends whatever money he gets on whiskey."

Shadow Hawk grunted softly. In his time, there were Indians who could not leave the white man's firewater alone, warriors who traded furs for whiskey, much to the shame of their families.

"Tell me, what was it like in the old days?" Bobby asked, his dark eyes glowing. "Was it wonderful?"

Shadow Hawk stroked the stallion's neck, his expression thoughtful. "It was a good way to live. A man knew who he was."

"What was it like to ride into battle?"

"To ride against an enemy tribe was a good thing. A man gained honor on the field of battle. It was a brave thing to count coup, to steal your enemy's horse, to take his weapons. But the white man does not fight for honor. He fights to kill, and he does not care whether he kills a man or a child. To him, it is all the same. He has no respect for the land, or the animals, or the people."

"It is the same today. They are polluting the water and the earth and the sky. They destroy the forests and kill the animals."

Shadow Hawk nodded. Was this why he had been sent to the future, to see the destruction of his people, of the land the Lakota held sacred? He looked at Bobby, dressed in the clothes of the white man, and felt a deep sadness that a young man should grow up ignorant of the ways of his people, ignorant of their language.

Bobby stared at Shadow Hawk, trying to imagine himself in the other man's place. All his life he'd wanted to be a warrior, to live in the old way, as his forefathers had lived, to follow the buffalo across the plains, to go to battle against the Crow. "Did you . . . ?"

"What?"

Bobby gestured at the scars on Shadow Hawk's chest. "You bear the marks of the Sun Dance. Did you also seek a vision?"

"Yes."

"Would you . . . do you think you could help me?"

Shadow Hawk nodded. "If that is your wish."

"When?" Bobby asked, his voice rising in excitement. "Today, tomorrow?"

"You must think about it. A vision is not something one rushes into. You must pray for guidance, and when you feel ready, we will have a sweat. And then you must go into the Hills, alone, and seek the Spirit."

"*Pilamaya*," Bobby said, his dark eyes glowing with excitement. "Thank you! Wait till I tell Veronica!" Jumping off the fence, he ran toward the house.

"So," Maggie said, "Bobby says you are going to help him seek a vision."

She had been sitting at the window watching the two of them, her eyes drawn, as always, to Shadow Hawk. Now he stood before her, talking of sweat lodges and visions, things she had read about and written about. Things she had never truly believed in until a Lakota warrior entered her life.

Shadow Hawk nodded. "It is a good thing, to seek the guidance of the spirits."

"Do you think he'll get one? I mean, I didn't think Indians did that any more."

"If his heart is right, if he truly believes, *Wakán Tanka* will grant him that which he seeks."

Maggie nodded, remembering that Hawk claimed to have seen her in his vision. When he'd first told her that, she had found it hard to believe, but no longer. She felt a kinship with Hawk, a spiritual bond that she could not explain, and it frightened her.

"I watched you riding the black today."

107

Hawk grinned, his pleasure in the horse obvious. "He would have made a fine war pony."

"He's yours."

"Does he not belong to Bob-by?"

"No, he belonged to me, and now he belongs to you."

"I have nothing to give you in return."

"Nothing is required."

"Why do you have a horse you cannot ride?"

"I have several horses I can't ride," Maggie reminded him, "but I bought the black because I thought he was beautiful and I liked looking at him."

Hawk nodded. "Come," he said. "I will take you for a ride."

"No." She shook her head vigorously. Once, she had loved to ride, but now the thought of being on a horse filled her with trepidation.

"Yes." He smiled at her as he lifted her from her wheelchair.

Maggie thought again how powerful that smile was, how quickly it changed her "no" to "yes." If she could only bottle that smile, she thought as she wrapped her arms around his neck, she could light up the world. And then, selfishly, she decided she wouldn't share him if she could. She wanted to keep Hawk to herself, for just a little while, because, too soon, he'd be gone, and she'd be in the dark again.

While Shadow Hawk bridled the black, she sat on a flat-topped rock near the corral watching his every move. Veronica had bought Hawk a pair of Levi's and a black T-shirt, but he continued to wear only his clout and moccasins, and she couldn't help admiring the dark bronze of his skin, the way his muscles flexed as he lifted her effortlessly onto the stallion's bare back, then swung up behind her, his movements as light and graceful as a dancer's.

She felt her heart quicken as his arm slid around her waist, and then they were riding toward the Hills.

The air was fragrant with the scent of pines and earth, alive with the hum of insects, the song of a bird. The sky was a clear azure blue, deep enough to swim in. Off in the distance, the gray mountain crags of the Hills rose in majestic splendor, the ever-green trees covering the slopes like a blanket of varying shades of green.

Hawk lifted the stallion into a trot and Maggie let out a sigh of delight. She'd missed riding, missed the sense of freedom it had once given her. Most men never understood why so many girls loved horses, but Maggie knew it wasn't just the sheer beauty of the animals that fascinated women, it was the feeling of power, of being in control of an animal that weighed ten times your weight, the sense of freedom and speed.

Men loved fast cars, but cars were just chrome and metal; they weren't living beings, capable of love and devotion.

Moments later, Hawk urged the black into a lope and Maggie felt her heart soar with excitement. It was wonderful, to feel the wind in her face again, to imagine that she could feel the surging power of the stallion beneath her.

The black ran effortlessly, its long legs carrying them ever closer to the foot of a low range of hills.

Hawk reined the horse to a walk and they began to climb upward. She was conscious of Hawk's broad chest at her back, of his arm around her waist, holding her tight.

Higher and higher they climbed until they came to a plateau. Hawk reined the black to a halt. Dismounting, he placed his hands around Maggie's waist and lifted her from the back of the horse to cradle her in his arms.

She stared at him, puzzled, when he didn't put her down, felt her breath catch in her throat as she gazed into the depths of his eyes.

"I . . . you . . . why don't you put me down," she stammered. "I must be heavy."

Slowly, he shook his head. She felt good in his arms. Her scent filled his nostrils, sweeter than the scent of the pines.

"Hawk, I . . ." Her voice trailed off as she realized she didn't know what she wanted to say, only that she liked to say his name.

"What is it, Mag-gie?"

"Nothing."

Still cradling her in his arms, he sat down, his back against a ponderosa pine. He gazed at her for a long time, and then he looked up the hill. The Sacred Cave. Was it still there?

"It's beautiful," Maggie said, following his gaze. "I often wished I could climb to the top."

Shadow Hawk nodded. "Bob-by will come here for his vision quest."

"I hope he's successful. He's a good boy. He's hoping to be accepted at one of the colleges this fall."

"College?"

"It's a place of learning."

"White man's learning?"

"Yes, he hopes to be a doctor, a modern medicine man, so he can help his people on the reservation."

"One learns this in college?"

"Yes. In the old days, I know that such things were handed down from one medicine man to the next, but things are more complicated now. A man needs a paper of permission to practice medicine. We have learned many things in the last hundred years or so."

"Have you? You have not learned how to live with the land. Or with each other."

He was very quick to comprehend what he saw and heard, Maggie reminded herself. He watched the news on television, appalled by the wars, the poverty, the murders. Some things were hard to translate. It was difficult to explain what AIDS was to a man who came from a culture where there was no such thing as casual sex. It was hard to explain child abuse, the drug scene, the high crime rate, the pollution of the air and the water, oil spills, abortion.

Maggie let out a sigh. Up here, where the sky was clear and the air smelled of pine, it was hard to think of the awful state the world was in. Sitting in Hawk's lap, with his arms around her, his breath warm upon her neck, it was hard to think at all.

"Tell me how you got your name?" she asked after awhile.

"During my vision quest, the shadow of a hawk merged with mine and for a time we were one.

The medicine man said I would be as strong and wise as a hawk if I followed the life path of the Lakota."

He was quiet a moment, remembering old Heart-of-the-Wolf, and then he gazed at Maggie. "I saw you that day, also, though I did not tell anyone. I did not see your face clearly, only the shadowed image of a woman with dark hair. I saw you again during the Sun Dance. And once, when I went to pray, I saw you as clearly as I do now."

His words washed over her, as warm as liquid sunshine. There were people who believed in reincarnation, who believed that spirits could travel between worlds. People who believed in ghosts, and in time travel. She had always been a skeptic, until now. She wondered why she found it so easy to believe he had come from the past, why she had never doubted it for a moment.

Hawk gazed deep into her eyes, his soul reaching out to hers. "The land of the *Paha Sapa* is in my blood. It is a part of me." His dark eyes caressed her for several moments, warming her from the inside out in a way no fire ever could. "Everything of value or importance in my life has come to me here," he said quietly, "in the sacred hills of the Lakota."

They gazed at each other for a long time and then, slowly, he stroked her cheek, the curve of her neck, the inner flesh of her arm. Heat flowed in the wake of his touch and she felt suddenly shy and awkward. She lowered her gaze, swallowing hard as she saw his broad shoulders, the muscular expanse of his chest.

Nervously, she licked her lips, wishing he would kiss her, just once. Wishing she was young and carefree, that she could take him by the hand and walk beside him in the sunshine, swim in the lake beneath the light of the moon.

Mute, her heart aching, she looked into his eyes. *Just one kiss*, she thought. What could it hurt? And leaning forward, she placed her lips to his. It was the lightest of touches, the merest whisper of a kiss, but it was more satisfying than anything she had ever known.

She drew back, embarrassed at her boldness. Hawk was looking at her strangely and it occurred to her that he might he married. The thought was like a knife in her heart. But surely he would have mentioned a wife if he had one. Then again, maybe not.

"Are you . . . I mean, do you have a family waiting for your return?"

"Only my mother, if she is still alive."

"Then you're not married, or anything?"

Hawk shook his head.

Maggie frowned. Were all the Indian women blind? "Why?" she asked. "Why haven't you married?"

Hawk looked at Maggie, at her curly black hair and deep blue eyes, eyes that touched the depths of his heart, and knew, for the first time, why none of the Lakota maidens had appealed to him, why he'd never courted any of the women who had made it known they found him desirable. He was in love with the Spirit Women, had been since he first saw her face in vision.

113

"Mag-gie." He whispered her name and then, very gently, he cupped her face between his hands and pressed his lips to hers.

Slowly, gradually, the pressure of his lips, and the beat of her heart, increased, until she was clinging to him, drinking from his lips as one who was dying of thirst might drink from the fount of life.

She felt his hands move in her hair and she twined her arms around his neck, reveling in his touch, his nearness. Too long, she thought, it had been too long since she'd been held in a man's arms, too long since she'd let anyone get close to her, physically or emotionally.

She was breathless when he drew away. Breathless and embarrassed. One kiss, and she reacted like a wanton. One little kiss, and she was ready to melt in his embrace. But she would not, could not! All her life she'd held her emotions in check, refusing to be like the other girls she knew, girls who slept with a guy just because he was cute, or sexy-looking, or because he drove a nice car. She'd wanted more out of life than just a good time, a quick thrill. She'd wanted love and romance and happy ever after. She still did, even though it was no longer possible.

"Spirit Woman." His voice was low and husky, his breathing erratic.

"Please, I . . . take me home."

"Do not be afraid of me, Mag-gie. I will not shame you."

But it wasn't Hawk she was afraid of, it was her reaction to his kiss. One kiss, and she was on fire for a man she hardly knew. It was too much, too fast, and it frightened her. "Please, Hawk, take me home."

"As you wish."

She held herself as far away from him as possible on the long ride down the hill. She was getting too fond of him, and she had to stop it now, before it was too late. She was too old for him, and he was too much of a man for her. He deserved a whole woman, not a useless cripple.

As soon as he put her in her chair, she went to her room and closed the door, hiding from Hawk as much as from herself, finally seeking escape in sleep. But he followed her there, as well, and in her dreams they walked together in the sun and she wasn't afraid any more.

Chapter Thirteen

Naked, Shadow Hawk and Bobby sat across from each other inside a sweat lodge made from the poles and tightly woven branches of a pine tree.

Bobby had been embarrassed at first. He had never done such a thing before, but Shadow Hawk had shed his clout and moccasins without the slightest hesitation.

And no wonder. Shadow Hawk had a powerful physique, Bobby thought with more than a trace of envy. He wasn't all arms and legs and thin as a sapling. Then and there, Bobby vowed to begin working out. He'd seen the way Miss St. Claire looked at Hawk, her eyes filled with admiration. He'd even seen Veronica staring at Hawk, and she was old enough to be his mother!

Now, he looked at Shadow Hawk expectantly, feeling anxious and excited as Hawk prepared the pit that would hold the heated stones, listening carefully as Hawk explained the purpose of the *hanbelachia* and the smoothed trail, then placed tiny bundles of tobacco on the vision hill. They had no sacred pipe, but Hawk had made a pipe that he hoped would serve the same purpose. It rested on the sacred hill, its stem facing east.

They had persuaded Veronica to help them, and when all was ready, Shadow Hawk called to her to pass in the first four stones. Then, as he had seen Heart-of-the-Wolf do, Shadow Hawk took the pipe and touched the stem to one of the stones.

"All winged creatures," he murmured, for his power came from the hawk. With great ceremony, he passed the pipe to Bobby, who puffed it four times before he passed it back, each of them taking turns puffing on the pipe until the tobacco was gone.

"All winged creatures," Shadow Hawk murmured again, and tossed a spoonful of cold water on the stones.

As steam filled the lodge, Shadow Hawk began to chant the sacred songs, imploring the Great Spirit to purify their hearts and minds, to cleanse their souls.

Eyes closed, he prayed for health and strength, for wisdom for himself and for Bobby. And as he prayed, he saw Heart-of-the-Wolf standing beside him, heard the old medicine man's voice assuring him that his mother was well, reminding him to follow the life path of the

Lakota, and to teach the young warrior to do the same.

Slowly, Shadow Hawk opened his eyes. Bobby was sitting across from him, a look of bewilderment on his face.

"What is it?" Shadow Hawk asked.

"I saw an old man," Bobby replied. "His skin was lined with the passage of many years, his hair was streaked with gray, and he wore a buffalo horn headdress."

"Heart-of-the-Wolf," Hawk murmured.

"Did you see him?"

"Yes."

"Did he speak?" Bobby asked, leaning forward.

"He reminded me to always walk in the life path of the Lakota. And to teach you to do the same."

Bobby swallowed hard. "I heard the same words."

"I know."

Bobby's eyes grew wide. "He spoke to both of us?"

Shadow Hawk nodded. He had shared Bobby's vision, and seen one of his own. He had seen Heart-of-the-Wolf standing outside the Sacred Cave, had heard the old man's voice speaking to him, the words soft yet clear.

It is not yet time, the old medicine man had said. *Only be patient and you will again be reunited with our people.*

It gave Hawk a sense of peace to know that Heart-of-the-Wolf was still watching over him, that he was not alone in a strange land after all.

118

"When will I seek a vision?" Bobby asked.

"In two days' time. You must go alone to the Hills, unarmed and unafraid. You must open your heart and your soul, your whole being, if you wish to hear the voice of *Wakán Tanka*. You must make an offering of tobacco or pollen to the earth and the sky and to the four directions. And you must listen, not with your ears, but with your heart and your soul. And you must not doubt."

Bobby nodded. He had known Shadow Hawk only a short time, yet he felt the greatness of the other man, the inner strength and self-confidence. He had seen few men on the reservation that he wanted to emulate, but Shadow Hawk was a man who inspired his trust.

Chapter Fourteen

Maggie's feelings grew more confused with each passing day. She tried to shut Hawk out of her life, tried to pretend that she didn't care for him at all, that his kiss hadn't warmed the innermost part of her being. In time, he would leave her, just as Susie had left her, as Frank had left her. It was better not to care at all than to risk being hurt again.

But Hawk refused to be shut out of her life. As fast as she built walls, he tore them down. Usually it took only a smile, or the sound of his voice, and barriers she'd thought made of stone melted like snow in the sunshine.

Sometimes she thought it was all a dream, that his presence was just a figment of her all too active imagination. And sometimes it seemed like Hawk had always been there, sitting across from her at the kitchen table, making her smile. She tried not to let him get close to her, tried to keep him away, but he had only to look at her through those fathomless dark eyes, speak her name in that voice like crushed black velvet, and she was lost.

She found herself taking more pains with her appearance, wearing long skirts and frilly blouses instead of jeans and a sweatshirt. Instead of tying her hair back in a pony tail to keep it out of her face, she let it fall free around her shoulders because he had once remarked that he liked it that way.

One night, while they were sitting on the sofa in front of the fireplace, she told Hawk about Susie, accusing herself of being negligent, foolish, a murderer, pounding on his chest with her fists as all the old pain and rage washed through her. He had let her scream, he had let her cry, and all the while he had held her in his arms, impervious to the blows she rained upon him, whispering that it hadn't been her fault, that it had been an accident, that her sister had died and she had lived because the Great Spirit had wanted it that way.

Maggie didn't believe him, didn't think she could ever forgive herself for what had happened, and yet, after that night, the nightmares that had intermittently haunted her dreams faded and she felt an inner sense of peace and acceptance.

Hawk had won Veronica's affection, as well. She cooked his favorite dinner, steak and fried potatoes, at least once a week, and because he had an insatiable sweet tooth, there was always something chocolate in the house be it cake or brownies or pie, and sometimes all three.

Bobby idolized Hawk, imitating the way he walked, trying to copy the soft way he spoke, following Hawk around the ranch whenever he went outside.

So quickly, Maggie thought, so easily, he had become a part of all their lives. How would she ever let him go?

It was on a cool cloudy morning when Bobby left on his vision quest. Clad only in a clout that his brother had sent him from the reservation, he vaulted onto the back of a long-legged gray gelding and rode off toward the Hills, carrying nothing but a small sack of corn pollen and a blanket.

Hawk stood outside, watching Bobby ride away.

Maggie sat at her bedroom window, watching them both. For a moment, she closed her eyes, praying that Bobby would find what he was looking for.

When she opened her eyes again, Hawk was still standing outside, his arms raised toward heaven, his head thrown back. Quietly, she opened the window, listening unabashedly to the sound of his voice, deep and rich, as he offered a prayer to *Wakán Tanka*.

"He, the Father of us all, has shown His mercy unto me. In peace will I walk the straight road. He has made the earth and the trees, the rocks, and all living things. This day is good. May this be the day I consider mine. Let all creatures be glad. Let all the earth sing."

After a moment, he lowered his arms to his sides and then, slowly, he turned around to face her.

Maggie blushed, embarrassed to be caught eavesdropping on something as personal as a prayer. But Hawk didn't seem angry to find her watching him. Instead, he smiled as he walked toward her bedroom window. Opening it all the way, he climbed over the low sill.

"Hawk, what are you doing?"

"Taking you to breakfast," he said, and lifting her from her chair, he carried her down the hall into the kitchen where Veronica was scrambling eggs and frying bacon.

"Morning," Veronica said, apparently unconcerned at the sight of her employer being carried into the kitchen in the arms of a man who was not her husband. "Breakfast is ready."

Shadow Hawk placed Maggie in one of the kitchen chairs, then sat down across from her. She looked especially pretty this morning. Her hair was unbound, falling free over her shoulders just the way he liked it, and he wondered fleetingly, hopefully, if she'd left it down to please him. She wore a flowing robe of some soft blue material that matched her eyes, and he thought he might willingly give up all the battle honors he had earned as a warrior if he could look upon her face each morning of his life.

Maggie felt the heat wash into her cheeks as Hawk smiled at her, his dark eyes warm. She smiled back at him, thinking how much more pleasant mornings had become since Hawk had arrived. He took such pleasure in eating that it made her enjoy her own food more. He seemed to have a limitless appetite and it had become a contest to see if Veronica could prepare more food than he could eat. This morning he wolfed down half a dozen pancakes, five strips of bacon, three eggs, and three cups of coffee.

Veronica grinned as she began to clear the table. "I thought that boy Bobby ate a lot," she mused, "but Hawk takes the cake."

"Cake," Hawk said. "You are baking again today?"

"Seems like I bake *every* day since you showed up."

"And it's beginning to show," Maggie said, patting her stomach. "I think I've gained ten pounds in the last couple of weeks."

"Looks good on you," Veronica retorted. "You were too thin."

Maggie made a soft sound of disagreement. "You know what they say, you can't be too rich or too thin."

Hawk sat back in his chair. He had come to enjoy the easy banter between the two women, just as he'd come to enjoy being the center of attention. In the village, there hadn't been much time to just sit back and relax. He'd spent many hours with Heart-of-the-Wolf, learning the ancient chants and healing skills of the Lakota. And because he was well liked by the other warriors, he was always invited to go along on a hunt or a raid. Though still a young man, he had been considered wise beyond his years and many of the young men had come to him seeking advice.

After breakfast, Veronica helped Maggie into the bathtub, then went into the laundry room to put in a load of wash. Alone, Hawk wandered through the house and then, on an impulse, he went into Maggie's room and sat in her wheelchair. He thought of the years she had been imprisoned in the chair by her inability to walk, and tried to imagine what it would be like if he were crippled. Would he want to live if he couldn't chase the buffalo across the vast sunlit prairie, or feel the wind in his face as he raced Wohitika across the plains? Would life be worth living if he couldn't stalk the wily elk, or stand beside Red Arrow and Crooked Lance to fight against the Pawnee?

Closing his eyes, he took a deep breath, breathing in the faint scent that was Maggie's alone. Sitting there, his hands fisted around the arms of the wheelchair, he seemed to feel Maggie's essence surround him. He felt her loneliness, the emptiness in her life. She was a beautiful woman, vibrant and alive. She should have a husband to cherish her, children to love. With all his heart, he wished he possessed the power to restore the strength to her legs, that he had the gift of healing that would allow her to walk again.

He looked up, feeling a little sheepish, as Veronica entered the room.

"It's all right," Veronica said. "We all do it."

"Is there nothing that will help her?"

"The doctor says she could walk if she wanted to."

Hawk ran his hands over the big black wheels. "I do not understand. If she can walk, why does she stay in this chair?"

"It's her guilt that keeps her there," Veronica explained. "The doctor says she feels responsible for her sister's death and that her refusal to walk is her way of punishing herself."

Shadow Hawk frowned. "I do not understand."

"I don't either. But when she wants to walk badly enough, she will. Now, I need the chair."

Wordlessly, Hawk stood up, wondering what he could do to make Maggie want to walk again.

Hawk stood alone under a starlit sky, his head back as he gazed at the heavens. For a moment, he thought of his people, his mother, wondering what had happened to them, frustrated because there was nothing he could do to help. Thinking of them, worrying about them, availed him nothing. He would go back to the cave when the moon was full and hope he could return to his people.

He let out a deep sigh as he closed his eyes, his spirit reaching out to Bobby. The boy had been gone for three days and Hawk yearned to know if he was well, if *Wakán Tanka* would grant the young man a vision.

Standing there, he heard the wind whispering through the pines that covered the Black Hills. He heard the gentle swoosh of wings as an owl skimmed the air in search of prey, heard the rustle of underbrush as a deer made its way toward a shallow pool to drink. His nostrils filled with the fragrant scent of the pines, of freshly turned earth where a skunk had dug a hole for the night. He felt the caress of the night wind on his cheek. And then, eyes still closed, he saw Heart-of-the-Wolf. The old man was dressed in white buckskins. White moccasins covered his feet. A single white feather adorned his hair; a thin slash of white paint bisected his left cheek.

As from far away, Hawk seemed to hear the sound of drums. He heard the rapid beat of an eagle's wings, and then Heart-of-the-Wolf was speaking to him.

Bobby Running Horse will now be known as Proud Eagle. It is because of you, Shadow Hawk, that this young warrior's dreams will come true. You have given him a new sense of pride in our people; you have set his feet on the Life Path of the Lakota. From this day forward, the Eagle will follow the Hawk.

The words were so clear that Hawk opened his eyes, expecting to see Heart-of-the-Wolf standing beside him.

Instead, he saw Maggie coming toward him, her wheelchair enveloped by a bright shaft of moonlight that seemed to follow her as she crossed the yard toward him.

For a moment, Hawk stared at her, the woman of his vision. Was she flesh and blood? Or a Spirit Woman he had summoned from the depths of his heart?

"Are you all right?" Maggie called softly. "You've been out here a long time."

"I am fine."

He couldn't take his eyes from her face. Shafts of silvery moonlight caressed her skin and danced in her hair, and suddenly he knew he must hold her or die.

He crossed the distance between them in three quick strides. Lifting her from the chair, he cradled her to his chest, afraid to hold her too tightly for fear of hurting her, afraid to let her go for fear she would vanish from his sight.

"Hawk . . ."

Slowly, he lowered his head toward hers, his lips finding hers in a kiss that was infinitely tender.

Maggie drew back, frightened by the power of his touch, intoxicated by the mere taste of his lips. Had he been as shaken, as moved, by what had just happened as she was?

She had a quick image of Hawk surrounded by women, beautiful Indian maidens with dark luminous eyes and smooth tawny skin.

"Have you kissed many girls?" Maggie asked brashly, and then wondered whatever had possessed her to ask such a question.

Hawk gazed down at her, his dark eyes alight with a fierce inner fire. "You are the first."

She couldn't hide her smile. "Truly?"

"Truly." His mouth descended on hers again, his kiss more ardent this time.

And Maggie kissed him back. She forgot all her fears, all her arguments that he was too young, that she was too old. Wrapping her arms around Hawk's neck, she forgot all about Frank and how much he'd hurt her, and thought only of the pleasure of Hawk's mouth moving over hers.

Boldly, she traced his lips with her tongue, heard his low groan, felt a tremor ripple through his body as his arms tightened around her and his tongue singed hers.

Thrilled by the rough magic of his touch, she tightened her hold on his neck, wanting to be closer, closer. She tangled one hand in his hair, loving the way it felt against her skin. He had beautiful hair. Long and thick, it fell to his waist like a black waterfall.

She closed her eyes as his lips moved over her face, placing light butterfly kisses on her eyes and nose, her cheeks and forehead, before returning to her mouth. She'd never known a kiss could be so intoxicating, or so arousing. She was warm all over, especially where his body touched hers.

Hawk began to tremble as their kisses grew deeper, more intimate, more impassioned. Her scent rose all around him, warm and womanly, inflaming his desire. Her skin was smooth and soft as new grass, her hair tickled his cheek, he could feel the heat of her breast against his arm. She tasted of apple pie and coffee laced with cream and he knew he'd never taste either again without remembering this moment when he stood in the moonlight with the woman of his dreams cradled to his chest.

Maggie let her head fall back over Hawk's arm so she could see his face. His eyes were like black pools of fire. His lips, slightly parted, issued a silent invitation and she placed her hand behind his head and drew him toward her, wanting to savor the taste of him again, and again.

Neither noticed as the minutes slid by. Hours might have passed, or only moments, but for Maggie there was nothing else in all the world, only Hawk and the sweet sorcery of his touch, the tenderness in his eyes, the strength of the arms that held her as if she weighed no more than a feather.

Soon, they'd have to go back to the house. She'd remember that she was too old for him, that he might disappear at any moment, that he could never be hers. Soon, she thought, but not now.

She was hardly aware that he was moving until he placed her on the damp grass beside the quiet pool on the west side of the house.

Silently, he stretched out beside her and took her in his arms again, holding her close. She breathed in the heady male scent of him, let her fingertips trace the muscles in his back and shoulders as she rained feathery kisses along his neck.

She was drowning in pleasure, floating on an ocean of sensation, and he was doing nothing more than holding her close. Her breasts were crushed against the unyielding wall of his chest, her face was buried in the curve of his neck. She could feel the warm whisper of his breath in her hair as he murmured her name, his voice filled with the same wonder she was feeling, his body trembling with the same passion that was turning her blood to fire.

Releasing a long shuddering sigh, Hawk loosened his hold and drew back a little.

"Mag-gie." He murmured her name, dazed by the unfamiliar emotions her nearness aroused.

He had never made love to a woman. To defile a Lakota woman was unthinkable; to lie with one of the captive women who sometimes exchanged their favors for food and clothing had been distasteful. In truth, he'd had little time for courting, or women. He had been too busy learning to be a warrior, a medicine man. And always, in the back of his mind, had been his vision of the Spirit Woman, making all other women seem uninteresting and unimportant.

Abruptly, he drew her close and stood up, carrying her with him, afraid if he lay beside her any longer the tight rein he had on his desire might snap, that he might force himself upon her and destroy the bond between them.

Maggie didn't argue as he carried her back to her chair. Her feelings, the depth of the emotions swirling through her like a restless tide, were too deep for words. She had a terrible feeling that if Hawk hadn't let her go, she would have willingly surrendered her body, and her heart.

The thought frightened her more than she cared to admit.

Chapter Fifteen

It was mid-afternoon the following day when Bobby returned to the ranch.

Hawk met the weary would-be warrior on the front porch, quickly taking in the lines of fatigue on the young man's face. He knew Bobby's vision had not come quickly or easily, but it had come.

"It was wonderful," Bobby said as he joined Hawk on the porch. "I don't know if I can explain it . . ."

"But you've been chosen by *Wakán Tanka* to be the next medicine man."

Bobby stared at Hawk, a look of amazement on his face. "How did you know?"

"Come," Hawk said. "Let us walk awhile."

They made their way out past the barn to a flat stretch of ground bordered by slender

132

pines. Sitting cross-legged on the thick grass, Hawk motioned for Bobby to join him.

Bobby closed his eyes a moment, trying to calm the excitement welling within him. "I did everything you told me to do. The first two days were hard. I couldn't concentrate. I was hungry and thirsty, the sun was hot." Bobby shrugged sheepishly. "My mind kept wandering to other things.

"The third day was worse. That night, I almost came home. But this morning! Hawk, this morning as the sun climbed over the Hills I saw an eagle. It seemed to come out of nowhere, and I heard it speak to me, telling me that the Eagle would follow the Hawk and finish the journey to the North Country. It was the strangest thing, but I knew somehow that it meant I would follow in your footsteps, that I would become a holy man."

Hawk smiled, feeling a warm sense of satisfaction as he saw the look of happiness on Bobby's face.

"But the strangest thing was that, for a time, I felt like *I* was an eagle. And I flew, Hawk, my spirit left my body and I could see for miles, and I felt different. Light. Powerful. It was . . ." He shook his head. "I don't know. I can't explain it. I flew over the Black Hills, and then I was flying northward, and then the strangest thing happened, I passed you and then I was flying toward Canada and I found a nest there, and I knew it was going to be my home. But that doesn't make sense, does it?"

Hawk shook his head, baffled by the boy's vision. How could Bobby be the next Lakota medicine man unless he stayed here, in the *Paha Sapa*?

"I saw the old man again, the one we saw in the sweat lodge. He said I'm to have a new name." There was a note of awe in Bobby's voice. "I'm to be called Proud Eagle."

"Wear it well, my brother. It is an honorable name."

"You knew all this before I told you, didn't you?" Bobby said. "How?"

"The old man you saw is Heart-of-the-Wolf. He was a powerful medicine man in our village. I think his spirit has followed me through time. Or it may be that he has come to help you know your own heart. But I feel that he is nearby."

Bobby nodded. "Do you think . . . I mean, would it be all right to tell Miss St. Claire about my vision?"

"I think she will insist."

Maggie watched Hawk's face, her mind racing, as Bobby related his experience. Imagine, an Indian in the twentieth century receiving a medicine dream! Who would believe it? It sounded so bizarre. And yet, as she searched her heart, she knew that Hawk believed every word. And so did she. One had only to look at Bobby to know that something extraordinary had happened to him.

"I'm happy for you, Bobby," she said, taking his hand in hers. "I know it's what you've always wanted."

"Yes, ma'am," he replied, his dark eyes shining with excitement. "I . . . would you mind if I took a few days off? I'd like to go home and tell my little brother what happened." A sad smile played over his lips. "My father probably won't believe me."

"Take all the time you need, Bobby," Maggie said, squeezing his hand. "You haven't had a vacation since you came to work for me."

"Thanks, Miss St. Claire. If it's all right, then, I may stay for a week or two."

"Of course."

Bobby clasped Hawk's forearm. "*Pilamaya*, Hawk. I never would have found the courage to seek a vision if it hadn't been for you."

"You did not need courage," Hawk said. "Only someone to point you in the right direction."

"Maybe. Anyway, I'm more grateful than I can say."

Somewhat shyly, Bobby gave Hawk a quick hug, kissed Maggie on the cheek, and hurried from the room before they could see the tears welling in his eyes.

"He's a good boy," Maggie said.

Hawk nodded. "He would have made a fine warrior."

"He'll make a fine doctor. Veronica's going to be sorry she didn't get to say goodbye."

It was Sunday, Hawk realized. Veronica didn't come to the ranch on Sundays, but stayed home to catch up on her own chores and go to church with her white husband. Hawk thought it odd that the white man felt the need to go to one of his square houses to pray to his God. But then, perhaps the god of the *wasichu* could not be found in the *Paha Sapa*. The white man's religion, like everything else, was hard to understand.

"Well," Maggie said, "I don't know about you, but I'm getting hungry. Shall we go see what Veronica left us for dinner?"

"If you wish."

Hawk sat at the table, watching as she warmed up the pot of beef stew Veronica had made, noticing for the first time that everything in the kitchen was built low so Maggie could reach it. It did not occur to him to help her. Lakota men were not accustomed to doing women's work.

Maggie hummed softly as she poured two cups of coffee, filled two big bowls with beef stew, buttered two slices of bread. Two, she thought. It was such a lovely number. She felt very domestic as she pulled two soup spoons from the drawer, placed napkins on the table. For a moment she found herself pretending that Hawk was her husband and they were sitting down to Sunday dinner like any other married couple.

But then she looked at Hawk and all pretense fell away. He would never be like any other husband. He was a man from the past, a warrior, with a warrior's inborn pride. He would never hold down a nine-to-five job, never be the kind of husband who helped with the dishes and the laundry. She couldn't imagine him diapering a baby, or mowing the front lawn, or driving the kids to soccer practice. He'd been born to hunt, to roam the plains in search of the buffalo, to fight the Crow and the Pawnee. And the white man. Trying to domesticate him would be like trying to turn a

136

zebra into a riding horse. It simply couldn't be done.

"What will you do when Bobby goes away to college?" Hawk asked after a while.

"I don't know." She guided her wheelchair up to the table and spread a napkin in her lap. "I guess I'll have to hire someone to take his place." It shouldn't be too hard, she thought. There were always young Indian boys who were anxious to work. She was only sorry she couldn't hire more of them.

"I will look after the animals while I am here," Hawk offered.

Maggie smiled her thanks. It would not offend his dignity to care for the horses, or feed the chickens, or keep her supplied with firewood.

She cleared the table after dinner, rinsed the dishes, and left them in the sink. Veronica would wash them and put them away in the morning.

When she'd finished in the kitchen, Maggie went into the living room. Hawk was stretched out on the sofa, watching an old Western on television. She placed her chair beside the sofa, thinking that maybe he wasn't so different from modern men after all. Her father had always gone in the den to watch TV while she and her mother did the dishes, and Westerns had been his favorite shows. He had loved watching "Bonanza" and "Wyatt Earp" and "The Rifleman."

Hawk liked to watch Westerns, too. Sometimes they made him angry, and sometimes they made him laugh.

Now he sat up, pointing at the television, as a horde of screaming Indians attacked an Army

137

patrol. "How is it that when the Indian wins, the battle is called a massacre, but when the white man wins, it is a great victory?"

"I don't know, but that's the way it always seems to be."

Hawk grunted, annoyed by the way his people were portrayed. Always, the red man was ignorant, savage, brutal, while the white man was heroic and noble. The whites who made the movies didn't seem to know one Indian from another, and he had seen movies where Indian warriors wore Pawnee scalplocks, Lakota war shirts, Cheyenne moccasins, and spoke Arapaho. But the message was always the same: the fort, or the ranch, or the woman would never be safe until the Indian was destroyed.

"Would you mind lighting a fire in the fireplace?" Maggie asked, hoping to draw Hawk's thoughts from the movie. "It's a little chilly in here."

She watched Hawk as he knelt before the fireplace, admiring the play of muscles in his broad back and shoulders as he took several pieces of wood from the box beside the hearth and arranged them on the grate. He still wore nothing but his clout and moccasins, and the sight of his bare back, though familiar, still did funny things in the pit of her stomach.

The kindling caught with a soft crackle of flames, the firelight playing over his bronzed skin, and Maggie closed her eyes, imagining Hawk dancing around a campfire, perhaps boasting of his exploits in battle. She could hear the rhythmic sound of drumming, smell the smoke and the dust, hear his voice filled with pride as he recounted how he had counted coup against the enemy.

Even with her eyes closed, she knew when he came to stand beside her. His presence was so strong, so vital, she was sure she could find him even if she were blindfolded in a dark cave.

She opened her eyes as she felt the weight of his hand on her shoulder.

"Come," he said, "sit beside me."

Maggie nodded, unable to speak past the lump that rose in her throat as he lifted her from her chair. She put her arms around his neck, marveling anew at how easily he lifted her, as if she weighed nothing at all.

But he didn't put her on the sofa. Instead, he sat down, holding her in his lap.

It was suddenly hard to breathe and she lowered her gaze to the muscular brown arm lightly circling her waist. How dark his skin was! His hands were callused and strong, his legs were corded with muscle. Was there another man in all the world as tall, as handsome?

His hand cupped her chin, encouraging her to look at him.

"Aren't you going to put me down?" she asked, her voice sounding uneven and strangely high-pitched.

"Do you want me to?"

Maggie shook her head, thinking she'd like nothing more than to be held in his arms forever.

A million butterflies seemed to be trapped in her stomach as his gaze moved to her lips.

He lowered his head toward hers, very slowly, giving her plenty of time to avoid his kiss if she desired.

It was the furthest thing from her mind. She closed her eyes as his lips covered hers, felt his arm tighten around her waist as his kiss deepened. His tongue delved into her mouth, gently exploring.

Desire uncurled deep within her, layer upon layer, unfolding like the petals of a rose. He kissed her for a long while before he drew back. His eyes, as black as ten feet down, smoldered with passion.

Maggie swallowed hard, amazed that something as simple as a kiss could so quickly enflame her senses.

"Ah, Mag-gie."

Hawk drew a deep breath, released it in a long shuddering sigh. Did she know what she did to him? Looking at her filled him with joy, touching her was the sweetest torment he'd ever known. He wanted to tear away her clothes and take her there, on the floor, before the fire; he wanted to undress her slowly and arouse her with infinite care and tenderness.

He wanted her.

Maggie read the desire in his eyes, felt it in the pressure of his hands, and it filled her with a sense of wonder. Since the accident, no other man had looked at her with such yearning, or made her feel like a woman instead of a cripple.

"What will you do if you can't get back to your people?"

Hawk shook his head. "I do not know."

He didn't speak of his people often, but Maggie knew he must be homesick, that he was worried about his mother and the welfare of his people. No doubt he missed his friends, and the familiarity of his own way of life. It was selfish of her to want to keep him here when he so clearly belonged to another time and place. Selfish and uncharitable and no doubt impossible, as well, and yet she needed him so desperately.

"You . . . you could stay here."

His dark eyes held hers in a long, measuring glance. "And take Bobby's place?"

"If you like."

She fidgeted with her skirt as she waited for his answer, knowing life would never be the same without him. He had become important to her. The house had taken on a new life since he'd been there. She had taken on a new life. He didn't seem to care that she was confined to a wheelchair. When he wanted to go for a walk, he simply picked her up and took her along. It was the same when he wanted to ride. And she began to think maybe it wasn't so bad, being unable to walk. She liked being held in his embrace; she liked the warmth and security of having his arm around her when they rode the big black stallion. Maybe her life wasn't over. Maybe she *could* have a husband, a family . . .

"Please don't go." She hadn't meant to speak the words aloud, but suddenly they were there, between them, demanding an answer.

Maggie held her breath, her pride withering under his steady dark-eyed gaze. She hadn't meant to beg, but she couldn't bear the thought of his leaving, of being alone again.

"I will stay, Mag-gie," he said. "If I cannot return to my own time and my own people, then I will stay here, with you, for as long as you want me."

Chapter Sixteen

Hawk stood outside, his gaze focused on the Hills rising in the distance.

Bobby had called early that morning to say he had received the grant he'd applied for and would be leaving for college in a couple of weeks. He had asked Maggie's permission to stay on with his family until then, and she had told him not to worry, she was doing fine. She had been happy and enthusiastic, offering to send Bobby money if he ran short, and promising to write.

Hawk had talked to Bobby, too, amazed that the white man had invented such a marvelous thing as the telephone, hardly able to believe that he was actually talking to someone many miles away.

Hawk had found a certain sense of satisfaction in taking Bobby's place on the ranch. He enjoyed looking after the stock. There were three other horses on the ranch besides the big black stallion: a pretty little chestnut mare and a matched pair of bay geldings.

The days had passed slowly. Caring for the stock and feeding the chickens didn't take more than a couple of hours, leaving him a lot of time to think.

Tonight, he found himself wondering about his people, hoping that most of them had survived the attack. He offered a silent prayer to *Wakán Tanka* in his mother's behalf, clinging, as always, to Heart-of-the-Wolf's promise that Winona was still alive and well.

He drew his gaze from the sacred Hills and looked at Maggie's house. It was strong and sturdy, made of stone and wood. Smoke rose from the chimney, light shone through the windows. He could not understand the white man's need to own land, to build a house and stay in one place, but he thought he could get used to the idea if he could share this house with Maggie.

He knew she was inside, sitting at her computer, writing the white man's words. Slowly, he shook his head. The *wasichu* might not know where the center of the earth was, he might not know how to live in harmony with Mother Earth, but he had created some amazing things.

Maggie had tried to explain how her computer worked, about the air waves that made television and radio possible, but it was beyond his comprehension.

He stared at the dark blue truck parked alongside the house. A Ford pickup, it was called. Bobby had once offered to teach him how to drive the huge metal beast, but Hawk had refused. Maybe someday, he had said dubiously, but not now.

A faint breeze stirred the leaves of the pines and caressed his cheek like a familiar hand and he felt a sudden loneliness, an aching need for home. He missed his own people, missed the familiar sights and smells of the village, the sound of children playing outside his lodge. He longed to hunt the buffalo with Red Arrow and Lame Elk, to ride into a Pawnee camp in the dark of night and steal some horses, to sit around a campfire and listen to the old ones tell the ancient tales of the Lakota.

He looked at the house again and in his mind's eye he could see Maggie, sitting at her desk, her slender fingers flying over the keyboard.

Heat washed through him as he remembered the kisses they had shared, the press of her body against his when he held her close. His arms ached to hold her again, and without conscious thought, he found himself walking toward the house, opening the front door, walking down the hall to the den.

His moccasined feet made no sound on the thick carpet as he crossed the floor and knelt beside the wheelchair.

Maggie glanced at him uncertainly. "Hawk, what is it?"

145

"I am lonely," he said quietly. "I miss my people."

"Of course you do." She laid her hand on his shoulder, her heart welling with compassion as she gazed into his beautiful black eyes. "You'll be back with them soon."

"Perhaps. But then I shall miss you."

His voice washed over her like liquid velvet and she felt a catch in her breath, a pain in her heart, at the thought of his leaving her.

"Mag-gie." He took her hand in his, his fingers gently cradling her hand while his thumb caressed her palm.

The touch of his hand, the sadness in his eyes, went straight to her heart. "Do you have to go back?"

"If I can. I must know if my people survived, if my mother is still alive. Heart-of-the-Wolf is dead. My people will need me."

"I need you." She had not meant to speak the words aloud.

"Ah, Mag-gie," he murmured, and rising to his feet, he lifted her into his arms and carried her out of the house and into the moonlit night.

The air was warm, fragrant with the scent of pines as he carried her toward the porch swing, then sat down, still holding her in his arms. Slowly, wordlessly, he rocked her back and forth in the swing, his heart hammering at her nearness. He had never been in love before, and he was afraid, so afraid, that what he felt for Maggie was more than compassion, more than affection.

He let out a deep sigh of helplessness. He could not love her. They were worlds apart. Years apart. But love her he did. Knowing that, how could he ever leave her?

He turned his head and gazed into her eyes, eyes as deep and blue as the quiet pool behind the house. Eyes that were haunted by old hurts. Eyes filled with the first stirrings of hope.

Ah, Mag-gie, he thought. *How will I ever leave you now?*

"Hawk." His name was a sigh on her lips, a whisper filled with longing.

She was watching him, waiting, and he could not deny her any more than he could deny himself. He put his arm around her shoulder and drew her close as his mouth slanted over hers. He felt her hand caress the back of his neck, felt the softness of her breasts against his chest as she turned more fully toward him, her arm wrapping around his waist. Their breath mingled, became one, as his tongue explored the sweetness of her mouth.

Maggie shuddered with pleasure, her fingers curling in his hair. She never thought to object as he pressed her down on the swing, his big body covering hers as he continued to kiss her, savoring the taste of her lips. His hand moved restlessly along her ribcage, barely stroking the curve of her breast.

Her gasp of pleasure and his groan of desire rose on a single breath, and then Hawk sat up, shaken to the depths of his being by how desperately he wanted to make love to her, frightened by the hot blood running through his veins, by the equally hot thoughts running through his mind, thoughts of taking her then and there, willing or not.

Closing his eyes, he drew a long shuddering sigh, reminding himself that she had been hurt before, that she was alone and vulnerable, that making love to her would be madness. She was a white woman, and he was a Lakota warrior. Loving her would only cause them both pain. And sooner or later, he would have to leave her. . . .

He felt her hand on his thigh, heard her voice, low and afraid as she whispered his name.

Opening his eyes, Hawk looked at her, saw her arms reaching for him, and knew he was lost.

He gathered her into his arms again, kissing her deeply, desperately, tasting the salt of her tears as she melted in his embrace. He covered her face with kisses, let his hands learn the softness of her skin, the fullness of her breasts, the length of her thighs.

And she was touching him in return, her hands exploring the width of his shoulders, the firmness of his flat belly ridged with muscle, the hard contours of his chest and arms.

Her fingertips traced the line of his fine straight nose, the planes of his cheeks, the sensual fullness of his lips, the curve of his jaw.

Cheeks flushed with pleasure, she gazed into his eyes, felt their heat encompass her even as the warmth of his breath caressed her.

"Hawk, I . . ."

He nodded, knowing what she wanted, what she couldn't say.

148

He kissed her again, and again, felt the tension building within him. And knew he had to let her go before it was too late.

He stood up, lifted her in his arms, and walked down the porch steps, his long strides carrying them around the house to the quiet pool located in the backyard. The water shimmered in the moonlight, its surface like dark glass.

Gently, he lowered Maggie to the ground, and then, in a fluid motion, he stripped off his clout and moccasins and plunged into the cold water, seeking relief for his heated flesh.

Maggie caught a brief flash of small firm buttocks and long bronze thighs before he disappeared into the pool. She wished, oh how she wished that she could join him there, that she could swim with him in the stillness of the night, that she could play and splash in the shallows near the water's edge, feel his skin, cool and damp, next to her own. . . .

He surfaced in the center of the pool, his hair and skin dappled with moonlight.

She waved to him, a wistful smile playing over her lips. And suddenly he was there beside her, removing her caftan and underwear, taking the slippers from her feet, lifting her in his arms.

She squealed as the cold water closed around them. And then he was swimming beside her, his hands easily supporting her weight in the water. It was wonderful to drift there beside him, to feel the water move across her skin. His eyes were as dark as the sky, as warm as the touch of his hand.

149

They circled the pool once, twice, before Hawk lifted Maggie in his arms and carried her out of the water.

He stood at the pool's edge for a long time, her body cradled against his.

Maggie remained quiescent in his arms, afraid to speak for fear of spoiling the intimacy of the moment. It felt so good to be in his arms, to feel his skin, cool and damp, against her own. She didn't stop to think of right or wrong, refused to think of the future, of what it would be like when he was gone. She wanted only this night, this moment, to treasure for the rest of her life.

She gazed up into his face, pleased with what she saw. He was beautiful, she thought, so beautiful. There was a wildness about him, a hint of violence, of untamed passion, that appealed to a part of her that she had never realized existed, something earthy and primal that lurked deep within her being.

She wanted him. Perhaps she had wanted him from the first moment she'd seen him. No matter that she was too old, that he was a man from another time, that he might disappear in the twinkling of an eye. She wanted him.

"Hawk."

She put all her wanting into that one word. For a moment, she thought he would take her there, on the damp ground. He kissed her once, briefly, and then gazed into her eyes.

"Have you ever been with a man?"

"No," she admitted, feeling her cheeks grow pink, "but it doesn't matter."

"It matters to me."

"Please, Hawk."

"No, Mag-gie," he said, and his voice was ragged and weary, as if he'd been waging a hard-fought battle. "I cannot."

"Why?" She heard the desperation in her voice and hated herself for it.

"It is not right. You are not my woman. I do not know how long I will be here. I do not want to hurt you. I do not want you to hate me when I am gone."

"I could never hate you."

"Think of how much you hate the man Frank."

"That's not the same thing."

"If I make you my woman and then leave, you will hate me much more. And I would hate myself for hurting you."

"It's because I'm a cripple, isn't it?"

"No."

"It is, I know it is! All those pretty words don't mean a thing. The truth is, you can't bear the thought of touching me!" She wriggled in his grasp, wanting to be out of his arms, hating herself for the tears that were stinging her eyes. Why had she thought he was different? He was just like Frank, just like every other man, wanting a woman who was whole.

"Mag-gie."

She heard the pain in his voice but she was too steeped in her own misery to care. She had practically begged him to make love to her and he had refused. And now she couldn't even get away from him.

With a sigh, Hawk sat down on a white wrought-iron bench in an arbor a few yards from the pool. Maggie remained stiff in his embrace, her face turned away from him, her shoulders shaking with the force of the silent sobs that rose in her throat.

"Mag-gie, do not make this any more difficult than it is. I do not wish to shame you, or myself. I have never defiled a maiden. Do not ask it of me now." He gazed deep into her eyes. "And never think that you are less of a woman because you cannot walk, or that I would desire you more if your legs were strong and healthy."

His words, softly spoken, and the heartfelt expression in his eyes washed over Maggie like a healing balm.

Sniffing back her tears, she rested her head against his shoulder and basked in the joy of knowing that he cared. What a man he was. Strong. Proud. With a deeply ingrained sense of honor. No wonder she loved him. She, who had vowed never to risk her heart again, had given it to a man who was as elusive as a will-o'-the-wisp. But she didn't care. Be it a day or a lifetime, she would make the most of each precious moment.

Chapter Seventeen

Hawk avoided being alone with Maggie for the next couple of days. He spent long hours outside, exercising the horses, brushing the animals until their coats were smooth as glass and their manes and tails flowed like silk.

Needing more to do, he moved to the woodpile and began chopping firewood, finishing the pile Bobby had started. He watered the front lawn, raked the leaves, mucked out the stalls in the barn.

"If you don't watch out, you'll soon be swilling beer in front of the TV every weekend, just like the *wasichu* ranchers," Veronica warned, but Hawk just scowled at her and asked her what else he could do.

Maggie understood why Hawk stayed outside, why he was reluctant to be near her, especially on

Sunday when they were alone in the house, but it hurt just the same. She supposed she should be grateful that he regarded her virtue so highly, that he was a man who believed in honor and chastity, but that was cold comfort in bed at night.

Holding on to her virginity had always been easy. She hadn't cared that saving herself for marriage was as old-fashioned as bustles and hoop skirts. But then, she'd never met a man like Hawk. Somehow, all her mother's teachings and her own sense of right and wrong evaporated when he was around. It was almost funny, she thought. She'd saved her virginity for so long, and now she couldn't even give it away.

She turned her attention to her novel, submerging herself in a love story where she was in complete control, where the hero behaved the way she thought he should, where nothing was impossible, not if two people loved each other enough.

She stayed at her computer until late at night, and in the space of three days she'd written one hundred and twenty pages. And it was good, all of it. There was a new depth of feeling in her writing, a deeper understanding of the relationship between a man and a woman, a vulnerability that she'd never explored before. And she owed it all to Hawk, to the feelings and emotions he had aroused in her.

The evening of the fourth day, Maggie was sitting at her computer, frowning at the blank blue screen, when Hawk entered the room.

"Veronica wants to know if you would like a piece of cake and a glass of milk before she leaves."

"What? Oh, not now. Tell her thanks."

Hawk crossed the room to stand beside her. He gestured at the blank computer screen. "You are having trouble?"

"Yes. I'm trying to write a scene that takes place in the Lakota village. I want my hero to do a scalp dance, but I've never seen one except in the movies and I doubt they're very accurate." Maggie glanced up at Hawk thoughtfully. "Maybe you could . . . would you . . . ?"

"Dance for you?"

"Yes. Would you mind?"

Hawk shrugged.

"Can you do it here? Now?"

"Outside is better."

Minutes later, Maggie and Veronica followed Hawk outside.

"A scalp dance usually takes place in the center of the village," Hawk explained. "It is a way of celebrating a warrior's victories. The men are joined by their mothers and sisters, who carry the trophies on poles while the men dance. Black face paint is worn by everyone as a symbol of victory."

Hawk stared at Maggie for a long moment, and then he began to dance, his steps now slow and deliberate, now fast and frenzied, moving to music only he could hear.

Maggie thought she had never seen anything more seductive, more provocative, than Hawk dancing in the light of the setting sun. He moved with masculine grace, the powerful muscles in his arms and legs rippling beneath his smooth bronze skin, his hair whipping over his shoulders, long and thick and black.

She stared at him in open admiration, at the broad shoulders and back that narrowed to a trim waist, and felt her heart skip a beat. He was wonderful to watch, untamed, primal, beautiful.

She slid a glance at Veronica, blushed when she saw the older woman watching her speculatively.

"He's something, isn't he?" Veronica murmured.

Maggie nodded. "I'll bet every young woman in the village had her cap set for him."

"And some of the older ones, too," Veronica remarked with a knowing grin.

Maggie applauded when Hawk finished his dance. "That was wonderful," she said, smiling. "Just wonderful." And then her smile faded as she realized the significance of the dance.

"Yes, wonderful," Veronica agreed, thinking the tension between Hawk and Maggie was thick enough to cut with a knife. "Well," she went on tactfully, "if you two don't need anything else, I think I'll head on home."

"Good night, Veronica. Give my love to Ed and the boys."

"Will do," Veronica called over her shoulder. "See you tomorrow."

An awkward silence fell between Maggie and Hawk as they watched Veronica drive away.

"Would you like some coffee?" Maggie asked.

"Yes."

He followed her into the house, sat across from her at the table, the coffee pot between them. It was the first time in almost a week that they'd been alone together.

"Would you tell me something?" Maggie asked.

"Yes."

"Have you ever . . . ?" She bit down on her lower lip, wondering if she really wanted the answer to the question on the tip of her tongue. "Have you ever taken a scalp?"

"I am a warrior."

It was, she supposed, all the answer she needed. "Very many?" she asked, surprised to find she had a rather morbid streak of curiosity.

"How many is many? Ten? Fifteen? A hundred?"

"A hundred!" She almost choked on the words, and then she saw he was teasing her.

"Does it make a difference, Mag-gie?"

"I don't know." She stared into her coffee cup. He had killed men. White men. Killed them and taken their scalps. It was a sobering thought. It was one thing to write about such atrocities, to know there had been horrors committed by both sides, and something else entirely to be sitting across from a man who had actually done such things.

A muscle flexed in Hawk's jaw as he watched the play of emotions on Maggie's face. She had found the scalp dance exciting, but she was sickened to think he had actually taken a scalp. Did she think less of him now, see him as a savage?

157

He stood up, his hands clenched at his sides. "Do you want me to leave?"

"No," she said quickly.

"It sickens you to think of it."

"Yes, a little. I know it was common practice. I even understand why it was done. I just never thought I'd know anyone who had actually done it." She tilted her head to one side. "Did you really take a hundred scalps?"

He shook his head, and then he smiled, and Maggie felt the warmth of it flood her being like sunshine.

Slowly, the smile faded from his face. His eyes, as black as ink, seemed to burn into her, searing her skin, firing her blood. The tension hummed between them like chain lightning.

Maggie opened her mouth to speak, but no words came out. She could only stare at him, her longing clearly mirrored in her eyes, in the quickening of her breath. She folded her hands in her lap to keep from reaching for him, wishing that, for just this night, he would forget he was a warrior, forget his honor, and make love to her.

He took a step toward her and she felt her heart begin to sing.

And then the phone rang. They stared at each other for several moments, unmoving. Maggie willed the infernal contraption to be still, but it continued to ring until, finally, Hawk answered it. He listened for a moment, then handed the receiver to Maggie and left the room.

Maggie watched him go, then put the phone to her ear. It was Veronica. Her husband had been in an accident at work. He was in the hospital at Rapid City in critical condition. Maggie listened to Veronica for several minutes, letting the older woman pour out her fears for her husband, wishing she had some words of comfort to offer Veronica, but in the end there was really nothing to say. And then Veronica began to worry about how Maggie would get along without her.

"I'll be fine, Veronica. Don't worry about me."

"What will you do? How will you manage?"

"For heaven's sake, Veronica, how can you worry about me at a time like this?"

"I hate to leave you in the lurch like this. I don't know how long Ed will be laid up. The doctor said it might be weeks." There was a long pause. "Perhaps months."

"I'll be fine, and your job will be waiting for you when you're ready to come back. Do you need anything? Money? Anything?"

"Maggie . . ."

"Veronica, promise you'll let me know if you need help."

"I will, Maggie. Thank you. I'd better go now."

"Keep in touch, Veronica."

"I will."

Frowning, Maggie dropped the receiver in place, then sat staring at the phone, wishing there was something she could do to help Veronica.

Going to the window, Maggie stared into the distance. Poor Veronica. If Ed passed away, she'd be left to raise her two sons alone.

159

Alone. Maggie swallowed the lump of self-pity rising in her throat. Veronica would never really be alone. Even if Ed passed away, Veronica would have her sons to comfort her, and years of memories to keep her company while, she, Maggie, had nothing, and no one. . . .

Disgusted with her maudlin thoughts, Maggie poured herself another cup of coffee. Tomorrow she'd put an ad in the paper. As much as she disliked the idea of hiring someone to take Veronica's place, it just wasn't practical for her to live alone. She needed help in and out of the tub, she needed someone to do the shopping, to pick up her mail from town. Even though there were a lot of things she could do for herself, she'd become accustomed to having Veronica do the dusting and the vacuuming, the laundry, the ironing and mending. And she hated to cook. Besides, having someone to look after the house gave her more time to write.

She emptied her cup, then went down the hall to her bedroom, but she was too worried about Veronica to go to bed. Instead, she went to the window and gazed out into the yard.

Somehow, she'd known Hawk would be out there. She stared at him for a long while. She never tired of looking at him, never saw him without a quickening in the pit of her stomach, a fullness in her heart.

She wondered what he was thinking, what he was feeling, what *she* would be feeling if she suddenly found herself in a world turned upside down.

She stared at the moon. It was yellow and bright, almost full. *Magic is always done best in the light of a full moon. . . .* That was what he was thinking. She knew it as clearly as if she'd heard him speak the words. Tomorrow night the moon would be full, and the cave was calling to him, bidding him to return to his own time, his own people.

The day she had dreaded was almost here.

Hawk stared at the *Paha Sapa*, clothed from top to bottom in evergreens. Near at hand, the Hills appeared to be an unchanging dark green. At greater distances they were black, and then blue. He had lived within the shadow of the Black Hills his whole life, camped in the verdant meadows, swam in clear blue lakes and streams shaded by spruce and birch and aspen. He had hunted the buffalo and the elk and the whitetail deer, fought the Crow and the Pawnee, raced his pony across a sea of prairie grass.

He lifted his gaze to the sky, to the bright yellow moon shining down upon him, felt his heart constrict with pain as he realized that his time with Maggie was coming to an end.

Tomorrow night the moon would be full. If the gods were with him, he would enter the Sacred Cave and follow the Spirit Path back to his own time, his own people.

But he didn't want to go. He didn't want to leave Maggie, could not bear the thought of never seeing her again. She was a part of him, more precious than the breath that gave him life.

She was watching him even now. He knew it as surely as he knew he must leave her. He could feel the warmth of her gaze resting on his back, could feel her spirit, lonely and unhappy, crying out to him, begging him to stay.

Spirit Woman, you must let me go.

Did he speak the words aloud, or were they only an anguished cry ripped from the depths of his heart? He felt torn, as if his heart and his soul were splitting apart. His soul demanded he return to his own people, that he take his place as the next holy man, that he go back and look after his mother. But his heart yearned to stay here, in Maggie's world. She needed him, wanted him. And he wanted her as he had never wanted anything, or anyone, else.

Ah, Maggie, what am I to do?

Slowly, he turned to face her. And then, as he had once before, he went to her window and climbed over the sill.

"You're leaving, aren't you?" Maggie asked tremulously. "Tomorrow night, when the moon is full. And I'll never see you again."

Only moments before, he had come to the same painful realization. But now, faced with the task of telling Maggie he had decided to leave, the words died in his throat. He did not want to go, and he could not stay. What was he to do?

A single tear glistened on her cheek and he knew he could not go. He could not leave her now, when she was alone. He would stay and look after her until Veronica returned. And then he would go to the Sacred Cave and hope he had not waited too long.

Chapter Eighteen

Hawk stared at the telephone, wondering if he should answer it. Maggie was in the bathroom and he thought maybe he'd just let it ring, but when it didn't stop, he picked up the receiver, trying to remember what Maggie said when she answered the phone. What was the word? Oh, yes.

"Hello."

"Well, hello." The voice was husky, female, and sounded surprised. "Is Maggie there?"

"She is . . . uh, busy."

"I see. Well, this is her editor, Sheila Goodman. Could you give her a message for me?"

"Yes."

"Tell her I'm going to a conference in Sioux Falls and I'll call her from there on Friday."

"Friday," Hawk repeated.

"Don't forget."

"I will not forget."

"Goodbye."

Hawk hung up the phone as Maggie wheeled into the room.

"Who was on the phone?" she asked.

"Sheila Goodman. She said to tell you she is going to Sioux Falls and will call you Friday."

"Oh, dear," Maggie said with a sigh. "She probably wants to know how my book's coming along."

She looked at Hawk, thinking that in some ways his being here had made her writing easier. He was a wonderful model for her hero and sometimes the ideas flowed like water, especially the love scenes.

And yet there were too many days when she sat in the den and didn't accomplish anything, days when she turned away from her computer and sat at the window to watch Hawk as he worked outside, her eyes drinking in the sight of him as he brushed the horses or raked the corral, days when she sat with her elbows on the windowsill, her head cradled in her hands, admiring the way he walked, the strength in his arms as he chopped wood for the fire. Days when there were no words to describe what she was thinking, feeling, days when the computer screen stared back at her, blue and empty like a cloudless sky.

Hawk lifted one black brow, wondering why Maggie was staring at him so pensively. "Is something wrong?"

"What? Oh, no, it's just that Sheila's going to want to know why I'm so far behind."

"Will she be angry?"

"Sheila? No, she never gets angry. But maybe I'd better try to get some work done before she calls."

Friday morning Maggie was procrastinating again. Instead of working, she was sitting at her easel, sketching Hawk as he exercised the black stallion.

A horse and a Sioux Indian played an important part in the novel she was working on and she wanted to make a few sketches in hopes that Sheila would use one of her ideas on the cover. So many covers featured buxom women falling out of their dresses. It was a marketing technique that Maggie had never understood. The women who read romance novels didn't want to see voluptuous blondes poured into scanty, low-cut dresses, they wanted to see the hero.

Hawk waved at her as he slid from the stallion's back and walked the horse down to the barn to cool it out.

Maggie waved back, then cast a critical eye at the drawing in front of her. It was good, she thought. She'd captured the latent strength of the stallion, the essence of the man.

She glanced over her shoulder at the sound of a car pulling into the driveway, shook her head in disbelief as she recognized the red-headed woman sitting behind the wheel.

"Sheila."

"Good morning, Maggie my girl," Sheila Goodman said. Sliding out of the car, she hurried toward Maggie, stooping to kiss her soundly on the cheek. "How's my number one author?"

"I'm fine." Maggie felt a faint twinge of envy as she took in Sheila's chic black silk suit, emerald green blouse, and black heels. The woman looked as if she'd just stepped off the cover of a fashion magazine "What on earth are you doing here?"

"Well, I was so close, I decided to come and see where my star author lives. My dear, I can see why you love it out here. It's beautiful. And so was that man on the horse. Who is he?"

"He's, uh, just someone who works here. Let's go in the house and I'll fix us some coffee."

"The house is lovely," Sheila said after giving herself a tour. "I hope you don't mind, but I read a few pages of your manuscript while I was in the den."

"I don't mind. What do you think?"

"Your fans will adore it. The hero's marvelous, and that love scene . . ."

"Thanks. Do you still take cream and sugar in your coffee?"

Sheila made a wry face and patted her hips. "Just black's fine. So, tell me more about that Indian who's working for you."

Stalling for time, Maggie added cream and sugar to her coffee. "He's Lakota, from Pine Ridge. Bobby's gone to spend some time with his family, and Hawk is taking his place."

"I see."

Maggie felt her cheeks grow warm. Sheila *did* see, she thought. In fact, she saw too much.

"How much longer until the book is finished?"

"At least another month. Maybe two."

"But it'll be done by the first of the year?"

Maggie nodded. "Did you see the sketch I was working on?"

"Yes, it's very good."

"I was hoping you might use something like it on the cover of *Midnight Hearts*."

"It's an idea. I'll talk it over with Max and see what he thinks."

"Good. I . . ." The words died in Maggie's throat as she heard Hawk's footsteps in the hall. She'd been hoping he would stay out of sight until Sheila left. How could she explain the way Hawk dressed? What if he said something about the cave?

Maggie stared at Hawk, her mouth agape, as he entered the room. He was wearing the clothes Veronica had bought him. The denim hugged his long legs like a second skin, the black T-shirt was the perfect foil for his swarthy skin and dark hair. She thought he looked sexier than Mel Gibson, Patrick Swayze, and Sean Connery all rolled into one.

A glance at Sheila told Maggie that her editor was not immune to Hawk's good looks, either. Indeed, the older woman was on the verge of drooling.

"You must be Hawk," Sheila purred, extending her hand. "I'm Sheila Goodman, Maggie's editor." She slid an arch glance at Maggie. "Now I know why you've been too busy to call me."

Because it seemed expected, Hawk took Sheila's hand in his. She was a pretty woman, with dark brown eyes and flaming red hair the likes of which Hawk had never seen.

"Hawk, would you like some coffee?" Maggie asked. A sharp twinge of jealousy darted through her as she wondered if Sheila was ever going to release Hawk's hand.

"Yes." Gently but firmly, he drew his hand from Sheila's and sat down in the chair across from Maggie.

Sheila stared at Hawk intently for a moment, and then snapped her fingers. "Now I know why you look so familiar," she exclaimed. "You're the Indian in the painting over the fireplace." Sheila looked at Maggie. "I thought you said the man in the painting was someone you saw in a dream."

"He is," Maggie said. She laughed nervously. "Isn't it remarkable how much they look alike?"

"Too remarkable to be a coincidence," Sheila replied dryly. "Tell me, Mr. Hawk, have you known Maggie long?"

Over a hundred years, Hawk mused. Aloud, he said, "Yes, I am an old friend."

Maggie bit back a grin. Old, indeed.

"I see," Sheila said. "Will you be staying here long?"

"I do not know."

Sheila glanced from Hawk to Maggie. She sensed an undercurrent between them, almost as if they shared a secret. What weren't they telling her?

For the next half hour, Maggie watched Hawk charm the socks off her editor. He answered Sheila's questions politely, offered her more coffee, lit her cigarette, and walked her to her car.

"Well," Maggie said when he returned to the kitchen. "That was the best performance I've ever seen. Where'd you learn to be so charming?"

Hawk shrugged, his expression sheepish. "Sometimes I stay up late and watch television," he said.

"What have you been watching?"

"Old movies, you call them."

Laughter bubbled in Maggie's throat as she imagined Hawk sitting in front of the TV watching old Cary Grant flicks. No wonder he knew how to light a cigarette and what words to say to flatter a woman.

"Why did you change your clothes?"

"You told me Indians today dress like the white man. I did not want your editor to wonder why I dressed so strangely. And I did not want you to be embarrassed."

"Oh, Hawk, you wouldn't have embarrassed me," Maggie said, touched by his thoughtfulness. And then she laughed. "But it's probably a good thing you changed. I think Sheila might have swooned if she'd seen you in just your clout. She could hardly keep her eyes off of you as it was."

Hawk looked at Maggie curiously. Was that jealousy he heard in her voice?

"She is very pretty," Hawk said, watching Maggie.

"I suppose, if you like the type," Maggie retorted, and then hated herself for being so catty. Sheila wasn't just her editor, she was a friend.

Hawk turned away to hide his grin. She was jealous. The idea pleased him very much.

*   *   *

The phone rang early the next morning. Groaning, Maggie picked up the receiver. "Hello?"

"Maggie? Sheila. Listen, on my way back to Sioux Falls, I had a marvelous idea. I called Max and told him about your Indian and then I sort of suggested it might be fun to have Raoul get some pictures of you and your Indian, you know, with the Black Hills in the background."

"Raoul, here? To paint us?"

"Yes! He's here in Sioux Falls with me. The writers all love him."

Wide awake now, Maggie sat up. "No, Sheila, I don't think that's a good idea. Besides, I don't want to be on the cover."

"But, Maggie, my girl, think of the publicity! Your fans will love it! And they'll adore Hawk. Besides, if he's a working man, he can probably use the money."

Maggie grinned, thinking that money was the last thing Hawk needed.

"We'll pay you, too, of course. One hundred twenty-five dollars an hour. It's nothing to sneeze at."

It was the standard rate, Maggie thought, but she didn't need the money and neither did Hawk.

"We'll be there tomorrow morning."

"We?"

"Well, darling, I'm coming, too. See you tomorrow," Sheila said brightly, and hung up before Maggie could protest further.

Maggie stared at the receiver in her hand. Sheila and Raoul were coming here to photograph her and Hawk. Raoul was one of the best romance artists in the business, and made upwards of seven thousand dollars a cover. His paintings were always in demand, some of them selling for as much as ten grand.

As she'd expected, Hawk was even less enthusiastic about the idea than she was.

"Take pictures?" he queried, frowning. "What does that mean?"

It was too hard to explain. Instead, she showed him her camera and then dragged out an old photo album and let him look through it.

Hawk studied the photographs carefully, especially the ones of Maggie. There were photos of Maggie standing between an older man and woman, photos of Maggie in various poses and places with a girl he knew must be her sister, Susie. It was strange to see Maggie standing up, walking, riding. In one picture she was wearing very short pants, and he couldn't help staring at her legs. They were long and slim and golden brown. He slid a glance in her direction, thinking he'd like very much to see her in those short pants.

Several times he looked at the pictures and then at Maggie, wondering how her spirit could be in two places at once.

"How?" he asked as he neared the end of the book. "How can you be beside me and in this picture?"

Maggie smiled indulgently, remembering that many Indians had feared to have their photographs taken, believing that the camera captured a part of their spirit.

"There's no life in the picture, Hawk. It's like a drawing of a winter count, or the pictures that warriors draw on the dew cloth of their lodges. Only these pictures are made with a camera instead of charcoal or paint."

Hawk grunted softly. Surely it could not be dangerous, or Maggie would not have so many pictures of herself in the book.

Maggie looked over Hawk's shoulder. The photos brought back so many memories. There were pictures of her mother and father, of their old two-story house in Los Angeles, of Susie, of her grandparents. There were pictures of her swimming in Bass Lake, horseback riding in Griffith Park, roller skating, riding the merry-go-round at Disneyland, playing tennis with Frank. . . .

"Your editor wishes to take pictures of us. Why?"

"To use on the cover of my next book. We've used your likeness before, from drawings I made, but Sheila thinks this will be better."

Hawk glanced at the bookrack that displayed Maggie's books, one black brow arching upward in amusement as he pointed to the cover of *Forbidden Flame.* "Will you dress like that?"

Maggie flushed as she glanced at the cover. The heroine was wearing a bright red dress that showed an ample amount of cleavage and a good deal of one thigh. "I don't think so."

Hawk grunted, obviously disappointed.

"We don't have to do it if you don't want to," Maggie said, though once Sheila had her mind made up, there was almost no way to make her reconsider.

"Is it something you want?"

Maggie started to say no, then realized it was something she *did* want. Not that she wanted to be on the cover of her book, but she would like to have some photos of herself with Hawk, and she knew Raoul would give her as many copies as she wanted.

Maggie nodded. "Yes, if it's all right with you."

Sheila and Raoul arrived early the following morning. After preparing a hearty breakfast of bacon, eggs, and pancakes, Sheila handed Maggie a vivid blue dress edged with white lace.

"I knew you wouldn't want to wear anything too revealing," Sheila remarked. "I think this is provocative without being immodest." Sheila looked at Hawk. "I don't suppose you have anything Indian you could wear?"

"Indian?" Hawk repeated with a frown.

"You know, one of those loincloth things."

"Yes, I have one of those," Hawk said.

"Good. Well, then, we're all set."

The blue dress was flattering, the neckline low and square but not indecent, the skirt long and flowing.

Sheila assured Maggie she looked terrific, but it was Hawk who held the older woman's gaze.

"You look . . . fine," Sheila said, and Maggie almost laughed out loud. Sheila had been around male models for years, had been to Chippendale's on numerous occasions, had been married three times, but it was obvious she'd never seen anything like Hawk.

"Shall we go?" Maggie asked.

"Go?" Sheila said.

"The pictures, remember?"

"C'mon, Sheila," Raoul said, taking her by the arm. "We're going to lose the light."

They drove around Maggie's property until Raoul found just the right place—a grassy meadow blooming with flowers. The Hills rose in the background, majestic and beautiful.

A small grassy rise provided just the setting he was looking for. It took twenty minutes before Raoul was satisfied with the pose. Hawk was on one knee with his back to the Hills, his hands resting on Maggie's shoulders, while Maggie sat at his feet gazing up at him, one hand spread over his thigh.

"That's good," Raoul said. "Hawk, I want you to look down at Maggie. Pretend you're a wild Indian and she's your woman. I want you to look savage, arrogant, possessive. Maggie, I want you to look up at him adoringly. You're his willing captive, his slave."

Hawk looked down at Maggie, one black brow arching in amusement at the photographer's words. *Pretend you're a wild Indian.* A muscle worked in Hawk's jaw as he heard the underlying disdain in the words, and then he grinned wryly. If they only knew how little pretending he had to do!

But then his gaze met Maggie's and the humor faded from his eyes. *And she's your woman.* Unconsciously, his hands tightened on her shoulders.

His woman. Maggie gazed up at Hawk, wishing it were true, wishing that she could be his woman

174

until the end of time. How many books had she read about white women abducted by Indians, women who fell hopelessly in love with their captors? She'd even written a couple.

As from far away, she heard Raoul call, "Perfect! Hold it!" But she was only aware of Hawk, of his dark eyes burning into her own, of the strength of his hands as he clutched her shoulders, of the muscular heat of his thigh beneath her fingertips. *His woman . . .*

"Okay, you can take a break now." Raoul looked at Sheila and shook his head. "I think they've forgotten we're here."

Sheila nodded, a faint look of envy in her eyes. She'd had three husbands and none of them had ever looked at her the way Hawk was looking at Maggie.

"Hey, you two," Raoul called. "That's it."

"What?" Maggie turned to face Raoul, felt her cheeks flush with embarrassment as she realized she'd forgotten that Raoul and Sheila were there.

"Well," Sheila said, "if the look in Hawk's eyes doesn't melt the film, we've got ourselves a great cover."

"I'm sure I don't know what you mean," Maggie said, not meeting her editor's probing gaze.

"I'm sure you do," Sheila retorted. "I'm also sure that it's time for me to go back to New York." She glanced at Hawk, then back at Maggie. "You behave yourself now, you hear?"

"It was a great shoot," Raoul said. He shook Hawk's hand, then Maggie's. "I'll send you the proofs."

"Thanks, Raoul."

The drive back to the ranch was uneventful. Sheila talked of a writers' conference she'd been asked to speak at later in the year, and of the American Booksellers Convention she'd attended in June, and then they were back at the house.

Maggie sat in her wheelchair on the porch, waving goodbye, more conscious than ever of the man standing beside her, of the way he had looked at her.

His woman. It could never be, but the mere idea sent a warm shiver of delight down her spine nonetheless.

Chapter Nineteen

Maggie stared into the refrigerator. It was empty save for a half-gallon of milk and a withered red apple.

They would have to go to town.

She frowned at the idea. She'd lived in the Black Hills for two years and never ventured beyond the boundaries of her own property. Veronica had done the shopping and Bobby had run whatever errands needed doing, and she had stayed home, as secluded as a monk. But that was about to change.

Taking a piece of paper from a kitchen drawer, she began to write a list: bread, eggs, bacon, potatoes, coffee, fruit, soap, toothpaste, canned goods, milk, orange juice . . .

The list seemed to go on and on. And then, abruptly, she stopped writing. How was she going to get into town?

"What is it, Mag-gie?"

The sound of his voice thrilled her as it always did. Was there any other man in the world who had a voice like his? Strong and deep and silky, like steel sheathed in layers of soft black velvet.

"We're about out of food."

Hawk nodded. Veronica always brought the food. It was something he could not quite comprehend, where it all came from, or how it was made. "Where must you go to get more?"

"Sturgis is the closest place."

"Then let us go."

"I don't have any way to get there."

"I will take you on the black."

"No, it's too far to go by horseback. And where would we put the groceries?" Maggie frowned thoughtfully. "Do you think you could drive the truck?"

"I do not know how."

"I could teach you."

Shadow Hawk looked doubtful, and then he shrugged. "We can try."

They practiced driving around the yard for forty-five minutes. At first, she was certain he would never learn. The truck lurched and jerked and bounced like a tumbleweed tossed by the wind as Hawk tried to coordinate steering, braking on turns, and working the gas pedal. Once, she thought he was going to run into the front porch, another time he barely avoided crashing into a tree, but finally Hawk got the hang of the gas and the brake and Maggie decided he'd be able to make the short drive to town and back.

178

Maggie glanced over at Hawk, attired in only a clout and moccasins, and frowned, wondering how she could tactfully suggest that he wasn't dressed quite right for a trip to town.

A slow grin spread over Hawk's face. "I will change," he said, obviously reading her thoughts.

"It might be best."

She waited for him in the truck while he went into the house to change. He reappeared moments later clad in the black T-shirt and jeans that Veronica had bought him.

Seeing him in regular clothes reminded Maggie of the photo shoot. Raoul had sent copies of the proofs, along with two checks from Sheila and a hastily scrawled note that read, "Standard pay for modeling. Sorry it couldn't be more. P.S. Give my love to Hawk. Sheila."

He had been amused when Maggie explained what the checks were for. Jokingly, she'd kidded him, saying that maybe if he stayed in her time, he could go into the modeling business and pose for romance covers. He had considered her suggestion gravely for a moment and then nodded, saying he wouldn't mind so long as she would always be the woman in his arms, and what had started as a joke quickly backfired because that was just what she wanted, to always be the woman in his arms.

Now, Maggie watched Hawk as he crossed the yard toward the truck, her pulse growing more rapid as she boldly admired him, unable to decide if he looked better in his clout or Levi's. Either way, he was drop dead gorgeous.

He looked at her for a moment when he reached the truck, a rueful grin on his handsome face, and then he climbed behind the wheel, turned the key in the ignition, and they started off down the dirt road that led to the highway.

For a moment, he concentrated on steering the truck, and then he asked the question that had been bothering him for days. "Mag-gie, tell me what happened to my people."

"What do you mean?"

"Where are they? Bob-by said they live on reservations. That they are soul sick and look for answers in the white man's whiskey."

"Yes, I'm afraid that's true." Life on the reservation was bleak, Maggie thought. Jobs were scarce. A single man received a measly fifty-six dollars from General Assistance every two weeks. She'd heard that teenage girls were getting pregnant just to get money from welfare. The homeless picked up aluminum cans to sell. What the reservation needed was industrial development, but the tribal council didn't want outsiders there, perhaps afraid they'd lose control of the reservation. Maggie couldn't fault them for that, considering past history.

"Why do my people live on reservations? Why does the white man control my people?"

"There were many wars in your day, Hawk. Do you know of Custer?"

Hawk grunted.

"Your people defeated him in a great battle at the Little Big Horn. It was the last great Indian victory. After that, the soldiers pursued the Indians until they were all hunted down and put on reservations. Crazy Horse was the last to surrender. He was killed at Fort Robinson, and after that, there were no more Indians living free on the plains."

Hawk stared at the yellow line that ran down the highway, trying to understand what Maggie had told him, trying to imagine his people defeated, living as the white man's prisoners on reservations. It could not be true. His people were born to the wind and the mountains. The thought of them living on reservations, stripped of their pride, their land, their way of life, was too painful to contemplate.

Slowly, he shook his head. "No . . ."

"I'm sorry, Hawk, but I'm afraid it's true. As near as I can tell, you came here from 1872, maybe 1873. In another four or five years, the life you knew will be gone."

"Could nothing have been done to change the fate of my people?"

"I don't think so. There were too many whites who wanted to move west, lured by tales of rich grassland and fertile soil. At first, the Army tried to stop them, but then Custer found gold in the Black Hills, and people poured westward. Miners and merchants and homesteaders, and there was just no way to stop them."

"So there is no hope for my people."

"I don't know. I'd like to think so. A lot of white people are beginning to feel ashamed of the way the Indians are being treated. Some of them are beginning to realize that your people knew how to take care of the land, that maybe some of the

Indian ways are better than ours."

Hawk's grip tightened on the steering wheel. Was this why he had been sent here? To learn the ultimate fate of his people? Should he go back and warn them not to fight, tell them it was useless, that there was no way to win? Or should he urge them into battle, for he knew now that it was better to die as a warrior than be penned on the white man's reservation, forced to live on his charity, never to be free again. Or should he live out his life here, with Maggie? There seemed to be no point in returning to his own time. He could do nothing for his people. Nothing but warn them of what was to come.

"Hawk . . ."

He glanced at Maggie as she laid her hand on his knee, his gaze moving briefly over her profile before he turned his attention back to the road.

"Hawk, I'm so sorry. I wish there was something I could do."

He nodded; then, feeling the need to touch her, he placed his hand over hers. They rode in silence until they reached the town.

Sturgis had originally been an annex to Fort Meade, one of the Army posts established to guard the Black Hills from Indian attacks on white settlers and miners. The Seventh Cavalry, re-formed after the Custer massacre, was the fort's first permanent garrison. A horse named Comanche was the only living thing found on the battlefield at the Little Big Horn. It had been officially retired with military honors at Fort Meade. In 1944, the old post had been turned into a Veteran's Administration Hospital.

According to a brochure Maggie had read, Sturgis was "a pretty and prosperous town lying in the red valley on the eastern border of the Hills, almost in the shadow of Bear Butte." It was here, at Fort Meade, that "The Star Spangled Banner" had been played for the first time.

Maggie groaned when they reached the outskirts of town. She had expected to find the quiet little town she'd seen the few times she'd come to Sturgis. What she had forgotten was that during one week every August, Sturgis welcomed over 80,000 bikers and spectators to the Black Hills Motor Classic and Rally, a week-long internationally famous motorcycle racing extravaganza.

And this was the week. Last year had been the fiftieth anniversary of the race and Veronica had told her that over 200,000 people had turned out to celebrate.

Thankfully, it wasn't as bad this year, but there seemed to be people everywhere. Men and women old enough to be grandparents rode down the main street on Gold Wing motorcycles; long-haired hippie-types clad in black leather lounged near the curb; a couple with blue hair were draped across a big Harley; a man in a pin-striped business suit was riding a big red, white, and blue Suzuki. She guessed the people dressed in plaid shirts and blue jeans probably lived in town all year long.

Hawk stared at the crowd, the fate of the Lakota temporarily forgotten. He had seen few whites in his day, but never any who looked like these. There were young girls in short skirts, in bathing suits, in halter tops and skin-tight pants. Some wore high heels, some were barefoot. He saw men in colorful shirts and pants, shirtless men in shorts, men in suits and ties, men in tight-fitting jeans and black leather jackets.

He looked over at Maggie and lifted one black brow. "I do not think anyone would have noticed what I wore."

"I guess you're right. This place is a madhouse. I don't know how we'll ever find a place to park."

Hawk drove around for a while, curious to see what the town looked like. Maggie looked out the window, unable to believe the crowds of people waiting at the McDonald's and the Pizza Hut. They passed a Super-Duper Market, and a Piggly-Wiggly. Shades of *Driving Miss Daisy*, Maggie thought with a grin. Most of the houses they passed were older, wood-framed buildings, although there were some newer, larger homes on the outskirts of town.

Driving down Junction Avenue, she saw the house where "Poker Alice" Tubbs, the Queen of Women Gamblers of the Old West, had lived.

Alice had been born in England, but she attended an exclusive girl's school in the United States. Later, she married a mining engineer named Duffield and they moved to Colorado, where her husband and his friends taught her to play poker. It seemed Alice was a natural and when her husband was killed in an explosion, Alice turned to gambling to earn a living, following the gold trail from Leadville to Deadwood. When the rush in Deadwood began to fade, Alice moved to

Sturgis where she raised three boys and girls.

The woman had lived an exciting life, Maggie thought, and made a mental note to visit her house some day. Perhaps she'd use Poker Alice in one of her books.

As Hawk drove on, Maggie saw Mom's Cafe where she'd once eaten lunch, and the Philtown Motel, and later, a modern-looking apartment building for senior citizens.

Hawk drove down Lazelle Street until he came to Lynn's Country Market and Maggie told him they'd shop there. After circling the block three times, he found a place to park. Maggie held her breath as he maneuvered the truck between a Toyota and a Dodge van. Hawk grinned at Maggie, then hopped out of the cab to get Maggie's wheelchair out of the back of the truck.

The wheelchair turned out to be a blessing in disguise, Maggie thought, as people parted before her like the waters of the Red Sea.

Inside the store, they moved up and down the aisles. For Hawk, it was an education, though he felt foolish pushing the metal shopping cart.

Maggie grinned at him. "I guess you have something in common with white men whether you like it or not," she remarked, "because most of them don't like to shop, either."

Hawk studied the cans he took off the shelves, looking at the pictures, frowning at the odd squiggles of the white man's writing. He thought perhaps he'd ask Maggie to teach him to read and write. It might be a wise thing for his people to learn.

185

At the meat counter, he stared at the neatly wrapped packages, trying to imagine how many such packages it would take to hold a buffalo, and thinking how easy it was for white women. The Lakota had to hunt the buffalo, kill it, skin it, cut up the meat, and haul it back to camp. White women had only to go to the store and the meat was laid out for them so that all they had to do was take it home and cook it. His mother would like that, he thought.

His mother . . . he gazed out the window, wondering if she was well. No doubt she thought him dead, killed in the battle along with Heart-of-the-Wolf. He wondered if she had gone to live with her cousin and his wife, if they were taking good care of her, if she had enough to eat . . .

He gazed at the mountains of canned goods and felt a wave of bitterness wash over him as he thought of the long winters when Lakota babies cried for food, when old ones refused to eat so that the young ones wouldn't starve. But the whites had enough to eat and more.

"Hawk?"

He glanced down at Maggie, saw that she was staring at him, her brow lined with concern.

"Are you all right?" she asked.

"Yes. I was just thinking of my mother."

"I guess she misses you."

He nodded. "As I miss her."

Maggie nodded, her own bright mood suddenly overshadowed by the thought that he would be leaving soon. She had managed to tuck that thought into the back of her mind, refusing to dwell on it, determined to live each day as it came.

In addition to canned goods and meat, they bought fresh fruit and vegetables, milk and ice cream, toilet paper—another miracle, Hawk thought with a wry grin. They bought sweet-smelling soap and toothpaste and finally, their shopping cart full, they made their way to the checkout counter. Hawk stared at the cash register, amazed once again by the white man's cleverness.

With their groceries paid for, they left the store and made their way down the crowded sidewalk. Maggie caught bits of conversation as she and Hawk made their way down the street, snide comments about tame Indians and white squaws. It was hard to believe, she thought with a rueful shake of her head. Hard to believe there was still so much prejudice between the whites and the Indians.

Maggie slid a glance at Hawk and saw that he, too, was aware of the rude comments. His expression was harsh, a muscle worked in his jaw. She saw his hands tighten around the handle of the shopping cart as a leather-clad biker with shoulder-length blond hair pointed a gloved finger in their direction.

"Damn redskins," the biker said with a sneer. "Why don't they stay on the reservation where they belong?"

Hawk was going to fight. She saw it in the way his body tensed, in the way his knuckles turned white around the handle of the shopping cart.

187

She reached up to grab his arm. It was rock hard, the muscle quivering with tension. "Hawk, don't. Please."

He looked down at her, his dark eyes filled with fury.

"Please," she said again. "It won't solve anything."

She was relieved when they reached the truck. Effortlessly, Hawk lifted her from her chair and put her in the truck, then loaded the groceries and the wheelchair into the back and climbed into the cab.

Maggie let out a sigh of relief, glad to be leaving, hoping that Veronica would be able to come back to work soon so that they wouldn't have to make another trip to town. She'd forgotten how she hated being stared at.

As they left town, she was glad to put it all behind her.

Chapter Twenty

When they reached the ranch, Hawk helped Maggie put the groceries away, his mind reeling with what she'd told him about the fate of the Lakota, with the wonders he'd seen in the market, with the taunting words of the black-clad *wasichu*.

He wanted to scream that it was unfair to jail his people on reservations simply because they were different, because they did not invent things that were amazing but of no real value. He wanted to yell at Maggie and tell her his people deserved to live free, as they had always lived free, that they didn't need cars or computers or grocery stores. But the fate of his people didn't rest in her hands, and yelling at her wouldn't solve anything. He wished there was a way he could change the future, a way that his people could learn to live with the whites without giving up their ancient laws and traditions and customs.

He wished he'd had a knife so he could have taught the loud-mouthed *wasichu* to have a little respect for a warrior.

He stared at the four walls of Maggie's kitchen and felt them closing in on him, smothering him.

Abruptly, he opened the back door and almost ran out of the house.

Standing in the yard facing the *Paha Sapa*, he took several deep breaths, his hands clenching and unclenching as he fought down the anger and the sense of helplessness churning within him.

He wanted to go home, to see his people, to live as he had always lived.

He wanted to stay here, with Maggie, to take her in his arms and make her his woman. Forever.

He knew suddenly that she was there, behind him. He inhaled a long slow breath, let it out in a long sigh before turning to face her.

"I'm sorry, Hawk."

"For what? You have done nothing to be sorry for."

"I'm sorry you're unhappy, sorry I can't help you get back to your people, but I don't want you to go."

A hint of a smile softened his features. "I do not want to go."

"But you're going."

"Yes, when the time is right."

She bit down on her lower lip, refusing to cry. *One day at a time,* she thought. "Would you like to go on a picnic?"

"Pic-nic?"

"I packed a lunch, and I thought we'd go up into the hills and eat it. That's what a picnic is, eating in a pretty place away from home." With someone you love.

"If you wish. Will we walk, or take the black?"

"Let's ride," Maggie said, smiling as she thought of sitting in front of him on the stallion, his arm around her waist, her head resting against his chest.

Ten minutes later they were riding toward the foothills. They couldn't have picked a better day, Maggie thought. The sky was clear and blue, the weather was warm but not too hot, the pines were whispering to each other, telling secrets only they knew.

With a sigh of contentment, Maggie closed her eyes and pretended it would last forever.

They stopped in a small grassy meadow surrounded by aspen and spruce. A narrow stream glistened in the sunlight. Birds called to each other in the tree tops, a gray squirrel watched them with dark curious eyes.

Maggie sat on the stallion while Hawk spread a blanket on the grass, her gaze lingering on the muscles that bunched and relaxed beneath the black T-shirt.

With the blanket spread beneath a tree, he took the picnic basket from her hands and placed it on the ground, then returned for her.

He stood beside the horse for a long moment, his hands spanning Maggie's waist, his dark eyes gazing into hers as if he thought to find answers to the questions that plagued him hidden in the depths of her eyes.

He was close, so close. They hadn't touched for days, and Maggie felt the breath catch in her throat as she gazed into his eyes. She knew that nothing had changed; that he would still leave her when he could, but she wished, oh how she wished that he would make love to her just once before he returned to his own time, his own people.

She rested her hands on his shoulders, felt him shudder at her touch. With pleasure, she wondered, or regret. He was so beautiful. Soon, he would return to his people and some woman would win his heart and he'd forget all about the crippled white woman and the weeks they had shared. She looked at the meadow, at the narrow stream and the bright blue sky and wondered if Eden could have been more perfect. She wanted to be Eve, just for today, and prayed that she could tempt Adam into her arms.

Hawk's hands closed around her waist as he lifted her from the back of the stallion and she smiled into his eyes, hoping he would read the longing there, that he would make her his woman, just for today.

Hawk held Maggie close for several moments, their bodies pressed tightly together. He read the longing in her eyes, saw the rapid beat of the pulse in her throat, felt his own body responding to her nearness, to the heat of her, the scent of her, and felt all his defenses crumbling. He wanted her, as she wanted him. Was he being foolish to deny himself the pleasure of her love?

And yet, how would he ever leave her once he had made her his?

"Ah, Mag-gie," he murmured, and then, reluctantly, he placed her on the blanket and sat down beside her. He took a deep breath, let it out in a long sigh, and then smiled at her. "What did you bring for lunch?"

"All your favorites. Roast beef sandwiches with Swiss cheese and tomato and lots of onions. Potato salad. Pickles. And chocolate cake for dessert."

Hawk grinned at her as she began to rummage around in the picnic basket, spreading a tablecloth over the basket, handing out paper plates and napkins, cans of soda, which he had learned to love, sandwiches wrapped in tinfoil.

He ate with more determination than appetite, ever aware of the woman beside him. The scent of her perfume, of woman, was carried to him on the breeze, making it difficult to think of anything else. He reached for a napkin just as she did, and the brief touch of her fingertips sent a frisson of heat racing up his arm, igniting his senses.

He raised his gaze to her face. Her eyes were bluer than the sky, deeper than the Missouri. Her lips, slightly parted, were full and pink, inviting his touch, his kiss. . . .

He could no more deny himself the taste of her lips than he could cause the sun to stop shining. Slowly, he leaned toward her, one hand sliding under her hair to curl around her neck as his mouth closed over hers. She tasted of mustard and mayonnaise and he thought he'd never tasted

Madeline Baker

anything sweeter or more seductive.

He watched her eyelids flutter down, heard her faint sigh of pleasure, felt the quickening of her breathing as his kiss deepened. He whispered her name, never taking his lips from hers, felt his blood begin to burn as she murmured, "Yes, oh yes," into his mouth.

With a low groan, he drew her into his lap, his arms wrapping around her, enveloping her in his embrace. He forgot the past, forgot the future. There was only this moment, and the woman in his arms.

Maggie's heart felt as if it would burst, she was so filled with happiness and anticipation. At last, she thought, her senses reeling with the wonder of it, at last he was going to make love to her. From this day forward, she would be his woman. . . .

He was bending her back, laying her on the blanket. She opened her eyes and saw only him. His eyes were dark with passion and then, abruptly, his expression changed from desire to alarm.

"Hawk, what is it?" she asked, but he paid her no mind. Rolling to his feet, he stared into the distance. And then she heard it, too, the roar of a motorcycle coming their way.

There were two of them. Big black Harleys ridden by men wearing faded Levi's, black leather jackets, and shiny black helmets.

Hawk moved to stand in front of Maggie as the motorcycles came to a stop. The two men removed their helmets before stepping from their bikes and Hawk recognized one of the bikers as the man who thought all Indians should stay on the reservation where they belonged.

"Well, Injun," the blond man said as he swaggered toward the blanket, "we meet again." He smiled at Maggie. "How you doing, little lady?"

She nodded, unable to speak past the fear rising in her throat.

"Ain't this nice? A picnic! I haven't been on a picnic since I was a little kid. You got any food left in there?"

"A little," Maggie said. She reached into the basket and handed the man a sandwich.

He grunted as he unwrapped it. "You got a beer in there?"

"No." She slid a glance at Hawk, who was standing motionless beside the blanket, his gaze moving from the blond biker to the other man still standing beside his Harley.

"Vince, come on over and get something to eat."

The man called Vince shook his head. "I'm not hungry," he said, his eyes sliding over Maggie's figure. "Not for food, anyway."

The blond biker grinned before devouring his sandwich in three big bites. And then he looked at Hawk. "Why don't you take a walk, redskin?"

Hawk shook his head, his whole body tensing as he waited for what he knew was to come. For the second time that day, he wished he had a weapon of some kind.

The biker stared at Hawk, one blond brow raised quizzically. "You wanna watch?"

"I want you to go and leave us alone."

"Yeah, well, you can't always have what you want." The biker reached into his jacket and withdrew a knife. It was a wicked-looking blade, six inches long with a serrated edge.

Maggie swallowed hard as the other biker came to see what was going on. Hawk stood between the two men. He was taller, broader, stronger, but he was unarmed and outnumbered.

"I always wanted to fight me an Injun," the blond biker remarked, running his thumb over the edge of the blade. "Maybe take a scalp."

The man called Vince grinned as he pulled a switchblade from his pants pocket. "Get on with it, Rocco," he drawled, glancing down at Maggie. "I never like to keep a lady waiting."

Maggie looked around, her gaze searching for something she could use as a weapon, but the deadliest thing she could find was a fork. Her hand curled around it and she slid it under her left leg.

Rocco stepped toward Hawk, the knife clutched in his hand, the blade weaving back and forth like a snake in search of prey. And then, almost quicker than the eye could follow, the blade made contact with flesh, opening a narrow gash in Hawk's left cheek.

But Hawk was moving, too, and before Rocco could strike again, Hawk grabbed his right wrist, curling his leg around Rocco's ankle at the same time and lunging forward with all his weight so that Rocco fell backward.

Hawk was on him before he hit the dirt, wrenching the knife from his grasp. He was raising the knife to strike when he heard Maggie's warning scream. He threw himself off Rocco, wincing as Vince's knife sliced through his T-shirt and across his back.

Rolling nimbly to his feet, Hawk whirled around to face Vince, the knife ready in his hand.

Maggie cried, "Hawk, don't!" as they began to circle, first left, then right. She saw Rocco scramble to his feet and she knew Hawk would never be able to fight them both.

Vince and Hawk came together, knives flashing in the sunlight, and when they parted, there was a long bloody gash in Vince's left arm.

Hawk drew back, his nostrils filling with the scent of sweat and blood. He sent a quick glance in Rocco's direction, then pivoted on his heel, his knife parrying Vince's blade. The ring of metal against metal was very loud in the stillness of the meadow.

Vince hurtled toward him, his knife slashing wildly. Hawk ducked under the man's arm and brought his own knife up, the Lakota war cry rumbling in his chest as he felt the blade slice into flesh.

Vince swore loudly, his free hand clutching his side in an effort to stem the blood that flowed in the wake of the blade.

"Rocco, here!" he hollered, and tossed the knife to the other biker.

Hawk whirled around to face Rocco. For a moment, they glared at each other and then they began to feint and parry, the blades moving with a kind of graceful beauty as they reflected the sun.

Maggie had been watching Hawk, mesmerized by the change in him. He looked every inch a warrior, even in jeans and a T-shirt. There was a feral gleam in his dark eyes as he wielded the blade, an expression of such hatred on his face that it was frightening. She spared hardly a glance for Vince until she realized he was beside her. He had torn a strip of material from his T-shirt and bound the knife wound and now he was on his knees beside her, his light brown eyes hot as he stared at her. She recoiled as he touched her. His hands were big, the backs covered with hair.

"Don't!" She clawed at his hands to no avail, turned her head to the side when he bent forward to kiss her. He smelled of stale beer and sweat and she cried out as he imprisoned her chin in one big hand to hold her still while he kissed her. She shuddered with revulsion and when he drew back, she grabbed the fork and jabbed it into his right cheek. He howled with pain, and then he hit her, hard, across the face.

Her scream broke Hawk's concentration and he darted a glance in her direction, his fury building when he saw the white man's hands touching her.

In that moment, Rocco lunged forward. Hawk saw the movement out of the corner of his eye and jerked sideways so that the blade meant for his belly skidded across his ribs instead.

With a cry of rage, Hawk hurled himself at Rocco, driving the other man to the ground, slamming his head against the hard-packed earth until he lay still.

Scrambling to his feet, Hawk hurled himself at Vince, catching the man off guard. His hands closed around Vince's throat, squeezing tighter, tighter, until the man's eyes rolled back in his head.

"Hawk, stop! You'll kill him! Please, please stop!" She grabbed his arm, shaking him, all the while begging him to stop.

With an effort, Hawk released his hold on the white man. Sitting back on his heels, he took several deep breaths and gradually the rage that had burned through him receded. Only then did he turn to face Maggie.

Her face was deathly pale save for the bruise on her left cheek. Her eyes were wide with fear as she looked at the blood dripping from his cheek, soaking into his shirt. "You're hurt."

"I am all right."

"You're bleeding."

He looked down at the blood oozing from his side, then lifted a hand to his back, wincing with the effort. "I am all right," he said again. Gently, his fingertips brushed her cheek where Vince had struck her. "Did he hurt you?"

"No." She uttered a shaky laugh. "Just scared me a little. You scared me, too. I was afraid you were going to kill him."

"He would be dead if you had not stopped me."

"Let's get out of here before they come to."

Hawk nodded. Rising to his feet, he quickly threw everything into the picnic basket, folded the blanket, lifted Maggie onto the back of the stallion. Then, knife in hand, he knelt beside Rocco.

Maggie held her breath as he grabbed a handful of the man's long blond hair and began hacking it off until only a quarter inch of stubble remained. Then he walked purposefully toward the two motorcycles.

Maggie watched as Hawk slashed the tires and the black leather seats. The civilized part of her knew it was wrong, but the other part, that primal part that longed for revenge, smiled with each stroke of the blade.

Vince and Rocco were beginning to stir as Hawk vaulted up behind Maggie and urged the black into a lope.

They rode out of the meadow without looking back.

Chapter Twenty-one

At home, Maggie insisted on treating Hawk's cuts, even though he said they weren't serious. He finally agreed to let her doctor him up, but only after he had taken care of the stallion and fed the stock.

Now he sat on a chair in the kitchen, clad once again in his clout and moccasins, while she washed the blood from his face and ribs and back. Her touch was gentle, innocently seductive. The ache of his wounds faded as he watched her. He closed his eyes as she began to smear a cooling ointment over the shallow cuts. She was close, so close. He inhaled the warm womanly scent of her as she bandaged his wounds, loving the touch of her hands on his skin.

Slowly, he opened his eyes, his hands reaching out to cup her face. "Mag-gie, what am I to do?"

"Whatever you want."

"I feel as if I am being torn in half," he murmured, his voice low and husky. "All my life I have been raised to be a warrior, to hunt, to fight."

"And you fight very well," Maggie said, smiling faintly.

"Any warrior would have done the same."

"Would they?"

"Any man worth the name would fight for his woman."

"But I'm not your woman."

The words pierced his heart like a knife. She was not his woman, and he had no right to touch her. Even with her consent, he could not make love to her, not when he knew he must soon leave her. He did not belong here. Even if he chose to stay, he would not belong here.

"Mag-gie, why do you live here alone? You are so beautiful, so full of love. Why do you not find a man to share your life?"

She gazed at him steadily, her clear blue eyes moist with unshed tears. "I have."

"Ah, Mag-gie," he whispered. "Do you know what you do to me when you look at me like that?"

Slowly, she shook her head. "Tell me."

"I wish . . ." The words died in his throat as a single tear slipped down her cheek.

"Do you know what I wish?" Maggie said. "I wish you would make love to me, just once."

"Just once," he repeated, and knew he was lost. He could not deny her, or himself, any longer. Right or wrong, he needed her, needed her as he needed food to eat and air to breathe. She was a part of his life, a part of every dream and vision he'd ever had. He was bound to her, as he was bound to the Black Hills, to the land of his birth. And she had called him here, perhaps for this very reason. But reasons no longer mattered. His blood was pounding in his veins; the desire that had plagued him since the day he first saw her face could no longer be ignored.

He put his arms around her and stood up, carrying her with him. He kissed her once, hard and quick, and then he carried her down the hallway to her bedroom. Stepping inside, he laid her on the bed and sat down beside her, a little hesitant now that he had committed himself. He had never made love to a woman. What if he disappointed her?

He took a deep breath, and then he kissed her and all his doubts faded away. Tenderly, he caressed her with his hands and lips, loving her gently, slowly. If he was to make love to her only once, he wanted it to last a long time.

Stretching out beside her, he drew her into his arms, their mouths fused together, their hands beginning a shy exploration.

Maggie let her hands slide over his arms, marveling anew at the muscles that rippled beneath his taut bronze skin. His body was as warm as the sun, as hard as the earth, strong and powerful. Just touching him made her ache to be touched in return.

She pressed her hands to his chest, let them drift down, down, to the ridged expanse of his

Madeline Baker

belly, felt the quick intake of his breath as she dared touch his thigh.

Hawk slid his hands under her blouse, letting his fingertips caress her breasts, marveling as their silky fullness filled his hands. He whispered her name as he struggled with her bra, and then, somehow, the covers were down and she was lying naked beneath him, with only his brief clout between them. They clung together, and he thought he had never felt anything more wonderful than the sweet softness of the woman beneath him, never known anything more intoxicating than the taste of her lips.

Maggie could not stop touching him. Her hands moved over his shoulders, slid down his arms, admiring the expanse of his bronzed chest, loving the feel of his bare skin against her own.

Boldly, she tugged at his clout and then, suddenly shy, she turned away as he quickly removed it.

Hawk groaned softly as the last barrier between them fell away and then he was kissing her again, urgently now. She could feel the tension coiled within him, the same tension that made her writhe beneath him. His voice was low and ragged as he whispered her name and then he was a part of her, his heat joined with hers, forging them together. He moved instinctively, his body possessing hers, branding her with his touch and his kisses, and she held him close, heat to heat and heart to heart, making her feel whole and complete at last.

Later, she held him close while he slept. She was his woman now, bound to him by love.

Perhaps she *had* called him here, perhaps the love they shared was meant to be. Perhaps she had been born in the wrong time, or perhaps he had, and this was Fate's way of righting a wrong, of bringing them together. It was a fanciful idea, but it pleased her.

Smiling, she stared out the window at the night. A full moon rode low in the night sky and she turned her back on it, refusing to think that the next full moon might take Hawk away from her.

She woke to the smell of coffee and frying bacon. Frowning, she pulled herself up, tucking the sheet under her arms. Had Veronica come back? She looked for her wheelchair, then remembered it was in the kitchen.

Her cheeks grew warm as she recalled the night past and she hugged herself, wanting to laugh out loud with the joy of it, the wonder, the magic.

And then Hawk was standing in the doorway, a tray in his hands. On the tray were two cups of coffee and two plates piled high with bacon and eggs and buttered toast.

"You cooked!" Maggie exclaimed.

"I was hungry," he replied solemnly, "and it looked like you were going to sleep all day."

"I was very tired," she said.

He bit back a grin. "I know."

"And now I'm very hungry."

Hawk grinned at her as he crossed the room. Placing the tray in the center of the bed, he sat down across from her, watching her face as she took a bite of scrambled eggs.

205

"They're good," she said, then blushed hotly as she realized the sheet had fallen into her lap.

Hawk sucked in a deep breath, his desire springing to life as he stared at her bare breasts and belly.

"Hawk . . ."

He understood her embarrassment. Rising, he found her nightgown and slipped it over her head, tugging it down over her breasts, kissing her as he did so. "Is that better?"

"Yes, thank you," she murmured, not meeting his gaze.

Smothering a grin, he sat down on the bed again and picked up a piece of bacon.

They finished the meal in silence, then Hawk took the tray and carried it into the kitchen. Maggie was frowning when he returned.

"What is wrong?" he asked.

"I need to . . . want to . . . take a bath." She'd been taking sponge baths since Veronica left, but this morning she wanted to soak in a hot tub.

"Ah." He knew Veronica usually helped her with such things, but Veronica wasn't here. "I will fill the tub for you."

"But . . ."

"There is no need for you to be embarrassed, Mag-gie," he said gently. "I will help you into the tub, and I will not look if you do not wish me to."

It seemed silly, to be shy about such things after what they had shared the night before, but she couldn't help it. After all, it had only been one night.

"Thank you, Hawk."

He nodded, then went to fill the tub.

When he returned, he was carrying the big bath sheet that Veronica always wrapped her in after her bath. He dropped the sheet in her lap, then left the room so she could take off her nightgown.

When she was ready and the tub was full, he carried her into the bathroom and deposited her, very gently, into the water.

With a curt nod, he left the room and shut the door, his imagination running wild as he thought of her sitting in the bathtub, surrounded by bubbles. What would it be like to join her there, to make love to her in the hot soapy water?

He uttered a low curse and left the house, heading for the barn. He brushed the black for twenty minutes, and all the while his mind filled with images of Maggie lying beneath him in bed, sitting in the bathtub amid a swirl of fragrant bubbles, smiling at him from the back of the stallion.

He should never have touched her, he thought. She had said she wanted to make love to him just once. Just once! How could he keep his hands off her now, when he knew the taste of her, the touch of her, the scent of her? How could he keep away from her now, when he knew what it was like to bury himself in her softness, to hear her soft cries of ecstasy? Now, when he knew what it was like to find fulfillment in her arms.

He was tense from head to foot when he returned to the house. After knocking on the door, he stepped into the bathroom, handed her a towel without looking at her, waited for her to cover herself before he lifted her from the tub and carried her down the hall.

When they reached her bedroom, he put her on the bed, got her wheelchair from the kitchen, and almost bolted from the room, afraid if he stayed one moment more he'd rip off his clout and take her, willing or not.

He was pacing the living room floor, wondering how he was going to keep his hands off her for the next month, when he heard a car pull into the driveway.

A moment later there was a knock at the door.

"I'll get it," Maggie said, and Hawk turned to find her smiling up at him. She was wearing black pants and a red silk blouse. Her hair, still damp, curled lovingly around her face.

Hawk swallowed hard. She was so beautiful. Just looking at her made him ache with desire.

Maggie frowned at the deputy sheriff standing on the porch. "Yes, can I help you?"

"Miss St. Claire?"

"Yes."

"I'm looking for an Indian known as Shadow Hawk. Chief Hollister said I might find him here."

"Is something wrong?"

"I have a warrant for his arrest."

"Arrest!"

"Yes, ma'am. He's being charged with aggravated assault and destruction of private property."

Maggie blinked up at the lawman, unable to believe that the two bikers had actually had the nerve to file a complaint against Hawk.

"May I come in?" Johnson asked.

"Of course."

Johnson threw a hard, assessing look in Hawk's direction as he stepped into the room. "You'll have to come with me, sir."

"But it was self-defense," Maggie said quickly. "They started it. One of them pulled a knife."

"Be that as it may," the deputy said, still watching Hawk, "I have a warrant for his arrest and I'm going to have to take him in for questioning."

The lawman drew his weapon as Hawk took a step back. "I wouldn't try that," he warned. "Turn around. I'll have to cuff you until we reach the jail."

Hawk stared at the lawman for a long moment, weighing his chances of making a run for it. The *wasichu* was tall and broad-shouldered. His skin was dark from long hours spent in the outdoors. One hand rested on the butt of the gun holstered at his side.

"Hawk, don't worry. Everything will be all right."

He didn't believe her. Almost, he was tempted to run, but the white man looked as if he would be only too happy to shoot him in the back, and in the end he turned around, flinching as the lawman snapped the handcuffs in place.

He was filled with a sense of dread as he got into the back seat of the car. He sent a last glance at Maggie, who was watching him from the porch, and then the car was moving down the driveway, going around the bend in the road, and she was out of sight.

*   *   *

The jail was in the basement of the court-house. They wrote down his name, his height and weight, searched him for weapons, removed the handcuffs, took his fingerprints.

The booking officer frowned when Shadow Hawk stated he didn't have a social security number, a residence, or a job. Muttering something about "worthless Indians," the officer locked him in a cell. Three sides were made of steel, the fourth was barred. There were four bunks in the cell, all empty. There were two other cells similar to his, and one large cell that had twelve bunks. All the other cells were full.

Hawk began to pace the floor, his anger building with each step. He had never been confined in such a small space, never known anything but freedom.

As his restlessness grew, an image of Crazy Horse flashed through his mind. Maggie had told him that the Oglala warrior would be killed at Fort Robinson while trying to escape from one of the white man's iron houses.

Hawk clenched his hands at his sides, wondering if he would meet the same fate. Wondering if he would ever see Maggie again.

Chapter Twenty-two

She sat on the porch until the police car was out of sight, and then she turned the wheelchair around and went into the parlor. Bobby didn't have a telephone, so she called the community center at Pine Ridge and left a message, asking the operator to repeat the message back to her twice to make sure she got it right.

Hanging up the phone, she looked out the window, frowning when she saw the truck parked alongside the house. If only she could drive the darn thing, she could go into town and get Hawk out of jail. She tried to imagine what he must be feeling, thinking. . . .

Her throat grew tight, tears stung her eyes as she pictured him locked up in some horrid little cell. How would she bear it?

She was crying now, the tears running unchecked down her cheeks as she maneuvered her wheelchair from room to room. They all held memories of Hawk. She remembered how he had followed her around, looking, touching, deeply intrigued by the phone and the TV and the stereo. He had been a little frightened, too, by the strangeness of it all, but he had hidden it well. After all, warriors didn't show fear. She smiled a little, thinking of how quickly he had come to like watching television, remembering how just that morning he had cooked breakfast for her. Remembering how he had made love to her. . . .

She cried all that day, her heart aching for him. How alone he must feel!

She had nightmares that night, horrible nightmares. Hawk was found guilty and sent to prison where he was ridiculed and abused until, finally, he lost all desire to live. . . .

The sound of the telephone woke her. Pulling herself into a sitting position, she reached for the phone beside the bed. It was Bobby.

"Oh, Bobby," she cried, "Hawk's in jail and I don't have any way to get to town to get him out."

"Jail!" Bobby exclaimed. "Why?"

As quickly as she could, Maggie explained what had happened, breathing a heartfelt sigh of relief as Bobby promised to leave for Sturgis immediately.

"Do you have enough money to post bail?"

"I'll get it, don't worry."

"Bless you, Bobby. Hurry, please."

"I'm on my way," he said. "Don't worry."

Replacing the receiver, Maggie gazed out the bedroom window. "Don't worry, Hawk," she murmured. "Help is on the way."

Hawk stopped in mid-stride, his head cocked to one side as he listened for the sound of her voice, and then he heard it again, the voice of the Spirit Woman, as clearly as if she stood beside him. *Don't worry, Hawk. Help is on the way.*

"Mag-gie." Her name was a sigh on his lips, a faint ray of hope in a world darkened with despair.

He had not slept the night before, only paced the floor, back and forth, back and forth, unable to relax, unable to rest. He had not eaten the food they'd brought him. Once, he had hunkered down on his heels in the corner and closed his eyes, only to be plagued by dark half-dreams of a life behind bars, and he knew he'd rather die than spend the rest of his life in prison, never to see the sunlit plains again, never to see the Black Hills. Never to see Maggie again.

"Hawk."

He turned to see Bobby striding toward him.

"You all right?" Bobby asked.

Hawk nodded, thinking he'd never been happier to see anyone in his life.

"Maggie told me you were here. I'll have you out of there in a few minutes."

A half hour later they left the courthouse. Since Bobby was a local resident, he'd been allowed to post an unsecured bond and no money was required. Hawk had sworn to apear

213

in court at the specified time and place to answer the charges against him, and they'd been free to go.

"Are you hungry?" Bobby asked. "I haven't had breakfast yet."

Hawk nodded. He'd had no appetite for food while locked up in the iron house, but now he thought he could eat a buffalo, horns and all.

"Any place special you want to go?"

"Go?"

Bobby grinned. "There are places in town where we can eat. They're called restaurants. Mom's Cafe has good food. Wanna go there?"

Hawk stared at the streets full of people. White people who stared at him as if he were some sort of strange creature. People like the lawman who had arrested him, refusing to believe a word he said, refusing to believe that the blond biker had started the fight. In Hawk's experience, no white man had ever believed an Indian; no white man had ever kept his word. "I would rather go back to Mag-gie's house," he said at last.

"Okay by me."

Bobby's car was parked behind the courthouse. It was an old beat-up Chevy with cardboard covering the back window and a busted tail light, what the whites called an "Indian car." But it got Bobby where he wanted to go. He slid behind the wheel, turned the key while Hawk climbed in beside him.

Bobby drove in silence until they were out of town. And then he cleared his throat. "Can I, uh, ask you something?"

"Yes."

214

"Do you think it's possible for people to be born in the wrong time?"

"What do you mean?"

"Did you ever have the feeling you didn't belong, that maybe you should have been born in another time? I don't know how to explain it, but I've always had the feeling that I was meant to be a warrior, that I should have been born a hundred years ago."

"I have always known who I was and where I belonged," Hawk replied. "Until now."

"Would you change places with me, if you could?"

Hawk started to shake his head, but then he thought of Maggie. If only it were that easy. If only he could send Bobby to the cave in his place.

"I was going to stay with my family until it was time for me to go to college," Bobby said. "But if it's all right with you, I'd like to stay at Miss St. Claire's. I thought maybe when you had a few minutes to spare, you might teach me how to be a medicine man in the old way."

"I will teach you what I know," Hawk said. "Though I feel that I still have much to learn."

Maggie was waiting for them on the front porch. She thanked Bobby profusely for his help, assured him that he was welcome to stay, smiled her gratitude when he said he thought he'd go take a look at the horses.

Bless the boy for realizing she wanted to be alone with Hawk, she thought, and then they were alone and she couldn't think of anything to say.

She gazed up at Hawk, who was standing near the edge of the porch, staring toward the Hills, and it was as if she could read his mind. Deep inside, he was angry, angry at Rocco and Vince who had tried to take his woman, then humiliated him by having him thrown in jail. He was angry at the officer who had taken him to jail, at everything and everyone that was white. Everyone except her, and it was tearing him apart. She was white, the enemy, and he loved her.

"Hawk, are you all right?"

He nodded curtly. His gaze focused on the Black Hills rising in the distance. He could feel the Sacred Cave calling to him, offering him safety and shelter within its walls. For a moment, he closed his eyes and he could almost feel the darkness hovering around him, promising to send him home.

"I guess it was awful, being locked up," Maggie said sympathetically. "I got you out of there as soon as I could."

"I am all right, Mag-gie," he said. But the anger was festering in his soul. It had been humiliating, being locked behind iron bars as if he were an animal instead of a man. And the worst of it was having Bobby see him like that.

Hawk spent the next two weeks instructing Bobby in the ways of a holy man. It was like a crash course, Maggie thought as she watched the two of them together. And even as the thought crossed her mind, she knew that was exactly what it was. Hawk was endeavoring to teach Bobby all he knew about healing and living off the land because he was leaving. She could feel him withdrawing from her a little more each day, almost as if he were building a wall between them.

She slid a glance at his profile, committing his finely chiseled features to memory, determined to paint him again before he was gone.

She began that evening, while he was outside with Bobby. She could see him clearly from her window and she began to sketch him, first his profile, then full-face, then riding the black stallion. Her fingers fairly flew over the canvas and when she finished the rough sketches, she knew they were going to be the best work she'd ever done. Her previous paintings of Hawk were good, but lacked vitality. These caught his strength, his honor, his pride.

Maggie smiled a secret smile. It wasn't that her skills had suddenly improved, she thought, it was only that she knew him now, knew him more intimately than she'd ever known anyone else. And that made the difference.

Leaning forward in her chair, she pressed a hand to her back, then went into the kitchen to prepare dinner, thinking how pleased Hawk would be when she served all his favorites: steak and fried potatoes, corn on the cob, hot rolls, and lots of coffee. She'd make a cake, too, chocolate, of course.

The cake was made and frosted, the table was set, and dinner was ready when she went outside to call Hawk and Bobby to come in for dinner.

Bobby stood up as she wheeled her chair onto the porch.

"Where's Hawk?" Maggie asked, looking around.

"He's gone."

"Gone?"

"He went for a ride."

Fighting down a surge of panic, she gazed up at the sky, assuring herself that the moon was still in its first quarter. He hadn't gone to the cave, then.

"Dinner's ready."

It was a quiet meal. Bobby ate quickly and then, sensing her need to be alone, excused himself and left the house.

Feeling listless and alone, Maggie cleaned up the kitchen, wondering where Hawk was. He'd seemed so angry lately, so withdrawn. Maybe he'd left, though she had no idea where he'd go. Still, he was a warrior. He could live off the land if he had to, disappear into the Hills, and she'd never see him again.

She tried to read for a while, but she couldn't concentrate. Every time she heard a noise she looked up, her heart beating fast, hoping it was Hawk coming home. She tried to watch television but the eleven o'clock news seemed even more depressing than usual and she turned it off, only to sit staring at the blank screen.

The house seemed suddenly small and empty and she went out the kitchen door and down the ramp that led to the back yard.

Maggie came to an abrupt halt as she saw

Hawk standing near the pool, his head thrown back, his arms lifted in an attitude of prayer.

She had never been one for praying, not since the accident. But she knew that Hawk prayed morning and evening. He seemed unaware of her presence and she stayed where she was, wondering if she should go away and leave him alone.

How beautiful he was, standing there in the faint light of the moon. The wind played in his hair, whispering over his skin, caressing his cheek, touching him as she longed to touch him.

He was silent for a long while, and then he was praying again, speaking in the Lakota tongue. It was a humble prayer, filled with thanksgiving and praise for *Wakán Tanka*, asking for nothing. And then she heard her own name fall from his lips. His voice was low and husky, filled with pain and an aching need that brought tears to her eyes.

She had to get away from here, she thought, before he knew she was there.

She started to turn around, intending to go back to the house before he discovered her presence, when Hawk's voice stopped her.

"Mag-gie, do not go."

He'd known she was there the whole time.

He lowered his arms to his sides and walked toward her. Wordlessly, he knelt beside her. She was so beautiful, it made him ache just to look at her.

"Are you all right?" Maggie asked tremulously.

"Yes."

"You missed dinner. You've been so withdrawn lately. And then you were gone so long, I thought maybe you'd left, that you weren't coming back."

"Where would I go?"

"I don't know."

She gazed up toward the Black Hills. The Sacred Cave was up there somewhere. On the night of the next full moon, he'd climb to the top of the mountain and she'd never see him again.

"Spirit Woman, you make me feel weak inside."

"Do I?"

"All my life I have known who I was, where I belonged, what path my life would follow. Until now."

"Is there nothing I can say that will make you stay?"

"I do not belong here."

"Maybe you do! Maybe that's why you were sent to me, because this is where you belong."

"Maybe I will not be able to go back. Maybe a man whose heart belongs to another, a man who is no longer whole, cannot travel the Spirit Path."

"Maybe," Maggie murmured softly, and prayed as she had never prayed before, hoping that the magic of the cave would be denied him, that he would be forced to stay here, with her. He'd never be sorry. She'd see to that. She'd be mother and father, brother and sister, lover and friend all rolled into one.

She stared up into his face, her lips parting as he drew her into his arms and kissed her.

220

At first, there was no passion in his touch, only an aching sense of need, of hopelessness. He was lost and alone and he reached out to her as the only familiar thing in an alien land.

Maggie held him close, wanting to comfort him. His eyes were filled with the same haunting sadness she had seen before and she longed to make him smile, to assure him that everything would be all right. But she had no words of comfort to give him, only the love in her heart

He kissed her again, the pressure of his lips increasing as the kiss deepened and became more demanding. He locked his arms around her waist, drawing the length of her body against his own, letting her feel his need.

She never thought to deny him. She clung to him with all her strength, kissing him back, whispering his name as he caressed the clothes from her body, his lips kissing each exposed area of flesh, teasing and tantalizing, as they made love, there, in the shadow of the Black Hills beneath a blanket of stars. The wind was cool against her skin, but he quickly warmed her, covering her with his body, his hands fanning the embers of desire to flame, his lips kissing her until she was breathless, caressing her, speaking to her in soft Lakota as he made her his, vowing he would never love another.

She wept then, her heart breaking for fear he would keep his word and spend the rest of his life alone, with only his mother to care for him.

And then she wept harder because she was only a woman, and a jealous one at that, and she knew that he'd forget her once he returned to his own time, forget her and find a lovely Lakota maiden who would bear him beautiful daughters and strong sons. And she would be left with only the memory of his touch, a memory that would fade in time until she was left with nothing.

Her fingernails raked the length and breadth of his back as their passion crested and in some primal corner of her mind she smiled as she dug her nails in deeper, hoping to leave her mark upon him, wanting him to be forever branded as hers.

They lay locked in each other's arms for long moments and then Hawk drew back, his gaze narrowed as he stared down at her.

"Mag-gie, why do you weep? Have I hurt you?"

She shook her head, unable to speak, ashamed of what she'd been thinking. She loved him and wanted only his happiness, and if he could not be happy here, then she would let him go and be glad for the time they'd had together.

A sob rose in her throat. It sounded so easy, so noble, but what would she do without him?

"Mag-gie, do not weep." His voice was low and deep, filled with love, and yet she heard a faint note of sadness as he whispered, "I will not leave you."

She blinked at him through her tears, not daring to believe.

"How can I go?" he asked, gently brushing a wisp of hair from her cheek. "I could not live without my heart."

"Hawk, oh, Hawk!" She threw her arms around his neck, tears of joy coursing down her cheeks, even as a distant voice warned her that it could never be.

He held her close, praying he had made the right decision, knowing he could never leave her now. He had made her his woman and he knew he could not go back to his own people and leave her behind, not now, when she might be carrying his child; not now, when he loved her more desperately than ever.

"Mag-gie, I do not know how it is among the *wasichu* when a man wishes to take a wife, but . . ."

"A wife," Maggie breathed. "You want to marry me?"

He nodded, confused by her reaction.

"But I'm older than you, and . . . and . . ."

He placed a hand over her mouth. "You are only a few years older than I, and it does not matter that you cannot walk. I will never want anyone else but you."

"Oh."

"What must we do?"

"I don't know. Get a license, I guess. Blood tests. Oh, Hawk!" she said, and threw her arms around his neck again.

"Does this mean you will marry me?"

"Yes," she said, feeling the laughter bubble up within her. "Oh, yes!"

Chapter Twenty-three

She was getting married! It was incredible. Only a few weeks ago she had been resigned to the fact that she would never have a husband, that she would spend her whole life alone, living her life vicariously through the lives of the heroines she created on paper, and then Hawk had come into her life and everything had changed. She was in love with a wonderful man. And today she would be married.

Sitting in her wheelchair in the middle of her bedroom, Maggie hugged herself, laughing out loud. She'd never been so happy.

Once the initial excitement of Hawk's proposal had worn off, she'd worried about the necessity of getting a marriage license, and the problems they might face where Hawk was concerned. He was a man from the past. He had no birth certificate, no identification of any kind. But that problem was easily rectified. She had called the office of the Register of Deeds and learned that all Hawk needed was two people with valid identification who would sign a form swearing Hawk was who he said he was. With that in hand and twenty-five dollars in cash—no checks, the man stated firmly—they could obtain a license that was good for twenty days. No blood tests were required. Both parties had to be present to obtain the license. It was all so simple. The whole thing had taken less than thirty minutes.

All that had been taken care of three days ago. Maggie and Bobby had signed the necessary paper, the license had been issued, and today was her wedding day.

Breathless, she gazed at her bed and felt her cheeks grow warm. Hawk had slept beside her every night since they'd made love beside the pool a week ago. They had not made love since that night, but it was wonderful to wake beside him every morning, to fall asleep in his arms every night.

This morning she had awakened to find Hawk watching her, his dark gaze so full of love it had brought tears to her eyes.

She heard his footsteps in the hallway, felt her heart quicken as he entered the room.

"Ready?" he asked.

"Ready."

Her wedding dress, made of white satin and lace, was already in the truck, as was the dark suit that Hawk had agreed to wear.

Madeline Baker

Hawk kissed her gently before they left the house, his dark eyes filled with promise. Bobby was waiting for them in the truck. Maggie smiled at him as Hawk lifted her into the cab and closed the door. After folding Maggie's wheelchair, Hawk placed it in the bed of the truck, then slid behind the wheel.

Veronica was waiting for them in Rapid City. Her husband was still in the hospital, but he was out of intensive care and the prognosis was hopeful.

Veronica smiled at Maggie as Hawk lifted her out of the truck and placed her in the wheelchair. "You look radiant," she whispered.

"I feel radiant," Maggie replied.

Veronica's two sons took Hawk and Bobby into the church and showed them where to change clothes while Veronica and Maggie went into the Bride's Room.

"Ed sends his best," Veronica said as she helped Maggie into her wedding dress.

Maggie squeezed Veronica's hands. "I'm sorry he can't be here, but I'm so glad to hear he's going to be all right."

There was a soft knock on the door. "Are you ready in there, Ma?"

"Yes, Jacob. We'll be out directly," Veronica called. She handed Maggie a bouquet of white daisies. "You're on," Veronica said. "Shall we go?"

Maggie nodded, too filled with emotion to speak.

Hawk stood beside the altar, fidgeting a little in his new suit as he waited for Maggie. He had never worn so many clothes in his life and he felt warm and uncomfortable. He had looked at himself in the mirror and thought his own mother would never have recognized him. The shoes were the worst, pinching his feet like bear traps. But he would wear them this once, for Maggie, and then never again.

Bobby stood beside him, dressed in a dark gray suit that also looked new.

There was no one else in the church save for the minister, clad in long black robes, Veronica's two sons, Jared and Jacob, and Sheila Goodman, dressed in a dark green skirt and matching jacket and sitting in the front row.

The organist began to play and Veronica walked down the aisle. She wore a dress of pale pink and carried a bouquet of lavender flowers. She sent Hawk a warm smile as she took her place at the altar.

Moments later, Maggie came down the aisle toward him, and Hawk forgot everything else. Never had she looked more beautiful. Her gown was long and white, the perfect complement to her curly black hair and dark blue eyes. White orchids and ribbons adorned the arms of the wheelchair, white ribbon had been wound around the spokes.

As she drew near him, the sun cast its light on the stained-glass window behind the altar, so that her face seemed to glow with a soft golden fire.

"Spirit Woman." He murmured the words, unaware that he'd spoken them aloud.

And then she was beside him, her hand in his, while the Black Robe spoke the white man's words that made Maggie St. Claire his woman, his wife.

There was a long silence while Hawk stared down at her, his heart filled to overflowing, his only regret that his mother could not be there, that he would never see her again.

The Black Robe cleared his throat discreetly, then said, in a loud whisper, "Young man, you may kiss the bride."

Dropping to one knee, Hawk cupped Maggie's face in his hands and kissed her softly, gently, with all the love in his heart.

And Maggie threw her arms around his neck and kissed him back, overcome with love and gratitude for the man who was now her husband, the man who had shown her what love was, who had given her a reason to live again.

Vaguely, she was aware of a cough, a snicker, a muffled laugh filled with happiness. Only then did she realize that she and Hawk had been kissing for quite some time, and remember that they weren't alone in the room.

Her cheeks were flushed when they parted, and then Veronica and Bobby crowded around, giving her hugs, shaking Hawk's hand.

Sheila Goodman stood nearby, waiting her turn, grinning broadly when she hugged Maggie.

"My dear," Sheila gushed, her brown eyes flashing with admiration, "we've got to use Hawk on the cover of your next book. Think of the publicity!"

Maggie nodded, but publicity was the furthest thing from her mind. She felt a twinge of jealousy as Sheila kissed Hawk full on the mouth.

Veronica had baked them a small wedding cake, chocolate, of course. Sheila offered a toast to the bride and groom, Veronica and the boys wished them well, Bobby said Jacob was going to drive him out to the reservation.

"Veronica said the two of you would probably want to . . . ah, be alone for a while," Bobby said, turning away so they couldn't see the heat climb in his cheeks.

Soon it was time to go.

Jacob put the wedding presents in the back of the truck along with their street clothes and Maggie's wheelchair. There were more hugs and more farewells, and then Hawk and Maggie were alone in the truck, driving out of town toward home.

"You look very handsome," Maggie said, smiling as her husband ran his finger around the inside of his collar.

She was tempted to tell him to remove his coat and tie, but he looked so wonderful, and she wasn't sure she'd ever get him into a suit again.

"And you are very beautiful."

His words washed over her like sunshine and she thought how wonderful it would be to spend the rest of her life with Hawk, to hear the sound of that voice, so deep and soft, speaking her name.

"Very beautiful," he repeated, and taking Maggie's right hand in his, he raised it to his lips, kissing her palm and then the tip of each finger. And each touch sent little shivers of pleasure, of anticipation, racing down her spine.

At home, Hawk parked the truck beside the house and Maggie felt suddenly shy as he lifted her out of the truck, placed her in the wheelchair, and pushed her up the ramp to the front door.

When they reached the door, she knew a moment of regret, wishing Hawk would carry her over the threshold.

She was wondering if asking him would ruin the moment when he swept her into his arms, his dark eyes shining as he opened the door.

"Veronica told me," he remarked, answering the unspoken question he read in Maggie's eyes. "She told me it is the custom of white men to carry their women into the house after the wedding."

Maggie's breath caught in her throat as Hawk lowered his head and kissed her before carrying her inside.

He gazed down at her, a glint of mischief in his eyes. "What do the *wasichu* do now?" he asked, his voice suddenly husky.

"Probably the same thing the Lakota do," Maggie replied innocently. "They change clothes and wash the breakfast dishes."

Hawk laughed out loud and Maggie thought she'd never heard anything more wonderful in her life.

"We will start our own custom, then," he said, his tone as solemn as a judge pronouncing sentence, and carried her quickly down the hall toward her bedroom.

Inside, he placed her on the edge of the bed and then, with great deliberation and reverence, he began to undress her, removing her veil and laying it aside, reaching around her to unfasten the small buttons at the back of her dress, sliding it slowly over her shoulders, kissing her neck and each exposed shoulder before removing her silky undergarments, her satin pumps. His hand slid down the length of each leg, marveling at the feel of silk beneath his hands before he slowly removed her stockings.

Maggie sat there, her mouth dry, her heart beating fiercely, her whole body tingling and warm under his ebony gaze, the look in his eyes making her feel more beautiful, more desirable, than she'd ever felt in her life.

"My turn," she murmured when he had finished undressing her, and he obligingly knelt before her so she could remove his coat and tie.

Her fingers trembled a little as she unbuttoned his shirt and slid it off his shoulders, revealing a broad expanse of flesh. She insisted he sit on the floor and put his feet up on the bed so she could remove his shoes and socks, then watched, a little breathless, as he stood up, his movements lithe and graceful, the muscles in his arms and shoulders rippling beneath his copper-hued skin.

She removed his belt, unfastened his trousers, and watched them fall to the floor at his feet. A rueful smile tugged at the corners of her mouth as she gazed at the sight of her husband, gloriously naked and fully aroused, leaving her to wonder what he'd done with the T-shirt and black bikini briefs.

But the whereabouts of his underwear quickly faded from her mind as his hands delved into her hair, moving softly, gently, sending shivers down her spine.

Maggie gazed into his face, saw the love that swelled in her own heart mirrored in the depths of Hawk's fathomless black eyes.

Filled with warmth and wonder, she drew him down beside her on the bed, letting her fingertips move over the face she adored, letting her hands thrill to the feel of his taut bronze skin. He drew her close, molding her body to his like satin to steel, and she thought she'd die from the sheer pleasure of it.

"Spirit Woman." He murmured her name, lost in the magic of her nearness, in the fierce intensity of his need for this one woman above all others.

Maggie basked in his embrace, in the knowledge of his love, returning kiss for kiss and touch for touch until he rose over her, his hand gently parting her thighs, his eyes dark with desire. His hair fell over his shoulders like a curtain of black silk, whispering against her breasts. She locked her hands behind his back and drew him close, closer, a soft sigh of ecstasy escaping her lips as she welcomed him home. He was her husband, her hero, a man from another time and place who had captured her heart and soul.

She whispered his name, speaking to him in Lakota, telling him of her love, as Hawk possessed her, two hearts and two worlds now made one.

*   *   *

They spent the next week and a half seeing the sights in and around Sturgis. It was amazing, Maggie thought. She'd lived here two years and had never been anywhere. But then, before Hawk entered her life, she hadn't had much interest in anything but her writing. They toured Fort Meade, rode to the top of Bear Butte, visited the Black Hills National Cemetery and the Ute burial ground.

And then it was on to Deadwood, only thirteen miles from Sturgis. After checking into the Adams House Bed and Breakfast, they went out to see the sights.

Deadwood was situated in a narrow gulch. Houses were built on the steep-sided hills on either hand and the roads that led to the houses formed terraces. Near the upper end of town, the gulch divided and buildings followed both valleys, the business establishments below and the houses above.

Walking through Deadwood was like taking a giant step into the past. Wild Bill Hickock and Calamity Jane had walked these streets. Poker Alice had resided here before moving to Sturgis. Other characters with colorful names had lived and died here: Potato Creek Johnny, Preacher Smith, Jack McCall, and Charlie Utter, who guided a dozen "soiled doves" into Deadwood in 1876, accompanied by Calamity Jane and Wild Bill Hickock.

They traversed historical Main Street, passing the Dakota Territory Saloon, the Bodega Cage, the House of Roses Museum. They stopped at the Franklin Hotel and Gambling Hall for lunch. A brochure stated that the Franklin had once been considered the finest hotel between Chicago and San Francisco, and Maggie had to admit the atmosphere was wonderful, the lobby beautifully restored.

Walking down Main Street was like strolling through the pages of history and Maggie fell in love with the town. It was here, in Deadwood, on August 2, 1876, that Jack McCall had killed Wild Bill Hickock in Saloon No. 10. Wild Bill and Calamity Jane were both buried in Mount Moriah Cemetery, while Jack McCall was buried in an unmarked grave in Potter's Field.

Deciding to set her next book in Deadwood, she picked up magazines and brochures everywhere they went.

One stop Maggie had to make was to the Midnight Star, which was owned primarily by Kevin Costner's younger brother, Dan. The building had been named after a saloon in the movie *Silverado*, which starred Kevin Costner; the third-floor restaurant was called Jake's, after Costner's character in the movie. Maggie couldn't help it, she'd always been star-stuck and Kevin Costner was one of her favorite actors, especially since *Dances with Wolves*. She loved seeing all the posters, photos, and costumes that had been used in the movie.

Leaving the Midnight Star, they spent several hours in the Adams Museum, which housed the first locomotive used in the Black Hills. There were numerous photographs of Deadwood, some dating as far back as 1876. And, of course, there were photographs of and artifacts that had belonged to Wild Bill and Calamity Jane.

Hawk seemed less than enthusiastic with their tour of the town, but she could hardly blame him. The discovery of gold in the Black Hills had ultimately led to the destruction of the Lakota way of life.

He was, however, intrigued by the Ghosts of Deadwood Gulch Wax Museum, which featured seventy full-size figures portraying various episodes in the settlement of the Dakota Territory. Some of them were remarkably lifelike, so much so that Maggie wouldn't have been surprised to see them move.

They had dinner at the Franklin Hotel, then spent a couple of hours playing blackjack. At first, Hawk watched Maggie, but then he decided to try his luck, surprising them both by winning over fifty dollars in ten minutes.

"Beginner's luck," Maggie muttered as he got blackjack for the third time in a row.

As the evening wore on, Hawk grew acutely aware of the people around him. He heard the whispers of those who stood around the blackjack table, speculating on whether he was a real Indian, and if so, what tribe he was from, wondering if maybe he was an actor. He overheard several tasteless jokes about scalps and massacres and Custer. And when he'd had enough, he picked up his winnings and walked away.

"Hawk. Hawk, wait. They don't mean it," Maggie said when she caught up with him.

"Don't they?"

"Well, maybe some of them do, but don't let it spoil our time here." She took his hand and smiled up at him. "Let's go back to our room, shall we?"

The anger he'd felt withered under her smile and he nodded, suddenly anxious to be alone with her. His woman. His wife.

Let the silly white men make all the jokes they wanted, Hawk thought as they made their way back to their hotel. He had won the best prize of all.

From Deadwood, they drove to Rapid City to visit Ed and Veronica and the boys. While there, they went to the Sioux Pioneer Museum. Hawk stared at the panoramas of Indian life, his expression wistful. He stood staring at a tribal calendar for a long while, studying the pictorial history, or "winter count" that detailed the annual highlights of a tribe beginning in 1796.

But it was an ancient Thunderbird shield that brought tears to his eyes.

"It belonged to Heart-of-the-Wolf," he replied in answer to Maggie's question. "I saw it often in his lodge."

He was visibly depressed when they left the museum, but she could hardly blame him for that. How awful, to see your own past on public display, to know that all you once held dear had been destroyed.

She should have known better than to let him talk her into going to visit the Badlands and the Pine Ridge Reservation. He was appalled by the small communities and towns on the reservation.

The houses, most built in the 1970s, were in sad repair, the paint peeling, the doors hanging, the yards filled with debris. The feelings between whites and Indians had not changed in the last hundred years. The whites were still worried and distrustful and tension was high.

He was quiet on the ride back home, his face set in hard lines, his eyes dark with despair. She knew what he was thinking, knew without asking that he was grieving for his people, for a way of life that was gone forever.

When they reached the ranch, Hawk kissed Maggie on the cheek, then caught the black and rode into the Hills.

He rode for hours, his thoughts bleak as he imagined what the future held for his people: the loss of their freedom, their land, their pride. He recalled driving on the reservation, seeing the ugly little houses, sensing the hopelessness of the people. Maggie had told him that drugs and whiskey and child abuse were big problems on the reservation. He felt sick inside when he thought of his people taking out their frustrations on their children. Such a thing was unheard of in his time. Children were a gift from *Wakán Tanka*, to be cherished and loved, and it made no difference if that child was red or white. All were welcome in the lodges of the Lakota.

He reined the black to a halt and stared into the distance. The setting sun was turning the sky to flame, the red making him think of blood . . . the blood of his people that would be shed so that the white man could lay claim to the Black Hills, to the vast grassy plains, to the mountains of the Little Big Horn. What a greedy people the whites were! They had owned all the land in the east, but it hadn't been enough. They had wanted the land of the Lakota as well, and they had destroyed the buffalo and a people to obtain it.

Dismounting, he sat cross-legged on the breast of Mother Earth, his head bowed, as he rocked slowly back and forth, mourning the death of his people, grieving for those who would survive, for a way of life that was gone.

He sat there for hours, sick at heart, wondering if he had made the right decision. Perhaps he should go back, if only to warn his people of what was to come so they might be prepared to fight, to die. Or perhaps he should go back and tell them that fighting was useless. . . .

He raised his eyes toward heaven, wondering if *Wakán Tanka* was angry with his red children. He stared at the moon and the stars, his heart and soul reaching toward heaven, but he heard nothing but the voice of the wind sighing through the pines.

It was after midnight when he swung aboard the big black stallion and rode back to the ranch.

A light burned in the front window and as he crossed the porch, he could see Maggie inside. She'd fallen asleep in her chair beside the window and he knew she'd been sitting there, waiting for him, her heart empty and afraid.

Entering the parlor, he knelt before her, filled with guilt because he had caused her pain.

"Spirit Woman." He took her hands in his, pressing his lips to the palm of one hand.

"Hawk?" she murmured sleepily, and when she saw it was really him and not a dream, she threw her arms around his neck, holding him to her breasts as she kissed the top of his head. "Oh, Hawk!"

"Mag-gie, I am sorry."

"It's all right. I understand."

He drew back to look up into her face. "Do you?"

The tone of his voice and the look in his eye turned her blood to ice.

"Do you?" he asked again.

"I think so, but Hawk, there's nothing you can do for your people. Nothing! You can't change history."

"I can try."

"But what could you do?" Silent tears slid down her cheeks. "You're just one man. You can't stop a whole civilization from expanding."

"I have to do something, if it is only to warn my people of what's to come."

"What good will that do?"

"I do not know. I only know I must go back."

"Why?" she cried.

"Because I feel so guilty," he replied quietly. "I cannot stay here knowing what's going to happen to my people and do nothing. They will fight, and I must be there to fight with them."

"But it won't do any good! Please, Hawk, we've been so happy these past few weeks. Doesn't that mean anything? Don't I mean anything?"

"Mag-gie."

239

There was such love in his voice, such anguish, she wished she could call back her words, but it was too late.

His dark eyes were filled with pain, a pain she could never fully comprehend. She had always been appalled at the way her people had treated the Indians, she felt sympathy for their plight, compassion for their misery. She sent money to the American Indian Relief Fund and to several other charities that were trying to make life better for Native Americans, but she could never fully understand how they felt.

No one had ever stolen her land or forced her into a way of life that was alien and unwanted. She had never been taken away from her parents and forced to learn the language of people she considered her enemy, or whipped for speaking her own tongue.

Sometimes she tried to console herself with the thought that it was their destiny. The Indians had fought amongst themselves for territory and the stronger tribes had driven the weaker ones out, taking the best hunting grounds for themselves. But the Lakota had not broken treaties. They had not imprisoned a whole race of people on a reservation, or tried to impose their own life-style on that of their enemy.

She gazed into Hawk's eyes and knew that he loved her beyond words. He did not want to leave her, but his pride and his inborn sense of honor demanded that he do whatever he could to help his people, even if it was only to prepare them for what was to come.

There was nothing more to say. He would leave her and she would have to let him go.

Wordlessly, she held out her arms.

Wordlessly, he picked her up and carried her down the hallway toward the bedroom.

Unable to put their feelings into words, they made love until dawn, and each touch, each tearful caress, was a renewal of the love they shared.

A renewal, and a goodbye.

Chapter Twenty-four

The next two weeks were bittersweet. Sometimes Maggie wanted to spend every minute with Hawk, to savor their remaining time together, to gather memories so she'd have something to look back on when he was gone. And at other times, she didn't want to see him at all. Better to get used to being without him now, she thought miserably, to wean herself away from the sight of his face, the sound of his voice.

On those days when she couldn't bear to be without him, they spent every moment together. He took her riding into the Hills, they swam in the pool behind the house, they went on another picnic.

One night, as they were making love, she prayed that she was pregnant, that she might have a part of Hawk to love and cherish after he was gone. She took countless pictures of him, shooting him from every side, every angle, trying to capture the essence of the man she loved.

She faced each sunset with growing dread, knowing that it meant she was one day closer to losing him forever. She told herself to be strong, that he was doing what he had to do, that he belonged back in 1872. But it was a losing battle, and it was tearing her apart inside.

Hawk was fighting his own demons. In the short time he'd spent with Maggie, he'd come to love her deeply. She was everything he had ever dreamed of, wished for, desired. She was truly a Spirit Woman, for she'd woven a spell around him from which he had no desire to escape. He loved her with his whole heart and soul; given time, he knew he could adjust to her world. And yet he couldn't stay. With each passing day, he felt more and more compelled to return to his people even though he knew there was nothing he could do to change their ultimate fate.

And then, too soon, the night of the full moon was upon them. They had tried to pretend that that day was like any other, but both had failed miserably and they had spent the afternoon and evening in each other's arms.

And now he was ready to go.

Hawk knelt beside Maggie's wheelchair, her hands clasped in his.

She gazed deep into his eyes. He had changed in the last few days and she sensed that even now he was shaking off the white man's words and ways. He was once again wrapping himself in the ancient customs and traditions of his people. She could readily imagine him riding to battle, his face streaked with war paint, a quiver of arrows slung over his shoulder.

But when he looked at her, she saw only the man she had grown to love, his dark eyes filled with the same sadness that tore at her heart.

"I will come back to you, Mag-gie," he promised. "If there is a way, I will come to you."

"You said you'd stay, that you couldn't live without me."

"It will not be living."

She clenched her fists, her nails digging into the palms of her hands. She had told him she understood; at the time she'd meant it. But now he was leaving and she couldn't bear it. He'd given her a taste of love, of happiness, made her feel like the princess in a fairy tale coming to life again after a long sleep.

"I do not want to go," he said, his voice thick with unshed tears. "But even now I can hear the Cave calling to me and I must answer."

"Then go!" She screamed out the anger and the pain that were clawing at her heart. "Go on, get out of here. Go back to your stupid cave! I wish I'd never met you!"

Her words sliced through Hawk like a knife, and even though he was certain she didn't mean them, they left him raw and bleeding. He wanted to take her in his arms, to soothe the pain in her eyes; instead, he stood up, his face an impassive mask. Perhaps it was better this way, after all. Perhaps her anger would dull the ache.

"Farewell, my heart," he murmured, and turning on his heel, he left the room without a backward glance.

It was the hardest thing he'd done and as he walked out of her house into the night, he knew he'd left the best part of himself behind.

He hesitated for a moment, wanting more than anything to go back to her, to see her one more time, but he knew it would only cause them both more pain. Resolutely, he swung aboard the stallion and rode out of the yard.

It was a beautiful night, clear and cool and quiet, with only the faint sigh of the wind and the sound of hoofbeats muffled by layers of pine needles to break the stillness. The *Paha Sapa* rose before him in the pale moonlight, beckoning him, calling him away from the woman he loved.

How would he live without her? What if she carried his child? He knew deep within himself that she was right. The future had already been written and there was nothing he could do to change it. And yet he had to try. He might not be able to save the entire Lakota Nation, but he had to know if his mother still lived, he had to try to help his people. Surely there was some small corner of the world where they could live without fear, where the old ones could die in peace, where the young could grow up unafraid.

He'd thought he could stay here, with Maggie, that he could turn his back on who he was, what he was. But the blood of warriors ran in his veins and he could not abandon his people.

Instead, he was deserting the woman he loved.

The thought left the taste of ashes in his mouth. He tried to rationalize by telling himself that Maggie's life wasn't in danger, that she would survive without him, while he might be the only hope his people had. He had seen the future. He knew, from what Maggie had told him, when and where battles would be fought, who would win and who would lose, who would live and who would die. He could not keep that knowledge to himself, not when it might save the lives of people he loved.

Too soon, he reached the Sacred Cave.

Hawk sat there for a long moment; then, expelling a deep sigh, he dismounted, only to stand beside the stallion, reluctant to enter the cave, to take the first step that would take him away from Maggie, perhaps forever. He wished now that he had thought to ask her for a photograph that he could carry back with him so that he might be able to look at it when her image began to fade from his memory, as it surely would, in time.

He rubbed the stallion behind its ears, then removed the bridle and turned the horse loose so it could make its way back to the ranch.

It was dark and cool within the bowels of the Sacred Cave. As he had done before, he made his way into the heart of the cavern; then, taking the small deerskin bag from his belt, he withdrew a handful of corn pollen and scattered a small amount to the east, the west, the north, and the south, to the Great Spirit above, to Mother Earth. And then, heavy-hearted, he faced east and sat down, staring into the darkness as he concentrated on his village. Closing his eyes, he sent a silent prayer to *Wakán Tanka*, asking to be sent home.

Maggie sat in the living room where Hawk had left her, staring out the front door. He was gone and she'd never see him again.

The thought was more painful than anything she'd ever known, worse than the guilt that had plagued her after Susie died, worse than the knowledge that she'd never walk again.

There is nothing wrong with your legs, Miss St. Claire. You can walk if you want to . . .

Hysterical paralysis . . .

Once you get over the guilt of your sister's death . . .

You can walk if you want to, if you want to, if you want to . . .

Oh, Lord, how she wanted to walk! She had to see Hawk one last time, kiss him once more, tell him she loved him, would always love him. She had to beg his forgiveness for the horrible words she'd hurled at him, tell him that she hadn't meant them, that she did understand why he was going.

And like a bolt out of the blue, she knew where his people could find safety.

Hawk, wait!

Biting down on her lower lip, Maggie put the foot rests aside, placed both feet squarely on the floor. Then, with her hands braced on the arms of her chair, she levered herself to a standing position.

You can walk if you want to . . .

She swayed for a moment, her heart hammering with fear: fear of failure, fear of falling, fear that she was already too late.

Another minute went by, and she was still standing, though her legs felt weak, so weak.

Putting one hand on the door jamb, she took a step forward, and then another one. Her steps were wobbly and uncertain, her legs felt as if they were made of Jell-O, but she was walking!

Left, right, left, right, she was walking!

She made her way down the hallway, her steps slow and uneven, her hands braced against the walls.

Wait for me, Hawk. Please wait for me.

She quickly changed her dress for a pair of Levi's and a red Western-style shirt. Sitting on the edge of the bed, she pulled on a pair of thick wool socks and her riding boots. Going to the hall closet, she grabbed a sheepskin jacket and left the house.

Outside, she let her gaze sweep across the Black Hills before hurrying to the barn to saddle the little chestnut mare.

I'm coming, Hawk, she thought, willing him to hear her voice. *I'm coming.*

Hawk gazed intently toward the east wall of the cave, wondering if he'd lost the power to summon the Spirit of the Cave, if he'd waited too long to try to make his way back.

He concentrated harder, willing the cave wall to come to life, willing the Spirit of the Cave to materialize and send him back to his own people where he belonged. But nothing happened. Perhaps Maggie had been right, he mused, perhaps this was where he was meant to be.

And even as he thought of her, he heard the sound of Maggie's voice echoing in the back of his mind, breaking his concentration, and he opened his eyes.

He frowned as he heard Maggie's voice again, louder this time, calling his name, begging him to wait for her.

Maggie! She was here, at the cave.

Hawk scrambled to his feet, his heart filling with dread as he remembered the fate of the white soldier who had dared to enter the cave during the cycle when the moon was full.

"Mag-gie, go back!" He screamed the warning as he ran toward the entrance, but it was too late. She was already within the walls of the cave. He could see her in the darkness, moving toward him like a faceless shadow as she called his name again.

"No," he cried, "No, Mag-gie, go back!"

He came to an abrupt halt, his heart pounding as he waited for the Spirit of the Cave to strike her down.

"Hawk! Oh, Hawk," she cried, stumbling toward him. "Don't leave me."

"Mag-gie." He held her close, marveling that she was still alive, wondering why she had not been stricken when she entered the cavern.

Abruptly, he put her away from him, his eyes straining to see her in the darkness. "Mag-gie," he breathed in awe. "You are walking!"

"Yes. I'll explain later. Oh, Hawk, take me with you."

She was walking. She wanted to go with him.
Was it possible? He drew her into his arms again,
wondering why she hadn't been struck down
when she entered the cave, when suddenly the
Spirit of the Cave was there, moving over him,
the darkness coming alive, surrounding him,
surrounding them both.

Hawk looked eastward, his mind filling with
thoughts of his people, of his mother, and slowly
the cave began to glow. He stared at the light
intently, overcome with an aching need to go
home.

He could feel Maggie watching him through
the thick darkness. She seemed to be able to read
his thoughts, for he sensed her growing horror as
cloudy images of death and destruction began to
fill his mind. Some deep instinct prompted him
to cover her mouth lest she speak and shatter the
moment.

Taking her hand in his, he closed his eyes,
shaking his head in silent denial as he dropped to
his knees, drawing Maggie down beside him. His
village had been destroyed, the lodges burned.
And what of his mother. . . .?

The darkness grew heavier, thicker, making it
difficult to think, to hear, to breathe. The images
in his mind grew sharper, and he saw the shadow
of a black hawk flying away from the *Paha Sapa*,
leaving the Black Hills far behind, and even as he
watched, an eagle swept past the hawk, heading
north.

He felt himself being drawn into the darkness.
As from far away, he heard Maggie's voice calling his name, felt her hands clutching his arms,

begging him not to leave her.

For a moment, there was nothing but swirling blackness, and then, slowly, he opened his eyes to find Maggie kneeling beside him.

"Mag-gie." He lifted her to her feet and then, her hand in his, he walked toward the entrance of the cave, only to come to an abrupt halt as his foot struck something.

He knew immediately what it was.

"Heart-of-the-Wolf," he murmured.

And knew he'd come home.

Chapter Twenty-five

They found the dead soldier near the mouth of the cave. Maggie couldn't help wondering how she'd missed stepping on it when she ran into the cavern the night before. The body had been mauled by predators and she pressed a hand to her queasy stomach as she followed Hawk outside.

It had been midnight when she entered the cavern; now the sun was shining brightly. Turning, she glanced down the hill. Her house was gone and in its place she could see the ruins of an Indian Village.

She shook her head. It wasn't possible, she thought, and then she laughed silently. She hadn't had any trouble believing that Shadow Hawk had come to the future, but she simply couldn't accept the fact that she was now in the past.

And yet there was no other explanation. She had known it when they stumbled across the medicine man's body. Shadow Hawk had told her that Heart-of-the-Wolf had died in the cave. It accounted for the fact that their horses were missing, too. Not missing, she amended. They were still there, on the other side of time.

She slid a glance at Shadow Hawk, all thought for her own welfare suddenly forgotten. He had come home to find his home destroyed, his village in ashes.

"Come," he said.

"Wait," Maggie called. "Shouldn't we bury Heart-of-the-Wolf and that soldier?"

Hawk shook his head. His people did not bury their dead in the ground. "Heart-of-the-Wolf will rest well enough in the cave. As for the soldier . . ." He shrugged. "The coyotes can have him."

She would have argued with him, but Hawk had already started down the hill and after a moment, she followed him, her mind reeling with the knowledge that she had traveled through time, that she might never see her home again. She thought of all the novels she'd written about white girls who had been captured by Indian warriors. On paper, it all seemed romantic, being carried off by a tall handsome savage, but she was sorely afraid that reality would not be quite as wonderful as fantasy. It was one thing to write about skinning a deer, living in a hide lodge, carrying water from the river, and another thing to do it.

She stood in the shade of a blackened pine

while Shadow Hawk walked through what was left of his village, stopping now and then to pick through the charred remains of a lodge.

It was quiet, so quiet, as if the whole earth were in mourning. People had died here, died violently. The thought sent a shiver through her.

Finally, after what seemed like hours, Shadow Hawk returned to her side carrying a bow and a quiver of arrows that he'd found lying in the dirt outside one of the lodges. There was a blanket over his shoulder, the edges scorched. A bone-handled knife was stuck in his belt. He carried a waterskin in his left hand.

Maggie made a gesture that encompassed the ruined village. "Hawk, I'm sorry."

He nodded curtly, afraid to speak for fear his anger would roll out in a loud scream of pain and anguish. Before he died, Heart-of-the-Wolf had assured Shadow Hawk that his mother was alive and well and he clung to that promise, his only thought to find her.

He sent one last look at the village, at the blackened poles that had supported his mother's lodge, and then he turned away.

"Come," he said. "We will go north, to the lodges of Sitting Bull."

Sitting Bull. Maggie had read about Sitting Bull, or *Tatonka Iyotake*, as the Lakota called him. He was a powerful medicine man. He'd been born in the Grand River region of South Dakota about 1834. His path often crossed that of Crazy Horse and Yellow Hand. It was Sitting Bull who was reported to have had a great vision that foretold the Custer massacre in 1876.

Following the Custer battle, he led a small band of followers into British Columbia. He remained there for several years and then, in 1881, Sitting Bull surrendered to General Miles. They left Canada on July 10. Ten days later, they arrived at Fort Buford, North Dakota, where they were put aboard a steamer and sent to Fort Yates where they were declared prisoners of war and moved to Fort Randall. In 1883, Sitting Bull returned to South Dakota.

Several years later, a Paiute Indian named Wovoka claimed to have had a vision which foretold the demise of all the white men and a return of the buffalo and all the Indian dead. The believers were told to join in the sacred Ghost Dance to prove their faith. Each convert wore a shirt which was to make them impervious to the bullets of the white man. The new religion spread like wildfire, offering hope where there was no hope. The Indians embraced Wovoka's doctrine, clinging to the will-o'-the-wisp promise that the new religion would bring back the life, and the freedom, they had lost.

The Ghost Dance was peaceful, advocating tolerance, honesty and nonviolence, but the reservation agents viewed it as a prelude to a new uprising. In November 1890, troopers were called to Pine Ridge. The Ghost Dancers, thinking they were being attacked, set fire to their lodges and fled into the Badlands. Reports from the agency, distorted and unclear, made the Ghost Dance sound like an outbreak of warfare.

At Standing Rock, the news triggered an order for the arrest of the Sioux. On December 15,

1890, in the early hours of the morning, Indian police dragged Sitting Bull from his lodge. The old medicine man was immediately surrounded by a crowd of outraged Lakota ready to defend him. A fierce battle followed in which twelve men, including Sitting Bull, were killed.

But she could not tell Hawk that, not now. He had enough grief to carry.

They walked for hours across the plains. Maggie removed her jacket. Wiping perspiration from her brow, she wished she had a hat. Hawk seemed oblivious to the heat. He walked steadily onward, his mouth set in a hard line, his dark eyes burning with a deep inner anger.

Late in the afternoon, he bid her to wait for him while he went hunting. He returned an hour later with a rabbit slung over his shoulder. *Dinner*, she thought, and felt her stomach churn as she stared at the limp gray body.

At dusk, Hawk decided it was time to make camp. With a grateful sigh, Maggie sat down on the blanket.

Shadow Hawk dumped his gear on one end of the blanket, then stared at Maggie quizzically for a moment, wondering if she knew how to build a fire, skin and gut a rabbit.

Maggie shook her head. "Sorry, Hawk," she said, reading his thoughts, "you killed it and I'm afraid you'll have to skin it, too. And cook it," she added with a wry grin. "I'll help you eat it, though."

He smiled for the first time that day. "You have much to learn, Spirit Woman," he murmured. "Watch carefully."

And watch she did, amazed as he gathered some dry twigs and started a fire with a fire drill he'd found back in the village. Drawing his knife, he skinned the rabbit, gutted it, and placed it on a spit over the fire. The sound of the juices dripping into the flames made her stomach growl.

Between them, they ate the whole rabbit and drank half the water.

Shadow Hawk buried the bones, then sat down on the blanket, staring into the darkness. He was home again, but his home was gone. For all he knew, his people had all been killed. His mother, too, might have been killed, he thought bleakly. Perhaps Heart-of-the-Wolf had been wrong. Perhaps she had not survived the battle. Sitting Bull would know. Any survivors would have made their way to his camp, knowing they would find food and shelter there.

He slid a glance at Maggie sitting beside him, saw the uncertainty in her eyes. "Spirit Woman." He murmured her name as he put his arm around her and drew her close. "I am sorry I cannot offer you the same hospitality you gave me." His smile turned bitter as he stared into the darkness again. "The *wasichu* have destroyed my home and everything in it."

"Hawk . . ."

He placed his hand over her mouth, stilling her words.

"We will not talk of it now. Tell me, how is it that you can walk?"

"I'm not sure. I guess the doctors were right. They always said I could walk if I wanted to

257

badly enough. And when I knew you were going, really going, and that I'd never see you again . . . I couldn't let you go." She smiled up at him. "I went to see a play called *The Phantom of the Opera* several years ago. There was a line in one of the songs that said 'wherever you go, let me go, too, that's all I ask of you.' That's how I feel. I want to go wherever you go."

He gazed into Maggie's eyes, not understanding why she hadn't been able to walk before, knowing only that he loved her, that they were destined to be together. Perhaps it had been the Spirit of the Cave that had put strength in her legs. Surely the power of the cave had remained dormant until she was there beside him, her hand in his.

Gently, he drew her down on the blanket, wondering what it all meant as he covered the two of them with her jacket. He had nothing now. His lodge was gone, his horses were gone. He felt all the old hatred for the whites rise within him as he thought of his village, remembering the day the whites had attacked, the screams of the women and children, the cries of the wounded, the scent of blood that had filled the air. . . .

Maggie snuggled against Hawk, sensing that he needed comfort, that he was grieving for his people.

"Hawk, I know where your people can go, where they'll be safe until all the battles are over."

"You think there is such a place?"

"Yes. Canada! Sitting Bull will take his people there after the Battle of the Little Big Horn.

Hawk, if you take your people there now, no one will harm them."

Hope. He felt it for the first time, a small ray of hope flickering to life.

"Mag-gie, I know now why the Spirit of the Cave did not strike you down. You have found a way to save what is left of my people."

"Strike me down? What do you mean?"

"Only holy men can enter the Sacred Cave. The *wasichu* that you saw there died when he entered the cave."

"I thought you had killed him."

Shadow Hawk shook his head. "No. The Spirit of the Cave struck him down."

Maggie shivered. *The Spirit of the Cave.* Thinking back, she remembered feeling a presence surround her, almost as though a living entity had been touching her, divining her thoughts. And while the Spirit of the Cave had surrounded her, it was as though she and Hawk had shared one heart, one soul. Perhaps that was the answer.

Perhaps love was stronger than whatever spirit possessed the cave; stronger, even, than time.

There was nothing to eat in the morning. After scattering the ashes of their fire, Shadow Hawk collected his gear and they began walking again. Maggie's stomach growled loudly as they made their way across the sun-bleached prairie. Unbidden came memories of Veronica's fluffy pancakes smothered in butter and syrup, rashers of crisp bacon, scrambled eggs, hot coffee. She took a long drink of water, but it did little to appease her appetite.

They'd been walking for about an hour when Hawk grabbed her by the arm and pulled her behind a tangled mass of berry bushes. Dropping to his knees, he drew her down beside him.

"Quiet," he whispered.

"What's wrong? Why . . ." The words died in her throat as she saw them, two dozen mounted Indians emerging from a fold in the seemingly flat prairie.

"Pawnee," Shadow Hawk said, his voice hushed.

Maggie nodded, her heart hammering as she watched the warriors ride by, so close she could smell the sweat of their horses.

The Lakota and the Pawnee were age-old enemies. For generations, they had counted coup on each other, stolen horses from one another. During the wars of the 1870s, the Pawnee had scouted against the Lakota, increasing the animosity between the two tribes.

She shuddered to think what would happen to them if they were discovered by the Pawnee. No doubt Hawk would be tortured and killed and her own fate would be as bad or worse.

Maggie glanced at Hawk. He was tense from head to foot, reminding her of a cat poised to spring at its prey.

Finally, the Pawnee were out of sight. Maggie hadn't realized she was holding her breath until it escaped in a long shuddering sigh.

Shadow Hawk waited another thirty minutes before he deemed it safe to move. He helped Maggie to her feet, slung his bow, quiver, and the waterskin over his left shoulder, the blanket over his right, and began walking again.

Maggie trudged after him, mile after mile, trying to ignore the blister on her right heel, trying to remember to be grateful that she could walk again. Visions of automobiles equipped with plush seats and air conditioning flashed before her eyes as morning gave way to afternoon.

Just when she thought she couldn't go another step, Hawk sank down on his haunches, his eyes studying the ground.

"What is it?" Maggie asked.

"Deer tracks."

She peered over his shoulder, her gaze following the twin sets of tracks that disappeared around a grassy rise.

"Stay here," Shadow Hawk said. Dropping the waterskin and blanket at her feet, he pulled an arrow from his quiver and began following the trail, putting his toes down first, then placing his weight on his heels to cut down on the noise.

Maggie spread the blanket and sat down, closing her eyes against the glare of the sun. If she weren't so hungry, if she'd had a pair of dark glasses and a bottle of suntan lotion, she might have worked on her tan. But all she could think about was how hungry she was.

She never heard a sound, but suddenly Hawk was there beside the blanket. He'd killed a young deer and she watched, fighting down a wave of nausea, as he began to skin the beautiful animal, slitting the belly, removing the entrails.

Unable to watch any longer, she went in search of wood and when she returned, empty-handed save for a few sticks and dried brush, Hawk told her to look for buffalo dung.

Maggie wrinkled her nose with distaste, but eating raw meat seemed the lesser of two evils, though it was all she could do not to gag when she began picking up the hard dried excrement. She found a few handfuls of berries on a nearby bush, and a scattering of greens that looked like cabbage.

The buffalo dung made a cheery fire, and the venison, the first she'd ever eaten, tasted wonderful.

Before he ate, Shadow Hawk held up a piece of meat and then tossed it over his shoulder and she heard him murmur, "Recognize this, Ghost, so that I may become the owner of something good."

It was an offering to the spirit of the deer he'd killed, Maggie thought, remembering that Indians considered all animals to be sacred to one degree or another. Unlike the white man, the Lakota did not kill for fun or for trophies, but for food.

After dinner, Hawk sliced one of the haunches into thin strips and smoked it over the fire.

Later, they sat side by side on the blanket. Maggie rested her head on Hawk's shoulder, content just to be near him. For this moment, she didn't think of what the morrow would bring.

There was only *Hanwi*, the moon, smiling down on them, and Hawk's arm around her, holding her close, whispering *"Mitawicu"* as his lips moved in her hair.

Maggie smiled as she repeated the word in her mind. *Mitawicu*. My wife. For better or worse, she mused, for richer or poorer, this was where she wanted to be.

She lifted her face for his kiss, saw the fire that blazed in his eyes, darker than the night, hotter than the glowing coals.

She nodded, her lips parting as his mouth slanted over hers, all her senses coming to life as he kissed her. She was aware of the hard ground beneath her, of the rough blanket under her back as he quickly removed her clothes, of the warmth of his skin as he covered her body with his own.

She heard the distant cry of a nightbird, smelled the smoke of the fire, felt the silent whisper of the wind as it kissed the grass good night.

She gazed up into her husband's face, his hair falling over her bare breasts like a waterfall of rough silk, his hands gently caressing her, teasing her, arousing her. She lifted her hips to receive him, joy bubbling in her soul as he made her his once again.

Chapter Twenty-six

Bobby smothered a yawn as he climbed the porch steps, then frowned as he saw that the front door was wide open.

Stepping into the parlor, he saw Maggie's wheelchair near the door. Thinking that his employer and Hawk were probably sleeping late, he started to leave the house when he noticed that the lights were on, not only in the front room, but in the kitchen and the hall, as well.

Feeling suddenly apprehensive, he went into the kitchen. Finding it empty, he walked down the hall to Maggie's room. The bedroom door was open. The dress she'd worn the night before made an untidy splash of color on the bed, the closet door was open, a wooden hanger was on the floor.

Leaving the bedroom, Bobby knocked on the bathroom door. "Miss St. Claire?"

No answer.

Hesitantly, he opened the door. The room was empty.

Where the devil had they gone?

He walked through the house again. There was no sign of foul play as far as he could tell. Nothing seemed to be missing.

Perhaps they'd gone for an early morning ride, he thought, though it seemed unlikely that Miss St. Claire would go off and leave the front door wide open and the lights on. But then, she'd been acting strangely for the last two weeks.

He went out to the back pasture where the horses were kept until cold weather set in, thinking that in a couple of weeks he'd have to start hauling feed out to the pasture.

He grunted softly as the two bay geldings trotted toward him, waiting for the chestnut mare to join them. She was a favorite of his, always nuzzling his pocket for treats, lowering her head so he could scratch her ears. But the mare didn't come.

Bobby leaned against the rail. If Hawk had taken Miss St. Claire riding, the chestnut mare would still be here. Unless Miss St. Claire had figured out a way to ride on her own.

Returning to the house, he turned off the lights, fixed himself something to eat, all the white listening for the sound of hoofbeats.

After breakfast, he went down to the barn to feed the chickens and the other animals; then, remembering that the pasture had looked pretty used up, he forked the horses some hay, pulled a dead branch from the creek.

By noon, he was really worried.

Going into the house, he called Veronica, hoping she might know where Miss St. Claire had gone, but Veronica hadn't heard from Maggie and when Bobby hung up, he was more worried than before.

He walked through the house again, trying to ignore what he was afraid was true, what couldn't possibly be true, but he had to know.

Saddling one of the bay geldings, he rode out of the yard, searching for sign the way Hawk had taught him.

He felt a thrill of satisfaction as he found the stallion's tracks, and then frowned. If Maggie was riding the chestnut, why was there only one set of tracks?

Not knowing what else to do, Bobby continued to follow the stallion's tracks. He knew a moment of relief when he cut the chestnut's trail.

A short time later, he found the black stallion and the chestnut mare cropping grass about halfway up the mountain.

Feeling a sudden sense of urgency, Bobby continued up the hill, winding up, up the side of the brush-covered slope until he came to a narrow ledge surrounded by trees.

The Sacred Cave.

He knew what it was though he'd never seen it before.

Dismounting, he walked toward the entrance, stood there peering into the darkness. There was nothing inside that could hurt him, he thought. It was just an ordinary cave, except at night when the moon was full.

Taking a deep breath, Bobby stepped inside, his body tensing even though he knew there was nothing to fear.

The Sacred Cave.

It was quiet, so quiet, as if nothing else existed. He cocked his head toward the entrance, listening to the silence.

Was it his imagination, or was the air inside the cave moving? He had a sudden, horrible feeling that he was no longer alone. He tried to shake it off, tried to tell himself it was just his imagination working overtime, but he could not dispel the notion that there was someone, or something, in the cave with him.

Proud Eagle, you must follow the Hawk.

Bobby spun around, his eyes probing the darkness. "Who's there?"

Follow the Hawk. The words came again, echoing in his mind, frightening in their intensity.

For the first time in his life, Bobby Proud Eagle knew real fear. And yet, who could blame him?

He knew what the words meant. He only hoped he possessed the courage to do what he'd been told.

Chapter Twenty-seven

They'd been traveling for three days and Maggie found herself thinking of all the wonderful modes of transportation that had been invented: buses, trains with luxury cars, airplanes that could get you across country in no time at all, taxi cabs, the silver BMW Frank had driven, her own pickup truck. She'd have settled for the old VW clunker she'd had in college if it meant she wouldn't have to take another step. How had the Indian women done it, walking mile after mile? They'd carried heavy loads on their backs before the arrival of the horse. No wonder they'd died young!

She looked at Hawk, striding along beside her. He never seemed to get tired. Didn't *his* feet hurt? Weren't his legs weary? Except for a fine film of perspiration on his chest, he didn't even appear to be sweating much. But then, he was a warrior, trained from childhood to go long distances on foot without food or water, if necessary, to live off the land.

Shadow Hawk glanced down at Maggie, easily reading the fatigue in her eyes, the faint look of irritation on her face. "What is wrong?"

"Nothing."

"Mag-gie."

"You!" she exclaimed. Coming to a halt, she planted her fists on her hips and glared up at him. "Don't you ever get tired?"

He nodded, confused by her outburst.

"Well, it doesn't show."

"That is why you are angry, because I do not look tired?"

She giggled at the look of amusement on his face, and then began to laugh. "Yes," she admitted between fits of laughter. "I'm mad at you because you never get tired."

Shadow Hawk stared at her for a moment, and then he laughed with her. It felt good to stand beside the woman he loved and laugh out loud.

"We can rest awhile if you like," he said when their outburst subsided.

"I feel better now," Maggie said, grinning up at him.

Shadow Hawk nodded. Taking her hand, he began to walk again, slower now, curbing his long stride to match her shorter one.

It was late afternoon when Hawk came to an abrupt halt.

"What is it?" Maggie asked. She followed his gaze but saw nothing to be alarmed about.

"There," Shadow Hawk said, pointing to a rising cloud of dust. "Riders. Coming our way."

"Pawnee?" Maggie asked.

Shadow Hawk shook his head. "I do not think so." He glanced around, looking for shelter, but there was none to be had. For miles, there was only the flat prairie.

He stared toward the cloud of dust. "*Wasichu*," he muttered. There were two of them, both heavily armed, both leading pack mules carrying picks and shovels.

He was reaching for his bow when a chunk of dirt exploded at his feet and the sound of gunfire flatted across the stillness of the plains.

"Don't try it, red stick."

The warning came from a heavily bearded man wearing travel-stained twill pants, a buckskin shirt, and a beaver hat.

But it was the rifle in his hands that held Shadow Hawk's attention. Wordlessly, Shadow Hawk lowered his arm to his side and then stood beside Maggie, his eyes wary as he watched the two white men.

"That's better," the bearded man said. He gestured at Maggie with the barrel of his rifle. "You white?"

"Yes."

"Thought so. Never seen no Injuns with curly hair."

"Good day to you, then," Maggie said, her gaze moving from the face of the black-bearded man to that of his silent companion.

"Not so fast, girlie," Black Beard said. "What are you two doing out here?"

"Minding our own business."

"Maybe your business is my business."

"I doubt it."

The bearded man looked at Shadow Hawk thoughtfully. "He Sioux?"

"Yes," Maggie said. "Why?"

The man leaned forward in the saddle, his deep-set brown eyes glittering with a strange light. "I heard tell there was gold in the Black Hills."

"So?"

"So the Hills are Sioux country," Black Beard exclaimed, a note of triumph in his voice. "And if there's gold hereabouts, he'd know where to find it."

"We don't know about any gold."

"And you'd tell us if you did?"

Maggie stared up at the man, wondering what to say. There was gold in the Black Hills, all right, but it wouldn't be discovered for another four or five years.

"Well, girlie, speak up."

"I don't know of any place where you could find gold," Maggie answered, boldly meeting his gaze. "And if I did, I wouldn't tell you."

The bearded man grunted. "You shackin' up with this red stick?"

"He's my husband."

"Man and wife. Well, ain't that cozy. Ask him where the gold is."

Maggie spoke to Hawk in Lakota, pretending to ask about the gold, when in reality she asked him what they were going to do.

"Tell them the gold is in the Sacred Cave."

The cave, of course! Pleased at her husband's

271

cleverness, Maggie relayed Hawk's words.

"A cave? I never heard of finding no gold in a cave."

"That's where he says it is."

The man rubbed his beard with his free hand, his eyes narrowed suspiciously. "You seen it?"

"No."

Black Beard contemplated Hawk for several minutes and then nodded, as though he'd made a decision. "Tell your red stick to drop his weapons. Ferdie, you tie him up. I think we'll just take them with us to make sure he's tellin' the truth."

Ferdie grinned as he removed a coil of rope from his saddlehorn and vaulted to the ground. He was tall and thin, with shaggy brown hair and tobacco-stained teeth. Maggie felt a chill as his hooded green eyes raked her from head to foot and she knew he wasn't thinking about gold.

A muscle twitched in Shadow Hawk's cheek as he saw the leer in Ferdie's pale green eyes. Unconsciously, he tightened his hold on the bow.

"Later, Ferd," Black Beard promised.

Maggie took a step backward as Ferdie walked in front of her to get to Hawk. It had not occurred to her that they might rape her. They were white men, after all. Foolish as it seemed now, she had thought they might be of help.

Ferdie was standing in front of Hawk now. Maggie's mind was racing as she reviewed and rejected a dozen ways to help Hawk, but in the end, Hawk didn't need any help.

Moving as swiftly as a striking snake, he drove the end of the bow into Ferdie's groin; then, as the man doubled over, gasping in pain, Shadow Hawk grabbed Ferdie by the shoulders and pushed him backward so that he crashed into his partner's horse. The animal reared, one iron-shod hoof striking Ferdie across the back of the head.

Muttering a curse, the bearded man toppled out of the saddle.

The Lakota war cry rose in the air as Shadow Hawk sprang forward. Grabbing the rifle that the bearded man had dropped, he jacked a round into the breech and fired a single shot into the man's chest.

Maggie stared in horror at the bright red stain that spread over the man's shirt, felt the vomit rise in her throat as a thin trickle of blood oozed from the corner of his mouth.

"Is he dead?" It was a silly question, she thought. No one could live with a hole like that in his chest.

"Yes. And the other one, too."

Slowly, Maggie looked over her shoulder. Ferdie lay face down on the ground, the back of his head covered with blood.

"I'm going to be sick," she murmured, and falling to her knees, she began to vomit.

Hawk was instantly beside her, his arm around her shoulders, supporting her. She retched until there was nothing left.

She closed her eyes, felt Hawk's hand in her hair, heard his voice speaking her name. He left her side for a few moments and when he returned, he wiped her face with a damp cloth, offered her a drink from a canteen that had obviously belonged to one of the dead men.

"I can't." Repulsed by the thought of drinking from the canteen of a dead man, she pushed it away.

Understanding how she felt, Shadow Hawk brought her the waterskin, held it while she rinsed her mouth, then took a drink.

"Mag-gie?"

"I'm all right now," she assured him, but it was a lie. He drew her into his arms as she began to shake violently. It was just a case of nerves, she thought, there was nothing more to fear. But she couldn't stop shaking. It could just as easily have been Hawk lying there with his life's blood staining the ground. And she would have been at the mercy of those men. . . . She realized that was why he had killed the bearded man, why he would have killed the other one, too, if necessary. Alone, he might have been able to make a run for it, to find a place to hide. But she was a burden to him.

Abruptly, she stared up into his face, her own going deathly pale. He had killed a man because of her. Killed him quickly, mercilessly. She had seen his face when he fired the rifle, his expression fiercely exultant, his dark eyes gleaming with a feral light as he shed the blood of his enemy. But there was no trace of blood lust in his eyes now, only love and concern.

She burrowed deeper into Hawk's embrace, seeking the warmth of his body to chase away the cold, the strength of his arms to rout her fear.

"You need not be afraid, Mag-gie," Shadow

Hawk vowed. "No one will harm you so long as I live."

She nodded, touched by the depth of emotion in his words, knowing he would die to protect her, yet unable to forget what would have befallen her if anything had happened to Hawk. She glanced at the bodies of the two dead men, feeling suddenly glad they were dead, and guilty for feeling that way.

"You . . . you won't scalp them?"

"No."

"But you would if I wasn't here?"

Shadow Hawk considered lying to her, but it was best she knew the truth. There must be no lies between them.

"Yes," he admitted. "I would have taken their scalps. Among my people, it is an honorable thing to take the scalp of an enemy."

Maggie nodded, remembering the night he had danced for her and Veronica out in the yard. He had told her then how a man's sisters or cousins carried his scalp stick while he danced. It was a matter of pride, of honor, to boast of killing one's enemy and taking his scalp. But it sickened her just the same.

She had nightmares that night, horrible dreams peopled with men who were dead. Men who looked like Ferdie and Black Beard. And she was back in her wheelchair, helpless to fight them. She screamed for Hawk, screamed her pain and fear, but he was out of reach, deep in the bowels of the Sacred Cave. . . .

"Mag-gie!" Shadow Hawk shook her again,

frightened by her screams, the paleness of her cheeks. "Mag-gie!"

"Hawk! Oh, Hawk." She threw her arms around his neck, clinging to him with all her might.

He held her close, whispering to her that he loved her, that there was nothing to fear. But deep inside he was afraid for her. She had told him what awaited his people, nothing but war and living death on the reservation. If he were killed in battle, she would be left alone, with no way to return to her own time, her own people.

"Mag-gie, I will take you back to the cave in the morning."

"What?"

"I think you must go back. You do not belong here."

He was going to take her home. She had never thought of her house in the Dakotas as home. It had only been a place to hide from the world. But it would be different now, with Hawk there to share it with her.

"We'll be happy there, I promise," she said, smiling up at him.

"I cannot go."

"What?"

"I cannot go. I must go to Sitting Bull and learn the whereabouts of my people, and then I will take them to Canada. But first I will take you back to the cave."

"I won't go back without you."

"Mag-gie, I am only thinking of you," he argued. "You know what lies ahead for my people. If we cannot make it to the Land of the Grandmother, if anything happens to me on the way, you will not be able to return to your own time. Are you prepared to spend the rest of your life here?"

It was a sobering thought. Much as she hated to think about it, Hawk could be killed. They'd already had two close calls. What would she do if something happened to him? Where would she go?

But then she looked into Hawk's face and knew she couldn't leave him. Even if she knew he would be taken from her in a day or a week, she would not give up whatever time they might have together. Better to live in a hide lodge, or in poverty on the reservation, than go back home and spend a lifetime without him.

"I'm staying here," she said. "Nothing you can say will change my mind."

Chapter Twenty-eight

Four days later, Maggie wasn't sure she'd made the right decision. Sitting on a low rise, she gazed down at the Indian lodges spread along the banks of a wide, slow-moving river.

Indians. Nothing but Indians as far as the eye could see. She had been fascinated with Indians for as long as she could remember, but she'd never seen so many at one time, in one place. She felt as if she were about to step into one of her own romance novels. *She felt like a white rose in a field of red carnations.* The line from one of her books whispered in the back of her mind.

She looked at Hawk, sitting on Black Beard's horse, saw the eager anticipation in his eyes.

"Ready?" he asked.

Maggie nodded, her heart pounding with trepidation, fear, excitement, and dread.

"Do not be afraid, Mag-gie. My people will not harm you."

"They won't like me, either."

"Not at first, perhaps. But it is only because you are a stranger to them." He smiled reassuringly. "When I tell them you are a Spirit Woman, they will honor you with gifts."

"Do you think they'll believe you?"

"My people live close to the gods. We have often been visited by spirits in times of need or trouble."

He took her hand in his and she felt his strength flow into her, calming her troubled heart. "Think of it as research," he remarked, and then they were riding down the hill.

Men, women, and children crowded around them as they entered the village. The Lakota were a comely people, Maggie thought as she gazed into hundreds of upturned faces. Most of the men were tall and handsome, though none were as handsome as Hawk. The women, too, were tall and attractive. They wore long doeskin tunics decorated with fringe and beads. And the children. They stared at her, their luminous black eyes filled with curiosity as they reached out to touch her.

She saw Sitting Bull striding toward them and the reality of where she was suddenly stuck her anew. This man was a legend. Though he was not a chief, his power over his people was strong and unfailing.

The crowd parted to let him through and she watched, wide-eyed, as Hawk swung down from his horse and embraced Sitting Bull. They spoke together for a time, then Hawk lifted Maggie from her horse and introduced her to the medicine man.

Flustered, Maggie muttered something about being pleased to meet him, then Sitting Bull took them to a vacant lodge and told them to make themselves at home. Maggie stood in the center of the tipi, too stunned to speak. She had met Sitting Bull, a man who had been dead for fifty years when she'd been born.

Shaking her head, she glanced around the lodge. It was just as she had expected, a tilted cone covered with buffalo hides, steeper up the back than the front, with the door facing east to greet the rising sun. The ground was covered with hides, there was a buffalo robe bed in the rear. Two willow-rod backrests, both covered with furs, flanked the fire pit.

From her research, she knew that the Indians considered the tipi a temple as well as a home. The floor of the lodge represented Mother Earth who gave life, the walls of the lodge were the sky, and the poles were a trail between the earth and the spirit world linking the occupants to *Wakán Tanka*.

Directly behind the firepit was a little section of bare earth which served as an altar on which was burned sweet grass, cedar, or sage in the belief that the smoke would carry their prayers to the Great Spirit. Some people believed that if you stepped over the altar, it would cause a storm.

Once, she had read the rules of tipi etiquette. She hoped she'd be able to remember them now.

She recalled that if the door flap was open, it meant company was welcome. Two sticks crossed over the door meant the owners were away. Men usually sat on the north side of the lodge, women on the south. On entering a tipi, a man went to the right to his place, a woman went to the left. Passing between the host and the fire was to be avoided.

After a while, she realized Hawk was watching her, his eyes narrowed thoughtfully. "What is it?" she asked.

"I was wondering what you were thinking."

"Nothing, really. I've written so many books about Indians, I'm glad to see that a real lodge looks pretty much as I described it."

Shadow Hawk glanced at the buffalo robe beds, the stack of firewood near the entrance, the willow backrests, and remembered the spaciousness of Maggie's home, the soft mattress on her bed, the refrigerator that kept her food fresh, the machines that washed and dried her clothes, the truck that went faster than any horse ever could.

How could she be happy here, bathing in a cold river when she was accustomed to soaking in a tub filled with scented bubbles? How long would she be happy to cook over a campfire when she knew the ease and convenience of a microwave oven? Would she be able to adjust to making her own clothing, her own moccasins?

If *he* already missed some of the miraculous inventions of the white man, wouldn't it be worse for her, when she'd been accustomed to them her whole life?

281

"We will rest here a few days. Will you be all right?"

Smiling, she walked toward him. "I'm always all right when I'm with you."

"Mag-gie." He swept her into his arms, knowing he would have regretted it the rest of his life if he had left her behind, yet still afraid of what the future held.

Shadow Hawk sat cross-legged, his hands resting on his knees, while Sitting Bull filled his pipe, offering it to the earth and the sky and to the four directions before passing it to his guest.

Shadow Hawk accepted the pipe reverently, puffed it several times, then passed it back to Sitting Bull.

As was customary, they did not speak until the tobacco was gone. Sitting Bull put the pipe aside, then turned to face his guest. "So, how can I help you?"

"I have come to ask the whereabouts of my people."

"Ah, yes. I received word of the battle only a few days ago. Some of my warriors scouted the area. They think the survivors have been taken to Fort Laramie."

"Do you know if my mother is alive?"

Sitting Bull shook his head. "I cannot say. The tracks show that many women were taken. Perhaps she is among them."

"Were all the men killed?"

"I cannot say. None have come here, but if any are still alive, they may have followed their women to the Fort."

Shadow Hawk nodded. He had to believe his mother was still alive, that he would be able to get the survivors away from the fort and guide them to Canada.

"Will you be leaving soon?"

"Tomorrow."

"I thought as much. My woman will provide you with provisions for your journey."

After thanking Sitting Bull for his help, Shadow Hawk returned to the lodge he shared with Maggie. She was standing in the doorway, waiting for him.

"Did he have any news of your people?" she asked, following him into the lodge.

"Yes. He said the survivors were taken to Fort Laramie. We will leave tomorrow."

It was raining in the morning, a strong steady rain that gave no indication of letting up any time soon.

With a sigh of discouragement, Shadow Hawk let the lodge flap fall into place. Alone, he would have ridden out of the village, but he could not ask Maggie to spend the day riding in the rain.

Restless, he paced the lodge, the need to find his people growing ever stronger within him. They would have to start their journey north soon, before winter shrouded the plains in snow, he thought, and then wondered if perhaps they should wait for spring. Gold would not be discovered in the Black Hills for several years. His people would have plenty of time to make their way to safety, and it would be easier to make the journey when the grass was new and the weather was warm and clear.

He glanced at Maggie, wondering if she was strong enough to endure the hardships of such a long trek, wondering if she would come to regret her decision to stay with him.

It was still raining the following day.

Maggie watched Hawk pace the floor until she thought she'd scream, and then, gently but firmly, she took him by the hand and drew him down on the buffalo robes, her hands lightly stoking his flat belly as she bent to kiss him.

"You've been avoiding me," she accused, nipping at his shoulder.

"Have I?"

"Yes. And I don't like it." She bit his ear lobe, then laved it with her tongue.

"Forgive me," he said, his voice growing deep and husky as her hands slid under his clout.

"I think I'll have to punish you first," she said.

He nuzzled her breasts as his hands caressed her thighs. "I'm ready," he said in mock horror. "Do your worst."

She laughed softly as she straddled his hips, her hands wandering over his shoulders and chest, then drifting down to remove his clout. She saw the heat flare in his eyes as she began to undress and then she lowered herself over him, her breasts crushed against his chest as she kissed him deeply, passionately.

He let her take control and she loved it. With her lips and her tongue she caressed him, adoring him with her hands, thrilling to the way he responded to her touch. His eyes glowed with a lambent flame, his breath grew shallow, his body rigid as she teased and tormented him, refusing to give him that which he sought until, with one deft move, he rolled on top of her, his lips claiming hers even as their bodies merged.

Ecstasy, Maggie thought, nothing but ecstasy in his touch. She gazed into his eyes, her hips arching upward as he surged within her. She drew him close, his name on her lips as she reached for that one elusive moment that felt like death and life all rolled into one.

There should have been fireworks, she thought, and brightly colored lights and sky-rockets. Instead, there was only the sound of the rain and the quick tattoo of her heart pounding in her ears. And then Hawk was whispering in her ear, telling her he loved her, as his life poured into her, filling her with warmth and peace.

They left Sitting Bull's village the following day. They would travel more comfortably now. Sitting Bull had given them provisions to last until they reached Fort Laramie, warm clothes and robes to turn away the cold. Maggie felt strange in her Indian garb, though she had to admit the dress was comfortable and the knee-high moccasins, lined with fur, were warmer than her boots. Her jeans, shirt, and boots were rolled up in one of the packs.

The air smelled clean and fresh after the rain, the sky was blue enough to swim in. It was wonderful to ride a horse again. When she'd been a little girl, it had been one of her dreams to own a horse. But her father argued that it was too expensive. *It's not buying the horse, you know, it's the upkeep*, he'd told her time and again. When she began making money with her writing, the first thing she'd bought was a new car, the second thing had been a horse.

She slid a glance at the man riding beside her. He was another dream come true, a warrior of her own. She knew now she would never have been happy with Frank, or any other contemporary man. They were all too ordinary, too tame. Without being aware of it, she'd been yearning for a real hero, a man who would fight for her, a man who had only to look at her to make her heart flame and her pulse race.

She'd have her happy-ever-after ending after all, she thought with a smile. They'd go to Fort Laramie, find Hawk's people, and take them to Canada where they'd be safe from the Army.

Shadow Hawk raised one black brow as he met her gaze. "Why are you smiling like that?"

"I've just written the end of the story," she replied, reaching over to squeeze his hand. "And they lived happily ever after."

"Who did?"

"We did, silly. Come on, I'll race you to that bluff."

Chapter Twenty-nine

Maggie groaned softly and burrowed deeper under the buffalo robe as Hawk shook her shoulder.

"Just another minute," she murmured, trying to get back to sleep, but he was shaking her again and she came suddenly awake as she heard the sound of hoofbeats, her heart pounding with dread at the thought that the Pawnee were coming.

She sat up, expecting to be scalped at any moment, then stared, open-mouthed, as a United States Cavalry patrol surrounded them. It was like something out of a B Western, she mused, the soldiers all dressed in sweat-stained Army blue, the guidon fluttering in the early morning breeze, the command "Halt!" being repeated down the line.

287

But this wasn't a movie and the rifles leveled at Hawk weren't stage props.

"Morning, ma'am." The lieutenant who addressed her was in his mid-thirties. He had dark blond hair, brown eyes, and a sweeping moustache reminiscent of the kind favored by General George Armstrong Custer.

"Good morning," Maggie replied, and then frowned as two troopers dismounted and walked purposefully toward Hawk. "See here," she said as they bound Hawk's hands behind his back, "what do you think you're doing?"

"My job," the lieutenant replied curtly. "We're rounding up hostiles and retrieving white captives like yourself, ma'am."

Maggie stared up at him, too surprised to speak. They thought she was Hawk's prisoner!

"I'm not his captive," Maggie said. Rising, she smoothed the wrinkles from her doeskin dress and combed her fingers through her hair. "He's my husband."

"That's all over now," the lieutenant assured her. "You've nothing to be afraid of."

"But . . ."

"We're in a bit of a hurry, if you don't mind, ma'am," the lieutenant said. "We've been on patrol for over two weeks. Lukovich, get the lady's horse. Daniels, drop a rope around that buck and bring him along." The lieutenant glanced down at Maggie. "Does that Injun speak English?"

She was about to say that he did when she saw Hawk shake his head imperceptibly. "No," she replied, wondering why Hawk didn't speak for himself.

"Too bad. Well, maybe one of the scouts can talk to him, find out where Sitting Bull's hiding out."

Maggie's protests fell on deaf ears as Private Lukovich led her horse forward.. She sent a helpless glance in Hawk's direction, frowning as a dark-haired trooper dropped a rope around Hawk's neck and snugged it tight, then resumed his place at the rear of the column.

There was nothing for Maggie to do but fall in line beside the lieutenant, who introduced himself as Lieutenant Jeffrey Collins. He and his men were garrisoned at Fort Laramie, he said, and eager to get back.

Maggie looked at Hawk. At least they were heading in the right direction.

They rode for several hours, pausing occasionally to rest the horses. Maggie's neck was sore from looking over her shoulder to see how Hawk was doing. He walked doggedly onward, his head high, his face impassive. Not once did he meet her eyes or look in her direction. When the column stopped to rest the horses, he dropped down on his haunches, refusing the water he was offered.

Once, when Maggie started to go to him, the lieutenant barred her way. "Best leave him alone, ma'am."

"I'm going to take him a drink," she replied firmly.

"No, ma'am."

"He's my husband. You have no right to keep me from him."

"Listen, Miss . . ."

"St. Claire."

"Miss St. Claire, I wouldn't tell anyone you're married to an Injun if you want to be accepted at the fort. Anyway, our government doesn't recognize marriages performed by heathens."

"But . . ." Maggie bit down on her lower lip. She couldn't very well tell the lieutenant she'd been married by a minister licensed by the state of South Dakota. For one thing, South Dakota hadn't been a state in 1872, and in the second place, she didn't know if a marriage between an Indian and a white woman would have been considered legal.

Frustrated, she sank down on the ground and stared at Hawk, willing him to look at her.

Shadow Hawk clenched and unclenched his fists in an effort to loosen his bonds and relieve the pressure on his wrists. He could feel Maggie watching him, hear her heart calling out to him, but he refused to meet her eyes. He knew that white women who took up with Indian men were scorned by their own kind. He had heard stories of captive white women who had been returned to their homes only to run back to their Indian captors rather than endure the ridicule and contempt of their own people. It would be better for Maggie if she had nothing more to do with him, at least for now.

Knowing that the soldier called Daniels would like nothing better than to drag him through the dirt, Shadow Hawk rose quickly to his feet as

Daniels gave a hard jerk on the rope around his neck. Staring at a distant point, he began to follow in the wake of the trooper's horse, staying to one side of the animal as much as possible to avoid the dust kicked up by the horse's hooves.

They were going to Fort Laramie. Once there, he would devise a way to find Maggie and escape.

In the days that followed, his anger at being a prisoner was swallowed up by his rising jealousy over the amount of time Lieutenant Collins spent with Maggie. The man was ever at her side, pointing out landmarks, entertaining her with tales of his bravery in battle, of his hopes of being promoted in rank. He talked of his home in the East, of his parents and his brothers and sisters.

Shadow Hawk watched Maggie carefully, his rage building each time she spoke to the *wasichu*, smiled at him, laughed at something he said. Jealousy clawed at his insides, sharper than the blade of a knife, more consuming than a prairie fire. Had she decided she would be better off with the paleface lieutenant than with a captive Lakota warrior? She had often remarked on the age difference between them, he thought angrily. Perhaps she had decided she'd rather have a man closer to her own age, a man of her own race.

He struggled to put his doubts and fears out of his mind, but it was impossible and by the time they reached the fort, he was certain that he had lost her, that she had decided she would be better off with Lieutenant Collins than with a homeless Indian. The lieutenant had bragged of the fine future that awaited him, while Hawk had nothing to offer her.

Maggie felt a deep sense of relief when they rode into Fort Laramie. She had endured the lieutenant's boasting, accepted his flowery compliments, in the hopes that he might be of some help in freeing Hawk when they arrived at the fort.

Dismounting, she watched as Hawk was led away, wondering if she'd ever see him again.

The lieutenant escorted her to the office of the post commander, promising to see her later that evening.

Maggie smiled noncommittally; then, drawing a deep breath, she stepped into the general's office.

For the next twenty-five minutes, she tried to convince the general that she had not been kidnapped, that she had freely and willingly become Hawk's wife. And when that failed, she broke down and begged to be allowed to see him.

Adamantly, General Sully shook his head. "You'll feel better in a few days, Miss St. Claire," he assured her in a fatherly tone. "Many women are reluctant to return to their own kind after being held captive, but please believe me when I say you have nothing to fear. We won't let this savage get his hands on you again, and I'm quite confident you'll feel more like your old self once you get out of those clothes and have a chance to, ah, get cleaned up."

There was nothing to do but agree. The general's orderly escorted her to an empty cabin on

Officers' Row and a few minutes later, a plump, gray-haired woman bustled inside. Introducing herself as Maud McKenzie, the subtler's wife, she quickly looked Maggie up and down and then hurried out again, promising to return with clean clothes, soap, towels, hot water, a brush, and pins for her hair.

An hour later, Maggie stood in front of a floor-length mirror, staring at her reflection. She had hidden her jeans under the mattress, knowing she'd never be able to explain what a zipper was should anyone inquire. Her shirt, jacket, and boots weren't that different from the clothes of the day.

Maggie grinned at her image in the mirror. She looked as if she'd just stepped out of the pages of one of her own romance novels. Maud McKenzie had brought her a cream-colored shirtwaist with long sleeves, a billowing burgundy skirt, and the required undergarments consisting of three starched petticoats, a cotton chemise, a corset, lace-trimmed drawers, and black cotton stockings. There were also a pair of black high-button shoes.

Maggie had thanked Mrs. McKenzie effusively though she'd had no intention of wearing the corset or drawers, preferring to wear her own bra and panties which she had washed and dried in front of the fire while she bathed and cleaned her hair. Looking at the high-button shoes, she decided her boots would do just fine.

She gazed out the window while she brushed her hair. Imagine, she was here in Fort Laramie, a place she had read about, written about.

It was here in April of 1868 that the government signed a treaty with the Brule and Oglala Sioux, giving the Indians all of what was now South Dakota west of the Missouri River as a reservation. It also gave them hunting rights in the territory north of the North Platte River and east of the Bighorn Mountains as unceded Indian lands.

Maggie shook her head. The government had broken the Laramie Treaty of '68 just as they'd broken every other treaty they'd ever made.

According to history, George Armstrong Custer would lead an expedition into the Black Hills to investigate reports of gold in the Black Hills, which he would confirm. At first, the Army would try to keep the resulting rush of prospectors out of the area, even arresting some of them. Other groups would be attacked by Indians for violating the Treaty of '68. The following spring, Colonel Dodge would set out from Fort Laramie to evaluate the gold deposits.

Meanwhile, the government would try to buy the Black Hills from the Sioux. Some of the Indians, like Chief Spotted Tail, would be willing to sell, but the government would refuse to meet his price, while other chiefs, including Sitting Bull, would adamantly refuse to sell so much as a foot of ground at any price. He warned the whites to stay out of the Hills. By then, the Army would have given up trying to keep the prospectors out of the *Paha Sapa* and miners would swarm into the hills.

Ignoring the existing treaties, the government would decide to force the wild Sioux onto their reservations. The Custer massacre, only four years into the future, would be the inevitable result.

Maggie laid her hairbrush aside. She was in a curious position, knowing what was to happen before it happened, knowing the outcome of battles. She wondered if she should tell General Sully to warn Custer to stay out of the Black Hills, and then wondered if it would do any good. The general would never believe she'd come here from the future. Likely they'd think her insane and lock her up.

But then, maybe it wasn't possible to change history at all. Maybe no matter what she did or said wouldn't make any difference because, in reality, she didn't even exist yet!

She was wondering what to do next when there was a knock at the door. It was Lieutenant Collins, looking as fresh as a daisy in a clean uniform and boots that practically sparkled.

"I've come to take you to dinner," he said, gallantly offering her his arm. "We've been invited to dine with the General and Mrs. Sully."

Dinner was an awkward affair. There were three other couples at the table besides the general and his wife. During the course of the meal, the men questioned her about the whereabouts of Hawk's camp while the ladies stared at her, obviously dying to ask her what it had been like to live with a savage but too polite to ask such intimate questions at the dinner table.

Following dinner, the men went into the general's study for brandy and cigars, while Mrs. Sully served sherry to the ladies. Pleading that she needed to use the facilities, Maggie hurried outside and practically ran back to her cabin.

Inside, she closed the door and sank down on a chair. Her behavior had been rude in the extreme, but she just couldn't face those women. Not now.

She stared out the parlor window, wondering where her husband was.

Shadow Hawk faced his captors defiantly, refusing to answer the interpreter's questions, refusing to tell them where they could find Sitting Bull's camp.

"Ask him again." The order came from a dark-haired major named Neville. It was obvious from the expression in his close-set brown eyes that he had no regard for Indians, and even less for human life. "And, Snider, ask him a little harder this time."

Shadow Hawk braced himself for the blow he saw coming, doubling over as Snider drove a fist the size of a cannon ball into his belly. The man, Snider, stood over six feet tall. He had legs the size of tree trunks and arms like steel. And he was very good at what he did, Shadow Hawk thought dully. Time and again the corporal's knotted fists connected with Shadow Hawk's flesh, driving deep into his back, his belly, his face.

Panting heavily, Shadow Hawk heard the mocking voice of the Pawnee interpreter ask him for Sitting Bull's whereabouts again. And again he shook his head, refusing to answer.

"He isn't gonna tell us anything," Snider remarked, rubbing his bruised knuckles. He glared at Hawk through narrowed ice-blue eyes. "You'd best tell the general he's buttin' his head against a stone wall."

"Corporal, why don't you just shut the hell up and hit him again? And this time, put a little muscle behind it."

The force of Snider's blow doubled the prisoner in half.

Teeth clenched against the pain, Shadow Hawk swallowed the bitter bile that rose in his throat, thinking he'd choke on his own vomit before he'd tell the major what he wanted to know.

After another fifteen minutes, Neville turned on his heel and left the stockade. The Pawnee interpreter trailed after him. Snider drove his knee into the prisoner's groin, just for the hell of it, then followed the major outside.

Alone, Shadow Hawk let out a low groan as pain spiraled through him. Dropping to the floor, he closed his eyes, waiting for the worst of the pain to pass.

Snider was very thorough, he thought bleakly. He hurt all over. His left eye was swollen shut, his lower lip was split, he thought his nose might be broken. But the worst pain was in his left side. Each labored breath sent fresh waves of agony through him and he guessed at least one of his ribs was broken.

Wearily, he leaned against the rough wooden wall.

"Spirit Woman," he murmured, and then everything went black.

Chapter Thirty

Maggie walked slowly around the parade ground, careful to keep her long billowing skirt out of the dirt. She had never envied pioneer women the amount of clothing they were required to wear and she dearly wished she had the nerve to don her jeans and shirt, but she'd given the good ladies at the fort enough to talk about. Seeing her attired in anything as scandalous as pants would likely set tongues to wagging all over again. By now, everyone knew she had left the general's house without so much as a fare thee well.

Leaving the general's house the night before had been rude. She knew it, and Lieutenant Collins had pointed it out to her rather bluntly earlier in the day. Swallowing her pride and her rebellion, Maggie had gone to Mrs. Sully and apologized profusely. Mrs. Sully had stared at her through cold gray eyes for several moments before accepting Maggie's apology.

But being rude was the least of her worries. She was frantic to know Hawk's whereabouts, but there was no one she could ask. Lieutenant Collins was in conference with the general and his officers and she had a sneaky feeling that Collins wouldn't tell her where to find Hawk even if he knew, which he surely did.

She wiped the perspiration from her forehead with the back of her hand. Where was Hawk?

She paused in mid-stride. Closing her eyes, she put everything from her mind but the face of her husband, wordlessly repeating his name over and over again. And it came to her then with cold clarity that Hawk was in trouble, in pain. In danger. She felt it deep within her and it filled her with a terrible sense of dread, of helplessness.

"Miss St. Claire, are you all right?"

"What?" She opened her eyes to find Lieutenant Collins standing at her elbow, his brow creased with worry. "Oh, yes, I'm fine. Just a bit warm, you know?" she said with a tight smile.

"You shouldn't be out here in the heat of the day," he admonished, taking her arm and guiding her toward a shady spot. "I . . . that is, I was wondering what your plans are. For the future, I mean?"

"Plans?" She stared past the lieutenant at the Lakota lodges visible outside the Fort. She wondered if any of the Lakota knew Hawk, if they would help her free him from the fort. It was a slim hope, she thought. The Indians she'd seen looked defeated, without hope, without the will to fight for themselves, let alone anyone else.

"Will you be staying on at the fort?" Collins prodded.

"I don't know." She stared up at him blankly. How could she make plans for the future when Hawk was in trouble?

"You'd be more than welcome. Women are scarce on the frontier."

"Yes, I've noticed. Two men proposed to me while I was walking."

"That's because you're so pretty," Collins said soberly. "If you were ugly, they'd have waited a week or two. Employment agencies back east often send young girls out west to work as domestics for the officers' wives. Captain Ayres' wife asked one of the agencies to send out the ugliest girl they could find in hopes of keeping the girl at work longer than a month before she up and married."

Maggie grinned. "You're making that up."

"No, it's quite true. Most men would rather have a wife waiting for them at home, even a homely one, than have to, uh . . ." His voice trailed off and he grew red around the ears.

"Satisfy their needs at the local hog ranch?" Maggie asked, and then could have bit her tongue at the look of shock that passed over the lieutenant's face.

"How do you know of such places?" he exclaimed.

"I . . ." Maggie shrugged. "I heard about a place in Texas near Fort Griffin called The Flat where men could buy whiskey and . . . things, and I just assumed there were such places wherever there were a lot of unmarried men."

"It isn't right for a decent woman to know about such goings-on," Collins said gruffly. "Come along, I'll walk you back to your cabin."

Maggie walked placidly beside him, thinking how shocked Lieutenant Jeffrey Collins would be if he found himself plunked down in the middle of downtown Las Vegas along about midnight on any given holiday. What had gone on at Lotte Deno's hog ranch in Texas during the Civil War would no doubt seem tame in comparison to the street walkers, gambling halls, bright lights, and nude shows.

Upon reaching her cabin, she pleaded a headache, bid the lieutenant good day after promising to go buggy riding with him the following afternoon.

She ate dinner alone in her cabin, and then sat at the window, staring out into the darkness, praying for a way to find her husband.

Shadow Hawk lurched to his feet at the sound of approaching footsteps. Backing against the far wall of his prison, he stared at the door, his stomach knotting with dread as he heard Snider's voice.

"I don't think the general would approve your methods, major."

"Well, then, we won't tell him, will we, corporal?" Neville retorted, and Shadow Hawk heard the thinly veiled threat in the major's voice.

Moments later, Neville unlocked the door and stepped inside, followed by Snider and the

Pawnee interpreter known as Bear Tracker.

"Ask him," Neville said curtly, and the Pawnee put the question to Shadow Hawk. "Where is Sitting Bull?"

Shadow Hawk shook his head, his gaze riveted on the long black whip loosely coiled in Snider's meaty fist.

"Tell him I'm only going to ask him one more time," Neville said. "Tell him if he doesn't answer, I'll have the skin flayed from his back."

The thought of seeing his enemy hurt and humiliated brought a smile to the Pawnee's face. In rapid Lakota, he told Shadow Hawk what the major had said.

"But know this," Bear Tracker added, still speaking Lakota, "even if you tell me what the white man wants to know, I will lie and say you refuse to answer, just so I may stand and watch them whip you like a dog."

Shadow Hawk glared at the Pawnee for a long moment and then spit in his face.

With a cry of rage, Bear Tracker drew his knife and lunged forward, the blade driving toward Shadow Hawk's belly.

Shadow Hawk sucked in a deep breath, let it out in a sigh of relief as Snider grabbed the Pawnee by the back of the neck and lifted him off the floor.

"Maybe later," Snider said with an easy grin. "Right now, he's mine."

"Bear Tracker, put that knife away," the major ordered brusquely. He glanced at the prisoner, then stared hard at the Pawnee. "What did you say to him?"

"Only that I would enjoy seeing him whipped like a dog."

Neville grunted. The age-old hatred between the two tribes was well known and was, in fact, one of the reasons the Pawnee made such good scouts for the Army. They were only too happy to see their old enemies defeated. "Get on with it, Snider."

Shadow Hawk watched in morbid fascination as Snider uncoiled the whip, shaking it out so that it slithered over the hard wooden floor like a living thing. His mouth went dry, his palms began to sweat, perspiration broke out across his forehead and trickled down his back as the major and the Pawnee stepped out of the way.

"Turn around," Snider said, grinning in anticipation. "Unless you want it in the face."

Shadow Hawk let out a deep breath as he turned to face the wall, wincing as his cracked rib made itself known. There was a long silence, like the quiet before a storm. He could feel the Pawnee's gaze on his back, feel the Pawnee warrior grinning in anticipation.

The first blow came hard and fast, without warning. The weighted tip of the lash bit deep into the center of Shadow Hawk's back, worse than anything he had imagined.

The second followed almost immediately and he stumbled forward, his left shoulder striking the wall, absorbing most of the impact.

"*Woglaka na!*" Bear Tracker demanded at Neville's urging. "Talk!"

Shadow Hawk bit back a groan as the whip came down again and again. He heard the soft tearing sound of his skin splitting beneath the force of the whip, felt the warm wet blood dripping down his back.

He tensed, waiting for the next blow, wondering how much longer his legs would support him. How much punishment could he take before pride succumbed to pain and he fell to his knees? How much more could he take before he begged them to stop, before he told them what they wanted to know?

Several moments passed. Just as he was hoping they'd finished with him, he heard the sibilant hiss of the whip slice through the air, felt the lash curl around his belly.

Pressing his head against the cool wooden wall, he closed his eyes. *"Winyan Wanagi,"* he murmured. "Spirit Woman."

Somewhere between consciousness and sleep, Maggie stirred restlessly as she whispered Hawk's name, praying that he was all right. Gradually, his image appeared before her. He was locked in a small wooden room that had iron bars on the window. He sat cross-legged on the floor, bent slightly at the waist, his chin resting on his chest. His hands were bound behind his back; his wrists were raw and caked with dried blood. One eye was black and swollen, his entire upper body was livid with bruises.

He'd been beaten. The thought seared through her mind, and even then she could feel the pain in his hands, in each breath he took.

"Hawk." Did she speak his name aloud or was it only an echo in the corridor of her mind?

An anguished cry brought her fully awake, and her head jerked up, Hawk's voice loud in her ears as he called her name. She glanced around the cabin. Had she dreamt it? But no, she could hear it still, his voice calling her name over and over again.

Rising from the chair beside the window, she hurried outside, the sound of his voice guiding her across the deserted parade ground toward a small square wooden building near the back wall of the fort.

Hawk was in there. She knew it.

Slowing her steps, she made her way to the rear of the building where she spied a small barred window. Standing on tiptoe, she peered into the room and quickly drew back, her hand covering her mouth to still the cry rising in her throat.

She took several deep breaths; then, her lower lip clamped firmly between her teeth, she stood on tiptoe and peered into the room again.

Hawk was facing the wall to her left, his forehead pressed against the wood. His hands, tied behind his back, were tightly clenched, the knuckles white, the muscles in his arms taut, his body shivering spasmodically. Three men stood behind him. She was shocked to see that one was an officer.

She flinched as the whip whistled through the air to land with a sickening thud against Hawk's mutilated back.

"That's enough," the major said, his voice filled with anger and frustration. "He's no good to us dead."

The major turned to the Pawnee. "Tell him we'll be back tomorrow night," he said, moving toward the door. "Tell him to think about what just happened. And tell him I'm not a patient man. If he doesn't tell me what I want to know tomorrow night, I'll let Snider finish him."

Bear Tracker waited until the major and Snider left the building, then, moving up behind Shadow Hawk, the Pawnee repeated what the major had said.

He laughed softly as he reached up and grabbed a handful of Shadow Hawk's hair. "And I will have your scalp," he added with a wicked grin. "My woman will be pleased with such a fine trophy."

"A woman who would take a worm like you for a husband should not be hard to please," Shadow Hawk retorted, then gasped as the Pawnee spun him around and kneed him in the groin.

"Perhaps I will take that scalp while you are still alive," the Pawnee threatened, and stalked out of the room, leaving Shadow Hawk blessedly alone.

With a groan, he fell to his knees, retching violently.

"Hawk?"

Slowly, he lifted his head. "Spirit Woman?"

"Over here."

Tears burned Maggie's eyes as she watched Hawk struggle to his feet. Hunched over against the pain that wracked his body, he walked slowly toward her.

"Oh, Hawk, what have they done to you?" His right eye was swollen shut, his body was a mass of bruises, and she thought, from the rasp of his breathing, that he might have a fractured rib.

Blinking back her tears, she reached up through the bars, barely able to reach his cheek with her fingertips.

Eyes closed, he leaned into her touch, sighing softly as she stroked his cheek. "Mag-gie. How did you know where to find me?"

"I heard you calling me, and I followed the sound of your voice."

He accepted her explanation without question, and it occurred to her that it was odd that she had heard his voice so clearly in her head, and even more odd that she hadn't thought anything about it at the time. Thinking about it now made her shiver.

"We are bound to one another heart and soul," Shadow Hawk remarked, rubbing his cheek against the palm of her hand. "If I could see you through a hundred years of time, why should you not be able to hear me calling you?"

Why, indeed, she thought.

"Mag-gie, I think I must sit down," he said, and dropped heavily to the floor.

"Hawk? Hawk!"

"I am all right," he assured her.

But he didn't sound all right. He sounded hurt, weak from pain and the loss of blood.

Grasping the bars, Maggie pulled herself up so she could see over the window ledge. Hawk was lying on his left side, his eyes closed. She could see the bright splashes of blood that covered his back, hear the painful rasp of each indrawn breath.

307

"Hawk?"

It required too great an effort to answer her. As from far away, he heard the sound of Maggie's voice promising help and he grunted softly, knowing there was no way she could help him. The Major would come back tomorrow night and Snider would whip him again and he knew he wouldn't be able to bear it. The mere thought of anyone, anything, touching his back made him shudder with dread.

He wanted only to sleep, to drift into blessed oblivion.

Closing his eyes, he surrendered to the darkness hovering all around him, smiling because Snider would never find him there.

Chapter Thirty-one

Maggie ran back to her cabin, her mind whirling. She had to get Hawk away before it was too late, before they returned to beat him again. He'd never survive another whipping; indeed, it was blatantly obvious that the major didn't intend for him to survive.

When she reached her house, she paused, one hand on the door knob. There was no way she could free Hawk on her own. She needed help.

Slowly, she glanced toward the entrance of the fort. And then, her mind made up, she hurried toward the gates, relieved to find them open to admit a wagon train of settlers. No one noticed her slip past. Picking up her skirts, she ran toward the Lakota lodges.

There were only a few people outside, mostly men, huddled around small fires. They eyed her curiously as she approached. White women were even more scarce in the Indian camp than in the fort, she thought as she smiled at the nearest man.

"I need help," she said, speaking Lakota.

Frowning, the man huddled deeper into a ratty-looking buffalo robe. "Go away."

"Please, I need help."

"Why?" His voice was curt and unfriendly, but his eyes were curious as he stared at her, bewildered at her knowledge of the Lakota language.

"My husband is a prisoner in the fort."

The man shrugged.

"He's Lakota."

The man looked at her more closely, his face twisted with doubt.

"It's true. His name is Shadow Hawk, and he's Oglala."

"Shadow Hawk is dead."

"No, he isn't. Please, you've got to help me. They'll kill him."

The man looked at her for a long moment, then, with an irritated shake of his head, he left the fire.

Maggie stared after him, wondering where he'd gone, wondering if he'd come back.

Five minutes later, the man returned, followed by a tall woman wrapped in a red blanket.

"Who are you?" the woman asked curtly. "What do you know of my son?"

"Winona?"

The woman blinked several times, then nodded.

"Shadow Hawk is my husband."

"No. He would not marry a white woman."

"But he did. And he needs help. Now. Tonight. Please, you must believe me."

"How are you called?"

"My name's Maggie St. Claire. But Hawk calls me Spirit Woman."

She didn't know what had possessed her to say such a thing, but the effect was startling. The woman pressed a hand to her mouth and took a step backward.

"*Winyan Wanagi*," she murmured. "My son has spoken of you often."

"Then you'll help me?"

"If I can."

"They're holding Hawk in a small building near the back wall of the fort. He's been badly beaten."

Winona took the man aside and they spoke for several minutes, then the man disappeared into the shadows.

"My cousin, Crooked Lance, has gone to ask Red Arrow to help him. They will climb over the wall when the moon is low. When they have Shadow Hawk, they will bring him here."

"No, this is the first place they'll look."

"If he is hurt as badly as you say, he will not be able to travel."

"He'll have to."

Winona frowned thoughtfully, then nodded. "I will gather my things."

"You're coming with us?"

"Of course. He is my son. Come, let us go into my lodge to wait."

311

The lodge was small and bare save for a buffalo robe bed and a few cooking pots and baskets.

Maggie was too nervous to sit still. While Winona packed her few belongings in a parfleche, Maggie paced the dirt floor, wishing she knew what was happening, wondering if the men would be successful in getting Hawk out of the fort, wondering where they could possibly go to hide.

She drank the cup of willow bark tea Winona gave her, hardly aware of what she was doing. Closing her eyes, Maggie tried to concentrate on Hawk, but her mind was in such turmoil she couldn't concentrate, and she began to pace again, praying that he'd be all right, that the waiting would soon be over.

It was almost two hours later when Crooked Lance and Red Arrow ducked inside the lodge, supporting Hawk between them.

Maggie stared at her husband in dismay. He was unconscious and when she touched him, she could feel he was burning with fever.

"You must hide him," Crooked Lance said urgently. With Red Arrow's help, he laid Hawk face down on Winona's blankets. "Already, the bluecoats are searching for him. I will get my horse and leave tracks leading away from the fort. Perhaps it will give us some time."

Winona nodded. "Go, quickly."

"I will keep watch outside," Red Arrow said, and followed Crooked Lance out of the lodge.

Maggie stared at Hawk. His face was swollen, his right eye puffy and black. His upper body was a mass of bruised and torn flesh. His breath came in shallow gasps. But it was his back that made her stomach churn with horror. There seemed to be hardly a place that had more than an inch of whole skin left.

"We must work quickly," Winona said. "You must sit beside him," she instructed. "Should he wake up, you must keep him quiet."

Maggie nodded. She dropped down on her knees beside her husband, unable to watch as Winona began to wash the blood from Hawk's mutilated back.

He lay as one dead for several minutes and then, as Winona touched a particularly deep gash near his left shoulder, his whole body went rigid.

"Hawk." Maggie whispered his name as she took his hand in hers. "It's all right."

He stared up at her, his right eye swollen shut, his left eye glazed with pain. "Where am I?"

"In your mother's lodge."

"*Iná?*"

"I am here, my son."

"How?"

"Later," Maggie said. "Rest now."

Hawk nodded. With a sigh, he closed his eyes. Questions, he thought; he had so many questions. But the pain in his body made it difficult to think of anything else and he hovered in a twilight world of light and shadow. The pain was constant, swelling and receding each time his mother touched him.

He clung to Maggie's hand, finding comfort in her nearness. As from far away, he heard his mother tell Maggie that several of the cuts in his back would require stitching.

"You must not cry out," Maggie said, leaning forward to whisper into his ear, and he nodded that he understood.

The first few stitches were agony. The pain sickened him and he turned his head to the side, his stomach heaving. The warrior in him felt a sense of shame as he retched helplessly, uncontrollably, while his mother and his woman looked on. And then Maggie was there, offering him a drink of cool water, holding his hand once again as his mother finished stitching his wounds.

He tried to tell them not to worry, that he would be all right, but the words wouldn't come, and then merciful darkness closed in around him, shutting him off from all thought, all feeling.

After what seemed like hours but was in reality only about fifteen minutes, Winona stood up, one hand pressed to her back. "I think he will be all right," she remarked.

"We've got to get him away from here," Maggie said.

"Perhaps tomorrow. He cannot travel tonight. The fever will get worse. He must stay warm and drink much water."

Winona went to the door of the lodge and called to Red Arrow. They spoke quietly for a few minutes, then Red Arrow drew his knife and began to dig a hole in the rear of the lodge.

"We will hide Shadow Hawk there," Winona said, answering Maggie's unspoken question. "I think you must go back to the fort. They will be looking for you also."

Maggie nodded. Winona was right, but she was reluctant to leave Hawk.

"I will take good care of him," Winona said.

"I know. Thank you for your help."

Leaving the lodge, Maggie hurried back to her cabin. Undressing, she climbed into the narrow bed, only to lie awake staring at the ceiling, wondering if Hawk would be all right, wishing she could ask the post doctor to look after him. She tried to tell herself that he'd be all right, that the Indians had managed to survive for thousands of years without the aid of modern medicine, but in the back of her mind she knew he might die. He'd lost a lot of blood, he had a high fever, and she thought, from his careful breathing, that he might have a broken rib as well. She wished she'd thought to tell Winona to check and see, but it was too late now.

She woke to the sound of someone pounding on the door. Rising, she wrapped herself in a blanket and hurried into the parlor.

"He's gone." The lieutenant's voice was brisk.

"Who's gone?" Maggie asked, smothering a yawn.

"That Injun. Is he here?"

"No."

"You wouldn't tell me if he was, would you?"

"No, but you're welcome to come in and see for yourself."

Collins grunted. "Where were you last night?"

"I was here."

"All night?"

"Of course. Really, lieutenant, I object to your tone."

315

"You're glad he's gone, aren't you?"

"Yes. He didn't deserve to be locked up. He hasn't done anything."

"Kidnapping a white woman is considered a serious charge out here," Collins remarked dryly. "Especially when the culprit is a redskin."

"I told you before, he didn't kidnap me. Now, if you'll excuse me, I'd like to get dressed."

With a curt nod, the lieutenant turned on his heel and walked toward the general's office.

Maggie felt a thrill of relief as she closed the door. At least they hadn't found Hawk yet! She dressed quickly, eager to go to him, and then paused. She couldn't go to him now. She had no logical reason for visiting the village. And if anyone saw her, they might report it to the general.

She spent the morning quilting with Mrs. Sully and a few of the Army wives. Much of the talk was about Indians, how they were all thieves and liars, running around the country causing trouble, killing innocent women and children.

Maggie kept a tight rein on her tongue, afraid to say anything for fear of offending her hostess. She had to play her part, pretend she was glad to be free of Hawk, back with her own people.

Later in the afternoon, she went walking with Lieutenant Collins, waiting patiently for him to mention Hawk, which he finally did.

"He's still missing," Collins said irritably. "I guess he's long gone by now."

Maggie nodded, careful to keep her expression neutral.

"Change your mind about him, did you?" Collins asked. "I thought you'd be upset at being left behind."

"No." She smiled up at him. "You were right. I want to be accepted here. I've missed my own people."

"So you don't consider him to be your husband anymore?"

"No," Maggie said, pained by the lie. "You were right about that, too. The marriage probably wouldn't have been recognized, anyway."

"Have you ever thought of marrying a career Army man?"

"No," Maggie replied with a coy smile. "Do you know a career Army man who's looking for a wife?"

"I might."

"Well," Maggie said, playing the game, "you must introduce me to him sometime."

"I will," Collins said. "You can count on it."

She bid him good day at her door, promising to dine with him at the general's house that evening, though she dreaded the thought of flirting with him, of listening to more talk about how terrible the Indians were. Why did everyone think the Lakota were wrong to fight for their land, to expect the government to abide by its treaties? Oh, it was so unfair!

She thought the evening would never end and then, when Collins had escorted her home, she wished she was back in the Sullys' home, safe from the lieutenant's advances.

"Just one kiss, Miss St. Claire," he urged, backing her into a corner.

"Please, lieutenant, we hardly know each other."

"I'm trying to remedy that," he said, grinning down at her.

Maggie gazed up at him, feeling as helpless as a cat treed by a dog. The lieutenant was a handsome young man, with an engaging smile and a charming manner. Under other circumstances, she might have found him attractive. But now, all she could think about was Hawk. She was frantic to see him, to make sure he was all right.

"Just one," she relented, and lifted her face for his kiss, thinking that it would be faster to give in and get it over with than spend an hour arguing about it.

The lieutenant smiled somewhat smugly as he lowered his head, his lips claiming hers as his arms drew her close.

It was a surprisingly pleasant kiss. His moustache tickled, his lips were warm and firm, gently beguiling . . .

Shocked to find herself responding to his touch, Maggie twisted out of the lieutenant's embrace. "Just one kiss," she reminded him, and slipping under his arm, she opened the door and stepped inside. "Good night, lieutenant."

She wandered through the cabin for over an hour, waiting for the fort to settle down for the night, before she slipped out the back door and made her way to the village.

Several warriors looked at her suspiciously as she made her way to Winona's lodge. She rapped on the lodge flap, her heart beating with eagerness to see Hawk.

Winona's face was grave when she threw back the flap and bid Maggie to enter.

"Where is he?" Maggie asked after a quick glance around.

"He is here," Winona said, and bending down, she uncovered Hawk, who was concealed in a shallow hole covered by the buffalo robe. It was, Maggie thought, a clever way to hide him.

She knelt beside Hawk, her heart going cold. He was going to die. She knew it. His skin was hot, so hot, his breathing rapid and shallow. He groaned softly as Winona lifted his head and urged him to drink from a waterskin.

"Spirit Woman?" His voice was thin and uneven.

"I'm here," Maggie said. She took his hand in hers and pressed it to her breast.

"Are you spirit or flesh?" He looked up at her, his dark eyes void of recognition.

"He's burning up," Maggie said. "We must bring his fever down quickly. Here." She grabbed a blanket and thrust it into Winona's hand. "Soak this in cold water."

Wordlessly, Winona did as bidden and Maggie spread the blanket over Hawk, tucking the ends over his shoulders and under his legs.

She sat beside him all night long, forcing him to drink the thin broth Winona made, replacing the water-soaked blanket when he threw it aside. He called for her over and over again, his hands reaching for hers. It grieved her that he didn't know she was there beside him.

He was going to die. The thought repeated itself in her mind even as she prayed for his fever to break.

He was going to die. She tried to accept the fact, to ready herself for the inevitable.

Toward dawn, Hawk fell into a deep sleep. It was then that Winona told Maggie that the soldiers had come during the day, poking into the lodges, questioning the men, finally deciding that Hawk had indeed stolen a horse and escaped. Red Arrow had seen a half-dozen bluecoats ride out of the fort, following the trail Crooked Lance had left the night they'd freed Hawk.

Maggie looked up, her eyes damp with tears, as Winona's handed her a cup of black tea.

"You love my son?"

"Yes, very much."

"How did he find you?"

"Do you know of the Sacred Cave?"

"Yes."

"He came to me through the cave, from your time into mine."

Winona frowned. "Your time?"

"The future."

"It is not possible."

"It is," Maggie said, and wondered how she'd get back to her own time if anything happened to Hawk.

"Mag-gie?"

"I'm here!" She whirled around to see Hawk gazing up at her, his beautiful dark eyes clear and rational. She placed her hand on his forehead, relieved to discover it was cool and damp. The fever had broken, thank God!

She felt tears on her cheeks. Glancing up, she saw tears sparkling in Winona's eyes, as well.

Three days later, Hawk watched his mother move about the lodge, rinsing out the dishes he'd used earlier in the day, stirring a large pot of mostly meatless stew, adding wood to the fire.

She looked older, thinner, wiser. Only twenty-three people, most of them women and young children, had survived the attack on the village. The soldiers had looted the village, burned the lodges, confiscated the horses and weapons. Hawk felt his hatred for the whites expand within him until there was no room for anything else. His people, once proud and free, had been slaughtered, the few survivors forced to become beggars and thieves to provide for their families.

The night before, after Maggie had returned to the fort, he had told his mother about Heart-of-the-Wolf's death, about emerging from the cave to find himself in another time.

"And what did you see there?"

"Wonderful things, *Iná*," he had replied, and he had told her of the wonders he had seen in Maggie's time, of cars and stoves and refrigerators, of soft beds and pillows, of chairs and tables, of electric lights and machines that washed clothes and dishes, of grocery stores where fresh meat was neatly cut and wrapped in shiny packages.

He paused, thinking of the things he'd seen on the reservation. Should he tell his mother of the poverty that awaited them in the future, of the loss of their homeland, the diseases that plagued them, the drunkenness?

"My son? Are you in pain?"

"Yes." He placed his hand over his heart. "In here." He shook his head as she bent toward him, her face lined with concern. "I am not sick, my mother. There is nothing you can do for me. I hurt for our people."

"I do not understand."

"I have seen things that I cannot forget, heard things I do not want to believe."

"In the future?"

"Yes."

Winona shook her head. "I find it difficult to believe that you have traveled to another time. Are you sure it was not another medicine dream?"

"It was real, my mother. The Spirit Woman is real. You have seen her."

"Yes. Rest now, my son. There is nothing to be done until you are well again."

Shadow Hawk nodded. His mother was right. There was nothing to do until he was well again. And perhaps not even then.

Chapter Thirty-two

Maggie stared at Major Neville, her fingers worrying a fold in her skirt as she waited for him to speak. This was the man who had flogged Hawk, the man who would have killed Hawk if he'd had the chance. What did he want with her?

"Miss St. Claire?"

"Yes."

"I'd like to ask you a few questions, if you don't mind."

Maggie shrugged.

"What, exactly, is your relationship to the Indian who was brought in with you?"

"I believe I explained all that to General Sully."

"Of course, but the general was called back East, and I'm in command now."

"I see. Hawk is . . . was my husband."

"You lived with him in the Indian camp?"

"Yes."

"For how long?"

"Not long."

"It's of vital importance that we find Sitting Bull. Do you know where his camp is?"

"No."

"Perhaps you don't understand. Since the red stick escaped, you're the only lead we have left."

"I'm sorry I can't help you."

"Perhaps I can help you refresh your memory. Snider!"

A quick shiver of apprehension skittered down Maggie's spine as the corporal entered the room.

"Yessir?"

"I've been questioning Miss St.Claire about Sitting Bull's whereabouts."

Snider nodded, one hand caressing the whip coiled over his arm.

Maggie stared at the whip, remembering how it had seemed to float through the air before striking Hawk's back, remembering the sound of it, sibilant and deadly as it sliced into her husband's flesh.

"She says she doesn't know where Sitting Bull's camp is." Neville leaned forward, his elbows on the desk top, his chin resting on his folded hands. "It would mean a great deal to my career if I could locate Sitting Bull," he said, his pale blue eyes boring into hers. "I'd do just about anything to find him. Anything."

"I wish I could help you," Maggie said, unable to still the quiver in her voice, or the shaking in her hands. "I'm sorry. I, uh, could I talk to Lieutenant Collins, please?"

"Collins is out on patrol. He won't be back for at least a week, perhaps longer."

She felt caught, helpless, like a rabbit in the jaws of a coyote. With the general and Collins away from the fort, she had no one to turn to.

"Snider, why don't you escort Miss. St. Claire to the interrogation room?"

"Yessir." Snider saluted, then stepped aside.

Rising, Maggie walked out of the major's office, her back rigid with fear.

Her heart began to pound with dread as she realized Snider was taking her to the same building where Hawk had been imprisoned.

She stepped inside, and her blood seemed to turn to ice as Snider closed and locked the door. Surely the major didn't intend to whip her. *I'd do just about anything to find him,* Neville had said with conviction. *Anything.*

Swallowing hard, Maggie went to the narrow barred window and gazed into the darkness. She refused to believe the major would abuse her. He was only trying to frighten her, nothing more.

And he was doing a heck of a job.

Shadow Hawk's gaze kept wandering toward the door of the lodge. It was far past the time when Maggie usually arrived and as the minutes passed, and she still didn't come, he began to worry that something was wrong.

With an effort, he stood up, panting from the effort. Knifelike pains caused by his broken rib accompanied each breath, each movement.

"What are you doing?" Winona exclaimed as she entered the lodge with an armload of wood.

"I must find Mag-gie."

"She will be here as soon as she can."

"No. Something is wrong."

"Shadow Hawk, you are not well. You must not move around or you will cause your wounds to bleed again."

"She needs me, *Iná*. I can feel her fear."

"But the soldiers . . ."

"They did not come looking for me today."

"Shadow Hawk, these are her people. Surely they will not harm her."

He did not argue with her further, only gave her a quick hug before leaving the lodge, a striped trade blanket over his head.

No one paid any attention to him as he walked toward the fort. His people were broken, beaten.

Silent as the shadow of a hawk, he made his way through the fort, skirting the parade ground, keeping out of sight as much as possible.

Maggie had told him where she stayed and he found her cabin without any trouble. The door was unlocked and he ghosted inside, pausing just inside the door.

The cabin was empty. He knew it even before he checked the bedroom.

Where would she have gone?

He stood there in the dark cabin, his eyes closed, his heart and spirit searching for Maggie, reaching out to her through time and space. Maggie . . .

*   *   *

Major Neville rocked back on his heels, his pale blue eyes void of compassion as he stared at Maggie. But it was Snider who held Maggie's attention, or rather, it was the long black whip in Snider's hand.

"How's your memory, Miss St. Claire?" Neville asked, his tone indicating he would wait all night for her answer, if necessary.

"My memory's fine," Maggie replied. "But I'm not familiar with this area," she said, shrugging helplessly, "so I'm afraid I can't tell you where the Indian camp is."

"I see." Neville pulled a cigar out of his pocket, unwrapped it, sniffed it appreciatively. "Was it near a river?"

"A river? I . . . yes, I think so."

"I knew you wouldn't let me down. I have to go now, but I'll be back tomorrow night. And I know you'll be able to tell me exactly where that village is, won't you?"

Maggie nodded, her gaze still on the whip in Snider's hand, her mind already working on the lie she was going to tell Neville when he came back.

Shadow Hawk paced the floor of his mother's lodge. For days, he had been confined to this small place and now he felt restless, weak from lack of exercise. And in the back of his mind was a growing concern for Maggie. Where was she?

Abruptly, he turned to face his mother. "We are leaving this place tonight."

"Leaving? Where are we going?"

327

"North, to the Land of the Grandmother."

"Why?"

"Because our people are going to be involved in many battles in the next few years. We will win some of them, but in the end, our people will be defeated. I have seen the future, *Iná*. We must leave here. It is the only way our people can survive."

Winona shook her head, not wanting to believe.

"I know it is hard for you to accept, but I speak the truth. I have seen the future. I have been there! Maggie told me of the wars that will come, of the defeat of the Lakota and our allies, the Cheyenne. Our only hope for safety lies in the north."

Winona nodded, knowing it was useless to argue, knowing, too, that her son was right. "I will tell the others."

Shadow Hawk gave his mother a quick hug; then, drawing a blanket over his head, he made his way toward Maggie's cabin, praying that she would be there, knowing even as he opened the door that the cabin was still empty.

She could not be with the paleface lieutenant. Everyone knew that Collins had ridden out of the fort several days ago. Had she made other friends among the *wasichu*?

Leaving the cabin, Hawk stared up at the sky. The moon was full and it seemed to be shining on the small building where he had been imprisoned only a few days ago. Could she be there? It seemed unlikely, yet he felt himself being drawn toward it.

There was a light inside the building and as he drew near, he could hear voices: Neville's, harsh and impatient, Maggie's hesitant and afraid.

His moccasined feet made no sound as he approached the door and peered cautiously inside.

Maggie stood against the far wall, her arms crossed over her breasts, her face pale, her eyes wide with fear. Snider stood to the left, Neville to the right. Both had their backs to Hawk.

Shadow Hawk saw the hope that flared in the depths of Maggie's eyes when she saw him and he shook his head, warning her not to give him away.

"Sitting Bull," she said, her words tumbling over themselves. "You want to know where Sitting Bull is? I'll tell you. I'll tell you anything you want, do anything you want, but please don't let him whip me."

The thought that Neville was going to let Snider whip Maggie drove all rational thought from Shadow Hawk's mind and he wanted only to kill the man who dared threaten his wife.

Maggie kept talking as Hawk crept up behind Neville. The Powder River, she said, her voice growing louder and more agitated, that was where Sitting Bull was camped.

Neville frowned, confused by her sudden turnabout, by the expectant look on her face.

Too late, he realized that someone had entered the building. And then that someone was yanking the gun from his holster.

"Snider!"

Neville's warning came too late.

Madeline Baker

The first shot drilled into the major's heart, killing him instantly. The second plowed into Snider's gut, promising a slow, agonizing death.

"Let's go!" Shadow Hawk said. Shoving the major's pistol into his belt, he grabbed Maggie by the hand and pulled her toward the door, stopping only long enough to knock over the oil lamp that illuminated the building.

The dry wood floor caught almost immediately and Hawk heard the sentry's cry of "Fire! Fire!" as they ran out of the fort.

Red Arrow had horses waiting and in a matter of minutes, all those who'd had enough of the white man's charity were following Shadow Hawk and Maggie across the plains, their escape swallowed up in the dark of the night and in the pandemonium caused by the roaring blaze.

Chapter Thirty-three

Bobby stood at the mouth of the Sacred Cave, wondering if he had the guts to take the first step inside.

That afternoon, he had called Veronica and told her what he was going to do, hoping, perhaps, that she would be able to talk him out of it.

And she had tried; perversely, all Veronica's arguments had only strengthened his resolve. The need to be a warrior, to prove himself in battle, had been stronger than all her arguments, and in the end, she had begged him to be careful and promised to pray for him.

Jared and Joshua had volunteered to stay at the ranch until Bobby returned, and that tied up all the loose ends.

Staring into the cave's darkness, Bobby took

a deep breath. He wore the clout and moccasins he'd worn on his vision quest. He carried no weapons. He'd fasted for twenty-four hours. He'd prayed for help and guidance. He carried a handful of sacred pollen to offer to the gods. All that remained was to take the first step.

The brassy taste of fear rose in his mouth, not fear of the cave, but fear that he didn't have what it took to be a warrior, that he didn't have the fortitude to step into the cave and face the unknown.

Raising his arms overhead, he prayed for courage, for guidance, his heart pounding a quick tattoo as he stared at the full moon that brightened the night sky.

It was time, he thought. If he was ever going to do it, the time was now, on the night of the full moon.

His mouth felt dry, his palms were damp, his whole body quivered with excitement, and fear— fear of the unknown, fear of failure, fear of the death that awaited him if he was not worthy to enter the cave. Hawk had told him what to do, what do wear, how to behave. All that remained was finding the courage to do it.

"I am Proud Eagle."

His voice was hardly a whisper and he repeated the words again, louder this time, stronger.

"I am Proud Eagle."

He closed his eyes and thought of his vision, of the power he had felt as he became one with his spirit guide. And then, in his mind, he heard again the words he'd heard in the Sacred Cave:

Proud Eagle, you must follow the Hawk.

And he knew it was time to enter the Sacred Cave and follow the Spirit Path that would lead to his destiny.

With a final prayer for guidance, he lowered his arms and took his first step into the enveloping darkness of the cave.

It was still and silent as the grave. The sound of his heartbeat roared like thunder in his ears as he took another step into the cavern, and then another.

I am Proud Eagle.

He said the words in his mind as he took another step into the Sacred Cave.

Sensations assailed him. The cave was cool but not cold. The ground at his feet was smooth and covered with sand. He took a deep breath, faced toward the east, and reached for the small bag of pollen tied to his belt. As Hawk had instructed, he offered a pinch of pollen to the sacred winds, to Man Above, to Mother Earth, and then he sat down on the ground and concentrated on his people.

Fear rose within him, primal and unreasoning, as he felt the darkness close around him, exploring him with hands that had no substance, sniffing him, reading his mind and his heart.

I am Proud Eagle. I must follow the Hawk.

He repeated the words over and over in his mind.

The darkness was all around him now, alive, breathing, a living entity with a mind and a heart of its own.

It was pulling at him, dragging him deeper into the darkness, into the very heart of the cave.

333

Madeline Baker

Knowing it was useless to fight, Bobby Proud Eagle surrendered to the blackness, felt himself falling down, down, into a swirling vortex that carried him into oblivion.

Chapter Thirty-four

They rode all that night and into the dawn and when it seemed Hawk would ride non-stop until they reached Canada, Maggie began to complain of being tired. Hawk called a halt immediately, as she had known he would. In truth, she *was* tired, but it was Hawk's well-being that concerned her. He looked pale and on the verge of exhaustion, and though he had traveled without complaint, she knew his broken rib must be causing him a great deal of pain.

In a matter of minutes, the women had small fires burning and were passing out jerky and pemmican. Maggie sat beside Hawk, studying him surreptitiously. Were his eyes too bright? Did he look feverish, or was it just her imagination?

He caught her worried look and grinned. "Maggie, I am all right."

"Are you sure?" She placed her hand on his forehead, relieved to find it cool to the touch.

"I am sure. Do not worry."

"I can't help it."

"Get some sleep. We will rest only a few hours."

"How long will it take us to get to Canada?"

"We are going to Sitting Bull."

"Sitting Bull? But why?"

"It will be winter soon. We will not make the journey to the Land of the Grandmother until spring."

Maggie nodded. He was right, of course. They'd had to leave their lodges and most of their belongings behind, and they didn't have enough warm clothes or enough food to see them through a long winter. It was now, in the fall of the year, that the Sioux would be hunting, storing meat to see them through the winter.

Maggie let her gaze wander around the small camp. Six men, four in their prime; nine women, most of them past child-bearing age, and eight children under the age of ten.

She couldn't help but wonder how many of them would survive the long journey north.

They reached Sitting Bull's camp a week later. Maggie was deeply touched as she watched Sitting Bull's people open their homes to what was left of Hawk's tribe. The Hunkpapa women gathered hides and quickly erected lodges for the married couples; single women were taken into the homes of elderly couples.

Maggie and Hawk shared a lodge with Winona. It was not a situation Maggie was particularly happy with. For one thing, she feared that Winona was less than thrilled at having a white woman for a daughter-in-law. For another, having Winona in the lodge left them no privacy at night, and she felt odd lying in Hawk's arms when his mother's bed was only a few feet away. But it was only temporary. In the spring, they would travel to Canada, and then they would have their own lodge.

Sighing, she snuggled closer to Hawk, felt his arm slip around her shoulders to draw her close.

Burying his face in her hair, Hawk began to caress her, losing himself in her nearness. Her skin was as soft as the petals of the wild roses that grew along the banks of the Rosebud, her lips as sweet as the berries that grew in the summertime.

Conscious of her mother-in-law sleeping nearby, Maggie whispered, "Hawk, not now."

"Spirit Woman." He whispered her name as he caressed her breasts and her belly, and then he drew back, a look of wonder in his eyes.

Maggie blinked up at him, a little disappointed that he had given heed to her words so quickly, and then she frowned. "What is it? What's wrong?"

"I feel life growing within you."

"What did you say?"

"I can feel the heartbeat of our child beneath my hand. You are carrying a new life within your womb. A son, Mag-gie. We will have a son."

Maggie shook her head. If she was pregnant, wouldn't she be the first to know it? She frowned as she thought of the symptoms she'd been having the last few weeks, the queasiness in the morning, the tenderness in her breasts, the fact that her period was late. She'd attributed her lack of energy and all the other complaints to tension and stress. It had never occurred to her that she could be pregnant.

"There's no way you could know such a thing," she said, stunned by his revelation. "It's impossible."

"Spirit Woman." He whispered her name as his hand slid reverently over her belly. "You should know by now that between us nothing is impossible."

Filled with wonder, Maggie placed her hand over Hawk's, and all the while she gazed into the depths of his eyes, feeling her soul communing with his.

And suddenly she felt it, too, the promise of a new life, the echo of a heartbeat beating soft as a butterfly wing, and in her mind's eye she saw a child, a beautiful little boy with smooth tawny skin and hair the color of a raven's wing.

Hawk's son.

A lasting link between the past and the future.

The following morning, the *Nacas*, the leaders of the camp, decided it was time to move the village. A crier rode through the camp, announcing that the village would be moving in two days' time. They would spend the winter in the sheltering wooded hollows of the Black Hills, camping where wood and water were abundant.

As soon as he heard the news, Shadow Hawk went to Sitting Bull and told him that they must not camp in the *Paha Sapa* that year, that it would not be safe.

"How do you know this?" Sitting Bull asked, his tone skeptical. The Lakota had always found shelter from the harsh winter storms in the sacred hills.

"I have traveled the Spirit Path of the Sacred Cave, and it was shown to me that any who winter in the Black Hills will be destroyed by the *wasichu*."

Sitting Bull considered Hawk's words for a long time. The legend of the Sacred Cave was known to all the Council Fires of the Lakota Nation, though only the holy man of the Oglala tribe possessed the power to enter the cave on the night of the Full Moon.

"I hear your words, my brother," Sitting Bull said gravely. "I will speak to the *Nacas*."

Two days later, the journey began.

It was an amazing sight, Maggie thought. Scouts rode at the head of the long column, followed by the warriors who rode their best horses and wore their best clothing. Following the warriors came the women and children, some riding and some walking, and then the vast horse herd.

They traveled leisurely, taking time out to rest, to hunt, to laugh and to play, to adjust the packs, to eat.

Maggie rode beside Hawk, fascinated by the speed with which the women had dismantled the lodges, amazed that a whole village could be moved so quickly and easily. She could find nothing to compare it to save the flight of the Children of Israel out of Egypt as depicted in the film *The Ten Commandments*. Indeed, that was how the Sioux traveled, carrying with them everything they owned, leaving nothing behind save a few old lodgepoles and scraps of hide.

But it was the thought of being a mother that occupied most of Maggie's thoughts. They had not told anyone their news, not even Winona, and Maggie held her secret close, cherishing it, dreaming the same dreams all women dreamed when they carried a new life under their hearts.

She looked at Hawk with new eyes now, seeing in him the epitome of what a father should be: a man who was brave and strong, protective and proud; a man who could defend her and provide for her, a man who would teach their son about loyalty and honor, respect for the land, respect for life itself.

He hovered over her, making sure she was comfortable when they stopped at night, making sure she had enough to eat, that she went to bed early.

Winona watched them through knowing eyes, remembering how it had been in those years long past when she had been pregnant with Shadow Hawk. Her husband, Gray Otter, had looked at her the way Shadow Hawk now looked at Maggie. It warmed her heart and made her sad at the same time. Knowing how much they yearned to be alone at this special time in their lives, she often left their temporary lodge in the evening, going out to visit with Sitting Bull and his family.

Shadow Hawk stared after his mother as she left the lodge, his expression thoughtful as he took Maggie in his arms.

"She knows," he remarked.

"Do you think so?"

"I am sure of it."

"Do you think she's glad?"

"Is not every woman happy at the thought of a new life?"

"I don't know. I don't think your mother likes me very much."

"She will, in time."

"I hope so." Maggie pressed her cheek to Hawk's chest and closed her eyes, content to listen to the steady sound of his heartbeat, to feel his arms around her. She didn't feel pregnant, and yet she knew in her heart that she carried Hawk's child. The thought filled her with joy, and fear.

"What is it?" Hawk asked, sensing the change in her mood.

"I . . . I'm afraid."

"Of what?"

"Having the baby."

"I do not understand."

Neither did she, not really. How could she tell him she was afraid of childbirth, afraid of the pain, afraid of dying, afraid of having the baby in the Canadian wilderness? He would think her cowardly, weak, unfit to be the mother of a Lakota warrior. But she couldn't help it. She was afraid.

"My mother will be there to help you," Hawk remarked.

"I know."

"There is nothing to fear."

"I know." But all the logic in the world couldn't change the way she felt. And the idea of having the baby here, in this time, made it all the worse. Women frequently died in childbirth. Babies were born dead, or died of diseases that, in the future, were no longer considered serious or fatal.

"Mag-gie."

"I'm all right," she said, but she didn't want to have her baby here. When the time came, she wanted a sterile hospital delivery room, and a doctor in a clean linen gown, and drugs to take the edge off the pain, and modern technology in case something went wrong.

She snuggled against him, seeking the strength of his arms, finding comfort in the strong steady beat of his heart beneath her cheek. She wouldn't be afraid. So long as Hawk was there beside her, she wouldn't be afraid.

Shadow Hawk held Maggie close, her fears now his. He had never given much thought to the mystery of birth. It was a thing best left to the understanding of women. But as he sat there, holding Maggie close, he remembered that Red Arrow's first wife had died giving birth to a stillborn child, and that, through the years, there had been many women who had died in childbirth, and many babies who had not lived more than a few days. The Lakota way of life was hard. Only the strong survived. That was the way it was, the way it had always been. As a child and a young man, he had not questioned such things, but now . . .

He gazed down at Maggie, pressed so trustingly against him, and knew he would make any sacrifice to keep her safe. He would pray for her each morning and each night, and in the summer he would offer his blood and his pain at the Sun Dance pole, beseeching the gods of the Lakota to watch over his woman and his son.

And then he thought of what Maggie had told him of the future. The white men would be coming soon. They would find the yellow metal in the Black Hills, battles would be fought and won, fought and lost, and in a few short years his people would be defeated, at the mercy of the *wasichu*, penned on a reservation. . . . It was the reason he was taking his people to Canada.

It occurred to him then, with crystal clarity, that he did not want to go to Canada, that he did not want to live in the Grandmother's country, that he wanted to live here, in the shadow of the Black Hills, where he had always lived, that he wanted his son to be born there.

But all that was impossible now, and for the first time, he realized what he was giving up.

Chapter Thirty-five

Slowly, Bobby opened his eyes, frowning when the darkness remained. Where was he?

It came back to him in a rush: the Sacred Cave, the blackness, the fear. Had he failed?

Rising to his feet, he raked his fingers through his hair, brushed the sand from his pants. He was stalling for time, he thought wryly, afraid to find out if he'd failed—and even more afraid to learn he had succeeded.

Squaring his shoulders, he walked toward the entrance of the cave. What would he find outside? Was it still 1993, or had he managed to find the spirit path that led into the past?

Heart pounding, he made his way toward the entrance and stepped out of the cave into the light of a new day. Hands clenched at his sides, he turned and looked down the hill toward Maggie St. Claire's house.

But the house was gone. His horse was gone.

He looked the other way, just to make sure, but there was no sign of human habitation, only the timeless Hills covered with tall ponderosa pines.

He uttered a quick prayer, praying that he was in 1872, and then, filled with a sense of exhilaration, he started down the far side of the hill, oblivious to the hunger clawing at his belly, oblivious to the fact that he had no food, no horse, no weapons. He would worry about those things later. For now, he must find Hawk.

When he reached the bottom of the hill, he saw the scattered remnants of what had been an Indian village. Hawk's village? The one destroyed by the Army?

He wandered through the ruined camp. Not much remained now. A few weathered lodgepoles, a few scraps of leather that had been chewed by rodents. Digging in the debris, he found a blanket that was only burnt around one edge. Laying it over his shoulder, he poked into the burned lodges, experiencing a sense of satisfaction when he found a long-bladed knife. The beaded sheath had been destroyed, but the bone haft and the blade were still intact, and he shoved it in the waistband of his clout, feeling better now that he had a weapon.

He spent another hour wandering through the village, but he found nothing else he could use. For a moment, he stood there, wondering which way to go, and then he started walking away from the village, headed for Fort Laramie for no other reason than it was the only landmark he knew that had existed in 1872.

He stopped at a shallow waterhole and quenched his thirst, then continued onward, grateful that he'd been working out the last few months.

Fear was his constant companion as he made his way across the plains, but he fought it down.

Follow the Hawk. Follow the Hawk. The voice in the cave had told him to follow the Hawk; the voice of Heart-of-the-Wolf had told him to follow the Hawk, and even now he seemed to hear the words repeating in the back of his mind. Surely it was his destiny to find Hawk. Surely the gods of the Lakota would help him if he didn't succumb to panic, if he held fast to his courage, to the conviction that he was doing the right thing.

As he walked briskly, Bobby's gaze shifted from right to left. The Black Hills looked different, yet the same. The main thing he noticed was the silence. The ranch had been quiet, set as it was in the little meadow away from the road, but there'd usually been noise of one kind or another in the background—Miss St. Claire's stereo endlessly playing the record of *The Phantom of the Opera*, the muted roar of airplane engines, the low hum of the air conditioner in the summertime, the ring of the telephone, the sound of Veronica's Ford Mustang. It was a little eerie, crossing the prairie with only the muffled sound of his footsteps for company.

He'd walked about five miles when he became aware of the faint sounds of battle, sounds that grew steadily louder as he topped a grassy rise.

He stared at the battle in disbelief. Horses raced back and forth across the short buffalo grass, their riders armed with bows and arrows, feathered lances, war clubs, and rifles.

Pawnee and Lakota. He recognized the two tribes at once. Neither party was painted for war and he guessed they were hunting parties that had run into each other.

There wasn't much killing going on, mostly warriors trying to count coup on one another.

He saw two men in hand-to-hand combat, fighting over a knife which lay on the ground at their feet, and he leaned forward, silently rooting for the Lakota warrior who, in a quick, graceful move, managed to slip out of the Pawnee's grasp. Diving for the knife, the Lakota rolled onto his back, the blade up, just as the Pawnee lunged at him.

The Pawnee let out a bone-chilling shriek as the knife pierced his stomach. The sound drew everyone's attention and all other fighting came to a halt. Slowly, the two hunting parties separated while two warriors went to look after the wounded man.

Bobby ran down the hill, calling to the Lakota until one of the warriors rode toward him.

"*Hau, kola,*" Bobby said. "Hello, friend."

The warrior looked at him suspiciously. "*Hau, kola.*"

"Can you help me?" Bobby said, still speaking Lakota. "I'm lost."

"Who are your people?"

"I have no people."

The warrior looked around and then grunted softly. "And no horse."

"And no horse."

Scooting forward a little, the warrior extended his arm and Bobby vaulted up behind him.

The warrior reined his horse around and urged the spotted pony into a lope, following his companions.

Bobby could hardly contain his excitement. He had found a band of Lakota. Perhaps one of these very men was related to him.

It was an exhilarating thought and it was all he could do to keep from laughing out loud. Deep down, he had never believed any of it, not for a moment. He had never truly believed that Hawk was from the past, never believed the cave held any magic. But now . . . he murmured a quick prayer of thanks to *Wakán Tanka*.

He was here and he was never going back.

Chapter Thirty-six

The hunting party caught up with the main body of the tribe three days later.

Bobby could only stare in awe at his first sight of Indians on the move. It was fascinating, incredible, a long procession strung out for miles.

Far ahead were the scouts, to the sides and rear were the Fox Soldiers, who were acting as police. Then came the warriors, followed by the women, some riding or leading pack horses, some walking. The old ones rode the travois ponies, sharing their horses with their grandchildren. Dogs ran everywhere, weaving back and forth, barking at the horses, chasing rabbits and prairie dogs. The horse herd brought up the rear, colts and fillies darting away from their mothers, then hurrying back again.

It was a sight Bobby knew he'd never forget.

As they neared the horse herd, the warrior who had befriended Bobby said, "See that big bald-faced roan? He is mine. Now he is yours."

The warrior, whose name was Buffalo Heart, pulled an extra bridle from his war bag. "If we get separated, look for me when we make camp tonight. My woman will prepare a meal for you, and then you will share my lodge."

"Pilamaya," Bobby said. Taking the bridle, he slid from the back of Buffalo Heart's pony and approached the roan gelding. The animal snorted and sidestepped, then stood docile as Bobby slipped the bridle over its head.

"Good boy," Bobby murmured. He patted the horse's neck for a moment, then vaulted onto the animal's bare back and rode after Buffalo Heart.

Shadow Hawk rode near the head of the column, just behind Sitting Bull, his heart swelling with emotion. He had not realized how much he had missed being with his own people.

Riding across the plains, he drew a deep breath, drinking in the smell of dust and sweat, of horses and leather, grass and sage. The sun warmed his back, a gentle breeze cooled his face. He found pleasure in the easy rhythm of the horse beneath him, and in the familiar sound of the Lakota language. He heard the piercing cry of a hunting hawk, the shrill whinny of a mare, the laughter of the women, and felt he had truly come home.

Glancing over his shoulder, Shadow Hawk saw Maggie riding beside his mother and he smiled at both women. Gradually, they were becoming friends.

The night before, Shadow Hawk had told his mother that Maggie was pregnant. Winona had looked at him for several seconds, one eyebrow raised.

"Do you think I am deaf and blind?" she had asked with a wry grin, and then she had hugged him and said maybe, just maybe, it wasn't so bad having a *wasichu* for a daughter-in-law.

He was about to face toward the front again when he saw a familiar face. He blinked hard, wondering if he was seeing things, but the face didn't change and it didn't go away.

Reining his horse out of the column, Shadow Hawk nodded to Maggie as she rode by, and then grinned broadly as Bobby Proud Eagle drew up beside him.

"Hi, Hawk," Bobby said, laughter bubbling in his throat. "I bet you never thought you'd see me here, did you?"

Hawk shook his head. "How did you get here? How did you find us?"

"I came through the Sacred Cave. I remembered all the things you told me, and I did it! Finding you was just a lucky coincidence. I ran into the hunting party and Buffalo Heart picked me up."

"But why have you come?"

"Do you remember I once told you I felt I'd been born in the wrong time? Well, the more you taught me about our people and the old ways, the stronger that feeling got. But that's not the reason I came."

Bobby ran his hand through his hair, then smiled. "Hawk, when you and Maggie disappeared, I went up to the Sacred Cave. While I was inside, I heard a voice saying, 'Proud Eagle, you must follow the Hawk,' and I remembered hearing the same words during my vision. At the time, I thought it meant what you said it did, that I would become a doctor and be the next Lakota medicine man back on the reservation. But when I went to the Sacred Cave, I knew it meant I was to follow you here, to your time. That I was supposed to find you."

"And so you have," Shadow Hawk exclaimed, pleased beyond measure at seeing the young man again. "Come, let us catch up with the others. We will talk more this evening."

An hour before dusk, the Indians made camp. Later, when they were settled for the night, Bobby came to visit.

Maggie threw her arms around Bobby and hugged him tight. It was so good to see a familiar face, so good to see someone from home.

"Bobby, what are you doing here?" she asked "How did you get here? I can't believe it."

Sitting beside the fire, Bobby retold his story. Winona listened quietly, politely.

Maggie could hardly sit still as Bobby told his tale. Bobby's eyes fairly glowed as he told of going to the Sacred Cave, emerging to find everything that was familiar gone. His voice rang with excitement as he told of climbing to the top of the rise and seeing the Lakota battling with the Pawnee.

"So," Maggie said excitedly, wondering at the pensive look on Hawk's face. "You're going with us to Canada! That's wonderful."

Bobby grinned. "I'm looking forward to it. Oh, and Miss St. Claire, don't worry about your house. Veronica's boys are looking after things." Bobby frowned. "They said they'd stay until I got back . . ." Bobby's voice trailed off. He wasn't going back. "Maybe you should worry."

Her house. Maggie shook her head. She hadn't even thought of her house. Or the book she'd left unfinished. What must Sheila be thinking!

"Did my editor call?"

"Yeah, several times. She sounded real mad, especially since I couldn't tell her where you were."

"No, I guess you couldn't," Maggie agreed. She looked at Hawk and smiled. She'd always wanted to live in the past, to be swept off her feet by a handsome warrior, and it had happened. "Well," she said with a laugh, "there goes my career."

Later that night, lying in the warmth of Hawk's arms, Maggie thought about Bobby and wondered what it all meant. Had he truly been born in the wrong time? Had she?

Drawing back a little, she looked at the man sleeping peacefully beside her. Her husband. She had never known it was possible to love another human being so much. Just looking at Hawk made her heart swell with tenderness. He was everything to her: father, brother, friend, confidant. He had exorcised her guilt over Susie's death, made her feel feminine and desirable, given her a reason to walk again, shown her how beautiful love could be.

They made their permanent winter camp four days later along the banks of a wide shallow river lined with cottonwoods.

Maggie helped Winona set up their lodge, marveling anew at how quickly and efficiently the Lakota women set up housekeeping. By mid-afternoon, it looked as if the village had been there for weeks instead of hours.

While Bobby and Hawk sat in the pale sunlight talking with Red Arrow and Buffalo Heart, Maggie walked along the riverbank looking for firewood. She nodded and smiled at the other women she met, glad for their friendliness toward her. She was, after all, a stranger, a white woman, but most of them treated her with courtesy and respect.

Still, there were a few who treated her rudely, ignoring her overtures of friendship. They called her names, their eyes dark with distrust and loathing. Maggie didn't blame them for their feelings. White men had killed their husbands, their sons. Perhaps, if she'd lost a loved one in battle, she'd feel the same.

When she returned to their lodge, she saw that Winona had a fire going. The family altar was in place in the rear of the lodge, a pot of venison stew was cooking over the fire, filling the air with warmth and savory smells.

A short time later, the men came inside and Winona handed them bowls of fragrant stew.

Maggie sat in the back of the lodge behind Hawk, her gaze never leaving her husband, her eyes drinking in the sight of his broad back and shoulders, the easy way he moved. Her heart warmed to the sound of his laughter, her fingers ached to reach out and caress the black waterfall of his hair. She wished they were alone in the lodge, wished he would take her in his arms and hold her close and promise her that everything would be all right.

Maggie learned a lot about being a Lakota woman in the course of the next few days. She learned that young girls were to be reserved and retiring in the presence of both men and older women. A proper Lakota girl was loving, industrious, and generous, kind to all people and all animals. A woman did not eat with the men. She kept to the left side of the lodge. She was to sit in a way that was modest and becoming. She spoke the female language. For instance, a man would say *Tokiya la hwo?* Where are you going? But a woman would say *Tokiya la he?*

Very young girls were expected to wash dishes, gather wood, pick berries, and keep the lodge tidy. In this, Maggie thought, Indian girls were not so different from their white sisters. As a girl grew older, she learned to cook and to tan a hide. Quilling and beading were also considered things a Lakota woman should excel at. If a girl had a younger brother or sister, much of its care fell to her.

The next few days passed tranquilly. The men repaired their weapons or fashioned new ones while the women put the finishing touches on new winter moccasins, shirts, and robes, and the boys began making sleds out of buffalo ribs in anticipation of the coming snow.

And then, overnight, winter was upon them in a howl of wind and a roar of thunder. Rain fell in great icy sheets, but inside the lodge it was warm and cozy. Grass had been stuffed between the tipi liner and the outer cover, providing insulation. A trench had been dug around the perimeter of the lodge to keep the rain out.

That night, Bobby, Hawk, and Maggie sat around the fire while Winona told the story of how the crow came to be black.

"In days long past," Winona began, "when the earth was young and the people were new, all crows were white. In those ancient days, the people had neither horses or guns. Like the people of today, they depended on the buffalo hunt to survive.

"The crows made things difficult for Lakota hunters because they were friends to the buffalo. Flying high above the prairie, they would cry, 'Caw, caw, look out, cousins,' to warn the buffalo that hunters were coming.

"The people held a council to decide what to do. There was among the crows an especially large one who was the leader, and the chief of the people decided they must capture the big crow and teach him a lesson he would not forget.

"The chief found a large buffalo robe, with the head and tail still attached, and put it on the back of a brave young warrior. 'Cousin, you must hide among the buffalo. They will think you are one of them, and then you can capture the big white crow.'

"Disguised as a buffalo, the young man did as he had been told and just as the chief had said, the buffalo thought he was one of them. When the young warrior was in place, the hunters came out of hiding. As they approached the herd, the crows began to call their warning and all the buffalo ran away, all but the young warrior who pretended to go on grazing on the lush green grass.

"Confused, the big white crow landed on the hunter's shoulders. Flapping its wings, it said, 'Brother, why do you not run away? The hunters are nearby. Run and save yourself.'

"Just then, the hunter reached out from under the buffalo robe and grabbed the crow by the neck. With a piece of rawhide, he tied the crow's legs together and carried it back to camp.

"Once again, the people sat in council to decide the fate of the crow.

" 'I will burn him up,' one of the warriors declared, and before anybody could stop him, he grabbed the crow from the hunter's hands and tossed it into the council fire.

"The string that tied the crow's legs together burned through right away and the big crow managed to fly out of the fire, but many of his feathers were singed and though he was still big, he was no longer white as the snow.

"Quickly, he flew away, promising that he would never again warn the buffalo. And so he escaped, but ever since that time, all crows have been black."

It was a wonderful tale, Maggie thought, and clapped her hands in delight, while Bobby begged for another story.

"Just one," Winona said, and began the tale of the end of the world.

"There is a place where the prairie and the Badlands meet and at that place there is a hidden cave. No one has been able to find it for many winters.

"In the cave lives a woman who is as old as the earth. She is dressed in deerskin. She has been sitting in the cave since the earth was young, working on a blanket strip for a buffalo robe. She is making the strip out of porcupine quills. Resting beside her is a big black dog named *Shunka Sapa*. The dog's eyes never leave the old woman.

"A fire burns a few steps from where the old woman is working. She lit the fire when the earth was young and has kept it burning ever since. Over the fire hangs a big earthen pot, the kind the people used before the white man came with kettles of iron. Inside the pot, *wojapi* is boiling. The soup, made of sweet berries, has been boiling ever since the fire was lit.

"Every now and then the old woman gets up to stir the soup. Because she is so old and frail, it takes her a long time to make the trip to the soup pot. As soon as her back is turned, *Shunka Sapa* starts pulling the porcupine quills out of her blanket strip. Because of this, the old woman never makes any progress on her quill work and her blanket remains forever unfinished."

Winona paused, her dark eyes intent on Bobby's face.

"And do you know what would happen if *Shunka Sapa* stopped pulling the porcupine quills from her blanket?" she asked, her voice hushed.

Mesmerized by the tale, Bobby shook his head.

Winona nodded slowly, her gaze moving over the faces of her audience. "Should that old woman ever sew the last porcupine quill into place and finish the design, the world will come to an end."

Winona said the words with such conviction that Maggie shivered.

Bobby laughed out loud, delighted with the tale. In the few short days that he had been among the Lakota, he had come to love and respect their way of life, their stories. This was where he belonged, this was the life he had been born to live. These were truly his people. He felt at home here as nowhere else.

He bid Hawk and Maggie good night, embraced Winona affectionately, and left the lodge. The rain had stopped and he stood outside, his face turned up to the leaden sky. And then he walked resolutely toward Buffalo Heart's tipi, because Buffalo Heart had a daughter named Star-on-the-Wind who was the most beautiful, graceful, delightful creature Bobby had ever seen.

He had met her the day they arrived at Sitting Bull's camp, and he had seen her every day since. Buffalo Heart didn't seem to mind that Bobby came calling and had, in passing, remarked that Star-on-the-Wind had refused to see any other young man since Proud Eagle arrived in the village.

Thinking of that now put a spring in Bobby's step and he hurried across the camp, oblivious to everything else.

Star-in-the-Wind stood near the door of her lodge, a heavy red blanket wrapped around her head and shoulders, her gaze constantly straying toward Shadow Hawk's tipi. Had Proud Eagle forgotten her? Only this morning he had promised to come courting.

Disappointment perched on her shoulder, black as the clouds overhead. Though she had known Proud Eagle only a few days, she knew he was the man she wanted to marry. He was so tall and handsome, just looking at him made her heart flutter like cottonwood leaves in a high wind.

It was growing late. Soon, her mother would call her to come inside. Star-on-the-Wind sighed. She was about to go into the lodge when she saw Proud Eagle hurrying toward her.

"Sorry I'm late," Proud Eagle said. He smiled into Star's midnight black eyes, felt his heart thump as she smiled back at him.

"I was afraid you had changed your mind."

Proud Eagle shook his head vigorously. "No. Winona was telling stories and I . . ." he shrugged. "I'm sorry."

Star-on-the-Wind lowered her lashes shyly as she opened the blanket, allowing Proud Eagle to share it with her.

For a time, they didn't say anything, just stood there in the sheltering folds of the big red blanket.

Proud Eagle took a deep breath, then slid his arm around Star's waist, wondering if she would rebuff him, wondering if he was moving too fast. But she didn't push him away; instead, she sidled closer to him until they were touching at shoulder, hip, and thigh.

"I've never gone courting before," Proud Eagle remarked, keeping his voice low so passersby couldn't hear him.

Star-on-the-Wind placed her hand over his and gave it a squeeze, pleased beyond words that he'd never been serious about another woman. "You are doing fine," she murmured.

"Must I court you for a long while?"

"Some courtships last several years," Star-on-the-Wind replied. Her tone was somber and thoughtful, though her eyes were filled with merriment.

"Several years!" Proud Eagle exclaimed.

"We have not known each other very long."

"I feel as though I've know you all my life."

She smiled up at him, her dark eyes luminous. "For me it is the same. Perhaps in the spring you could bring horses to my father's lodge. My mother and father think very highly of you. I do not think they will make us wait too long."

"Another day will be too long," Proud Eagle murmured, but he knew he would wait months, years, if necessary, so long as he could have Star-on-the-Wind for his wife.

Chapter Thirty-seven

Within a few days, everyone in the village knew Proud Eagle was courting Star-on-the-Wind. He tried to be discreet, but his gaze followed her whenever she was in sight. Somehow, he managed to be at the river each morning when she went for water. He was always nearby when she gathered firewood in the afternoon.

Just as everyone knew Proud Eagle and Star were courting, they knew that Buffalo Heart and his wife approved the match, and that when Proud Eagle sent someone to speak for him, Star-on-the-Wind's parents would give them their blessing.

Proud Eagle took a lot of good-natured teasing from Shadow Hawk and Winona, but it rolled off his back like water from a duck. He was happy, happier than he'd ever been in his life.

Two weeks after his courtship began, he went
to one of the Buffalo Dreamers for a Big Twisted
Flute. All flutes were considered *Wakan*, or holy,
and as such, they were always crafted by men
who had dreamed of the buffalo.

Big Twisted Flutes, however, were only effec-
tive when accompanied by the music of love
which the shaman received in a dream. They
were made of cedar wood and carved with the
likeness of a horse, the most ardent of all animal
lovers. Men placed great faith in the power of
these flutes, and in the music of love composed
by the Buffalo Dreamer. Some believed that the
melody of the flute was so powerful that a girl
would leave her lodge to follow the music. Some
flutes were believed to have such magic that a
man had only to touch a woman with it and she
would follow him anywhere.

But Proud Eagle didn't want to enchant Star-
on-the-Wind, he wanted only to express his love
for her. And so, on the first snowy night after
everyone had gone to bed, he went to her lodge
and played his flute, hoping the soulful notes
would tell her of his love and devotion.

Inside their lodge, Maggie rolled closer to
Hawk, smiling as she heard the faint trilling song
of the flute. It did indeed have a magical sound,
she thought, and wished for a moment that she
was a Lakota girl and that Hawk had courted her
beneath a big red courting blanket, that he had
sat in the snow behind her lodge and poured out
his love in the notes of a Big Twisted Flute.

Shadow Hawk drew Maggie close, his hand
caressing her cheek, the curve of her breast,

before settling on the slight swell of her belly. He listened to the music of the flute for a moment before he turned on his side and pulled Maggie more fully against him, letting her feel his rising desire as he kissed her eyes, her lips.

With a soft sigh, Maggie began to caress him in return, her fingertips sliding over his hard-muscled arms and chest, slipping ever so slowly down his thigh. Pleasure washed through her as he groaned softly. It still amazed her that she had the power to arouse him, that their bodies fit together so well.

His breath was warm as he nuzzled her breasts, his hands gently caressing her hip and thigh, the touch of skin against skin sending shivers of delight along her spine, making her blood flow hotly within her veins.

His kiss was filled with love and desire, with the primal male urge to possess, to dominate, and yet he was infinitely tender, iron sheathed in silk, strength veiled in velvet.

The sound of his voice was low and husky. The notes of the flute were soft and sweet. The buffalo robe beneath her was warm against her bare skin. And Hawk was all around her, his scent filling her nostrils, his body molding itself to hers, making her heart sing.

She watched his face as they became one, saw the passion flare in the depths of his beautiful black eyes, felt the rough silk of his hair brush her cheek as he moved slowly within her, and everywhere he touched, her skin turned to fire.

And then she was reaching, climbing toward the fulfillment that only he could give her. She sighed his name as she burst into the sun, felt him shudder as his own release came a moment later.

Sated, they clung to each other, the rasp of their breath and the faint notes of the love flute the only sounds within the dark cocoon of the lodge.

Maggie woke feeling as if she had swallowed a ray of sunlight. Smiling with the memory of the night past, she gazed at the man sleeping peacefully beside her, felt her heart swell with love as she lifted a lock of his hair and wound it around her finger. She wished she could tell Bobby just how much magic his Big Twisted Flute possessed, and then she laughed softly, thinking how embarrassed they'd both be if she told him about last night.

"Are you laughing at me, *mitawicu*?" Shadow Hawk asked, his voice filled with mock reproach.

"I wouldn't dare," Maggie replied. "Not after last night."

"Last night," he murmured, and a slow smile of remembrance curved his lips. "I must tell Proud Eagle that his flute does indeed work magic and ask him to play his flute often."

"Don't you dare!" Maggie said. She punched Hawk on the shoulder as she imagined him telling Bobby about the night past. Men! She could just imagine the two of them grinning at each other and slapping each other on the back.

Hawk covered his face with his arms, laughing uproariously as Maggie continued to pummel him with her fists.

"Are you laughing at me?" she demanded.

"No, *mitawicu*," he said, gasping for breath. "I would never laugh at you."

"Oh, you!" Maggie exclaimed, and, changing tactics, she began to kiss Hawk's arms and hands, licking his fingers.

Before she quite knew what had happened, she found herself on her back looking up at her husband, her hands imprisoned in one of his.

"Something wrong?" she asked innocently.

"I am thinking of last night," Hawk replied. "And thinking that you are just as tempting in the light of day with no flute playing in the background."

"Are you?" Maggie whispered, surprised that she could speak at all for the sudden, fierce pounding of her heart.

Shadow Hawk nodded. Slowly, he bent to place a kiss on her brow, the tip of her nose, her cheek, her chin.

"Your mother . . ." Maggie said. "She . . ."

"I will secure the lodge flap, and she will understand."

"We can't shut her out of her own house."

"Yes," Shadow Hawk said firmly. "We can."

He left her just long enough to secure the door, then slid under the buffalo robes again, his arms reaching for her eagerly as he caught her close.

Later, Maggie admitted it was just as wonderful in the morning.

When they left the lodge an hour later, they saw that it had snowed the night before. The whole world was covered in a spotless blanket of white.

Winona's lips twitched slightly as she nodded to her son and his wife before ducking into the lodge.

Maggie felt her cheeks grow hot, but Hawk just grinned.

"There is no need to be embarrassed," Hawk said. "My mother was young once. Her blood warmed at my father's touch. How do you think I came to be born?"

"I know, but . . ." Maggie shrugged. "I just never thought I'd be locking my mother-in-law out in the snow while I made love to my husband."

Shadow Hawk laughed and the sound of it washed over Maggie like sunshine. It occurred to her that she had rarely heard Hawk laugh until they came here. It was a wonderful sound, deep and filled with happiness.

She smiled up at him, her eyes reflecting the love in her heart.

Impulsively, Hawk lifted her into his arms and twirled her around. "It is a good day to be alive," he said, smiling into her eyes. "May all our days be the same."

"And may our son be as handsome as his father."

"And as giving as his mother," Shadow Hawk said fervently.

"And as strong as the love that binds us together."

Shadow Hawk nodded solemnly as he set Maggie on her feet. For a moment, they gazed into each other's eyes, oblivious of the comings and goings of others in the camp, and then Winona called them in for breakfast.

That afternoon, a couple of young men, Red Arrow among them, set up a target and they began shooting at it, bragging about who was the best.

Gradually, more and more people gathered around to watch, and what had started as a way to pass the time became a contest to see who was the most skilled with bow and arrow.

Shadow Hawk was urged to take part, as were Crooked Lance and Buffalo Heart. Proud Eagle stood beside Maggie as the men took their places. When all bets were made, the contest began.

It was evident from the start that Hawk and Buffalo Heart were the best of the bunch. They matched each other shot for shot, placing their arrows in the center of the target every time.

Gradually, the target was moved farther and farther away, and now Hawk's skill proved itself.

"He's great," Bobby said, his voice filled with awe. "I wish I could do that."

"You will," Maggie said, but she doubted that anyone could ever attain Hawk's speed and accuracy. Or his fluidity of movement. He was wonderful to watch. His eye and hand coordination was flawless, his movements graceful and smooth, without wasted motion. Each arrow went exactly where it was meant to go.

Eventually, Hawk beat out every other competitor and was declared the winner. There was a lot of talking and laughing as bets were paid off, some cheerfully, some with mock reluctance, while wives and sweethearts consoled the losers.

Foot races were the next event, with races for children, women, and men according to age. The first race was for young men. The course was two miles long, a mile down and a mile back over a course brushed clear of snow.

Maggie shivered as the men who were going to participate in the race stripped down to their leggings and breechclouts.

More bets were made as the runners warmed up.

Bobby stood between Maggie and Hawk, undecided about whether to enter or not, until he saw Star-on-the-Wind join the crowd.

Taking a deep breath, he stripped off his shirt and handed it to Maggie.

Shadow Hawk shot Proud Eagle a knowing grin as he patted him on the back. "May *Wakán Tanka* give your feet wings," he murmured.

With a nod, Bobby went to join the other men at the starting line.

The runners were tightly bunched during the first half of the race. Maggie clenched her fists as she leaned forward, willing Bobby to run faster. Around her, she could hear people shouting encouragement to their favorites. She slid a quick glance at Star-on-the-Wind, smiled as she saw that the girl's gaze was fixed on Bobby.

As the runners made the turn at the halfway point, Bobby was in fourth place.

Maggie screamed his name, jumping up and down as he began to pull ahead. Into third place. Second.

"Run, Bobby, run!" she yelled, and then hollered with excitement as he overtook the leader, crossing the finish line first.

Breathless, Bobby stood at the finish line, his sides heaving, certain he'd never be the same again. He'd been working out at the ranch for a couple of months, but the men he'd run against had been training their whole lives. It was only his need to look good in Star-on-the-Wind's eyes that had given him the strength to finish the race, the will to win.

When his breathing was less erratic, he looked over his shoulder.

Star-on-the-Wind was standing only a few feet away, her beautiful dark eyes glowing with pride and affection. She held up the buffalo robe she had wagered on the outcome of the race, and then held up the fine buffalo robe she had won.

Bobby smiled back at her, thinking he'd never been more pleased about anything in his life.

The next race was for men over twenty-five.

Maggie looked at Hawk as he stripped off his shirt. "You're going to run?"

Hawk grinned at her. "I must. Red Arrow has entered the race. We have run against each other every year since we could walk."

"Who's going to win?"

Shadow Hawk shrugged. "I cannot say. I won last year. He won the year before that. And the year before that, it was a tie. But that was among our own people. I do not know how fast Sitting Bull's warriors can run." He grinned at her as he handed her his shirt. "Wish me luck, *mitawicu*."

Maggie smiled at her husband, then kissed his cheek. "You've got it."

Buffalo Heart gave the signal to begin and the crowd cheered as the men took off. Hawk and Red Arrow went right to the front, closely followed by a Hunkpapa warrior. Women and children yelled at the tops of their voices, calling for their fathers or brothers to run like the wind. But the race was between Hawk and Red Arrow and the Hunkpapa warrior, and the lead changed several times as they reached the halfway mark.

Maggie cheered for Hawk as he headed down the homestretch, her voice hoarse from screaming his name. She laughed with pleasure as he crossed the finish line first, then threw her arms around Winona and gave her a hug.

Hawk's mother smiled, delighted by her daughter-in-law's enthusiasm and affection. In the beginning, she had not been in favor of the marriage, but now she knew that Hawk had found the right woman. Though Maggie was white, she had a good heart, a deep love for the Lakota people and their way of life. She was quick to learn their ways, eager to know more. She did not view their life-style with derision, she did not mock their beliefs but embraced them as fully as any Lakota maiden.

"He won!" Maggie exclaimed, blushing a little at her emotional outburst.

Winona nodded. "I always thought he was part horse, he could run so fast. Now, I must go find Red Arrow's wife. She wagered a pair of quilled moccasins against my red blanket. It is time she paid up."

Maggie chuckled softly. The Lakota, both men and women, loved to gamble. Any game, any contest, was sure to be wagered upon.

She watched Hawk as he teased Red Arrow, accusing his best friend of getting too old and lazy to run a mere two miles. Red Arrow gave Hawk a good-natured thump on the shoulder and promised to get even next time.

When the races were done, the people went back to their lodges to rest and eat the noonday meal. And then Red Arrow and his wife and son came to visit. Little Owl crawled into Winona's lap and begged for a story and she agreed to tell him one if he promised to take a nap when it was over.

At his solemn nod, she began to tell one of the Sioux creation stories. Maggie remembered the story Hawk had told her, but this one was different. This wasn't about the creation of people, but the creation of the earth.

As Maggie listened, she realized that Winona's story was very similar to the story of the creation found in the Bible, for her story also told how *Maka*, the earth, was formed, from *Inyan*, the rock, and how *Wakán Tanka* created the heavens, which he called *Skan*. He also created the great waters and divided the light from the darkness, so that there was night and day. Day was called *Anpetu*, and the light of day, or the sun, was called *Wi*, and *Wakán Tanka* called the darkness *Han*, and he called the moon *Hanhepi wi*.

Maggie let out a deep breath as Winona finished her story. It was a beautiful tale, filled with wonder and mystery, so different from the biblical creation of the earth and yet so similar that she felt a new closeness with Hawk and his people.

As promised, Little Owl went to take a nap, and Winona left the lodge to visit Star-on-the-Wind's mother, leaving Hawk and Maggie alone.

Shadow Hawk studied Maggie's face, the faint smile that curved her lips, the peaceful look in her eyes. She seemed happy here with the Lakota, but he couldn't help wondering if she missed her own people. Her life was so different from his. He found it hard to believe she could be happy here, when every day was a struggle for survival, that she didn't long to return to her own house, to all the modern wonders that made the life of the white man so easy, so comfortable.

Odd as it seemed, sometimes *he* missed the marvels of her age, the luxury of a hot bath, the sweet taste of chocolate, even watching television. She had known those things all her life.

"Are you happy here with my people? With me?" he asked quietly.

Maggie basked in the deep, rich sound of his voice, warmed to the depths of her heart by the love shining in his eyes.

"Oh, yes," she whispered, her voice thick with emotion. "More than I can say."

"You liked my mother's story."

Maggie nodded. "It's very like what my people believe." She took his hand in hers and pressed it to her lips. "Someday, we will tell it to our children, and our children's children."

Hawk grunted softly, his love for her filling him with such tenderness it was almost painful.

"Ah, Mag-gie, you are like *Wi*, filled with warmth and light."

"And you are like *Inyan*, strong and powerful, yet you make me feel weak."

Shadow Hawk's fingertips caressed her cheek. "Are you weak now?" he asked, his voice husky with desire.

"Weak with wanting you," Maggie whispered, and felt the familiar flutter deep in the core of her being as Hawk drew her into his arms and kissed her.

Ever mindful of the new life she carried, his hands were tender, gentle as they moved over her body. His dark-eyed gaze lingered on her face, the look in his eyes more eloquent than a thousand words.

And Maggie gave herself to him willingly, wholly, holding nothing back.

He was *Inyan*, the rock upon which all her hopes and dreams were built.

And she was *Wi*, the sun, giver of life, who filled his world with light and warmth.

And for Maggie there were no fears.

And for Hawk there was no darkness.

Chapter Thirty-eight

Maggie had a chance to see her first Lakota ceremony a few days later. Buffalo Heart's youngest daughter, Tashia, was six years old and her mother had decided that it was time for *Nonge Pahloka*, the ear-piercing ceremony.

It was a happy time. By performing this ceremony, Tashia's parents and grandmother were displaying their love for the child.

Shadow Hawk had been chosen to pierce Tashia's ears. It was an honor, for only a man of respect, one esteemed for his bravery and wisdom, was chosen for such a thing.

Maggie sat between Winona and Star-on-the-Wind, caught up in the festivities. Tashia's grandmother had prepared a great feast of roast venison and the people ate with gusto, knowing this would be the last big feed before winter closed in.

Maggie felt a wave of gratitude to Veronica for teaching her to speak the Lakota language. It was wonderful to be able to converse with Winona and Star-on-the-Wind. Knowing their language eased the barriers between them, making Maggie more readily accepted by the Indian people. Many were surprised to learn she could speak their tongue fluently. Women who had looked at her with suspicion and distrust looked at her through new eyes when they discovered she could speak their language.

Tashia's parents placed the girl on a large blanket. All around her were gifts that would be given away as a token of their love for their daughter. The most valuable gift, a Winchester rifle, was given to Hawk.

Tashia was very brave as Hawk took a sharp awl and pierced her ears.

Afterward, the gifts were handed out.

Later, Maggie and Hawk walked hand in hand along the river. It was peaceful and quiet, with only the soft calling of crickets and frogs to mar the stillness. Overhead, a million twinkling stars smiled down on them.

Maggie smiled up at Hawk. "It was a great honor for you, wasn't it, to be chosen to pierce Tashia's ears?"

"Yes. I had thought they would ask Sitting Bull."

"Why didn't they?"

"I don't know. Perhaps because Bobby is my friend and Buffalo Heart and his wife wished to honor him through me."

Maggie nodded. "He's very much in love with Star-on-the-Wind."

"Yes. I think they will be married soon."

Maggie smiled, eager for Bobby to find the same kind of happiness she had found. "He's adapted well to life here."

"It is in his blood to be a warrior."

"Perhaps he was right," Maggie mused. "Perhaps he was born in the wrong time, after all."

"He will be happy here," Shadow Hawk remarked. "But what of you, Mag-gie? How long will you be content to stay here?"

"What do you mean?"

"Do you not miss the ease of your old life?"

Maggie shrugged. "There are things I miss," she admitted, "but none of them compare to you. After all, you can't make love to a microwave, and curling up in your arms is much more satisfying than curling up in front of the TV."

Shadow Hawk grinned. "Then you will be content to spend the rest of your life here, with me?"

"I'd be content to spend the rest of my life with you anywhere," Maggie said emphatically, and kissed him soundly, putting an end to the last of his doubts.

The weather was mild for the next few days and then, without warning, winter returned. The wind blew down out of the north, its teeth sharp and cold. Rain pummeled the lodge skins, thunder shook the earth, and lightning danced across the skies, occasionally striking one of the tall pines.

A week later it began to snow. Unlike the last time, when the snow had lasted only two days, this storm lasted for a week.

Maggie and Winona stayed inside the lodge, huddled around a fire. Occasionally Bobby and Hawk went outside to check on the horses and search for game. And like every other able-bodied man in the village, they took their turns at keeping watch, ever mindful that the wily Crow liked nothing better than to creep up on a winter village and steal horses and scalps.

Sometimes Star-on-the-Wind came to the lodge, ostensibly to visit Maggie and Winona, but Maggie noticed that Star-on-the-Wind never seemed to come calling when Bobby was away from the lodge.

Star was a beautiful young woman. She was tall and slender, with smooth, clear skin and dancing black eyes. The three women spent many afternoons together and Maggie soon learned how to make moccasins, how to quill, how to make leggings and shirts.

Maggie had never been one for sewing, but now she found it was an excellent way to pass a wintry day, and relaxing, as well. She took a great deal of pride in the first shirt she made for Hawk, pleased with the fit, the design of dyed porcupine quills that adorned the yoke, the way the fringes on the sleeves swayed when he moved.

As winter progressed, they began to make baby clothes. Winona made a small robe of white rabbit fur, Star-on-the-Wind made several soft clouts, while Maggie sewed a half-dozen sacques similar to ones she'd seen in the stores. It wasn't anything as fine as infant wear by Carter's, but, all in all, she was pleased with her handiwork.

Since Maggie was not versed in all the Lakota ways, and since she didn't have a mother to guide her, Star's mother, Blue Fawn, made two "sand lizards" explaining that one of the two little pouches would hold the child's umbilical cord. She went on to say that the amulet was fashioned after a lizard because lizards were hard to kill, thus it was fitting that the lizard's protective powers should be used to guard the child's substance. One pouch would be used for the cord, the other was a decoy to guard the child against malevolent forces.

Maggie had trouble believing that carrying her son's umbilical cord in a pouch shaped like a lizard would protect him from anything, but she accepted Blue Fawn's offerings politely and stored them with the baby's other things, eagerly waiting for the day when her son would be born, when she could hold Hawk's child in her arms and see the visible proof of the love that had spanned time and space.

She was touched by the love and generosity of Winona and Star and Blue Fawn, but it was the cradle that Hawk made for their son that brought tears to Maggie's eyes. Usually, the father's sister made the cradle, but Hawk had no sister and so he made their child's first bed himself.

Looking at it, Maggie saw his love for their unborn child in the delicate carvings in the headboard, in the shape and texture of the wood, in the strip of softly tanned hide that lined it.

Sometimes, late at night, he lay with his head on her breast, his hand resting lightly on the gentle swell of her belly, and told her of his childhood, of growing up with Red Arrow, of his first clumsy attempt with a bow, of his first pony and how he'd cried with shame the first time he tumbled off the animal's back.

Listening, Maggie could imagine her own son following in his father's footsteps. She'd never been able to imagine Hawk changing diapers or driving their son to soccer games, but she could picture him hunkered down beside their son, teaching him how to track a rabbit to its hole, how to distinguish between the tracks of a dog and coyote, how to follow the buffalo.

Closing her eyes, she imagined herself surrounded by black-haired children, boys who would grow to be tall and handsome as their father, girls who were beautiful and modest.

Winter was mild that year. They had enough to eat, and if Maggie grew weary of jerky and pemmican, at least they didn't go hungry.

Gradually, the days grew warmer. Slender green shoots poked their way through the snow. Soon the trees were clothed in bright new emerald gowns, the sky turned from leaden gray to azure, and a bright profusion of flowers blossomed seemingly overnight.

Newborn foals frolicked in the greening meadow, birds sang in the trees, and Maggie felt the first faint flutter of new life.

It was spring. The Lakota shook off the lethargy of winter in much the same way the horses shed their winter coats. Lodges were swept, robes were aired. The men went hunting. The children threw off their heavy shirts and ran barefoot in the sun.

And on a bright clear afternoon, Bobby Proud Eagle asked Shadow Hawk to speak to Star-on-the-Wind's parents.

Shadow Hawk grinned at the eager look on Bobby's face. "So, the time has come," he said, slapping his friend on the back.

"I can't wait any longer," Bobby said. "Please, Hawk, go today."

"Have you asked her?"

"Of course."

"And she said yes?

Bobby nodded impatiently. "Go! The horses are outside."

Shadow Hawk lifted an inquiring brow. "Horses?"

"Where do you think I've been the last four days? I've been out stealing horses from the Crow."

Seeing Maggie's astonished look, Shadow Hawk laughed out loud. "Truly, Proud Eagle, you are one of us. I shall be proud to carry your wishes to the brother of Star-on-the-Wind."

Winona offered Bobby something to eat, but he was too nervous. He knew Star would marry him, but what if her brother refused the match? What if he didn't think the horses were good enough?

Maggie and Winona exchanged amused glances as Bobby paced the lodge. Everyone in the village had been expecting this day. Everyone, except Bobby, knew that Star's parents and brother had agreed to the marriage.

Bobby whirled around as Hawk entered the lodge. "Well? What did Owl Feather say?"

Slowly, Shadow Hawk shook his head, hiding a teasing grin by looking down at the ground. "I am sorry, Proud Eagle. The elder brother of Star-on-the-Wind said no."

Bobby stared at Hawk. "He said no?" Bobby's face contorted with anger. "He said no! Then we'll run away!"

Shadow Hawk lifted a restraining hand. "Wait! He did not say no. It is all arranged. The marriage will take place in a month's time."

"A month," Bobby said, groaning.

"It is to give Star-on-the-Wind and her mother time to gather hides for a lodge. The time will go fast, *sunkaku*. There is much for you to do, as well."

The time did go fast. A month later, on a bright sunny morning in late April, Bobby Proud Eagle took Star-on-the-Wind as his wife. It was, of course, an occasion for a feast, for the exchange of gifts, for dancing.

Star-on-the-Wind pitched her new lodge near Winona's and the couple set up housekeeping. Maggie was disappointed to learn that the newlyweds would not have a honeymoon, but Hawk explained that such a thing was not wise due to the constant warfare between the Lakota and the

Crow and the Pawnee. However, for the next few days, Bobby and Star-on-the-Wind were seldom seen outside their lodge and Maggie decided they were having what might be called an in-house honeymoon.

In early May, the *Nacas* decided it was time to move the Hunkpapa village back to the Black Hills, and Shadow Hawk began making preparations to take Hawk's people to Canada. Surprisingly, several of Sitting Bull's people expressed an interest in going to the Land of the Grandmother. The thought pleased Shadow Hawk. Instead of traveling with mostly women and children, there would be over twenty seasoned warriors riding with him.

It was hard to say goodbye. Star-on-the-Wind wept as she bid farewell to her parents, and Maggie choked back tears of her own as she hugged Buffalo Heart and Blue Fawn, certain she'd never see either of them again. Bobby put his arm around Star, holding her close as they watched Sitting Bull's people ride southward.

"I'll miss them," Maggie murmured.

Shadow Hawk nodded, but there was no time for melancholy feelings. It was time they were on their way.

"Come," he said, "we have much to do before we leave tomorrow morning."

They left early on a bright clear day. Maggie was eager to begin. Years ago, she'd gone to Canada on vacation with her parents and she remembered it as a beautiful place, lush and green.

But once the journey began in earnest, much of her excitement dissipated. Riding a horse six or seven hours a day was a lot different from a pleasure ride, especially when you were five months pregnant. The constant jarring made her back ache. Her increasing girth made her feel clumsy and awkward. She had to stop frequently to empty her bladder. Sometimes she walked, but she tired easily and then, when all she wanted to do was sleep, she had to climb back on a horse and ride until it was time to make camp for the night.

She grew increasingly grateful for Hawk's mother. Winona was always there to share the work. Maggie had always thought it would be awful to have to live with her mother-in-law, but Winona treated her with love and respect and Maggie found she enjoyed having the older woman around. It was nice to be able to share the complaints of pregnancy with someone who understood, someone who could tell her that what she was feeling was perfectly normal, someone she could ask for advice.

Hawk was unfailingly kind and attentive. He did his best to make Maggie comfortable. In the evenings, he rubbed her back and shoulders, massaged her feet, her neck. He held her in his arms when she cried for no reason at all. Some nights, he brushed her hair. Other nights, he carried her away from the camp to some private place where he undressed her and bathed her as if she were a child, drying her with a soft cloth, then rubbing her skin with sage.

The days passed slowly for Maggie. At intervals, they made camp for several days at a time while the men went hunting. It was wonderful to have fresh meat again, to stuff herself on nuts and berries and wild plums.

She was an old hand at putting up their lodge now and she took great satisfaction in doing it as quickly and efficiently as the Lakota women. Indeed, except for her curly hair, she looked pretty much like an Indian herself. Her skin was deeply tanned; she wore moccasins and a doeskin dress beaded and fringed in the manner of the Sioux.

She felt a sharp pang in her heart the day the Black Hills came into view for the first time. This was home, she thought. It would always be home, even if she never saw it again. It would be good to see the majesty of the Hills again, she mused, if only for a week, good to inhale the fragrant scent of the pines, to walk in the tall prairie grass, to swim in the lakes, to see the deer grazing in the quiet meadows at dusk.

That night, she lay in Hawk's arms, wondering what he was thinking. He had been born here. The land was in his blood, a part of him. If it was hard for her to say goodbye, how much harder must it be for him?

He had decided they would spend a week here, replenishing their supplies, hunting for buffalo, before they moved on. Maggie knew in her heart that it wasn't really a need for meat or supplies that had prompted his decision, but a desire to spend a little more time in the place that would always be his home.

Chapter Thirty-nine

Blood. A smear of bright red blood staining her thighs. Maggie looked at it in horror, wondering if she was losing the baby. But there were no pains, no contractions, just that little bit of blood.

She didn't say anything to anyone that day, or the next, but the bleeding didn't stop, and her fear grew stronger. Something was wrong. She tried to remember everything she'd ever heard about miscarriages and childbirth, but all she could remember was that blood was never a good sign.

She kept hoping it would pass. After all, there wasn't a lot of blood, but when the cramping began she knew something was terribly wrong. That night, she told Hawk, and Hawk told his mother.

Winona sent Hawk outside while she examined Maggie. Her face was grave when she finished. Rising, she went outside to prepare Hawk.

"What is it, *Iná*?" Shadow Hawk asked anxiously.

"I have seen this before, in other women," Winona explained sadly. "Always, the baby is lost." She laid her hand on Hawk's arm. "And sometimes, the mother."

"Is there nothing to be done?"

"I know of no way to stop the bleeding. She is having pains, also. I think you must expect the worst."

"No!"

Winona patted her son's arm sympathetically and then, sensing his need to be alone, she returned to the lodge to comfort Maggie as best she could.

Shadow Hawk walked away from the camp, the pain in his heart worse than anything he had ever known as he contemplated the loss of his son. He could bear that, he thought bleakly, if he had to, but he could not bear to think of living without Maggie.

Standing in the darkness of the night, he felt himself being torn in half. It was a familiar feeling, and he remembered another time when he'd had to make a painful decision, a decision between his heart and his soul.

And now he must make such a decision again, a decision between the lives of his child and his wife, and the welfare of his people.

Raising his arms overhead, Shadow Hawk lifted his face to the sky and began to pray, asking *Wakán Tanka* for guidance.

For a time, he heard nothing but the sound of the wind soughing through the trees, and then, in an instant, he knew all the answers.

The Eagle must follow the Hawk.

Shadow Hawk knew then, as certainly as if he'd heard the words aloud, that it was Bobby's destiny to lead his people to Canada. Maggie had been the catalyst that had drawn the two of them together. She had been the link between the two worlds. Her love for the Lakota and the land had bridged the gap between the past and the future.

Bobby Proud Eagle did indeed belong in this time. He was the medicine man his people needed. It was his fate to take the people to Canada. He would make his home there with Star-on-the-Wind, while Shadow Hawk remained behind, in the Black Hills.

He stared at the moon, bright and full, and knew it was time to take Maggie home. He could not risk her life, and their son's life, by staying here. Life on the plains was perilous at best. Even if they didn't make the long ride to Canada and stayed with Sitting Bull's people instead, there was always the chance of attack by soldiers or an enemy tribe, the possibility that they would have to fight, or take flight in the dead of night. It had happened before; it could happen again. And he knew that such exertion would be fatal for the child, and perhaps for Maggie, as well.

She'd been crying. He knew it the minute he entered the lodge. With a smile of encouragement, Winona went outside, knowing they needed time alone.

"Did she tell you?" Maggie asked.

"Yes."

"I'm sorry, so sorry. I wanted so much to give you a son."

"We have not lost this one yet."

"But we will," Maggie whispered, and a fresh flood of tears coursed down her cheeks. "Oh, Hawk . . ."

He slid under the buffalo robe and drew her close, one hand gently stroking her hair while she cried.

When her tears subsided, he wiped her face. "I am taking you home tomorrow, Mag-gie," he said quietly.

"Home?" This was home. Didn't he want her any more?

"Back to your time."

Maggie stared at him, a sudden ray of hope making its way through her tears. Of course, Hawk was taking her home because of the child, because their son's only chance for life was there, in the future, where modern medicine could stop her miscarriage.

She smiled at him then, certain that everything would be all right. They would go to her time until the baby was born, and then come back here. With childlike faith, she clung to his hand and fell asleep.

Shadow Hawk held her all through the night. He had never loved anyone as he loved Maggie. She was a part of him, would always be a part of him. They belonged together, perhaps forever, perhaps only for a short time.

Tomorrow he would take Maggie to the Sacred Cave. It was the only way to save the child.

Shadow Hawk stood outside his lodge, watching his people ride away. All their goodbyes had been said. Maggie had wept as she embraced Winona and Bobby and Star.

Strangely, Shadow Hawk felt no sadness at his mother's going. She had adopted Star-on-the-Wind and Bobby as her own, and he knew she would be well cared for into her old age. And somehow, deep in his heart, he knew she would be well and happy with her new life.

When they were out of sight, he bridled his horse, then went into the lodge to get Maggie. Very carefully, he lifted her onto his horse, then swung up behind her. It was a bad time of year to be traveling the plains alone. The *wasichu* would be swarming into the Hills in search of gold; the young men of the Crow and Pawnee would be eager for scalps, but perhaps, like the Lakota, they would be too busy hunting fresh meat to stray into the Land of the Spotted Eagle.

He should have asked Red Arrow and Crooked Lance and a few of the other warriors to ride with him, but it was too late now. He would travel slowly, carefully. Fortunately, the Sacred Cave was not far. With any luck, he could get Maggie there before it was too late. He did not think beyond that, but he could not shake the feeling that his life was about to change in some way that would be irreversible.

The thought of death crossed his mind and he

wondered bleakly if perhaps he was going to die, if he would not survive another journey down the Spirit Path. He did not fear death, it was a part of the circle that formed the Great Mystery of life, but he knew he would miss Maggie, even in the Land of Shadows.

Maggie rested against Hawk, her eyes closed, her thoughts confused. She had been so certain that Hawk had traveled through time to find her, that they had been fated from the beginning of time to be together. But now Hawk seemed to think he had been sent to the future to find Bobby, that it was Bobby's destiny to lead Hawk's people to safety in Canada.

"It was my destiny to find him," Hawk had said, his voice firm with conviction. "And it is his destiny to lead my people to Canada. It is what he was born for."

"And what about us?" Maggie had asked.

"I think we were meant to be together, Maggie," he had replied, his voice tender with affection. "Perhaps forever, perhaps only for a short time. I only know that I love you more than my life, that I loved you even before I knew you."

No matter what other reason Hawk might have had for coming to her time, she would always believe it was because they were meant to be together.

With every fiber of her being, she knew she belonged to Hawk, in his time or hers, it didn't matter.

Yet maybe she was wrong. Maybe it was just a quirk of fate that they had found each other. Somehow, she knew that wasn't true. Hawk had come to the future and Veronica had found a new sense of pride in her heritage. Bobby had received a vision to guide him through life. And she had received the greatest gift of all. Hawk had given her a reason and the courage to walk again. Not only that, but Hawk had saved the life of Sitting Bull and his people by persuading them not to winter in the Black Hills.

Maggie considered that at length. Sitting Bull's vision and leadership would have a profound effect on the Plains Indians in the next few years. Without his guidance, the Sioux and Cheyenne might have been defeated at the Little Big Horn, George Armstrong Custer might have survived the battle and run for President.

She tried to project what kind of effect such changes would have had on history, but there were too many factors to be reckoned with, too many unknowns to contemplate, and she put it out of her mind. All that mattered was that Hawk was here and she was with him.

Shadow Hawk kept the horse to a slow but steady pace, making frequent stops so Maggie could rest. She was sleeping now, her head cradled in the hollow of his shoulder. His arm tightened protectively around her waist and his heart swelled as he felt a tiny foot move beneath his hand. Thank God, the child still lived.

He urged the horse onward. Soon they would stop for the night; tomorrow they would finish their journey to the Sacred Cave.

He gazed at the Hills looming before them, closer now, and he felt it again, the premonition that his life was about to change, that he was

saying goodbye to all he had known and loved.
He knew then that he would never see his mother or Bobby again, that his old life as a Lakota
warrior was over.

But it didn't matter. Nothing mattered but
Maggie and the child. If he could just get
her safely to the Cave, everything would be
all right.

Shadow Hawk drew rein shortly before sundown. Spreading a buffalo robe on the ground,
he lifted Maggie from the back of the horse and
gently placed her on the robe before he began to
build a fire.

"I should be doing that," Maggie said.

"You should be lying still," Shadow Hawk admonished gently. "I know how to make a fire."

Maggie smiled at him, her eyes shining with
love. "I know."

He handed her a strip of jerky and the waterskin. "We will reach the Cave tomorrow afternoon."

Maggie nodded. She knew Hawk had picked
the easiest trails, that he was trying to make the
trip as easy as possible, but she would be glad
when they reached the Cave, glad when she was
home in her own bed.

She knew a moment of regret as she thought
of all they'd had to leave behind: the people
she'd grown to love and respect, the funny little sand lizards, the beautiful cradle Hawk had
made with his own hands.

"Aren't you going to eat?" she asked, offering
him the waterskin.

"No. I must fast before entering the Cave."

"Oh. Should I be eating?"

"Yes. You need the nourishment." He smiled wryly. "And you are not a holy man."

Maggie finished the jerky, then wearily closed her eyes, thinking she'd never been so tired in her life.

She was asleep in moments.

Shadow Hawk sat before the fire for a long time, listening to the sounds of the night, thinking of Heart-of-the-Wolf, of Winona and his father, of Bobby Proud Eagle. And then, inevitably, of Maggie. Whatever the future held, he would be eternally grateful for her love, for the happiness she had brought him.

Maggie stirred as he slid under the blanket beside her. "Is it morning already?" she murmured.

"No, beloved. Go back to sleep."

"I love you," she whispered.

Shadow Hawk nodded, his throat thick with emotion as he realized this might be their last night together.

"Is something wrong?" Maggie asked. She sat up, suddenly wide awake without knowing why.

Shadow Hawk gazed up at the moon shining brightly overhead. It was full and white, so bright it almost turned the night to day.

"No, *mitawicu*," he said with a sigh. "Everything is as it should be."

Chapter Forty

Shadow Hawk heard the soft snuffle of a horse, the sound of hoofbeats. Too late, he reached for the rifle that was now in the hands of an enemy.

There were three men, all heavily armed. Two were riding double on a big blood bay mare. The man who held Hawk's rifle was on foot.

Shadow Hawk stood up, his expression impassive as he placed himself between Maggie and the three men. "What do you want?"

"You speak English? Well, that makes it easier." He gestured at the man on foot. "My partner here lost his horse, so we'll be taking yours."

"No."

The man looked at Shadow Hawk in amazement. "What did you say?"

"I said no."

The man jacked a round into the breech of his rifle. "I don't think you're in any position to argue."

"My woman is with child. She is not well enough to walk."

"Yeah, well, that's too bad, but we're in a kind of a hurry ourselves."

"Wait, La Jeunesse. He said something about a woman."

"Forget it, Conner. We ain't got time to dally with no squaw."

"She is not a squaw," Shadow Hawk said, his voice cold.

Conner stepped past Shadow Hawk and stared at Maggie, who was sitting up, the blanket pulled up to her chin. "Well, now, she ain't no squaw, that's a fact. She's a white woman."

"Dammit, Conner, I don't care if she's the Queen of Sheba, we got no time for this now."

"There's always time for a woman."

The man riding pillion on the bay slid to the ground. "Come on, Conner, La Jeunesse is right. We need to be makin' tracks."

"All in good time, you two," Conner said affably. He smiled at Maggie, then reached out to touch her cheek with a hand that was dirty and stained with tobacco.

A moment later, he was flat on his back, staring death in the face as he tried to pry Hawk's fingers from his throat.

Irv and La Jeunesse watched a moment, then Irv drew his revolver and brought the butt down on Shadow Hawk's head, just behind his ear.

Hawk fell sideways, his body limp. With a grunt of satisfaction, La Jeunesse reached down and pulled the knife from Hawk's belt and stuck it in his own.

With a cry of despair, Maggie rose to her feet and started toward Hawk. He lay so still, she was certain he was dead. But the man called Conner dropped a heavy hand on her shoulder and held her back.

"Conner, I don't want any more trouble," La Jeunesse said. "Get the Injun's horse and let's get out of here."

Conner shook his head, one hand rubbing his throat, his gaze on the woman. "Let's take her with us."

"She's breedin'," Irv said irritably. "La Jeunesse is right. Let's get movin' before that Injun comes to."

"One kiss, then," Conner insisted. "Just one. I ain't seen a white woman in months."

"Hurry on with it then," La Jeunesse muttered, regretting the day he'd met Conner. The man had been nothing but trouble. It was Conner's fault they were hightailing it out of the territory. He'd raped a woman and killed her husband, then, to top it off, his horse had stepped in a prairie dog hole and broken its leg. And now this.

Le Jeunesse shook his head, thinking it might be easier to ride on and leave Conner behind. Hell, they didn't need a woman. All they needed was a horse.

Maggie backed away, repulsed by the lust in the man's eyes, by the filthy hands that reached out for her. She screamed as Conner's hand clamped down on her arm.

The sound of Maggie's cry pierced the darkness and the pain. Feeling groggy, Shadow Hawk stared at the scene before him through narrowed eyes, anger building within him as he saw one of the white men holding Maggie. She struggled in his grasp as he tried to kiss her.

The other two men stood nearby and Shadow Hawk assumed they were waiting their turn. Through half-closed eyes, he saw his rifle propped against a rock. He heard Maggie cry out as the man called Conner pressed his mouth to hers.

Rage overcame caution. Rolling to his knees, Shadow Hawk grabbed his rifle, jacked a round into the breech, and fired three times in rapid succession.

The sound of gunfire echoed and re-echoed in the stillness that followed.

Shadow Hawk stared at the three men. He felt no regret at killing them. They had frightened Maggie. They would have stolen his horse. They had laid hands on his woman.

Throwing the Winchester aside, Shadow Hawk hurried to Maggie's side. She was shaking violently, her face as pale as death as he pulled her into his arms, turning away so she couldn't see the dead men, or the blood staining the ground.

He rocked her back and forth, the hot blood of vengeance roaring in his ears. Killing the *wasichu* with a rifle had been too quick, too easy. The man who dared touch Maggie should have died slowly, inch by painful inch. He longed to hack the man to pieces, to cut off his filthy hands. Instead, he murmured words of comfort to Maggie and slowly, gradually, the lust for blood lessened.

"Are you all right?" he asked after a while.

She nodded, wishing Hawk had not killed those men, understanding why he had and feeling guilty anyway.

"Mag-gie?"

"I want to go home," she whispered. Home, where the only real violence she saw was on the ten o'clock news. Home, to the serenity of her ranch in the shadow of the Black Hills, where the only men who carried guns were lawmen or deer hunters.

"I will take you home, Mag-gie," he promised. He felt her tremble in his arms, and then she was clinging to him, her face buried in his neck as she cried.

Later, when the horror of the moment had passed, she insisted on examining the gash in his head. He flinched as she probed the wound. It wasn't deep and had stopped bleeding, but his hair was matted with blood. She washed it as best she could, thanking God that it wasn't worse, that Hawk was the kind of man he was. Without his courage and quick thinking, they might both have been killed.

When she'd finished looking after Hawk, he turned the tables on her. The look on his face told her that she was bleeding again. Fear, colder than winter ice, stabbed at her heart as she wrapped her arms over her belly, wishing she could protect her unborn child as ably as Hawk had protected her.

After retrieving his own rifle and hunting knife, he carried Maggie away from their camp and made her comfortable in the shade of a squat yellow bluff while he went back to dispose of the bodies and turn the extra horse loose.

Lying there, Maggie tried to clear her mind of the grotesque images, but every time she closed her eyes, she saw blood spurting from the back of La Jeunesse's head. And though she tried to think of something else, she could not help but wonder if Hawk would take their scalps.

But this time, she didn't ask.

They reached the plateau of the Sacred Cave late in the afternoon.

Dismounting, Hawk spread the buffalo robe beneath a leafy pine so Maggie would have shade. When she was comfortable, he turned the horse loose, then left his rifle behind a clump of brush.

When that was done, he walked a short distance from the cave entrance. Removing his shirt and leggings, he lifted his head and began to pray, beseeching *Wakán Tanka* to grant Maggie safe passage through the Spirit Path, to spare their son's life, to give Maggie strength to endure the rest of their journey, to bear their child in safety. He asked nothing for himself.

Drawing his knife, he made several shallow cuts in his chest, offering his blood and his pain to *Wakán Tanka* as a token of his willingness to sacrifice his own life in exchange for Maggie's safety and the life of their child.

It was near dark when he returned to the Cave.

"Hawk, what happened?" Maggie asked, gesturing at the blood that streaked his chest.

"Nothing."

"Nothing!"

"I was praying, Mag-gie. The blood was an offering to *Wakán Tanka*."

"I see."

"Are you ready?"

"Yes."

Hawk nodded. Removing the knife from his belt, he tossed it away, then removed the coup feather he wore in his hair. That done, he lifted Maggie into his arms and took his first step into the Cave of the Spirit Path.

The dark of the cavern swallowed them up as Shadow Hawk made his way deeper into the Cave.

It was as he remembered it, the air cool, the floor covered with sand. When they reached the heart of the Cave, he laid Maggie on the ground, then withdrew a small sack of pollen from his belt. He held it in his hand a moment, recalling that it had been a gift from Sitting Bull, a token of friendship from one medicine man to another.

Standing beside Maggie, Shadow Hawk offered a pinch of sacred pollen to the Powers Above, to the Four Winds, to Mother Earth, praying softly as he did so, and then he knelt beside Maggie. Taking her hand in his, he faced the east wall of the Sacred Cave and concentrated on the future, specifically Maggie's ranch house nestled in the little meadow in the Black Hills.

For a time, nothing happened. Silently, he called out to the Spirit of the Cave, pleading

Madeline Baker

for its help, praying that Maggie would be sent back to her own time even if he could not go with her.

Please, Wakán Tanka, be merciful to my wife and child. Please Father, send her home that my child may live. Do as you will with me, but grant Maggie and my son a long and healthy life.

Slowly, the darkness within the Cave grew thicker, heavier. Shadow Hawk could feel the Spirit of the Cave closing in around him, could feel the Spirit's breath upon his face. He held tight to Maggie's hand, felt her tremble in his grasp as the darkness came to life, surrounding them with its power.

He sensed her fear and he placed one arm around her shoulders, hoping his closeness would comfort her, even as he pressed a finger to her lips, reminding her to be silent.

Maggie nodded that she understood, but she couldn't still the trembling of her limbs as the blackness closed in around her, enveloping her, wrapping her in a cocoon of darkness and warmth.

Shadow Hawk continued to stare at the east wall of the Cave, all his energy, all his thoughts, now focused on Maggie's home in the meadow. He pictured it in his mind's eye, the house, the red brick chimney, the corrals, the barn, and as the wall of the cave grew light, the images in his mind grew stronger, sharper, the details becoming clearer, until he could almost touch the house, feel the wood beneath his hand.

He felt Maggie clutching his arm, felt her shivering uncontrollably. He knew a moment

402

of panic as he felt her slipping away from him, and then he felt himself being pulled down, down, into darkness blacker than night, deeper than eternity, a darkness so consuming it felt like death.

Awareness returned slowly. When he opened his eyes, he saw only darkness and for a moment he thought he was traveling the Dark Road to *Wanagi Yatu*, the Place of Souls.

And then, as from a great distance, he heard Maggie's voice calling his name, felt her hand clinging to his as if she would never let go.

"Hawk?" Her voice was louder this time, closer.

"I am here." He stood up slowly, feeling as if he were climbing through layers of quicksand, and then he reached for Maggie, lifting her carefully into his arms.

He could feel her shivering against him as he walked toward the mouth of the Sacred Cave, and he sent a silent plea to *Wakán Tanka*, praying that they had returned to Maggie's time, that it wasn't too late to save their child.

He was holding his breath as he crossed the threshold of the Cave into the pale dawn. Turning, he glanced down the mountain, felt a warm rush of relief as he saw Maggie's house in the distance.

"We made it!" Maggie exclaimed, and then sighed in defeat. Her house looked a million miles away. Strong as Hawk was, he couldn't carry her all the way down the hill and across the meadow to the ranch.

Hawk was thinking the same thing. "I must leave you here, Mag-gie," he said. Squatting on his heels, he made her comfortable in the shade of a pine. "I will return as soon as I can. Do not move."

"I won't."

Hawk nodded. Leaning forward, he kissed her cheek and then he was gone.

She watched him run effortlessly down the hill until his long legs carried him out of sight.

Hawk ran as if his life depended on it. And it did, he thought somberly. If anything happened to Maggie, he knew all the joy would be gone from his life.

He ran steadily onward, ignoring the thorny brush that scratched his arms and legs, concentrating on keeping his balance as he plunged down the hill.

Running was something every Lakota boy excelled at. As a young warrior, he had run for miles at a time to build the muscles in his legs, to increase his breathing. Sometimes they had run with a mouthful of water and any boy who had swallowed the water before he reached the end of the course went away in shame. He was glad now for the many miles he had run.

At length, he reached the foot of the hill. He paused only a moment, and then he began to run again, his gaze focused on the house. There was smoke rising from the chimney, and for a moment he thought how surprised Jared and Joshua were going to be to see him, and then he put everything from his mind but the need to hurry.

His legs felt weak, his side was aching by the time he reached the house. It had been a long time since he'd run so far, so fast, he thought as he sprinted up the porch stairs and opened the door.

Jared and Joshua were in the kitchen drinking coffee. They looked at Hawk and then at each other as if they didn't believe their eyes.

"I've no time to explain," Hawk said. "Joshua, get a doctor out here right away. Jared, I want you to bring the truck to the bottom of the hill and wait for me."

"Sure, Hawk," Jared said, "we'll take care of it."

With a curt nod, Hawk left the house and ran to the corral. The black nickered a friendly greeting as Hawk approached. Minutes later, Hawk was riding hard for the Hills.

With a yawn, Maggie closed her eyes. How long had Hawk been gone? It seemed like hours, though it had probably only been twenty or thirty minutes.

She placed her hand over her belly, a faint smile turning up the corners of her mouth as she felt the baby kick.

"Thank you, Lord," she murmured fervently.

It was peaceful, lying there in the shade. A faint breeze talked to the trees, a bird chirped in the distance.

Lying there, on the brink of sleep, she thought of names for the baby. Adam, because she hoped he would be the first of many? John, because he was beloved even before birth? Jason, perhaps, because the name meant "one who heals" and she

405

knew Hawk would be pleased if his son wanted to be a medicine man.

She was almost asleep when she heard the sound of hoofbeats. Moments later, the black stallion crested the ridge. Foamy lather streaked its necks and flanks. And then Hawk was kneeling beside her, lifting her into his arms, placing her on the stallion's back.

Agile as a cougar, he swung up behind her. Holding her in his arms, he urged the horse down the mountain.

Jared was waiting for them at the bottom of the hill. "Dr. Lansky's on his way, Hawk," Jared said. He stared at Maggie, his eyes worried, as Hawk dismounted.

"Thanks, Jared." Dismounting, Hawk lifted Maggie from the stallion's back and carried her to the truck.

Jared opened the door, then stood back while Hawk settled Maggie on the black leather seat.

"Cool the black out for me, will you?" Hawk asked as he slammed the door.

"Sure."

"See you at the house," Hawk called, and without waiting for an answer, he climbed into the truck, turned the key, and headed for home.

Maggie tried to bite back the groan that rose in her throat as the truck hit a rut. She knew Hawk was driving as carefully as he could, but the long night in the cave and the ride down the hill had sapped her strength. And she was bleeding again. She could feel the warmth of it on her thighs.

"Mag-gie?"

"I'm all right," she said.

Hawk slid a glance in her direction and knew she was lying. Her face was pale. There were dark shadows under her eyes.

He cursed softly, repeating a string of words he had heard on television, and found the experience strangely satisfying.

Joshua was waiting for them on the porch. "The doc should be here in about ten minutes."

"*Pilamaya.*" Hawk spoke in his native tongue without thinking.

He carried Maggie to her room, placed her carefully on the bed. "Can I get you anything?"

"No."

Hawk nodded, then frowned. He would have to get her out of those clothes before the doctor came, he thought, and closing the bedroom door, he eased Maggie out of her blood-stained doeskin dress and moccasins.

Going to the kitchen, he returned with a bowl of warm water and a washcloth and gently bathed her from head to foot.

That done, he pulled a clean nightgown from the dresser and slid it over her head, easing it over her breasts and past her hips, careful not to jar her or move her too much.

"You know this doctor who is coming?" he asked as he drew the gown over her legs.

"Dr. Lansky? Yes, I've seen him a few times."

Hawk grunted. He had little faith in white men, but he had seen the magic of their inventions. Perhaps there was magic in their medicine as well.

He was tucking Maggie under the covers when the doctor knocked on the door.

Hawk stared at the man through narrowed eyes. There was nothing in this *wasichu* to inspire confidence. He was tall and thin, dressed in a rumpled gray suit and tie. His hair was gray, his eyes were gray.

Ed Lansky couldn't help staring at the man who opened Maggie St. Claire's bedroom door. Lansky had been born and raised in South Dakota. He was no stranger to Indians, but he'd never seen one dressed quite like this— clad in nothing but a clout and a pair of moccasins.

"What seems to be the trouble?" Lansky asked.

"My wife is pregnant. She is bleeding."

Lansky grunted softly. He glanced from the Indian to Maggie St. Claire and back again. He'd heard rumors that she'd married an Indian. It seemed that, in this instance, the rumors were not rumors at all.

Lansky cleared his throat, hoping the Indian would take the hint and move out of the doorway. The man's very posture was intimidating, and, to his chagrin, Lansky discovered he didn't quite have the nerve to shoulder his way into the room.

Seeing the doctor's hesitation, Hawk moved away from the door.

"You'll, ah, have to wait outside," Lansky said.

"No."

"I think I'll have to insist."

"Please do as he says, Hawk. I'll be all right."

Hawk sent a single warning glance in the doctor's direction, then left the room, quietly closing the door behind him.

Joshua looked up as Hawk walked into the kitchen. "Is everything all right?"

"I do not know. She is with child."

Joshua nodded, his cheeks flushing. It was obvious that Miss St. Claire was pregnant.

"Something is not right. I fear she may lose the baby."

"I'm sorry," Joshua said. "I . . . I'm sorry."

Hawk nodded, too worried about Maggie to indulge in conversation. He wondered about the doctor, if he knew what he was doing, and what magic he carried in his black bag.

Worried and restless, he walked through the house, pausing in the front room to stare at the picture over the fireplace. His likeness stared back at him, haughty and proud, a flat image devoid of life. That was how he had been, he thought, before Maggie entered his life.

"Mag-gie." He breathed her name like a prayer.

Leaving the parlor, he wandered into her den to stand staring at the computer where she had spent so many hours, at the framed book covers that adorned the walls.

He glanced at the pile of clutter on her desk, at the unfinished manuscript. Curious, he picked up a page, wishing, for the first time, that he could read the white man's language.

He heard Jared enter the house, heard the two boys talking to each other in hushed tones. And then Lansky was calling him.

"How is Mag-gie?" Hawk asked anxiously.

"She's experiencing what we call placentia praevia," Lansky replied. "It means the placenta is separating from the wall of the uterus. That's what's causing the bleeding."

"Will she be all right?"

Lansky nodded. Unbidden came the memory of a movie he'd seen where a white doctor had been called to treat the son of an Indian chief. The main thing he remembered was the chief's threat to kill the doctor if anything happened to the boy. Though he was pretty sure he wasn't in any real danger, Lansky was glad that Maggie St. Claire was going to be all right.

"And the baby?"

"Fine, as far as I can tell. I want you to make sure Maggie stays in bed until the bleeding stops completely. She's not to get up for anything," Lansky said, stressing the last word. "Do you understand?"

"I understand."

"Good. Once the bleeding stops, she can get up for short periods of time, but she needs a lot of rest and no physical activity of any kind." One gray brow lifted. "Is that clear?"

Hawk nodded. Now that he knew Maggie was out of danger, he was amused by the wary look in the doctor's eyes. Did the doctor think he would be scalped if something went wrong?

Lansky cleared his throat. "Well, call me if you need me. I'll be back in a couple of days to check on her."

"*Pilamaya*," Hawk murmured sincerely. "Thank you."

Maggie was asleep when he returned to her room. For a long moment, he stood beside the bed looking down at her, at the dark cloud of her hair spread across the white pillowcase, at the soft swell of her belly.

Then, with a weary sigh, he left the room.

"Anything we can do, Hawk?" Jared asked.

"No."

"I know Ma will be glad to do anything she can," Joshua remarked. "Just say the word."

Hawk nodded his appreciation. "Why don't you two go on home? There is nothing you can do here."

"Sure, Hawk. I hope Miss St. Claire gets better soon."

Hawk nodded. He sat in the parlor, staring into the fireplace, while Jared and Joshua gathered their things.

"Let us know if you need anything," Joshua said.

The silence was very loud after the boys went home.

Going out onto the front porch, Hawk gazed at the Black Hills, knowing, without quite knowing how, that he would never again be allowed to summon the Spirit of the Sacred Cave, that by choosing to follow Maggie back to her time the door from the past to the present had been closed.

Bobby Proud Eagle had gone home where he belonged.

But what of the Hawk?

411

Chapter Forty-one

Maggie smiled at Hawk as he brought her a glass of milk. A week had passed since they returned to the ranch and in that time Hawk had been the soul of courtesy and kindness. He looked after her every want, her every need. He brushed her hair, bathed her with all the gentleness of a mother washing a new baby. He massaged her back, her shoulders, her legs, her feet. He made sure she took the vitamins and the medication the doctor had prescribed, that she drank plenty of liquids, that she took a nap in the afternoon. He sat beside her on the bed in the evening, and they talked of their hopes for their son, or played blackjack, or watched television.

She remembered the night they had watched *Dances with Wolves*. Hawk had watched without much interest until Lieutenant John Dunbar made contact with Kicking Bird, the Lakota holy man. From that moment on, Maggie knew Hawk had forgotten she was in the room.

Maggie had watched the emotions play across Hawk's face as the story unfolded, her heart aching as she saw the longing in his eyes, the yearning for the old days, the old ways that were forever gone. Of course, he was homesick, she thought, but he'd get over it, she'd see to that.

In bed that night, he didn't say anything, just drew her into his arms and held her tight against him.

For the first time, Maggie wondered if he was thinking of going back to his own time, his own people. And if he did, what would she do? As much as she loved Hawk, as much as she had grown to love his people, she wanted her son to be raised in the here and now. She knew there were no guarantees in life, but she wanted the best for her children, food and shelter and security, a good education.

Veronica came to visit several times. Her husband, Ed, was back at work. Joshua had found a job in Rapid City. Jared was dating a girl from Pine Ridge.

"And how are you?" Veronica asked, sitting forward in her chair. "What was it like, traveling through time? Gracious, Maggie, I can't believe you really did it!"

"Sometimes I can't believe it, either. I don't know how to describe it." Maggie made a vague gesture with her hand. "It was like being sucked into a dark tunnel, and yet I was never really afraid." She shook her head. "I guess you had to be there."

"Did Bobby make it?" Veronica asked.

"Yes. And he loved it. He said it was where he was meant to be and he'd never come back. And he got married."

"Married! Bobby?"

"Yes, to a lovely girl named Star-on-the-Wind."

"Bobby married," Veronica mused with a shake of her head. "My, my. So, the past was everything he hoped it would be." Veronica grinned. "And what about you? Are you ready to trade in your house and your computer for a horse and a hide lodge?"

Maggie shrugged. "Living in the past wasn't as romantic as I thought it would be, and yet, in some ways it was wonderful. I loved the people. They had such an appreciation for life, such reverence for the land. White people go to church on Sunday, and most of them don't think about their religion the rest of the week, but the Lakota lived their religion every day. I'd like to have that sense of oneness with the land, with God.

"Oh, and I got to meet Hawk's mother. I don't think she liked me much at first, me being a white woman and all, but after we got to be friends, she was great. And Sitting Bull, Veronica. I actually met Sitting Bull! He's . . . he was, an amazing man."

Veronica shook her head. "You know, if you wrote this down, no one would believe it."

"I'm going to write it down," Maggie said with a grin. "As soon as I finish *Midnight Hearts*, I'm going to write it all down."

"I can't wait to read it," Veronica said dryly.
"Well, I guess I'd better start back. Ed will be
home soon. Call me if you need anything."

"I will, Veronica, thanks."

Outside, Veronica gave Hawk a quick hug.
"Everything okay?" she asked.

"Yes. The doctor said the baby is fine."

Veronica placed a motherly hand on Hawk's
shoulder. "And what about you, Hawk?" she
asked quietly. "Are you fine, too?"

But he had no answer for her.

After three weeks in bed, Maggie felt much
better. The bleeding had stopped and she was
eager to be up and busy, but the doctor had
advised her to get as much bed rest as possible
and Hawk refused to let her stay up for more
than an hour or two at a time.

"I'm going stir crazy," Maggie complained. "I
need something to do."

"Can you not work on your book?"

Maggie smiled. Of course, why hadn't she
thought of it before! Soon, with the aid of her
lap top computer and a pillow propped behind
her back, she was busily engaged in writing the
last few chapters of *Midnight Hearts*.

Hawk wandered around the ranch while Maggie worked on her book, at a loss as to what to
do. He was a warrior, a hunter. He was accustomed to providing meat and protection for his
people. But there was no need for a warrior in
Maggie's time.

He exercised the horses, riding across the
meadow and up in the Hills, though he never

rode near the Cave, never heard its voice calling to him.

He fed the stock, cleaned the corrals and the barn, chopped wood even though it wouldn't be needed for months.

Sometimes he took Maggie's truck and drove along the back roads, finding a nameless satisfaction in being behind the wheel of a machine that could go twice as fast as the fastest horse he'd ever owned.

And sometimes he simply sat on the front porch staring into the distance, wondering what he would do with the rest of his life. Maggie had her books to write. Soon she would have a child to care for. And when she was on her feet again, she would cook their meals and keep the house clean and do all the other tasks women had been doing since time began.

He often caught Maggie staring at him, a puzzled look in her eyes. And finally, one night, she asked him what was wrong.

Without meeting her gaze, he shook his head. "Nothing is wrong."

"Are you sure? Sometimes you seem so far away."

"I feel like an old woman. There is nothing for me to do here."

"But you do plenty!" Maggie exclaimed. "You exercise the horses and look after the stock. I don't know what I'd do without you. You do the shopping, and the laundry. You cook most of our meals. You do the dishes. You're taking care of me better than anyone else could."

"Woman's work!" he retorted disdainfully. "I am a man, a warrior, but there is nothing for me to do here."

Maggie bit down on her lower lip, fighting back the tears that threatened to surface. "Are you going back to your people?"

"I cannot."

She flinched at the anguish in his voice, hurt because it was so obvious that he wanted to go back, hurt that he'd thought about it at all.

"You don't have to stay because of me," she said, unable to keep the bitterness out of her voice. "Veronica will come and stay with me."

"Mag-gie."

"Go on, go back if you want to."

"Mag-gie . . ."

The sadness she read in the depths of his eyes wrenched at her heart, obliterating her anger, reminding her of how much she loved him. Whither thou goest, she thought.

"We can go back, Hawk, if that's what you want. After the baby is born."

"I cannot. I have lost the power to travel the Spirit Path."

"Have you tried?"

"No."

"Then how do you know?"

"I know." He said the words with such conviction, such pain, that she knew it was true, just as she knew that it had something to do with her, with his decision to bring her back to the present to have the baby.

For the first time, she realized what he had given up when he brought her back home.

417

"Hawk, I'm sorry, so sorry."

"It is not your fault, Spirit Woman. I knew what I was doing."

She could think of nothing to say to him, no words of comfort. He had given up his people, his family, his way of life, so that their son might live.

Chapter Forty-two

Maggie shook her head as Sheila went on and on about how inconsiderate it had been of Maggie to take such a long vacation without telling her.

"I'm sorry, Sheila," Maggie apologized for the third time. "Truly, I am. Now, do you want to go on ranting and raving at me, or do you want me to tell you that the book's finished and in the mail? You should get it in a day or two."

"Finished! Bless you. Oh, and Maggie, wait until you see the cover! It's fabulous. You look wonderful, of course, but Hawk is going to have every woman in America drooling, and every other author in America is going to be green with envy."

"Send me a couple copies, will you?"

"Of course. And listen, girl, now that you're on

419

your feet again, how about an author's tour after the baby is born?"

"No, Sheila, I'm sorry. I'm going to take some time off, and then I've got an idea for another time travel book."

"I was afraid you'd say no, but I can hardly blame you. I wouldn't leave home either if I had a gorgeous hunk hanging around. Well, listen, sweetie, I've got to go. Let me know when the baby's born."

"I will. 'Bye, Sheila."

Maggie hung up the phone, then sat back against the pillows, staring out the window, wondering what she could do to put a smile on Hawk's face, hoping that the baby would bring him out of his melancholy mood.

Spring gave way to summer and Maggie began counting the days until the baby would be born. She fretted because she couldn't go shopping for a layette. She didn't have a single thing for the baby, not a diaper, not a gown, not even a bed for it to sleep in.

Hawk seemed resigned to remaining in the present. Not sad, not happy, just resigned. Some days she seldom saw him at all and she wondered where he went and what he did.

And then one morning early in June he took the truck and went into Sturgis. He was gone for a couple of hours and Maggie spent the whole time wondering what he was doing there. He didn't know anyone, so he wasn't visiting. He'd done the marketing the day before, so he hadn't gone for groceries. . . .

Maggie smiled sadly. She'd never thought to see Hawk doing anything as domestic as shopping, but he'd learned to do it because she couldn't, because he loved her enough to sacrifice his male pride to do what he considered women's work.

He'd learned to do the laundry and change the sheets on the bed. He could cook a variety of simple meals. He'd become quite adept as a ladies' maid, too. And she felt guilty as hell for being the cause of it, especially because he never complained.

And each day she loved him more.

Her heart skipped a beat as she heard the truck pull into the yard. The back door slammed shut, and then she heard the faint whisper of Hawk's footsteps as he walked down the hall toward the bedroom.

"Hi," she said, smiling brightly as he peered into the room.

"I thought you might be asleep."

"No. Where did you go?"

"I went shopping."

"But you bought groceries yesterday."

"I did not buy groceries."

"Oh?"

He looked somewhat sheepish as he stepped into the room, his arms laden with packages. One by one, he placed them on the bed.

"What's all this?" Maggie asked.

"Presents."

"Presents? What's the occasion?"

"Open them."

Feeling like a child on Christmas morning,

Maggie unwrapped a large box. Inside she found a delicate blue baby quilt.

"Hawk . . ."

"I asked Veronica what things the baby would need," he explained, "and she gave me a list."

Maggie felt a prickling behind her eyelids as she reached for another package. It contained several cotton gowns. Other packages revealed diapers, blankets, booties, sweaters, and tiny stretch pajamas.

"You are pleased?"

"Yes. You used the money from the photo shoot, didn't you?"

Hawk nodded, then pointed at the last package, partially hidden by wrapping paper and ribbon. "You missed one."

Maggie opened the last present and the tears came. It was a nightgown, sheer black silk.

"You do not like it?" he asked, puzzled by her tears. The saleswoman had assured him that any woman would be delighted with such a gift, but perhaps she had been wrong.

"I love it, Hawk," Maggie said, blinking back her tears, "and I love you."

"There is one more gift," he said, and turning on his heel, he went out in the hallway.

When he returned, he was carrying a cradle similar to the one he'd made before, the one they'd had to leave behind.

"Oh, Hawk," Maggie murmured, and knew she'd never loved him more than she did at this moment. She held out her arms as he crossed the room toward her.

Placing the cradle on the floor at the foot of

the bed, he took Maggie in his arms and held her tight. "Ah, Mag-gie," he whispered softly. "Do not weep."

"I can't help it. You knew how I loved the cradle you made, and you made me another."

"My child must have a bed to sleep in," he said, trying to lighten the mood between them.

"Sometimes you seem so far away. I look at you and I feel your sadness. If you'd married a Lakota woman, you wouldn't be stuck here waiting on me hand and foot. You'd be with your own people, and . . ."

"Shh." He placed his fingertips over her mouth. "I do not want a Lakota woman, Mag-gie. I want you. You are my people."

"But you're not happy here. I know it. I can feel it."

"Mag-gie, I am where I want to be."

"But you're not happy here."

He could not argue with the truth. He was not happy, but only because he felt his life lacked meaning and purpose. He did not mind looking after Maggie. In many ways, he enjoyed taking care of her. She was his woman, his wife, the mother of his son. He would live and die for her. But how was he to fill his days when she recovered and no longer needed his care?

He held her close that night, listening to the soft sound of her breathing as she slept, tormented by the sweet feminine curves pressed against his groin. Her breasts were full and heavy in his hands, the scent of her hair filled his nostrils, the scent of woman aroused his desire.

With a low groan, he closed his eyes, his body aching for hers, but he dared not take her.

He reminded himself there were only a few more weeks until the baby came and that thought cooled his ardor. He was afraid for her, for the child. She had told him not to worry. First babies usually took hours to be born. They would have plenty of time to get to the hospital.

He placed his hand over her swollen abdomen, felt his child's lusty kick. Surely there could be nothing wrong with a baby as active as his son seemed to be! He could feel the tiny foot pressing against his hand and he was suddenly eager to see his son, to hold his child in his arms.

Lying there, holding Maggie close beside him, he fell asleep with a prayer in his heart that all would be well.

He woke to the sound of thunder. Turning his head, he saw that Maggie was still sleeping. Slipping out of bed, he pulled on his jeans and T-shirt and left the house.

It started raining as he ran toward the barn where he forked the horses some hay, threw some feed to the chickens.

Sprinting back to the house, he turned on the light in the kitchen, put the coffee pot on the stove, then stood looking out the window at the rain. Another rumble of thunder shook the house and it began to rain harder.

In a matter of minutes, what he'd thought was merely a summer shower became a raging storm. Lightning rent the clouds, wind flattened the meadow grass and moaned under the eaves.

Pouring two cups of coffee, he carried them into the bedroom, intending to crawl back into bed with Maggie and enjoy the rain.

He'd expected to find her still asleep, but she was sitting up in bed, one hand pressed to her stomach, her eyes wide and scared.

"What is it?" he asked.

"I think I'm in labor."

Setting the coffee cups on the top of the dresser, Hawk went to sit beside Maggie. "It's too soon. The baby is not due for another month."

"Dr. Lansky said it might come early. Maybe you'd better call him and see what he says."

With a nod, Hawk picked up the phone, then frowned. "It makes no sound."

"What?"

He handed her the receiver. "It makes no sound," he repeated.

Maggie listened for a moment, but there was no dial tone, only an echoing silence. "The storm must have knocked one of the lines down," she mused, replacing the receiver. "I guess . . ." She went suddenly rigid as a sharp pain threatened to split her in half. A moment later, her water broke.

"Hawk!" She looked up at him, more frightened than she'd ever been in her life. "I don't think this is going to take hours."

Hawk looked out the window, wondering if he dared try to drive Maggie into town, wondering if they had time to get there before the baby was born. He frowned as lightning sizzled across the blackened skies. What if they made it part way and the roads became impassable? What if he got a flat tire, or ran out of gas? He couldn't take a chance of being caught out in the storm. No, they were better off here. Indian women had babies all the time. But some of them died. . . .

He shook the thought from his mind, turning back to the bed as a Maggie moaned his name.

"Mag-gie, tell me what to do?"

"Heat some water," she said, breathing through the pain. "Get a knife to cut the cord. And some twine. It's . . . in the kitchen drawer . . ." Another pain knifed through her and she grabbed his hands, squeezing tightly. "Clean sheets for the bed . . . a blanket for the baby . . . hurry!"

He eased her down on the bed, then went into the kitchen and put a pot of water on the stove to warm. While the water was heating, he found a sharp knife and the twine, pulled a receiving blanket from the dresser drawer. That done, he put fresh sheets on the bed, covered Maggie, and went to check on the water. It was boiling and he turned off the burner, then covered the pan before returning to the bedroom.

"Mag-gie." He breathed her name as he took her hand, wincing as her nails bit into his palms.

The next half hour was the worst he'd ever known. Unable to help, he watched her writhe in pain as the contractions came harder and faster. She clung to his hands, her grip like iron, as her body fought to dispel the child.

She screamed only once, as the baby's head crowned, and then, quickly, it was over and Hawk was staring down at his son. The baby's first cry was the sweetest music he'd ever heard.

For a moment, he could hardly breathe, so awed was he by the miracle of birth. And then he placed the child on Maggie's belly, cut and tied the cord. He washed the baby, terrified he'd drop it, it was so small and slippery, and then he wrapped his son in a blanket and placed him in Maggie's arms.

"It is a boy," she murmured. "You were right all along."

Hawk smiled through a mist of tears, thinking he had never seen anything more lovely than Maggie cradling their newborn son.

"Thank you, Hawk," she said, smothering a yawn. "He's beautiful, just like you," she added with a lopsided grin, and promptly fell asleep.

Hawk gazed at his wife and son for a moment, and then he went to stand at the window. Raising his arms overhead, he offered a heartfelt prayer of thanks to *Wakán Tanka*, and as he finished the prayer, the rain stopped as abruptly as it had begun. And there, stretching over the Black Hills like a promise from God, he saw a rainbow made by the rising sun.

Chapter Forty-three

Hawk sat on the front porch, his legs crossed, his arms folded across his chest as he watched a handful of baby chicks follow their mother around the yard. From inside the house, he could hear Maggie singing to their son as she put him down for a nap.

Two months had passed since the day their son was born and Maggie and the baby were both strong and healthy. Dr. Lansky had come out the day after the delivery to examine mother and child, Veronica had arrived the next day, arms loaded with flowers and presents, declaring she had come to stay and look after things for a few days whether he liked it or not. Hawk had put up a token protest, insisting he could look after Maggie and the baby just fine, but, secretly, he was glad for her help. Delivering a baby was one thing, looking after it was another.

His son. Every time he looked at the baby, he saw a living, breathing miracle. The boy was so small, so perfect, from the top of his black-thatched head to the soles of his tiny feet. Maggie had mentioned wanting another child in a year or two, but Hawk wasn't sure he would ever put her through the pain of childbirth again. He'd felt so helpless, so damned helpless, while she lay there struggling to bring their son into the world, her face pale and sheened with sweat, her body convulsing with pain that he could not begin to imagine.

Woman's work, he mused, and felt a new reverence and respect for his wife, his mother, for all women who had walked the Shadow World to bring forth a new life.

He was dozing when the sound of hoofbeats roused him. Rising, Hawk stared down the road to see a young Indian boy riding toward the house.

Descending the stairs, Hawk walked down the driveway to meet him.

"Is this Miss St. Claire's house?" the boy asked as he drew rein.

"Yes."

A look of relief crossed the boy's face. "Is Bobby Proud Eagle here?"

"No."

"Are you sure? I need to find him real bad."

"Who are you?" Hawk asked.

"I'm Bobby's brother, Glen."

Hawk took a deep breath and let it out in a long slow sigh. "Why have you come looking for Proud Eagle?"

"Our father died. I've got no one else to stay with. The elders were going to send me to live with a foster family, but I want to live with Bobby, so I ran away. You're the Indian he told me about, aren't you? Do you know where he is?"

Hawk frowned, wondering how to explain Proud Eagle's whereabouts, wondering if the boy would believe him if he told him the truth.

Glen shifted impatiently on his horse. "Do you know where my brother is, or don't you?"

"Yes," Hawk said at last. "I know where your brother has gone."

"Where is he?" Glen asked, his dark eyes shining. "Tell me, and I'll be on my way."

"You cannot go where he is."

The light went out of the boy's eyes. "He's . . . he's not dead?"

"No. We will discuss it later," Hawk promised. He studied the boy for a moment, taking in the lines of fatigue on his face, the dust and grime that covered his plaid shirt and blue jeans, the mud crusted on the badly worn shoes. "What is a foster family?"

"Somebody who takes in kids who don't have anybody else."

"And you do not want to stay with these people?"

"No. And if you try and make me go back, I'll run away again!"

Hawk grunted, amused by the look of defiance in the boy's eyes. "How long ago did you leave the reservation?"

Glen shrugged. "Three, four days ago."

"When did you eat last?"

"Day before yesterday."

"Come," Hawk said. "We will look after your horse, and then we will find you something to eat."

Maggie was fixing lunch when Hawk entered the kitchen, followed by a young boy of perhaps eleven or twelve.

"Well," she said with a smile, "who have we here?"

"This is Bobby's brother, Glen."

"Bobby's brother!" Maggie exclaimed. Wiping her hands on her apron, she gave Glen a hug. "I'm so glad to meet you at last. Here, sit down. Would you like a glass of milk?"

The boy nodded eagerly, his eyes watching Maggie's every move as she opened the refrigerator and poured him a tall glass of milk which he downed in half a dozen long swallows.

"Would you like some more?" Maggie asked, and refilled the glass at the boy's nod.

Taking Maggie into the hallway outside the kitchen, Hawk told her that Glen's father was dead and that he'd run away from Pine Ridge.

"We'll have to let them know," Maggie said. "They'll be looking for him."

"He does not want to go back. He said they will send him to a foster family."

Maggie glanced over her shoulder. "Doesn't he have any other kin?"

"No. I want to keep the boy here."

Maggie's heart went out to the boy, but she had her hands full with a new baby. And she'd heard

some awful stories about people who opened
their homes to needy kids. She knew the stories
couldn't all be true, but it was enough to give
her pause, especially with a new baby in the
house.

Feeling guilty, she said, "I'm sure he'll be all
right, Hawk. A lot of orphan kids live with foster
families."

"I want to keep him here," Hawk repeated.

"But, Hawk . . ."

"I know what I want to do with my life, Maggie," he said, his voice tinged with excitement.
"I want to bring boys who have nowhere else to
go here and teach them the old ways. I want to
teach them to speak Lakota, to think Lakota, to
walk the Life Path of the Lakota."

With a start, Maggie realized that Glen Running Horse was the answer to her prayers. Hawk
would teach Glen the Lakota way, instill within
the boy a sense of pride in his heritage, teach
him to value the land. With Hawk's help, Glen
would learn the ancient customs and traditions
of his people, and, in time, he would pass them
on to his own children.

It was the Lakota way, the warrior's way, to
hand down the lessons and legends of the past
to the young.

And someday, God willing, Hawk would teach
those same lessons to their grandchildren and
their grandchildren's children.

"Will you help me, Mag-gie?"

How could she deny him anything when the
mere sound of his voice still had the power to
make her knees weak? "Maybe."

"Maybe?"

"I think I could be persuaded if I was coaxed just right."

Hawk smiled, his dark eyes alight as he drew her into his arms and kissed her, the seduction of his tongue stealing her breath away.

Maggie sighed as the kiss deepened, her heart soaring at his touch. After all, how much trouble could one little boy be? She would let Hawk bring home ten children, twenty children, if he would kiss her like this for each one.

With a sigh, she nestled against his chest, secure in his love, a smile of satisfaction curving her lips because she knew he would finish "persuading" her later, when they were alone.

And she would say yes because she loved him too much to deny him anything within her power to give, loved him beyond description, beyond words.

He was her husband, her hero, the warrior of her dreams, and she knew they would live happily-ever-after, because that was the way all true romances ended.

Hand in hand, they went into the kitchen to welcome Glen to the family.

Epilogue

It was late afternoon on a beautiful spring day. Maggie sat on the front porch, her five-year-old daughter, Ashley, sitting on her lap while her seven-year-old son, Adam, showed off his riding skills in the yard. Glen Running Horse, now a tall, lanky young man of eighteen, was instructing two young Lakota boys in the art of the bow and arrow. Other boys could be seen at various endeavors—cleaning the stables, grooming horses, painting the barn, weeding the garden. She heard the sound of laughter as several girls left the house with baskets over their arms. There would be berry pie for dessert tonight, Maggie thought.

She let out a long contented sigh as she bent down to check on baby Amanda sleeping peacefully in the cradle beside her rocking chair.

Maggie looked up and smiled as she saw Hawk rounding the corner of the porch, their twin sons, Stuart and Steve, perched on his broad shoulders. Her heart warmed as she looked at her husband, clad in tight-fitting, well-worn jeans, a white T-shirt, and scuffed boots, his long black hair adorned with a single feather. Each day he grew more handsome, more beloved. She could not have asked for a better father for her children, a more loving husband.

They had harvested quite a crop, she thought with a touch of pride.

At first, they had taken in only boys, but now, in addition to their own five children, there were thirteen Lakota boys and seven Lakota girls between the ages of three and eighteen living on the ranch, and they all idolized Hawk. He was their role model, the epitome of what a Lakota warrior should be. He was proud, resourceful, patient, loving, strong, wise in the ways of his people, honest and even-tempered, firm but fair. The boys imitated him, the girls adored him, and his own children thought he could do no wrong.

In the beginning, Maggie had thought Glen would be the only outside addition to their family, but after Glen came Tommy, and then Brent and his younger brother, Greg. Soon the reservation was calling the St. Claire Ranch for help whenever they couldn't find a home for this boy or that girl.

After the first year, they'd had to hire extra help. After the second year, they'd had to add on to the house. In the third year, they'd built dormitories—one for the girls, one for the boys. But money had never been a problem. Maggie's books were doing well, the last one had made the *New York Times* Best Seller list, and whenever they needed money in a hurry, Hawk flew to New York and did photo shoots.

Since *Midnight Hearts* had been published, Hawk had become quite a celebrity and romance writers everywhere wanted him on the covers of their books. He'd even made the cover of *GQ* as the hottest male model in America. And his fan mail was staggering—hundreds and hundreds of letters from women of all ages who wanted autographed photos, bookmarks, anything with his picture on it.

Hawk found it all very amusing. He'd once told her he couldn't imagine white women falling all over themselves to be in his arms, but now it happened every time they left the ranch.

And now Hollywood was after him to star in a movie based on one of Maggie's novels. She thought it ironic that they wanted Hawk to play himself, for the novel they were interested in was the fictionalized account of Hawk's journey through time.

But the lights and glamour of Hollywood held no appeal for either of them. This was home, this little patch of ground in the shadow of the Black Hills. Everything Maggie had ever hoped for, everything she'd ever dreamed of, was here.

She let her gaze wander over the ranch. Chickens scratched in the dirt, dogs napped in the shade. A few red and white cows grazed in the distance. There were goats and sheep and rabbits.

The corrals were filled with horses. Each child who came to the ranch was assigned a horse which they were then expected to look after.

There were even a few head of shaggy buffalo in the east meadow, and every couple of years, Hawk took the older boys on a hunt. It was an event that was anticipated for months and talked about for weeks afterward. The kids were all given the opportunity to sample the raw heart and liver, if they desired. Few boys ever refused; few girls, including Maggie, ever accepted. The kids all learned how to skin a buffalo, how to make jerky and pemmican. For days afterward, they had buffalo steak or ribs or tongue for dinner.

When their son Adam started school, Hawk took Maggie aside and asked her to teach him to read and write so that his children would not be ashamed of him. It had not been easy for him. He was still a warrior at heart, proud and stubborn, but eventually he learned to read and to write. Maggie could hardly contain her tears the first time she saw him reading one of her books.

Now, she stood up as Hawk climbed the stairs, lifting her face for his kiss.

Hawk draped his arm around Maggie's shoulders, feeling the same sense of homecoming he always felt when they were reunited at the end of the day. He knew now that this was where he belonged, where he had always belonged.

Sometimes, late at night, they still talked about it, wondering if Bobby had lived a long and happy life with the Lakota. Maggie was convinced that Hawk and Bobby had both been born in the wrong time, and that Hawk had been called to the present to take his rightful place at her side, while Bobby had been sent back in time where he was meant to be.

And perhaps she was right, he mused. Who was to say?

"Spirit Woman." He murmured his name for her, his heart quickening as always at her nearness.

The sound of Hawk's voice moved through her like dark honey; the look in his eyes warmed her to the core of her being, the brush of his lips against her cheek made her pulse race.

They'd been married eight years, Maggie mused, and his touch still had the power to make her heart soar. She hoped the wonder of it, the newness, the rightness, would never grow dull, that his face would always be the first thing she saw in the morning and his voice the last thing she heard at night.

Maggie shivered with anticipation, looking forward to the time when all the children would be safely tucked in for the night, when Hawk would take her by the hand and lead her out to the quiet pool behind the house.

There, in a cocoon of darkness beneath a leafy green umbrella, he would take her in his arms as he had so many times before, renewing the love that was ever new between them.

A secret smile curved Maggie's lips as she thought of the new life she carried beneath her heart, knowing that Hawk would be pleased when she told him another child was coming to share their happiness.

Hawk smiled at Maggie, the Spirit Woman who was his wife, the mother of his children, and blessed the moonlit night he had entered the Sacred Cave and followed the Spirit Path to Maggie's arms.

Sioux Glossary

AI - yes
ANPETU - day time

CETÁN - hawk
CETAN NAGIN - shadow hawk

HAN - darkness
HANBELACHIA - vision hill
HAN-YETU - night time
HAU - hello
HEY-AY-HEE-EE! - a call to the Great Spirit
HEYAH - no
HTAYETU WASTÉ - good evening
HUNONPA - bear

INÁ - mother
INIOWASPE - pit

INYAN - rock

KOLA - friend

MAHPIYA LUTA - Red Cloud
MAKA - earth
MATANYAN YELO - I am fine
MATOHOTA - grizzly bear
MITAWICU - my wife

NAGI TANKA - great spirit
NITUWE HE? - who are you?
NUNWE - so be it

PAHA SAPA - Black Hills
PILAMAYA - thank you
PTE - buffalo cow

SINTKALA WAKSU - sweat lodge
SKAN - sky
SUNKAKU - younger brother

TATANKA - buffalo bull
TATETOB - the four winds
TUNKASILA - grandfather

UNKTEHI - water monster

WAKÁN ANKANTU - great holy
WAKÁN TANKA - god
WAKINYAN - thunderbird
WANBLEE GALESHKA - spotted eagle
WASICHU - white man
WASICUN WINYAN - white woman

Madeline Baker

WASTÉ - good
WAZUSTECASA WI - July
WI - sun
WICASA WAKÁN - holy man
WICOTI MITAWA - my village
WINYAN WANAGI - spirit woman
WIWANYANK WACIPI - Sun Dance
WOHITIKA - to be brave
WÓYUTE - food

YUMNI - whirlwind
YÚTA - eat

442

MIDNIGHT FIRE

MADELINE BAKER

"Lovers of Indian Romance have a special place on their bookshelves for Madeline Baker!"

—*Romantic Times*

A half-breed who has no use for a frightened girl fleeing an unwanted wedding, Morgan thinks he wants only the money Carolyn Chandler offers him to guide her across the plains, but halfway between Galveston and Ogallala, where the burning prairie meets the endless night sky, he makes her his woman. There in the vast wilderness, Morgan swears to change his life path, to fulfill the challenge of his vision quest—anything to keep Carolyn's love.

__3323-2 $4.99 US/$5.99 CAN

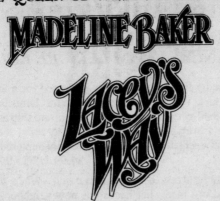

BRIMMING WITH PASSION...
BURSTING WITH EXCITEMENT...

UNFORGETTABLE HISTORICAL ROMANCES FROM *LEISURE BOOKS!*

The Magic by Robin Lee Hatcher. Destined for a loveless marriage to a virtual stranger, Cassandra Jamison finds herself instead swept aboard a notorious pirate ship and into its captain's arms. How can she hope to resist the most devastatingly seductive man she's ever encountered?
_3433-6 $4.99 US/$5.99 CAN

Ryan's Enchantress by Connie Harwell. When tomboy Susan Bradford meets her handsome new neighbor, she is shocked to realize that she longs for his tender caresses, longs to wipe the mocking grin off his face and show him how much of a woman she can be.
_3436-0 $4.99 US/$5.99 CAN

Fleeting Splendor by Julie Moffett. Trapped in a marriage of convenience with broodingly handsome Nathaniel Beauchamp, Alana MacKenzie makes the surprising discovery that love can sometimes blossom in the most unexpected places.
_3434-4 $4.50 US/$5.50 CAN